D0282157

PETER DOYLE was born in Maroubra, in Sydney's eastern suburbs. He worked as a taxi driver, musician, and teacher before writing his first book, *Get Rich Quick*, which won the Ned Kelly Award for Best First Crime Fiction. Two more novels followed, *Amaze Your Friends* and *The Devil's Jump*, as did two more Ned Kelly Awards.

No one knows Sydney (especially its murky past) quite like Peter Doyle. He combed through the archives of the Sydney police department to put together a highly acclaimed and long-running exhibition of crime-scene photographs and mug shots, as well as an accompanying book, *City of Shadows: Sydney Police Photographs 1912-1948*, and recently curated *Pulp Confidential*, an exhibition of Australian pulp publishing, at the State Library of NSW. Doyle teaches writing at Macquarie University.

LUC SANTE is the author of numerous books, including *Low Life: Lures and Snares of Old New York* and *The Other Paris: The People's City*. He has also contributed introductions to crime novels and memoirs by Georges Simenon, Richard Stark, and Charles Willeford.

J M C P L
DISCARDED

Also by Peter Doyle

THE BIG WHATEVER

PETER DOYLE

with an introduction by
LUC SANTE

DARK
PASSAGE

VERSE CHORUS PRESS

© 2015 Peter Doyle
Introduction © 2015 Luc Sante

All rights reserved. No part of this book may be reproduced, stored in or
introduced into a retrieval system, or transmitted in any form or by any means
(digital, electronic, mechanical, photocopying, recording, or otherwise), without
the prior written permission of the publisher, except by a reviewer, who may
quote brief passages in a review.

 A Dark Passage book
Published by Verse Chorus Press
PO Box 14806, Portland OR 97293
info@versechorus.com

Design and layout by Steve Connell/Transgraphic
Dark Passage logo by Mike Reddy

Printed in the USA

Library of Congress Cataloging-in-Publication Data

Doyle, Peter, 1951-
The big whatever / Peter Doyle ; introduction by Luc Sante.
     pages ; cm
   "A Dark Passage book."
   ISBN 978-1-891241-44-4 (softcover) — ISBN 978-1-891241-79-6 (ebook)
   1. Organized crime—Fiction. 2. Sydney (N.S.W.)—History—20th century—
Fiction. I. Title.
PR9619.3.D69B54 2015
823'.914--dc23
                              2015010045

INTRODUCTION
Luc Sante

Peter Doyle, in addition to being a crime novelist, is also a social historian, slide guitarist, university professor, and authority on popular culture, police photography, and recording acoustics. He has acquired fantastic amounts of learning, on disparate subjects of all orders of magnitude. Unsurprisingly, he has done a lot of living, in settings of assorted highness and lowness. It has primarily occurred in Australia. That country, which happens to also be a continent, is a bejeweled anomaly in the American conception of the world. The Australians are assuredly not us, but neither are they entirely them. English-speaking, forward-looking, ex-colonial, dismissive of old-world hierarchies and formalities, inclined to avert its eyes from a gutted and abject indigenous population – Australia is like the United States on another planet, complete with flora and fauna that seem nearly extraterrestrial to foreign eyes.

Putting it that way might seem like the typical American view of the world, in which other cultures are relevant only to the degree to which they reflect – or threaten – the American project. But the two countries' ties are long and largely subterranean. Over the past two centuries, Australia and the US have done a brisk, reciprocal trade in boxers, sailors, con artists, and evangelists. Their body of lore and mischief can be glimpsed in the slang terms they hauled back and forth. Then, after World War II, America redoubled its effort to "colonize our subconscious," in the famous phrase from Wim Wenders's *Kings of the Road*. It was handy that rock and roll came about just when the Americans badly needed a propaganda weapon that would reach the adolescents of the world. The Australians, through their port cities, received the gospel in tantalizing bits, and yet they were hip enough to be down with the Cornel Wilde look even before the accompanying music clocked in.

The absorption of American style is a continuous theme in Doyle's four novels, which form a loose chronicle of those years. *Get Rich Quick* (1996) begins in 1952; Little Richard makes an appearance, quite literally. *Amaze Your Friends* (1998) starts in 1957; you hear Lloyd Price and "Jumpin' with Symphony Sid." *The Devil's Jump* (2001) leaps back to 1945; boogie-woogie plays throughout. *The Big Whatever* hops back and forth between the years 1969 and 1973, and between funk and "longer and longer songs, with drum solos that went on forever." The books feature Max Perkal, the boy wonder of the 88s, perpetually just one hit away from becoming the biggest star in Australian pop history. They are narrated by his best friend, Billy Glasheen, whose purity of heart fails to prevent him from spending a great deal of time on the other side of the law.

Because for all that music is continuous in the books, skulduggery is twice as prominent. The shenanigans usually feature some toxic blend of drugs, gambling, confidence schemes, and governmental corruption – dimly but not obtrusively, the foreign reader suspects there are entire strata of allusions, in-jokes, and historical corrections going on outside one's ken. The plots take long, sinuous routes across time and space, gathering characters, generating subplots, exploding into sporadic violence, frequently ending on a note of pastoral calm. They are as involving and as difficult to reconstruct afterward as any of your Chandlers. *The Big Whatever* is similar to its predecessors but different. The times have changed, emphatically – youth rebellion has become political, and at least some of the drugs are psychotropic – and they demand a different sort of storytelling. The vehicle is a book within a book, *Lost Highway to Hell*, a very pointed roman à clef directed from one character to another as a coded message, yet dressed up as pulp, observing all the pulp conventions of plot and character. The nested paperback is, in effect, the back story in semi-transparent disguise, and it presents the reader with the – pardon my French – hermeneutic challenge of translating its fictions into the actuality of the main story. This is a tactic I've seen employed nowhere else, especially not in a crime novel.

In *The Big Whatever* Billy and Max are up to their usual sort of grift, although the youth culture they've long cultivated for their own purposes has, in 1969, become imbued with the chimeric promise of revolution. This is fine with them, up to a point – revolution can provide cover for all sorts of mayhem, but it can also bring additional unwanted interest on the part of the police. But all precautions fall to the wayside anyhow, thanks to the novel's greatest creation, its agent of discord, Cathy Darnley. "Polymorphously loose," she was a "party girl and former stripper" – "pure trouble" – "who knew everything and did anything;" "she had powers, heavy powers." Cathy is beautiful, highly sexed, highly intelligent, and as stable as nitro. She is always the one urging direct, violent action, who takes all the insane chances and makes everyone else go along with her. Thanks to Cathy the gang stage a spectacular triple coup under cover of a Vietnam Moratorium march, and thanks in part to her it all goes terribly wrong. But that was then, and now it's 1973. The party is conclusively over; the years of lead have descended. Everyone is lying low. Wild poets and drug addicts have gone to ground as blandly respectable shopkeepers in sleepy country towns. Nevertheless, the past is unquiet, and mysteries hover over the story like ghosts, demanding resolution. As a crime novel about bitter survivors confronting the excesses of their radical past, *The Big Whatever* has a genre nearly to itself, barring only Léo Malet's *Fog on the Tolbiac Bridge* and maybe some things by Didier Daeninckx.

Part of the book's appeal is, inevitably, Australia itself, especially in the extended tour of isolated hamlets in northern Victoria and western New South Wales taken by Billy late in the book, a panoramic sequence that manages to sound idyllic despite the anxieties that await the hero at every port of call, and that convincingly renders the landscape while almost entirely avoiding the longueurs of description, employing chastened language to sketch only as much as the reader's inner eye needs to see. And then there is the music of the Australian language itself, a matter-of-fact tongue with no illusions, impatiently given to abbreviating any word over two syllables, since after all "afternoon" takes longer to say than "arvo."

There is the celebrated rhyming slang, which makes "moreton" mean "gig" by way of the intermediary "Moreton Bay fig." And there are coinages of breathtaking directness, such as the irreducible "standover man," meaning "extortionist," which plays out an entire vignette in two words.

Doyle's great appeal as a writer lies in his position always as the sadder but wiser man, who has played with fire in his day and been sufficiently burned as to render him forever hesitant to pass judgment. He is tender with his characters – excepting of course the traitors and weasels and double-dealers – noting their humor and pathos and vain hopes. "Down these mean streets a man must go who is not himself mean" – well, they're not always on the side of the angels, either, or not in most obvious ways. They need cash, they need drugs, they need to preserve their hides. And yet, like denizens of the Old West, they observe a code, while it generally turns out that the forces of order, who have the same corrupted human needs, are very much less inclined to moral strictures. Doyle's heroes are fully paid-up members of the Johnson Family, the mind-your-own-business gang. In William Burroughs's words, 'To say someone is a Johnson means he keeps his word and honors his obligations'." Doyle knows that everybody's unavoidable task in life is to avoid the other side: the shits, who often tend to be the ones wielding power.

The Big Whatever concludes with a mystic vision of a Johnson nation, surviving after earthquake or meteor has taken out large parts of the world, in which "a band of outlaw surfers . . . wait on the high ground for each new apocalypse set to arrive. . . . Anarchists, hippies, heads, blackfellas, musicians, fortune-tellers, separatist lesbians, artists' co-ops, angelheaded hipsters." Motor vehicles made from scrap parts are involved. Perhaps we then remember that a leading character's name is Max, and that he's possibly not quite right in the head. But that's par for the course: Doyle's people are always offhandedly inventing the future.

THE BIG WHATEVER

SYDNEY, 1973.

The taxi was outside the Professor's house as usual, the motor ticking as it cooled. I dropped my bag in the boot, slammed it down twice before it caught, walked round and got in. It smelled of stale tobacco and air freshener. The fuel gauge looked okay, but sometimes you couldn't tell if it was short-filled until you'd driven for a few hours. I rummaged through the glove box – a few paperbacks, a broken pair of sunglasses, a cigarette lighter – to find the docket book. Filled out a worksheet, turned on the two-way and drove off.

I picked up the crippled kid from Drummoyne Boys' High School. Asked how he was, he said he was very good thanks, and I dropped him home without us exchanging another word. Then the pathology run to the city. After that I collected a couple of bank parcels and took them to North Sydney. Copped a street hail in Clarence, which doubled my take for crossing the Bridge. All except the street hail were regular jobs. They went with the cab.

At six I stopped into Barrack Motors. A dozen drivers were standing around the food van, gossiping, reviewing controversial radio job allocations, telling stories about their idiot passengers. I listened for a few minutes and drifted away.

A Legion cab on the opposite side of Oxford Street pulled up sharply enough the tyres screeched, then hung an illegal u-turn at the lights and pulled onto the drive. A guy with long curly hair and half a beard hopped out from behind the wheel and came over, grinning broadly. Brian.

He asked how it was going. All right, I said. How about him? He shook his head. "First job?" he said, "straight to fucking *Earlwood*." A driver hovering nearby groaned in sympathy. Brian gave a quick sideways bob of his head and we moved away.

"Got any of the old smokables?" he said quietly, but with a comical eyebrow triple bounce.

"Maybe later. See you on the Cross rank? After eleven."

"Ace," he said, and drove off as quickly as he'd pulled in.

Back on the road. The sun nearly down, traffic easing off. Time for the private jobs. I stopped into a hotel in Croydon. A fellow in the front bar, perched near the door, was waiting for me. I bipped once and he slid in, said in a flat monotone, "G'day Bill, how's it going?" I told him it was going good. He directed me to a street in Gladesville, then down a long driveway to a garage behind a brick house. We filled the boot of the cab with transistor radios, still in their boxes – they were the mini type, much preferred by off-course punters. Not much passed between us beyond the directions he'd given me and the money I gave him.

I took the radios to an address on the northern beaches, which I'd hoped would dovetail with the pickup at Avalon. I unloaded the radios, received a wad of notes, then made a phone call from a booth at Brookvale. Avalon was ready to go.

I drove to the cottage on the headland where Katie, tan-skinned, dark-haired wife of one-time surf legend 'Mullet' Jackson, was waiting. A green garbage bag was by the door, tightly packed. It gave off a musty smell, but nothing too strong.

"Looks all right," I said.

Katie nodded. "It is. But it might be the last for a while. Comes from out the back of Lismore. It's tough up there now . . . the helicopters."

She made coffee and gave me something grainy and macrobiotic to eat.

"Heard from Mullet?" I said.

"Three nights ago. Hawaii went very well, he said. Showed the film to the locals. Got a good crowd."

"Showed it where?"

"Some old hall where they put on music films, head films and all that."

"Like a scout hall?"

"Maybe, yeah. He'll be in California by now."

I picked up the garbage bag and headed for the door. Katie said to send her love to Terry and Anna.

I took the stuff straight to Duke Street. Terry and Anna were expecting me. When we opened the bag the smell filled the room. I put a handful of heads in a sandwich bag, then popped into my flat, a sleepout above an old stable at the back of their house, and took a fifteen-minute nap. I was driving again by ten.

I saw Brian at the Kings Cross rank, slipped him enough gear for a smoke or two, told him to make sure he took a joint down to Steve in the radio room, kept going.

I ran hot for a while on street hails, then it went quiet. That was all right; I was heading for a 35, maybe 40 dollar night, easy, not counting the other business. So near midnight I pulled up at St James rank and turned the two-way down low. Took a look at the paperbacks in the glove box. A Western, a Carter Brown, a book of golfing jokes, and a slim one called *Lost Highway to Hell*. The picture on the cover showed a bosomy girl in beads and a headband, dancing, with a gun in her hand. To one side of her was a bloke with an afro, hunched over a keyboard, while a hard man in the background looked on. I opened it. The title page had been torn out. I started reading.

I sucked on the square of blotting paper and checked out Cathy in the go-go cage. Shaking and twisting. Her hair swayed and swung and flew. Sweat ran down the side of her face. I kept pounding that Hammond B3, man, playing a fat seventh chord with my right hand, syncopated just the way I knew she liked it. She started to shimmy, and the fringe on her dress, and all those sweet bits underneath, shimmied right along. Dig the wavy lines. A Van Gogh pin-up. With neon colours. How long had I been playing that seventh? Who knows? I was out of my goddamned tree, dig?

I looked out at the crowd. Johnny Malone, alias Johnny the Lurk Merchant, his pockets stuffed with trips, stood in front of the bandstand, still as a statue, surrounded by dancers, staring at Cathy. Had he seen her smiling at me?

Another four choruses of soloing, the music pouring out of the big Leslie speaker like nectar, sweeter with every chorus. I had the holy ghost in me. I mean, I was *preaching,* children. The tune was Ray Charles's, 'What'd I Say?' Archie took over and played his sax like a crazy angel for another, what, fifteen minutes? My time-sense was blown to hell. The music flowed on and on and the sound turned into a swirling blaze of colour. It filled the discotheque, starting at the ceiling and working its way down, until everybody, Cathy, Archie, the Maori bouncers, Mick at the bar, even my sad-sack partner Johnny, was surrounded by pulsating haloes. Sweet LSD 25!

And it was like everybody else was seeing the same lights I was. Cathy smiled at me again, and I felt it – I mean *physically*. Watching the beautiful vibrations coming from all those people in the crowd, I imagined that instead of it being 1969 in the Joker Discotheque in Kellett Street, Sydney – the sweet home of funk I co-owned with Johnny, we were time travellers in some freaky space ship, cruising distant galaxies, and we didn't need speech to communicate anymore, we just understood each other's thoughts – you dig? – and when we *did* need to say something, we used pure musical vibration. Ray Charles was our crazy, blind, all-seeing navigator, steering us through meteor showers, alien attacks and shit like that, just *sensing* where we should go, and wherever he took us, that would be cool. We'd meet up with other searchers, crazy sweet like us, but in different ways – outlaws, poets, surfers, musicians, sacred prostitutes, mystics, artists, blessed anarchist lunatics – brothers and sisters all.

Right about then a fight started somewhere up the back of the room, and the Maori bouncers moved in. The bad energy was coming from a strung-out R&R guy named Eddie, one cat who was maybe *not* quite ready for lysergic acid diethylamide. Negative conditioning by the *military-industrial complex* and the CIA, plus a Nam skag habit – had turned Eddie's brain, which was no doubt once beautiful and angelic, into something vicious and twisted, and whenever he tried to turn on, things got VERY WEIRD. Anyway, the bouncer whacked Eddie, and he fell in a heap. End of story, dig? Another heavy picked him up and carried him out. Goodnight Eddie. Kind of changed the vibe for a while there, but hey, that's the world, sweethearts, and your correspondent Mel 'the Cool One' Parker has no illusions about such things. So bros and sisses, I grooved on regardless, and lo, the room and everyone in it sweetened again.

At three that morning I smoked a joint in the back lane with Cathy and we sipped cognac from a bottle I'd taken from the bar. Cathy did a dance, right there in the alley way. Not the fucking Watusi or the Boogaloo, but pure, free, arms-waving, tribal goddess MAGIC. Dig, Cathy had powers. That's not a figure of speech, little ones, I *mean* it. She was possessed by Lilith. She was the Hindu goddess Mohini. She was Delilah. She was Cleopatra. She was Gilda. Morgan le Fay. Medusa. And don't forget Beatrix. She was angel, siren and succubus. She was *She*.

Actually, dear friends, I exaggerate. She was just another chick, right? Like everyone is just another whatever they are. It doesn't do to make out this one or that one is *that* special, dig?

So, truly, Cathy? you ask. Now harken unto the good doctor Mel. She was like this: About five foot six or seven. Good height. Thin, slightly foxy face, brown hair, which she sometimes grew long and was never less than shoulder length. Light brown eyes, large, but not gormless large. Taking-everything-in, never-miss-a-trick large. She leaned a tiny tad forward nearly all the time – gave you an impression of energy and enthusiasm, and even when she was stoned that drive and animation was there. Her brow was clear and even, but deep furrows would suddenly appear if she was laughing or concentrating. They were cute. She gave it all she had, everything, all the time. She didn't fuck around. Metaphorically speaking.

Which leads me to the bod: nicely stacked, but not too much of anything. She could walk into any dancing, stripping, lewdly-displaying-the-wanton-flesh-type gig any time she wanted. But it was never a dumb thing with her. She kept a knowing eye on the staring palookas, and probably picked up a lot more about them than they did about her.

Anyway, Cathy had it all going on that night in the laneway out the back of the Joker. She danced in big circles while I was slouched against the wall, clutching a bottle of firewater. She sauntered over and slowly, beautifully leaned against me. I kissed her cheek, then her nose, then her lips, while she swayed and wiggled.

Then I shook my head and pushed her away.

"It's not right."

"Hmm," she said, moving her hips, "why not?"

"You know, Johnny," I said. "Where is he, by the way?"

"He split when the fight started." She moved forward again. "Forget him. He'll be all right." She nuzzled into my neck and whispered, "Let's go home and fuck."

I looked at the cover again. The author's name was given as 'Mel Parker.' The blurb on the back said, *They live for thrills – drugs, sex, music and MURDER. The shocking truth about Australia's freaked-out generation.*

There was a hesitant tap on my window. A man in a suit, leaning forward, said politely, "Excuse me. Are you free?"

I shook my head, switched on the NOT FOR HIRE sign, started the cab and drove away. I could see him in the rear-view mirror, standing in the street staring after me.

I drove back to Five Dock and filled up at the Victoria Road Shell. Dave asked if I was going to pop into the game out the back. I shook my head. The petrol bill was high for the miles I'd done. Another short fill.

I left the cab back outside the Professor's place, quietly slipped the pay-in under his door and hailed a cab back to Balmain. I knew the driver slightly, and he tried to chat. I was having none of it.

His two-way was turned down low, but like any proper taxi driver I was never *not* conscious of what was happening on the radio, even if I was talking to a passenger. So I distinctly heard Steve call me in. "Car 370 on this channel? Message for 370."

The driver looked at me. "That's you isn't it? You're Bill, right? Bill Glasheen?"

"Don't worry about it," I said, but the bloke already had the mic in his hand. "22 in. Got him right here with me, basey."

"Having an early one?"

"Apparently."

"Tell him there's a message here. Ring his mother."

The driver turned to me again. "Get that?"

I said nothing, so he shut up. We rode in silence until I asked him to stop in Darling Street, two blocks from Duke Street. I paid and walked the rest of the way home.

Lights were on downstairs, sounds of carousing came from the big front room. The Forth and Clyde crowd, smoking the stuff I'd brought over earlier.

I walked quietly down the side of the house to my room above the garage, drew the blinds before turning on the light, sat down at the small table and took the paperback out of my bag.

So Cathy and I went back to the Castle. We made love. Crazy acid love. Cathy knew everything and did anything. Mad sweet bad Cathy, who'd gone to Vietnam as a nurse, become a go-go dancer, made a pile as a booking agent, yet somehow come back to Australia stony broke. Cathy who'd smoked opium with soul brothers in the fleshpots of Saigon, who'd spent 1966 in Paris with the anarchists. Cathy who knew everything. Cathy who RUINED MY GODDAMNED LIFE. The sad truth, my young hellions.

But back on that night, all was warm and soft and dark, and I was the most blissed-out cat in the world.

We slept until two the next day, made love again – slooooooowly – then slept some more. I woke up with the sun low in the sky. Whoa – bad, weird, too bright, wrong-time late afternoon vibe!

I lit a slim joint and got my head nearly right. I was sitting there propped up in bed, slowly coming to, grooving on the early evening sounds when the phone rang downstairs and I heard Cathy's voice.

Half an hour later, Dutch Harry was waiting for me in the lounge room, listening to a Miles Davis record, drinking white wine from a flagon. Big, red-faced, long-haired, wild-eyed.

"At last!"

"Hiya Harry. Where's Cathy?"

"Out there. I'm here with money, my friend."

"Oh yeah?"

"*Fucking* yeah!" He waved a roll of notes in front of me. "You got weed? Like, a pound."

I scratched my head. The phone in the kitchen went off again. Cathy picked it up on the first ring

"It's for this guy I know," Harry said. "He might even go for two pounds if you can get it."

"I'll make a call," I said.

Out in the kitchen, Cathy was smoking a cigarette.

"What does *he* want?" she said quietly.

I held up one finger, then two.

"Ounces?"

I shook my head. "Pounds. Who was on the phone?"

"No one." Cathy went out of the room.

I rang Alex direct, breaking protocol slightly – Johnny normally dealt with him.

Alex, better known as 'the Greek,' didn't seem to mind. He wasn't holding now, he said, but something might be on a little later. He'd make a call, ring back in five. He was oddly nervous.

I left Harry playing records and drinking his flagon, and went upstairs to wait. It was warm, so I opened a window. Cathy was lying on the bed. I lay down beside her and put my arm out to her, but she reached over and lit a smoke.

"How much money has Harry got?" Cathy said.

"Why do you ask?"

Downstairs the phone rang. I ran down, got to it in time. The Greek. He was onto something. Afghani hash. Really good, he said, but we'd have to be quick – it had just arrived, and it was all happening that afternoon. A hundred an ounce, minimum purchase half a pound.

Jesus, big amounts. "I can't manage that," I said.

Cathy had followed me into the kitchen and was waving at me.

"What's he say?" she whispered.

"Hang on a minute, Alex." I cupped the phone. "Hash. He's got ounces. Good gear, but eight ounces is the minimum buy."

Cathy bit her thumbnail, then whispered, "Tell him we'll take it."

"What?"

But she was gone.

"Alex," I said into the phone. "Just wait another second."

Cathy skipped back into the room. "Harry wants the hash. Better than weed. I can flog the rest."

I looked at her.

"Go on, tell him. I'll ring my buyer." She put her head down and gave me that look. "This will work out for us, Mel."

"All right," I said to Alex, "It's on."

He told me to meet him in Oxford Street in an hour.

I took Harry's money and sent him away, told him I'd ring him as soon as I had the gear.

When I went back to the kitchen Cathy was on the phone again. She waved me away. I hesitated. She turned around, whispered, "Mel, *please*."

I stood there and looked at her.

19

She said, "Hang on" into the phone, covered the mouthpiece, fixed me with that incredible gaze and whispered calmly, "Listen, babe, why don't you go fill your station wagon, check the oil and water and all that. We'll do this deal. We'll get some nice cream off the top." She gave me a deliciously evil smile. "And then let's take a long, long drive."

"Where to?"

"Wherever. *What*ever. This is it, Mel, right now. No time to waste." She stepped up closer to me, laid her hand on my chest, let it slip down below my waist, slowly, and said, "You for it?"

Christ, was I for it? She had me. Those beautiful legs, that auburn hair, those breasts, that wonderful devious mind, they all had me, and I was GONE GONE GONE. I didn't think about where we were heading. I didn't think about the trouble I was making for myself. Like the fact that officially Cathy was still hooked up with Johnny, my lifelong best pal and a beautiful soul, but maybe not the smartest cat in the world, nor the most honest, to tell you the *real* truth (Sorry Johnny, if you're out there, but I'm just telling it like it is). No, I was lost, and I didn't think or care, and even if I'd known we were setting off on a GHOST HIGHWAY DEATH TRIP I probably still would have gone. That, my friends, is how fucking crazy Mel Parker was.

So I took the car and tanked up while Cathy cooked up her crazy bitch's brew.

DRIVE BABY!

When I got back Cathy was ready. She wore jeans and an old collarless shirt, no makeup, hair tied back. That pony tail – man, I could write a fucking book about the way it bounced.

"All right," I said, "Let's go."

She shook her head. "First things first."

She rooted through her shoulder bag, brought out a pill

bottle, tipped out four purple hearts.

"Here you go, lover boy," she said and dropped them in my palm, then tipped out another four for herself.

I washed the stuff down and my goddamn brain *EXPLODED* with *ASTRAL FUCKING ELECTRICITY!* I knew in my head and in my heart that everything would be cool, that whatever was to go down, there was no wrong move for us, no mistake, no false step.

But we don't know what lies before us, and if we did know, would we do anything differently? Plenty to ponder there, my young lonesome travellers. Me, I wasn't doing *any* thinking that night – I was just reading the charts, playing my part, not knowing the arranger had scored a coda of pure mayhem for Crazy Daddy Mel Parker. Right then, I was blowing the sweet solo of the angels.

We drove to a big old house in Paddington. Cathy had me wait in the car around the corner while she ran in. She came back five minutes later smiling, waving a fat envelope in my face, "Got money, baby!"

"Whose?"

She shook her head. "Mugs," she muttered. "Forget 'em. Let's go."

I stopped just before Taylor Square. Alex was outside the Oxford Gate, chewing on a shish kebab. Long curly hair, a thick beard, patent leather shoes – he looked half spiv, half hippie. I tapped the horn and he strolled over. He eyed us slowly – baby, we were *HIGH!* – and then told me to drive to Bondi Junction, park near the corner of York Road and wait.

We drove along Oxford Street, my hands white-knuckled on the wheel, teeth grinding. We turned into York Road, parked and waited.

After fifteen minutes the Greek came to the window, leaned over, nervous. "Five ounces?"

I nodded.

"Give me the money. Take your car out of the way around the corner. I'll bring it to you there."

"I'm coming with you."

"You can't."

"No try, no buy."

He looked at me hard, then shook his head. "Jesus, all *right*. But you'll have to give me the tax, just the same. Park the car. Don't bring the girl." He walked off.

"He's desperate," said Cathy quietly.

I took Cathy's money, put it with Harry's, counted out the necessary, put the rest in my back pocket.

Alex was waiting at the corner. We walked a couple of hundred yards down the road to a nondescript semi with an unmown lawn. He knocked quietly. Thirty seconds later he knocked again. The door was opened on the last knock by some long-haired Rasputin cat. We went in. Two bikeys with bandit moustaches, a straight-edged, short-haired bloke, a surfie, and a bearded guy were sitting in the lounge room. There were open cans of beer on the coffee table. No one was speaking.

"Take a seat," said the long-haired bloke. "They'll be here in a minute."

I sure didn't feel like waiting. I glanced at the bikey blokes. They looked like trouble. The smaller one saw me staring.

"What's up your arse, grandpa?"

I said to the Greek, "Fuck this, if there's no dope I'm going home."

There was a knock at the door and Rasputin got up again.

I heard the door open and two or three voices. Rasputin came back in, then he and the surfie disappeared into the kitchen. The surfie came back a minute later, gave us the thumbs-up sign, gestured for us to wait there, went back to the kitchen. I got up and followed him in. The Greek, behind me, whined, "Mel! *Jesus*."

The kitchen reeked of greasy, pungent hash. *Good* hash. Sitting at the table was a guy named Drew, a shifty piece of work, ex-private school, disgraced playboy, widely regarded as a slime and rip-off merchant. In front of him on the table were blocks of hash wrapped in cellophane, each about the size of a half-pound pack of butter, and a cutting board, a knife, a set of chemist's scales. Somebody was noisily taking a leak in the toilet. Drew, who didn't like me (and who, for the record, I didn't like in return), glanced my way then back to the scales, on which sat a big cube of hash.

Rasputin was over at the kitchen bench rolling a joint. "I said to wait outside, man." He started walking towards me, shepherding me out. "I'll bring a smoke out to you."

At that point the back door opened and Cathy walked into the kitchen holding my Smith and Wesson.

Okay, you're wondering why would mellow cat Mel Parker own a fucking roscoe? Well that's just how it is, all right? I've never hurt anyone with it, not really, but it's helped me out of more than a couple of tight corners.

So there was Cathy, holding my pistol. As steady as you like, too. Of all the things I was thinking right then, the main one was that she was fucking magnificent.

The room became very still, everyone staring at Cathy. She pointed the gun at Rasputin and then at Drew. She said to me, "The dope any good?"

"What are you doing?" I said to her.

She ignored me. To Rasputin she said, "Light that joint and give it to me."

He did. She inhaled deeply, still holding the gun in her right hand. She kept the smoke down for a good while, let it out slowly, took another quick toke and passed it to me.

"My compliments to the cook. Get it, Mel, and let's go."

"What?" I took a toke and passed it to Alex.

Johnny Malone came out of the toilet buttoning his fly. He looked at Cathy, the gun, the dope, then at me, and stopped, his face expressionless.

The bikey came in from the lounge room, clocked the crazy tableau and said, "The fuck's this?"

Drew stood up from the table, took a step towards Cathy. She lifted the gun at him, gave it a shake. He grinned and took another step. She shot him in the middle of the chest. He fell like a sack of cabbages, a hundred and ten percent dead.

She pointed the gun at Rasputin, then the bikey. The surfie had seen enough already. The others piled into the kitchen, and stopped. Cathy stood there holding the gun like nothing much had happened.

"We're taking the dope," she said. "We'll leave one block. You can divide it up among yourselves. Gratis. You can tell your people we took it all, if that helps." She pointed at the body on the floor. "Mel, check his pockets."

There were three fat rolls of twenties in his kick. Cathy motioned for me to put them on the table. "A quick whip-round now, boys," she said, pointing the gun from one to the other. They slowly emptied their pockets. Every man present had been set on scoring, so the money pile was not inconsequential.

The Greek said, "Jesus fucking *shit!*" He looked at me and shook his head. "Oh no." He flopped onto a kitchen chair. "This is so heavy."

With her free hand Cathy separated a roll of twenties from the money pile and put the rest in one of the bags of dope. She pushed the role of twenties towards the stunned dope fiends.

"Tell whoever you're scoring for that you got ripped. You needn't tell them about this—" she nudged the roll of twenties with the gun barrel.

She turned to Johnny. "I'm sorry." Back to the open-mouthed drug dealers. "As for this one" – she nodded at Drew's corpse – "I'm sorry, okay? But, you know? Anyway I'll leave you lot to deal with it. Call the cops if you think you can handle it. Or just take care of it your own way."

She looked at me, made the "let's go" sign, and backed towards the door she'd come through. I followed. Then I stopped. "Wait a sec."

Cathy was standing with the screen door pushed half open behind her. She tilted her head, waiting.

Now this Drew character was – had been – an unloved piece of work: he'd been disowned by his rich family, who were no doubt a pack of cunts but maybe had a point in this case, because the guy was without scruples of any kind.

Being of the moneyed class however, he was also a member of the yachting fraternity. And that corpse lying there, bleeding now, was super tanned, the hair sun-bleached. So Sherlock Mel gerried: he was just back from a voyage – he'd brought the hash in. And was suddenly convinced: there was more stuff here, dope, who knows what.

To Cathy I said, "We're not finished here. Keep your wits about you."

Next to the chair Drew had recently vacated was an overnight bag. I peeked inside. A couple of plastic shopping bags. Smaller bags inside them. A lot more . . .

I closed it up, slung it over my shoulder. "All right, Cath. Off we fuck."

We couldn't go back to the Castle, obviously, because Dutch Harry would have wanted some dope or his money back. Even with the .38, neither of us was too keen on another showdown right then. But we couldn't exactly hang around either.

The Joker was closed that night, so we drove to the back entrance, took Drew's overnight bag inside and checked our booty.

Three more blocks of hash and what looked like a hundred or so tabs of acid. Also a sandwich bag of double-O caps, with sparkly white powder in them that we judged to be cocaine. Now this may sound strange to you youngsters, but back in 1969 – not so long ago, but in some ways another fucking epoch – people weren't so interested in powder drugs, especially coke. A touch of heroin laced on a joint for special occasions, okay. But powders generally? Nah, not really.

There was one more sandwich bag with a dozen buddha

sticks in it. And at the very bottom a bottle of mandies – that's Mandrax to you sticklers for accuracy, or what the R&R blokes called Quaaludes. I dropped a mandy to ease the jingle-jangle. All grist for the mill.

We had a drink, then decided to drive to Melbourne, five hundred miles away. Right then. Fuck it. Why not? It seemed like the idea just kind of materialised naturally, on its own. When I thought back, of course it had come from Cathy. Anyway, sights were set on Melbourne, cool sister city of the south. But first we needed to get shit sorted out.

I lugged my Hammond into the station wagon – I'd chopped the thing down years before, best thing I ever did. It was still a bastard to move, but I could do it on my own with a dolly, and the thing was worth the hassle – it was my meal ticket. I took some bread from the safe – Sorry again, Johnny, but I was more than slightly CRAZY by that stage – and grabbed a change of clothes (I kept stage gear there), then we split. We stopped by Cathy's pad, the Koala Motor Inn near Taylor Square, cleared out her stuff, topped up on purple hearts . . . and we *HIT THE ROAD*.

The wee small hours. We were on the Hume Highway eighty miles out of Sydney.

It was too bad about the dead guy back at Bondi Junction. Don't get me wrong, my friends, I believe in the sacred law of karma and I wholly and unreservedly subscribe to the principles of peace and non-violence. But it was hard to think anybody in the world would really miss Drew. Maybe in some crazy way, Cathy had played her part in the cosmic drama by shooting him, just as I was playing mine by driving us to Melbourne with my Hammond B3 loaded in the back, those bags of dope hidden about the car, and a couple of fat money rolls in my pocket. Theologians and philosophers among you can go figure that one out.

In truth, I felt much worse about Johnny, about leaving him stuck in the middle of it all. Before we'd left the kitchen back there, Cathy had asked him – did he want to come with us? Because the moment Drew copped that bullet, there was nothing else for it but to run. But Johnny just looked at her, shook his head slowly.

Thinking about it as we barrelled down the Hume Highway, I figured maybe that was just as well. If there was one soul in all the world who could slip out of a tricky situation, even one as tricky as that, it was our Johnny. So if you're out there, bro, I pray that it's all cool with you and me today, and if not, well maybe we'll meet again some time and straighten it out over a couple of cool ones and a couple of hot ones.

Ten miles outside Goulburn, the highway empty but for the odd truck lumbering over the ranges, Cathy said, "Look out for an all-night Golden Fleece. It'll be along here somewhere."

"It's okay, we've got plenty of petrol."

"Do what I say, Mel. Stop at the Golden Fleece."

I looked at her. Man, had this chick gone COMPLETELY CRAZY? The closer we got to Goulburn, the more nervous she became.

The servo was on the near side of town. When I pulled in, Cathy was out of the car and across the road before I'd even put the handbrake on. I had the kid put a few bucks worth of juice in the tank while I stretched my legs. I went inside, paid for the juice, and when I got back to the car there was a bloke sitting in the back seat with Cathy. Young guy, wiry, short dark hair, green overalls. Head down.

I got in and turned around, but Cathy said, "Drive away, Mel. Keep cool and just fucking drive."

So I did.

No one said a word until we were ten miles out of Goulburn. Then Cathy and this guy had a huge pash session, after which she straightened up and said "Mel, this is Stan. We're giving him a lift to Melbourne. That okay with you?"

This Stan character leaned forward eagerly, patted me

on the shoulder. I glanced back and saw a smiling face. A direct look, maybe sincere. A hand offered. We shook.

"Mel," he said. "I can't thank you enough, brother. I owe you for this, and I won't forget it." He wound down the window and looked into the dark, breathing deep. Then he sat back and said to Cathy, "Got anything?"

She rummaged in her bag and handed him a joint: "Starters." They lit it and swapped it, then offered it to me, but I passed.

She gave him the cognac and he took a long swig. Then the sparkle powder was broken out, and mandies for good measure. Then they settled down together, all mellow and nice.

But man, I was wound tighter than a .013-gauge E string.

Soon afterwards, murmuring, squelching sounds started coming from the back seat. Holy Jesus, I thought to myself, she's making the bloke *right* at home.

I'd long since got hip: the guy was an escapee from Goulburn Jail, and Cathy had it planned all along. The sex and drugs were just to make sure I'd be a willing driver. The dope score, Drew, the hoist – she'd made all that up as she went along, improvising her crazy twisted melody, jamming WILD CRAZINESS.

I remembered that Cathy had been hanging out with some armed robbery boys. Was one of them Stan Something? Yeah, could be. They'd been tight one time, then came a big bust. Bye-bye Stan, good luck with sewing mail bags, and the buggery.

Now he was with us. Problem was, if the cops weren't already looking for us, they'd be after escapee Stan before long. How soon would the alarm be raised at the jail? No later than six.

But if the law *was* after us that night, we saw neither hide nor hair of them. We hit Gundagai with the sun coming up. I needed something in my stomach but Cathy said to keep going, don't stop this side of the Murray River.

It got hot. Baby, it got VERY HOT. The head gasket blew outside Holbrook. We limped to the edge of town. I pulled up and left the motor running, kicking and hiccuping, blowing steam, while I took a leak. By the time I came back it had stalled, and try as I might I couldn't start it again.

"That's it," I said. "It's a job for a mechanic now."

Stan said, "I can't stay here." He turned to Cathy, "I'll get us some transport," and walked off towards Holbrook. Ten minutes later he was back with a newish Ford Falcon.

"I'll never get my organ into *that*," I said.

"Come on," Stan said, "we have to move. *I* have to move."

I looked at Cathy. "I can't leave the Hammond. Or the car. We should let Stan go on while I get this looked at."

She looked me in the eye. I heard it coming: "Stan needs my help, Mel." She put her hand on my shoulder, touched the side of my face. "Get the car fixed and meet us in Melbourne. Or buy yourself another car. Whatever you think, there's plenty of money. I'll make it up to you."

"But where'll we meet?"

Stan said, "The George Hotel at St Kilda. The publican there's staunch. We'll get a couple of rooms."

Cathy said, "But we can't leave the dope in your car, not if there'll be a mechanic crawling all over it."

"I'll stash it," I said.

She shook her head firmly. "Not a good idea. We'll take it with us."

So we transferred the shit to the Falcon. Cathy and I split the money fifty-fifty. I took just an ounce of hash.

Stan shook my hand, firmly, looked me in the eye. "I won't forget what you've done for us. Get to Melbourne quick as you can. I'll look after you down there. You're solid, Mel, and I can dig it. Mind if I take the gun?"

Cathy gave me a long, lingering, full-body-contact kiss. "See you in St Kilda." And then they were gone.

I was stuck in Holbrook until the next afternoon. The motor had a cracked head. But a good cat named Theo dug up a second-hand Holden head and put it all back together, better than it had ever been. Thanks, Theo – you have a mystical connection to the Holden 186 motor, my brother, and I salute you.

I drove on for an hour then had to stop. The purple hearts, the acid, the grass, they'd all drained out of me and I came down hard, wide-eyed and exhausted at the same time. The few remaining molecules of dope in my system bounced around like pinballs, lighting up a frazzled nerve ending every now and then. Man, I was low. Friends, I was staring right into the big fucking infinite zero, the bardic abyss.

In fact, I was somewhere near Albury. I pulled into the scrub and slept for a few hours, drove into Melbourne late that night and went straight to the George in St Kilda. There was no sign of Cathy and Stan.

I put the book down and rubbed my eyes. It was one in the morning. Muffled music came from the main house. I set the kettle on the gas burner, toasted two pieces of bread, made a pot of tea, took it all over to the table. Ate a bite of toast, took a sip of tea, looked at the cover of the book again. I thought, how long since I'd had a ciggy? Nearly two years. I went to the kitchen drawer, got out the pack of B&Hs I kept on hand, lit one and drew deep. Two and a half years without a drink. I got the rum from the cupboard, took a swig straight from the bottle. I sat down, smoking the cig, drinking from the bottle, my mind racing. A gentle knock on my door.

It was Anna. "I saw your light on," she said. "You coming over for a joint?"

I shook my head. "Thanks, not tonight."

She was stoned, and a bit pissed. She shrugged cutely, glanced at the ciggy burning in the ashtray, the bottle of rum. Then she peered more closely at me. "Are you all right?"

I picked up the paperback. "You ever seen this?" I said.

She walked over to the table, then shook her head slowly, smiling. Waiting for the joke.

"It's about Max," I said.

She tilted her head a little. "Really? Well, he is kind of posthumously famous, I suppose."

"And it's about *me*."

She stopped smiling. "Some of the fame rubbed off. Who wrote it?"

I held up the cover.

"Mel Parker? Never heard of him."

"Mel Parker . . . Max Perkal. Get it? And the character who's me is called Johnny Malone. It's written like a novel, but it's obviously about Max and all that happened. It *sounds* like Max. Actual Max, raving off his head. Not someone trying to sound like him. *Him*."

She looked at me, waiting.

"Max has been dead for three years, Anna. More than three years."

"Is it that long?" She took the book from my hand, turned it over, flipped through it. "Where'd you get it?"

"It was in the cab."

She was thumbing for the title page.

"It's not there," I said. "Ripped out."

"Hey, that's pretty fuckin' weird all right," she said, and handed it back to me. "*Someone's* got their eye on you." She smiled again. "Anyway, come over later for a smoke, if you feel like it."

I locked the door after her, sat back down. When I picked up the book, my hand was shaking. I put my head back, closed my eyes, started replaying the old tapes.

❖ ❖ ❖

Back then. A warm autumn night. The whole job, start to finish, is sweet as can be. Within a minute of the truck backing into the loading dock, the roller door opens from inside. Multi is already making progress on the vault out the back. He has it busted within thirty minutes, all alarms disabled. The four men work quietly and steadily for the best part of an hour until the vault is empty, the truck full. The nightwatchman remains absent, as arranged.

Electronics. Small components in boxes. All sorts of things, but the most valuable is some sort of new computer gear just arrived from America. Schottky Bipolar Ram. Except for Multi, none of us even know what it does, but it's valuable, and a handful of in-the-know people in South Africa, New Zealand, Hong Kong are prepared to pay plenty for it.

After less than an hour we drive away slowly through the dark streets of Alexandria and pull into a warehouse about a mile away. The gear is unloaded, sorted into groups, and repackaged. Over the next two days it gets delivered to our buyers. Our last job had been a furniture shop – lounge and dining suites, fridges, stereograms – so everyone involved just loves this stuff.

Two weeks later the crew gets together at a house in Collaroy to divide the whack. The money has come in from the on-sellers with no big complications. Everyone is happy. A perfect hoist. Beers, scotch and wine are drunk. Soft drink for the kiddies. Multi lifts a glass of champagne, and says, "To miniaturization, the way of the future," and everyone laughs. Then we happily go our separate ways.

I'm left with a nice bundle for my contribution, which involved getting the right hoisters together, and doing a bit of driving. My pal Max Perkal, noted Sydney musician and ratbag, had a stake in the job too, a smaller one. But between us we now have the wherewithal to expand our current, sort of legitimate, enterprise.

The year before, the US military had done a deal with the Australian government: henceforth many planeloads of US servicemen would arrive in Sydney each week to blow off steam before being shipped back to Vietnam. This "R&R" – rest and recuperation – promises to give Sydney its biggest night-life boom ever.

For two weeks we watch the hordes of bored Yanks milling around the Cross. Then we rent a place in Glebe, a big room on

Bridge Road, and put the word out to the R&R guys, big party this Friday night. We invite some girls. Max and two other musos do a human jukebox thing, playing Beatles, Stones, Creedence songs. We charge a goodly snip at the door, offer free mugs of flagon wine, and turn a blind eye to joints smoked, pills dropped. We let the girls run their own race, but insist they do nothing out of line on the premises. At the end of the night the cash box is bursting.

So we do it again two weeks later, then again a week after that, then we open up Saturday nights as well. I work the door while Max holds the stage, plays MC. The cops come around, but since we aren't selling grog, just giving it away, we're not technically breaking the licensing laws, so there isn't much they can do other than accept a small consideration and a glass of plonk.

All in all, a not bad way of turning a modest dollar. The last of the good times.

Just before Christmas, eleven at night. The place is three-quarters filled. Party lights, music, boys and girls. Abe Saffron and the biggest Maori lad I've ever seen wander up the stairs, stop at the door, look inside. There's a hundred and fifty people in the room, dancing under the lights. The band in the corner is playing loud. I'm sitting right there at the door, taking the cover charge.

Abe's face crinkles into something that could be a grin, could be a grimace, and shakes my hand. "Bill Glasheen, it's been far, far too long. We miss you. You should come and visit." He doesn't introduce the Maori bloke, but slowly looks around the room again, nodding. "You've done pretty well here, pretty well." He looks back at me, and says, "Congratulations."

My blood runs cold. "Abe, it's not that much."

"No really," he says, "You've shown the mugs something."

Max is on the bandstand singing "Love, Love Me Do," in his strangled cocky voice. Abe nods in his direction and laughs. "The fifth Beatle, eh!"

"He likes to sing his songs," I say. "So, Abe, what brings you here?"

He grin-grimaces again. "Let's get away from this row, so we can chat. Lucas here will mind the door for you."

We go downstairs, sit in Abe's Merc.

It comes out soon enough. After praising our get up and go once more, Abe delivers a more studied assessment of the business. He quickly identifies our most vulnerable point: the crappy location. And he's right. Each week we have to spend two or three days handing out leaflets at the Cross, otherwise no one is going to troop across town to a forlorn, semi-industrial precinct, no matter how rocking the party might be.

Abe sympathises and then, as though he's thinking aloud more than putting forward a proposition, "I've got this room upstairs in Oxford Street," he says. "Got it on a long lease. Doing nothing at the moment."

"Yeah?"

"Used to be a dance academy or something. Has a good floor, a small stage. A block down from Taylor Square. It's not the Cross exactly, but a good spot for—" he nods back towards the room, "that sort of thing. No neighbours."

Then he stops, looks at me, and waits.

"You're about to put it to me, Abe, so go ahead."

"We've had our dealings, Bill. I know you're reliable. A man can make an advance to you and it'll come back on time. I don't trust your mate up there so much, but I trust you, and that's good enough."

"So?"

He lays it out: We take over the Oxford Street space. Abe will get us a liquor license, put in a couple of slot machines, maybe later on run a game out the back. We'll keep the door and the bar, but kick back a percentage to him. It's more or less extortion, in that we don't have much choice. But the deal itself isn't too bad, and the way things are going it could work out well for us.

So in the new year we move. We call the club the House of Cards. We get the license. And Abe's right, of course. It's much easier to get a regular, big-spending R&R crowd to the Oxford Street place.

We have to do some fixing up first: the old joint is pretty drack. A dance hall originally, up a flight of stairs. Thommo's was there for a couple of years, it was a physical fitness gym for a while, then used for storage by the furniture shop downstairs. The old hardwood floorboards are split and worn, plaster is falling off damp spots on the walls. It needs rewiring. It needs a proper bar. But this just happens to coincide with the Alexandria electronics hoist. So we have our share of the readies.

It costs a lot, but it gets done. Abe's people work the bar. They're ripping us off, but within reason. And we're charging high prices. We have to pay proper bouncers now, and we have to kick back to the licensing police, the vice squad, the council, the health department and the fire brigade. We're obliged to serve food – barely edible spaghetti bolognaise – for which we need a kitchen and a cook, of sorts.

But still, by the end of the year we're ahead. Just barely, but the trend is in the right direction.

By then things are rocky on the home front. Eloise and I have more or less gone our separate ways – our mutually relaxed attitudes to foreign orders didn't play out so well in the long run. In theory I still live at the big house in Woollahra, but sometimes three or four days go by without us seeing each other. I try to take the kids out once a week, and always sling some spondulicks into the kitty, make the mortgage payments.

In her mid-thirties now, my wife still looks as impressive as ever with her billowing brown hair, her kaftans, her Black Russians. She affects the to-the-manor-born demeanour she learned when her dad Donny – then the licensee of a scungey Ultimo pub, starting price bookmaker, and occasional on-seller of stolen goods – sent her off to the very best ladies college on the North Shore, where she must have stood out at first, until she got properly tooled up for life among the upper crust. But Eloise understands the ways things really work in this town, did then and does now, and she backs me up when it's needed without having to be prompted. Most of the time.

When we're stuck she comes down and pulls drinks or works

the door at the House of Cards. Calls the punters "darling" in her posh voice, with the saucy inflection. She brings the kids along sometimes for an extra-special treat, just like Donny did with her when she was a sprout. "It's good for the tots," she says, "to see how their daddy's money gets made."

Max Perkal is having a good time, too good. He keeps up there with purple hearts and joints, sometimes acid. Max with a bellyful of purple hearts and alcohol can play rhythm and blues pretty well, but anything non-musical he's likely to stuff up. So when Cathy Darnley returns from Vietnam and starts dancing in a go-go cage at the House, there are emotional complications all round. Things move quickly.

The House of Cards, under Abe's protection and with the cooperation of various civil authorities, naturally becomes a bit of a drug market. Not always and not every day, but if you need to do a deal, the House isn't the worst place in town for it to happen. You give the house a cut, of course. So when Max and Cathy pull their stunt, wise heads mutter that they saw it coming.

The rip doesn't take place in a house in Bondi, as whoever wrote the book has it – it happened late one night in the House of Cards, after closing. I wander in on proceedings, more or less as the book describes, maybe not buttoning my fly exactly, but kind of. A shot is fired, amid much drama. But no one actually gets hit. Which is not as big a distinction as you'd think, because a bridge has now been crossed: guns have been produced at a marijuana deal, and that's a scary new thing.

There is present, as the book describes, a motley gathering of heads and hangers-on, and the deal is indeed orchestrated by a doper of Greek extraction, name of Alex Politis. After everyone on the premises has been relieved of their drugs and money, the safe is emptied. Cathy walks out looking pleased and proud. Max is sheepish, shrugging at me as though it's all out of his hands.

And that's the last I see of Max. Ever. I hear later that he's in Melbourne, then later still that Cathy has cleared out, that Max is playing in some band. But by then I'm not inclined to go after him. I know there'll be nothing to recover anyway. The nearest I'll get to Max Perkal again will be two years later, standing by his casket at Waverley Cemetery while Marty Mooney plays "Just a Closer Walk with Thee" on tenor sax, and a couple of hundred aging beatniks, jazz-dags and stoned young heads whimper into their hankies.

Back at the House of Cards, the night of the rip, I'm left with a safe full of nothing. My problems – or "the Troubles," as I come to think of them – are about to begin. And in short order they will have me living semi-incognito in a sleep-out behind a falling-down hippie house in Balmain, driving a cab on the night shift, neck-deep in unmoveable debt.

❖ ❖ ❖

I woke with a start. It was two thirty in the morning. The music from Terry and Anna's had stopped. I got out of the chair and made another pot of tea. I wasn't going to sleep much anyway. I sat back down, lit another cig and picked up the book. Just holding it gave me a strange and creepy feeling, like I was being watched. I recognised the feeling, of course, the old paranoia. But this was something more.

THE JAM!

I took a room at the George. The next morning I sought out the publican, a harmless-looking old cat. I told him I was supposed to be meeting a bloke named Stan who'd said he was a friend of his. He said he didn't know who I meant. I looked into his eyes. Not a flicker.

I bought the local papers. Nothing about a jail escape in New South Wales, nothing on the radio either. I went to the municipal library that afternoon. The Sydney papers came in at three. There was a story on page two of the *Tele*.

An escape from Goulburn Jail last night. A bloke serving

five years for armed robbery (the Commonwealth Bank at Bexley). Whereabouts unknown. Believed to be dangerous. But nothing, zero, not a word, about any cold-blooded murder in Bondi.

I went to the milk bar and thought about my situation. The mob at the house had got rid of the Drew's corpse after all. It's harder than you might think – take it easy, my little ones, don't ask how I know – but not impossible. Maybe Johnny stepped to the fore there.

The drug rip was a bad scene, sure, and the boys back at that house would be spewing. But they were in Sydney, no doubt stoned off their dials by now, one way or another. I couldn't see them coming five hundred miles after me, even if they knew where I was. So my resolution was: stay clear of Sydney, and with luck, further unpleasantness could probably be avoided. (Tip for hip ones: stay away for long enough and pretty much *anything* can be forgiven and forgotten. Hear me talkin' to ya!)

Cathy. Yeah, bad shit there. Cathy had been a mistake, as bad as mistakes get. Oh brother, she had powers, heavy powers, Christ knows what, white magic, voodoo, some twisted Vietnamese juju. Acid magic, too. LSD bestows weird and dangerous potencies upon certain souls, makes it so they can read minds, bend others to their will, even move matter by thought alone. I've seen all those things. I'm not for burning people at the stake and so on, but phew, heed me friends, don't fuck around with the acid priestess.

Strangely though, my thing for Cathy had gone. Pretty much. Which was further proof the girl had hoodooed me. Now the thrill was gone, the spell was broken, there was nothing in my heart but a big fat fucking ZEEEEEEEEROOOOOOO.

The main thing weighing on my mind: I'd left Johnny in the hot seat. But if anyone in the southern hemisphere could slip out of knots it was our Johnny. And on the other side of the ledger, he still had our nightclub, which returned a handsome dollar – not that I'm *into* money, which is a capitalist mirage we'd be better off without – being as the Joker was party headquarters for an endless stream of American servicemen desperate for rocks-offedness and all manner of diversions. So yeah, when things quieted down I'd return, but meanwhile Johnny could pocket the whole take.

The more I mulled it all over, the better things looked. I was in a new city. I had a car, a Hammond B3 (the sacred instrument of the electric gods, as revealed by their prophet, Saint Jimmy Smith), enough bread to cool it for a while, and a good chunk of hashish. I could feel the karmic current moving me. I had that tingle in my cells, a surge in the blood, that told me: Mel baby, something is about to happen. Have your wits about you, because fate just remembered your name and phone number.

I needed to be prepared for untoward events, just the same. So that afternoon I went to a certain pub in South Melbourne, mentioned a certain name, a name I'd been given one time back in Sydney. No one knew the bloke whose name I mentioned. I waited around, but nothing happened. I went back next day, waited again, drinking just enough to avoid suspicion but not enough to get drunk. Eventually a hard old gaffer moseyed over, dropped the name I'd mentioned, and we had a nice little chat. Nothing was said outright, but later that night I swapped a wad of money for a clean .38 Special. Even if I didn't expect to encounter Dutch Harry, or the Greek, or any of the Sydney crew, it was nice to know that if I did, I'd have some bargaining power.

I checked out of the George the next day, drove down to Geelong, and took a room in a run-down but comfortable enough guesthouse.

The weeks went by. I'd left Sydney needing a haircut, but I let my hair grow longer, grew a beard too. Killed time reading, smoking hash, practicing scales. It wasn't too bad, especially with the good gear. A simple schedule: wake up, smoke something, go for a stroll along the beach. A bite to eat, mucho coffee, the newspapers, then back to the pad to practice.

The dope was holding out better than the money, but no urgency with either just yet. I could've carried on this way for months. But with all that practice I was itching to make real music. And – more wise words from old Mel – it's a thousand times easier to make money when you've *got* money than when you don't.

So one mild and mellow morning I packed the B3 into the station wagon, paid off the landlady and took my leave. I headed around the bay into Melbourne, all the way to St Kilda, put down a bond and a month's rent on a furnished flat on an out-of-the-way block, stuck between a garage and a vacant warehouse.

The place was one block back from the beach, but it had glimpses of the bay, and a lock-up garage, too. (Now hear me, brother and sister musicians: a lock-up garage is a *must* for those late nights when you get home too drunk or stoned to unload your gear).

That night I hit the bricks.

All right, hipsters, I know what you're thinking – Melbourne! Trams and quiet Sundays. Glen Waverley and Moomba. Blokes in grey cardigans going home through grey streets to grey wives and grey kids. Industrial shithole or suburban death zone. Yeah, I know. Well, listen to your Uncle Mel, because I'm right here telling you, Melbourne that year was the funkiest town in the country. Nay, fuck that, *in the southern motherloving hemisphere*. Oh sure, the discotheques were dry, the pubs closed early, the streets were empty. And there was nothing like Kings Cross, with its clip joints and nightclubs and brothels, all existing solely for the extraction of dollars from the pockets of Yankee soldiers on R&R, which it had been ordained, MUST and could only happen to the non-stop accompaniment of funkful soul music, preferably played by one or another band led by your faithful correspondent and teller of truths, Mel 'Wild Man' Parker.

But I digress. Melbourne didn't do it that way. Down there it was hidden doorways and signs that said "For Madmen Only." It was a crazy lodge, with secret handshakes and arcane signals. Nothing to see on the outside, but inside – madness and anarchy. Music, drugs and dancing to make Sydney look half-arsed.

Three days later I'd hooked up with a jazz-fusion group called the Bright Lights. A lucky break. We were playing three, four gigs a week. Wild parties afterwards in ramshackle mansions around East Melbourne, terrace houses in Carlton, mad farmhouses out Eltham way.

Within a few weeks I was also moonlighting with a rock'n'roll band called the Rods, playing suburban dances for greasy, leather-jacketed bodgies and purple-mohair, beehive-hairdo widgies who didn't know what year it was.

Theatre, too. Don't be surprised, my darlings, Mel Parker is an initiate of the thespian arts. I got a gig playing abstract accompaniment to a nonsensical piece of theatre at the Old Bakery. Never worked out what the hell it was about, but the writer, a young guy known as "Spinner," told me I wasn't supposed to, I should just keep doing what I was doing.

But it is ordained that such times can't last. One night, as we writers like to say, I was playing with a little pickup jazz group in a St Kilda café. Standing outside, taking a break, a tap on the shoulder. I turned around: Stan.

"Hiya, Mel." He stuck out his hand. "How's everything?" We shook. For my part, the handshake was not enthusiastic. But Stan's was. He patted me on the back like we were old, deep friends. "Great to see you, bro." And fuck me, he sounded sincere.

Now, let me give you the mail on Stan. Last time he'd not been at his best, having just crawled, climbed and clambered out of Goulburn Jail. I for my part had been suffering a bad case of the Hume Horrors, so all I'd registered was a raggedy-arsed desperate in the back seat.

He was a different character now. He looked lean and

fast. His hair was short on top, longer at the back, in the Melbourne style. His eyes were clear, his gaze direct, ready for anything. He had on Levis, a red and blue striped T-shirt, both clean and new. There was another bloke with him, hawk-nosed, fair-haired, his head down, sucking on a cigarette. The back-up.

Later on there would be all that talk in the press and on the radio about Stan and me and the others, and the shit we did. Every idiot journalist and politician in the country would come up with some crazy theory or other – international criminal conspiracies, the harmful effects of drugs and music and leftist politics, the rising tide of contempt for law and order – Oh brother, and they said *we* were out of our trees – and people cast around for a mastermind who was orchestrating it all. Well I'm here to tell you children, it didn't happen that way. There was no master plan. One thing just led naturally to another. We thought we were paddling our own canoe, but we had no idea where it was heading until we were halfway over the falls.

But mark my words: none of it would have happened if it hadn't been for Stan. He had brains and he had guts, and he had something else, a quality I've only seen in a few people, something sweet and visionary that swept other people along with him. People wanted Stan around, they wanted to do what *he* wanted. He wasn't some kind of Svengali character, though, despite what a certain fuckwit journo later suggested. He was the front man of the operation, but he wasn't the leader exactly. He had no more of a grand vision of what was going on than anyone else. He was just having fun, going that one step further, upping the ante with each move, because that seemed the only thing to do. Not that I knew any of that outside the café in St Kilda that night.

"You're still at large," I said.

He shrugged. "Got to tell you. The George Hotel business. Makes me feel bad." He shook his head. "We lobbed there, and it didn't feel right – I saw a bloke drinking in the front bar, a notorious dog. So I split. *We* split, me and Cathy. She said you'd sort yourself out, and we could make it up to you later."

"Cathy?"

Stan shook his head. "She's not with me now. Beautiful chick, but . . ." He lit a ciggy, looked around. "This is Jimmy." We shook. Jimmy grunted at me.

"Listen," said Stan, "Let's get off the street." He bent his head towards a Fairlane parked around the corner.

After we all got in, Stan said, "You want a toot?"

I shook my head.

He pulled a cap from his shirt pocket, tapped some powder out onto a cigarette pack, worked it into two lines with a penknife, put it on the seat between us. He rolled a twenty-dollar note and sniffed up a line. "Try that. Best speed you'll ever have."

I hadn't had any go-fast since that big night in Sydney. "No thanks."

"Sure?"

"I've been taking giddy-up since before you lit your first cigarette. I know what I want and don't want. Thanks anyway."

Stan grinned. "Munching the sponge from a Benzedrine inhaler? Aspros dissolved in Coca-Cola?"

Jimmy snorted from the back seat. "Jiving to Benny Goodman records?"

Stan chuckled. "*This*—" nodding at the line of powder between us, "is the new thing. But suit yourself."

Fact is, there's always been some part of me, the seeker you might say, or maybe the idiot, that wants to change. Change up, change down, change fucking *sideways*. Doesn't matter what, just . . . be altered. Oh yes, comrades, there was a crystalline sparkle to that white powder, and it was beckoning to me.

"Gimme that." I took the rolled-up note, leaned over, snarfed up the other line. It stung like a bastard, but a moment later I felt my scalp contract and my heart thumped hard. I felt goooooooood.

After we'd shared a few silent moments, Stan said quietly, "Back then. You did the right thing by me."

"Ahh. Doesn't matter."

"No, mate, it does. And now I want to do the right thing by you. Got a business proposition for you."

I WALK ON GUILDED SPLINTERS

I'll spare you all the I saids, he saids and we saids – this is Mel 'Mr No-Bullshit' Parker talking, after all, not Leo Fucking Tolstoy.

Nutshells-ville: one of Stan's crook overlord mates had come upon a batch of factory-made amphetamine sulphate, the by-product of a warehouse robbery. Totally pure, so very strong. And very much of it. As a gesture of hail fellow, welcome home, and many thanks for not gobbing off when you got pinched over the Bexley bank heist, said crime czar had given Stan these numerous pounds – yes, you heard me, kiddies – *pounds* of white powder to help him get back on his feet.

Yours truly was to be a kind of local rep, responsible for supplying powdered go-fast to musicians, artists, writers and other deadbeats. I was suspicious at first – you would be too, right? My question to Stan was, Why the hell me? His line was, Because you're a staunch cat, Mel, solid as a rock, like a brother, and I'm back at him, Yeah sure, whatever you say, now give me the *real* story. He gets uncomfortable and lets it out in dribs and drabs. He personally hasn't a clue how to go about retailing the product.

The thing was, Stan may have been a criminal visionary, with genuine charisma, but back then he wasn't connected. He'd grown up in the rough and tumble of beer, footy, bashings, thievery and union politics, among the cop-hating, IRA-sympathizing, undeserving working class of Collingwood. He knew that world pretty well, and it knew him, but he was a newcomer to the underground. Pot was a novelty to him, he'd only dropped acid once or twice, and for all I knew he still listened to Roy Orbison records. Back in Sydney, before his last arrest, he'd made the scene with Cathy. He'd introduced her to his crowd, to gunmen and second-storey boys, and she'd dragged him around to freak parties, art galleries, Balmain poetry readings and Trotskyist meetings. He was just starting to get the hang of all that when he was pinched for the Bexley job.

I did another line while we sat there in the Fairlane, Stan laying out his grand money-making speed-flogging plan. I told him I was sort of interested, then went inside and finished the gig – I was playing guitar that night. Later on we gabbed our way into a party at Brighton – me, Stan and 'Jimmy the Thug,' as the backup guy was known.

Stan's people were a noisy, rough and hell-bent crowd, rangy, loose-cannon psychos. Rock'n'roll records were playing, glass was breaking. I saw a boy and girl, nine or ten years old, smoking cigs and getting pissed. No one seemed to care. A couple of women had a brawl out the back, and fought as rough as any men. In the kitchen a dog was trying to fuck a cat.

Stan was the big hero. As an escapee on the run, of course, but more than that. The people watched him almost shyly, they deferred to him, men and women equally. He spoke quietly, but when he did they listened.

The sun came up and we were still flying, hard-edged, clear-eyed, speed-mad. All that day we went from house to house, pub to pub, taking a sniff every few hours.

When I rolled up to my job at the Barrel Discotheque that night – by then I was playing the funk-filled Hammond B3 two nights a week with Bobby Boyd and the Oracles – I was packing a pocket full of speed deals, neatly folded in foil. I was primed to kick off the retail venture in fine style:

Bobby and the boys and their various wives, girlfriends and hangers-on were dopers, every man jack of them.

But drugs were iffy in those days: you could never rely on them being there when you wanted them. Someone would go to Bali for a few weeks, bring back some buddha, sell a bit, give the rest away to friends. Someone else would have purple hearts now and then. Hashish was a delicacy, hash oil even rarer. Junkies had their tame doctors and their chemist busts, but they were in a separate world. You wanted your drugs regular, you had to leave the country. So me, with my supply of high-quality powder, offering consistent deals, neatly packaged, at stable prices – that was a whole new thing.

Listen to me now, you lot, let me lay on you some heavy tips regarding the purveying of mind-fucking substances. With the exception of Bobby Boyd himself, who'd been in the game almost as long as me, who'd played hillbilly, rock'n'roll, rock, soul-funk, fusion, and who knew the truth, that music was a gift of the gods, and who also knew that to help us play it, they, the gods, had given us drugs and alcohol, and who had therefore fallen upon my new-found supply of amphetamine with expressions of joy and thankfulness – with that sole exception, my questing ones, every single person I sidled up to that night, I mean every last one of them, told me the same miserable, useless, sorry-arsed, bullshit story. They liked pot, they told me, or they liked acid, or they liked magic mushrooms, or morning fucking glory seeds, or opium, or even the occasional line of smack or what-fucking-ever, but none of those fiends – that's right, not a single one – would cop to liking speed. A frown, a turning-up of the nose, a shake of the head. Oh no, not speed. Speed's a *bad* drug, speed fucks your brains, speed makes you paranoid, speed ruins your teeth, and so on. One chick even told me the problem with speed was, it keeps you awake.

Oh, but offer one of those scoffers a free line, my pets,

and they'll fucking well horn it up in the blink of an eye, all the time telling you, too bad it's not [here insert their drug of choice]. And then they'll continue to bang on for the next seventeen hours about how much they don't care for your speed, which they will continue to sniff up every time it's offered, all the while making out they're doing you a favour. And then the next time you see them they'll tell you again, in case you'd forgotten, how much they don't like that shit, in tones of outright condemnation – but hey, you wouldn't happen to have a snort with you by any chance? Because it's going to be a long night and just this once it might be the thing they need to get 'em over the hump. Oh, hear me, impressionable ones, selling speed to heads is tough work.

After two nights on the trot at the Barrel, a quarter of an ounce of sparkling sulphate had disappeared up greedy nostrils and I had scarcely a shekel to show for it. I rang Stan that night with a sales report: plenty of stock moved, poor cash-flow situation. Like me, Stan hadn't really slept the past few nights, and a volatile reaction to the news would not have been unexpected. But he took it well. He was icy cool, in fact. Said yeah, same story his end.

It is not the way of Mel 'Psychonaut' Parker to give up easily, however. I knew the product was first-rate, it was just a matter of finding the right market. I got on with my business, drawing water and chopping wood as the ancients counsel. I was doing my thing, playing my part, vamping the chords, dear ones. There *would* be a key change, I knew, for such is the nature of things. The big question: would yours truly be ready?

I woke up with the book open across my chest. Eleven a.m., sunny outside. I made a cup of tea, ate more toast. Smoked a cigarette. Walked up and down. Had another cup of tea, another cig, then went to the corner phone booth and rang the Professor to tell him I wasn't going to drive that night.

Before I could get to that he said, "Phil is looking for you. He's rung here twice."

"Right."

"He said he tried you on the network."

"Yeah. Listen, I can't drive tonight."

"Just like that?"

"Yeah." I said nothing more. There was still time for him to get a driver for the three p.m. start.

After a moment he sighed and said, "All right. But ring Phil for Christ's sake, will you? I don't want the cunt on my hammer."

"While I've got you," I said. "There was a book in the glove box. Cover has a chick with big tits, dancing, a couple of shady blokes in the background. Know the one I mean?"

"The shit you blokes leave in that glove box, I tell you. There's always a few books in there, aren't there?"

"This one's a kind of thriller."

A pause. "I'm not with you, mate. Did you lose it?" Sounding genuinely perplexed.

"Never mind."

So I rang Phil.

"Bloody hell have you been?"

"Nowhere. What do you want?"

"I need you to do a little something."

"Yeah?"

"No need to sound so enthusiastic. I want you to go see the Lebs again. I need them out of there."

I said nothing. A Lebanese family was renting one of Phil's old houses in Annandale. He'd been trying to get rid of them for months, had me go and see them a couple of times. They'd been friendly but apologetic. They weren't going anywhere too soon.

The silence dragged on a few seconds, until Phil said, "Billy! You there? Hear me?"

"I'm here."

"Well fucking answer then."

"Answer what?"

"Tell me, 'Yes Phil, I'll do it.'"

I sighed. "I'm busy for the next few days. I'll drop by when I get a chance."

"I'd like you to go there next Saturday. In the morning. No more bullshit. I'm sending Barry along with you."

"Barry *Geddins*?"

"Yeah."

"He's a liability."

"I want him to be there. And I want *you* there to keep an eye on things."

"Keep an eye on him, you mean?"

"That too. Meet him outside the Toxteth at eleven."

I bought a newspaper and a bottle of milk from the corner shop. As I turned back into Duke Street, there was a new yellow P76 parked a little way down the street. A hundred yards away, a bulky figure was opening the front gate of the place a couple of doors down from mine. Barry, the liability we'd just been discussing.

I watched for a minute without him seeing me. The householder came to the door. There was a short exchange, Barry standing a little too close to the householder, the householder pulling back, Barry closing the gap again. Then he left, tried the next door. Big friendly smile on his face. I could imagine his line. "I'm looking for an old mate named Billy, late thirties, sandy-haired bloke. Lives in this street, but I've forgotten which house." It wouldn't take him long to find Terry and Anna's.

I called to him before he could knock on our door. He turned around and walked back to the footpath.

"Where have *you* been?" he said, still grinning. "Phil is looking for you."

"I spoke to him just now."

Barry looked around. "Yeah? Did he tell you about us going to see the Lebs?"

"How did you know to come to this street?"

He smiled. "Ah, so you *don't* know everything, do you?"

"The taxi driver, right?"

He pointed to the derelict house across the street. "Is that one yours?" he said, guffawing.

I didn't answer.

"Just kidding." Barry waited, staring at me for way too long. I held the stare, but it wasn't easy. Then he shook his head. "Jesus, you're a hard cunt to be friendly to." He shook his head. "No need to be so hostile," he said quietly, an ever-so-slight note of hurt in his voice.

He walked off, turned around when he got to his car. A forced smile now. "See you at the Tocky."

I walked back up the street, away from my flat, and watched him drive away. I came back only when I was sure he'd gone.

I went inside and packed a couple of suitcases, then went to the back of the main house. Anna and Terry were in the kitchen drinking tea. The place was tidy, no sign of last night's partying except for a box of empties by the back door.

Anna was a psych nurse at Callan Park. She was wearing denim overalls today, her hair in a plait, smoking a roll-your-own. Terry was early thirties. Beard and long hair, but not scruffy. Hair parted in the middle, tied back and clean. His official job was as a cook at Balmain hospital. Unofficially, he was a trader in old furniture and an unlicensed dealer in second-hand cars, one a fortnight, sold through the *Herald* classifieds. A bit of dope in the mix, too. And now, like me, he was an investor in the film industry.

I sat down at the table. Anna smiled and pushed the teapot and a mug my way.

"Eloise rang a little while ago, said to ring her," she said.

"Okay," I said. I pulled out my wallet, counted out fifty dollars and put it on the table. "Rent. I'll be away for a few weeks." I asked Terry, "Can I borrow your ute for an hour or two this afternoon?"

"Sure."

Anna looked serious. "Everything all right?"

I nodded and said, "It's unlikely, but if anyone comes around looking for me—"

Terry put his hand up. "We know, Bill. It's okay."

They did know. That's what I liked about them.

Anna said, "That book you showed me last night . . ." and trailed off.

I shook my head. "Not sure about that," I said. "Gotta straighten a couple of things out." I drank the tea, got up.

Anna said, "Eloise said for you to ring her."

"Yeah, you told me."

"She said I was to tell you twice."

I drove out to Matraville with my bags. Turned off Bunnerong Road, followed a track through a gate, past the Chinese market gardens, around a sandhill, then another one, to an old shack. I hadn't been here in a while, and the spiders and rodents had moved back in. I spent an hour cleaning up, airing the place out, firing up the kero fridge. The bushes had grown since the last time, but that was good, it made the place even less visible.

I bought groceries at Maroubra Junction, stocked the fridge, which had cooled nicely, took the car back to Balmain. I hailed an RSL cab – no one at that network knew me, I hoped – and had the driver take me to Kingsford. From there I took the bus back to Matraville. When I walked past the gardens, not one of the Chinese working in the paddock even looked up. That's what I liked about them. I hacked out some weeds growing around the door of the shack, upsetting a clumsy blue-tongued lizard in the process. It got late.

Standing at the front door, I could see in the distance the back of the drive-in screen, the white oil tanks at Boral, the top of the crematorium chimney, and the very tallest of the smokestacks over at the ICI complex. Nothing else. No houses. Not even a road. Just the track leading to the cabin. I went inside, pumped up the pressure lamp, lit a mosquito coil and sat down. I felt the need for a cigarette, bad as I ever had.

❖ ❖ ❖

Monday morning at the House of Cards, three days after the rip. The place looks forlorn by daylight, and it smells of stale cigs, cheap perfume and spilt booze. An emergency meeting of the Combine has been called.

Abe's bought an offsider, not Maori Lucas this time but a bulky, mean-looking sergeant-major type named Jim. He has a big mo, a pommy accent, and is clearly itching for trouble. He silently sets up chairs and a table in the middle of the room.

The Greeks arrive. No smiles, none of the usual "Life's a crazy party, so let's have a drink and lose the long faces." Today it's business. Joe Dimitrios is there in person. Quiet, dark, wearing heavy-rimmed glasses, not unlike Abe in size and stature. Two younger toughs with him, Mascot boys, looking elaborately casual. They take their places against the wall. One of them nudges the other, points to the shattered glass on the floor opposite, where Cathy's single gunshot the previous Friday night had taken out the old dance academy mirror. The lads smirk.

Alex, Joe's nephew, sits at the table, a hangdog look on his face. Next to him is Danny, a large, youngish bloke, hunched over. Not too bright, but mean. He'd been present last Friday night, he's one of the "bikeys" referred to in the book. Works as a bouncer for Joe sometimes.

Another dark-haired bloke comes in, smiling amiably. Heavy-set going on pudgy, but well-groomed. At first glance you might think he's an easygoing spiv. His name's Phil, he's a property speculator, doing well building flats and town houses around Glebe and Annandale. He waves vaguely at everyone and takes a seat, catches my eye and shakes his head sadly. It's meant as sympathy. But he's a shark, and he can smell blood.

Heavy steps on the stairs and Detective Sergeant Fred Slaney walks in, puffing. He glances around at the gathering and grins. He looks at me and winks, grabs a chair from against the wall and joins the circle. And at my right is my father-in-law Donny, in his white shoes and Ban-Lon sports shirt, his grey hair plastered down, smoking a Senior Service, trying to look at ease. He's anything but. A former publican, for the last few years he's been mixed up in the second-hand motor trade, runs a yard on Parramatta Road. He's doing something on the side with Joe and Abe, something involving stolen cars and cleaned-up spare parts being sold as new. Donny wouldn't normally be considered a big enough fish to sit in on a top-level meeting of the Combine, the car parts rort notwithstanding. But sometimes they let him hang around, if they think he might be useful. He's smiling ingratiatingly at no one in particular.

I stand up. "Okay, that's everyone. Drinks?"

Mumbled replies. No drinks. So I sit down again.

Abe starts. "Thanks to all of you for making the time today. We have a bit of a fucking mess on our hands, but I'm sure we can deal with it like grown men. Our combine can deal with this, I think, so long as we listen to everyone's point of view and—"

Joe's voice cuts across him. "This fool—" he nods at Alex on his left, "lets a girl steal from him. His problem, not mine. But Mr Danny—" he nods to his right and the bikey straightens up a little, "and I have dealings with one another. So Mr Danny and his friends are very upset. And this one—" again he nods at Alex, "is my nephew. So it's my job to do something about it." He looks at his watch.

That glance at his watch makes Joe's meaning clear. Let's not waste any time. Just punish the next person in line. Bill Glasheen. And take everything he's got as compensation.

The meaning isn't lost on anyone, and there's a moment of dead silence. Then Abe says, nodding, "Yes, Joe, we all understand. But it's complicated. Bill didn't really have a hand in this, even though his putz of a friend did. And this place here—" he gestures around the room "has a future. And we have a big stake in that future. So . . ."

He lets that hang there. His meaning is equally clear: "We" means Abe, and Abe isn't going to let Joe take anything from him.

Abe continues. "So let's look at what's practical here." He looks in my direction. Wants me to make an offer.

"All right," I say. "It's simple. You figure out what you're owed and get it from Max and Cathy, wherever they are. Nothing to do with me. That's all there is to it."

The Mascot boys brace. Joe shakes his head. Abe is stony faced.

I've gone this far, so I go on and fill the silence. "I get where this is heading. You want to take this place from me. After the money I've spent. The work I've done. Well, forget it. Now, with respect, I'd like you all to fuck off and let me go about my business." I stand up. No one else moves.

I go downstairs and out onto Oxford Street, to the espresso bar a few doors up.

Two minutes later Fred Slaney and Donny find me there, seat themselves either side of me.

Slaney says, "Got a gun?"

I'm not armed. I don't even own a gun. I shake my head.

"You really want to take them on?'

I look at Slaney. The question's genuine. Big, ruddy-faced, coarse-featured. But clear-eyed and shrewd. And eager for trouble.

Ten years earlier, Detective Sergeant Fred Slaney shot a man dead in cold blood just to make an impression on me. Extorted big bugs out of me. Nearly killed me. Later I nearly killed him. Then four years ago, in 1965, he knocked on my door and politely said he wanted to talk. I told him to fuck off.

He did, but he came back a month later, and again I fucked him off. Again he left. Then a month after that came again. I told him I'd give him one minute to explain himself. Right there at the front door.

"I want to square up with you," he said. He was off the drink, a reformed character. "I'm making amends to some of the people I've wronged."

"That'll be keeping you busy," I said. I told him to fuck off.

He shrugged sadly and fucked off.

Six months later a thing I had going on went sour unexpectedly. It was messy, but my hands were tied – I had a wife, a kid, another on the way, couldn't attend to the mess properly. Slaney fixed things, without me asking. He did it quietly, and no one knew. I only found out by accident much later that he'd intervened. I was angry. I hadn't asked for his help, didn't want it. But he kept doing me small favours here and there, looking after my interests. After a while it became just the way things were.

Eloise asked me one time whether I trusted the bloke.

"No." I said, "Not a bit. But I'm getting used to him."

Now, sitting in the coffee bar, Fred says, "The natural solution for that lot—" nodding vaguely in the direction of the club, "would be to shoot you. Right now. A deal of any sort, that's a special concession as far as they're concerned. That big Scottish cunt is tooled up. The Greeks probably are as well. On the other hand, Abe would hate any trouble right here and now, in broad daylight."

"My, that's a huge relief," I say.

Slaney looks away, shakes his head. "Abe's way would be to come back later and burn you out. Place full or empty – wouldn't matter so long as there was some insurance to collect."

"Fuck him."

"Yeah, fuck him. But if you do go up against them, you'd want a strong team."

He glances at Donny, who sees the look and comes in hastily, "Well, you know you can count on me, Bill. I can get a few good blokes together. Just give me the word." He bares his teeth in a tight, hostile grimace, punches his left palm with his right fist, says, "Bang!" The response is too hasty. He looks down at the floor right after. It's an empty promise.

A few seconds later Donny goes on. "But the thing is, it's not just you and me. If we turn on a blue, then everyone is in line. Eloise. And the kids, for chrissake."

I say nothing.

"They've got you by the short and curlies."

"It sticks in my craw, letting those arseholes take the business."

"Early days yet," says Fred. "But while we're at it, how good is the business anyway?"

In fact, R&R numbers are tailing off and trade has been levelling out. Max and I had discussed it: if we were to carry on, sooner or later we'd have to either turn the joint into a rock music club, for kids, or a gambling joint like the 33 or the Forbes.

I don't say that to Fred or Donny. "So what are my choices?"

"Right now, you've got to blue with them, or strike a deal."

I sit there for a moment, doing my best to think it through. Donny next to me, talking tough. It's true, he has a whole team of dodgy characters, car salesmen, thieves, fences, mechanics. Crooks and spivs to a man. But they're not gunmen. Slaney is all I've *really* got on my side. One psychopathic killer. Not enough.

"All right," I say. "No blue."

❖ ❖ ❖

When it was fully dark outside I cooked a pan of sausages on the primus and then made a pot of coffee. Flying ants flitted about the room, gathered on the kero lamp.

I drank the coffee then went outside, walked around the cabin, followed the track a little way towards the road. Just checking. Lights were on in the bungalow. I had no idea how many Chinese kipped there, who they were, or where they were from. Apart from them, there wasn't a soul around.

I went back inside the cabin, gave the Tilley lamp a good pump, hung it from a rafter, and sat down on the cane chair. I picked up the book, put it down again, stood up and walked around. After another half an hour of that I finally sat down to read.

TAKE ME TO THE BRIDGE!

Winter was becoming spring, and I was the speed Santa of the Melbourne discotheque scene. People had finally started picking up on the new powder thing. Parties would start after midnight and go through the next day and night. Cats were grinding teeth, bobbing their heads, dancing like dervishes, drinking without let or hindrance. Musos were jamming high craziness for hours, even days on end. The whole damn town was *raving*.

I'd been making free with the shit, and was digging the heady round of boogaloo parties as much as anyone. Each day I'd resolve to give not one grain away, then that night I'd be chopping up lines for all and sundry. I was the Wizard of Whizz, the Guru of Go-Fast, the Master of the Good Ship Giddy-Up. Dig this, children: if you're going to play Captain Trips, then be free and open-handed about it. You'll fill your pockets just the same. But it never hurts to put a little something in the poor box, so to speak.

Anyway, that groovy Melbourne spring – music, parties, speed. Beautiful ladies with long straight hair and willowy figures, cool, amused and reckless. Tech college and art school students, earnest university girls. Chicks who worked in clothes shops, ran market stalls, or sold matchbox-fulls of smoking dope. Young lads who were playing at being musicians, painters, poets or freelance philosophers. Ne'er-do-wells and no-hopers, most of them, trust-fund playboys and Toorak tramps, still too young for their character flaws to show. Funsters, though. There were a few Maoists, forever gobbing off about the violence that liberates and the violence that oppresses, property being theft, and so on and so forth, while horning up the free drugs on the side. Would-be Neal Cassadys, soldiers of fortune, itinerants, vagabonds, mad scientists, fugitives, bikey types and crazy visionaries. Queers and lesbians flitting in and out. Petty criminals and hard men from Stan and Jimmy's crowd, mellow and sweet on dope and music.

Gradually a core group formed. There was Bobby Boyd, the bandleader and singer. Bobby was King of the Heads. The President. He sang in a big-voiced soul-blues style. Bobby was a solid cat, then and always.

There was Denise, photographer, arts student, freelance

journalist, and aspiring novelist. Younger, a big girl, just the right side of plump. Thick blond hair parted in the middle in kind of a supercharged Bardot style. Wore R.M. Williams with Cuban heels, straight-leg Lee jeans, bulky knitted jumpers – Afghan or some shit – carried a big shoulder bag, flicked her long straight hair around. Private school, equestrian, confident. She first turned up at the Barrel saying she was writing an article about Bobby for a student paper. We talked, we took drugs, we made love, we moved on.

There was a bloke named Clive, another journo. A fop. Wore a linen suit. Trying to look like Tom Wolfe, was my guess. He had plenty to say, pontificated about the "Carlton Underground" and such things. Took lots of drugs but was never seen to pay for any, or bring along any of his own. Wrote music reviews for a Sunday paper.

Another character who was usually still there when the rest had finally gone home was this heavy-drinking toff, a large, fruity bloke, always calling people "dear boy" and so on. Said to be ex-military, but he had a taste for the new-fangled drugs. I'd never seen anyone put away as much. With a certain roguish charm, even old seen-it-all Mel had to admit. They called him 'the Captain.'

Stan stuck pretty close, too. *His* crowd of old-school crooks and roughnecks mostly thought drugs were a long-haired degenerate poofter thing, but Stan was getting good mileage hanging around the Barrel and other discotheques, tagging along to the inevitable all-nighter at my flat or someone else's. Usually with Jimmy the Thug in tow. No one, but *no one,* in the scene knew the speed was coming from Stan.

Over time the money side picked up, thanks to a knock-about guy named Vic, who arranged the muscle for some of the rougher suburban rock'n'roll gigs I still did from time to time. Vic was a pill-popper from way back, but I'd turned him on to powder speed one day, and Jesus god he took to it. Came back the next day and bought – yes, *bought* – half a dozen caps. Same again a few days later.

Vic was a bikey, but not your stereotypical kitten-drowning, flying-booted brute. He was a short, nuggety bloke, ginger-haired, with a broken nose and a pugnacious air, yet quietly spoken, a thinker of sorts, who always figured the odds, planned his play. A good person to sell dope to. Stuck to his word, was good for credit. Vic made the Barrel scene too, and palled up pronto with Stan and Jimmy, who recognised a fellow hardhead.

When the booze was all gone and the partyers had drifted off, it'd be those same few diehards remaining – me, Stan, Jimmy, the Captain, Denise, Clive, Bobby and Vic – still playing records, jamming, sniffing lines of speed as the sun came up.

The Oracles had been working plenty that winter, but they had started heading in what I considered to be square and unhip directions. Bobby had taken to wearing long robes, with little mirrors and shit sewn into them. His afro hairdo was big enough to hide a cat in. Me, I still wore my beret, sunglasses, black skivvies and such. I had long since reverted to my bad hombre moustache, but the fellers in the band had begun nagging me about the "look," saying I needed to grow my hair longer. They wanted me to wear the kaftan, beads and so forth. Dig, chillen, this tragic shit was uttered to yours truly, Mel Parker, King of the Hipsters! But since my hair is naturally curly, I grew it out, and let Bobby's hairdresser girlfriend Maysie turn it into an afro. With my swarthy Levantine complexion, I was quite the white negro.

But yeah, the aforementioned unhip directions: the band was playing longer and longer songs, with drum solos that went on forever. The guitarist had two amps now, and played loud enough to be heard in Antarctica. Audiences stopped dancing and took to squatting on the floor instead, zombie-staring at the band. A head named Zack put on a light show, and the group no longer played dances or discotheque gigs – no, that was old-hat shit. Now it had to be art. Performance. An *experience*. And the band name was changed to Oracle, singular, without the "the." I mean, what kind of bullshit was *that*?

Not that I was dead set *against* the psychedelic music thing – hey, my little astral travellers, hadn't I been an acknowledged acid pioneer nearly a decade earlier back in Sydney? Oh yeah, I could tell you stories about visions and other worlds, and those old doors of perception. (And for that matter about what lies beyond, the League of Secret Rulers of the Fallen World and whatnot, who are responsible for nearly everything. But alas, another time for that one.)

Because that spring, late 1969, was when acid really took hold. Each month more and more recruits were turning on for the first time, and thereafter doing all the acid they could gobble down. And behaving accordingly. Just as many, maybe more, trod a little more warily: they'd drop a trip or two, and then go, yeah thanks very much, very interesting, now I'd like a nice beer and a smoke of hash, if you don't mind.

When I'd first dropped acid, it took me deeeeeeeeep into Ornette and Albert and Miles, into art and philosophy – don't scoff, my young smartarses – but for Bobby and his crowd, acid turned everything into a harlequin-coloured playground, and them into fairy children. Which I could dig, but only so far. Plus I'd kind of vowed not to take any more acid. Gave me funny aftershocks. And – full disclosure – yeah, I'd spent time in a certain Sydney funny farm, following what they used to call a 'nervous breakdown.' Despite the electric jolts and the two-week stretches of sleepy time, I could still recall some *non*-drug-induced trippy sequences, not pleasant ones, and the acid sometimes brought those back too.

Given all that, I could see the day coming when I would drop out of the performance side of Oracle, whether it was my own doing or Bobby's. So I did my homework, practised my scales, brushed up on technique. I hung out at the St Kilda flat, working up songs, recording demo tracks on my tape recorder.

I still did the occasional gig with those marooned-in-time old bodgies the Rods, who played well, no denying it, and I also did a few dates with my jazz-fusion pals. There was always a bit of work there, generally paid union scale. Some of it loose and creative, a lot of it by the numbers. Weddings. Supper clubs. Private functions. You noodle away in the background, play pop songs. Do a bossa nova when the suburbanites want to cut loose on the floor. The Hammond was a work ticket.

But dig, other pursuits were occupying your artistically inclined correspondent. Denise's parents presented her with a new typewriter, so she gave me her old Olympia portable. Surprise you though it may, little ones, I'm no stranger to the ways of the scribbler. I even wrote a book once, years ago (long story, never mind). But now, with a typewriter sitting on the kitchen table, I was tempted once again to wax verbal. And holy shit, my young questers, I *knew* I had a story to tell, full of funkfulness and revelation and angelheaded whatnots. And guns of course, those staples of the storyteller's art. But such jottings would be incriminating in the extreme, and I decided I could bide my time on that front.

But I could sense the big wheel was still turning, and who the fuck knew where or when it would come to rest? Not me, young seekers. So I tapped away at the Olympia, bits of song lyrics and such, and kept the big story in my mind, waiting for the right time to tell it.

RIPPING

So there I was at home, listening back to a two-track I'd recorded that morning, when there came upon my door a loud, rapid banging. When I opened up, Stan, Denise and Jimmy the Thug stormed in, laughing and stumbling like ecstatic fools, carrying armloads of stuff: silk blouses, dresses, men's suits, jackets. A 35mm camera, a pair of binoculars. Denise was beside herself. Even the Thug was chatty.

"The five finger discount, mate," he said, to my raised eyebrow enquiry.

I shook my head and muttered, "High risk."

Stan looked at me, reached into his pocket and thumped a handful of jewellery down on the table. A gold chain, a pair of silver earrings, a brooch.

Denise, flushed and grinning, said, "These boys are the *champions!*"

Stan looked me in the eye. "Mel. A favour, mate. We need to leave this here for a couple of hours."

I shook my head.

"Give you ten percent," said the Thug.

I said nothing, but the stuff stayed there for two days.

Thereafter the three of them regularly used the flat to store swag.

I didn't want any part of the actual shoplifting – I knew I wasn't cut out for it, had found out years before. Yeah, and I'm no good at poker either – what Mel feels, Mel expresses. But early in the piece – just once, at Denise's enthusiastic insistence – I tagged along to observe her and Stan and Jimmy in action.

As arranged, I got to Myer's before them. I was well-dressed, making like an independent shopper. I pottered around, picking up this and that, checking out socks and ties and whatnot.

A little while later Stan and Denise sauntered in. Playing a couple of straights, chatting, giggling, like they were planning their wedding. Denise was dressed smart and voluptuous, like a Toorak heiress. Jimmy came in a few minutes later, looking like maybe a respectable bachelor. Stan and Denise glided about aisles for a while, taking their sweet time then they latched onto a shop assistant. Stan flirting with her, Denise being as sweet as pie. I lost track of Jimmy, and didn't see anyone lift anything.

When I got back to St Kilda later that day the table was

covered with booty – a pocket radio, a leather wallet, a couple of handbags, gloves, scarves, silk ties. All with Myer's tags.

"But I was watching you," I said, "and I saw nothing!"

Stan grinned and hugged Denise. "This one is a natural," he said, and kissed her.

I shook my head. "And you, a nice girl from Bentleigh East."

She bowed her head, curtsied. "Property is theft," she said.

Next day they brought home a new electric guitar (a Les Paul Gibson, no less), a leather coat and a bottle of cognac, and gave them to me.

By late spring their thievery had hit such a level that serious police attention was inevitable. Jimmy and Stan could spot a floor walker or plain-clothes man a mile off – they had the instincts – and they were seeing more and more of them.

Instead of backing off, they grew more audacious. Sometimes they'd create elaborate distractions, like paying a mob of urchins to start a fight inside Buckley and Nunn while they stripped the racks elsewhere in the store. They pulled the same stunt in three different shops. Another time they started a fire in a loading dock at Chadstone, so that one whole section had to be evacuated. They stampeded out the door with the other panicked shoppers, except *their* bags were stuffed with swag. There were close scrapes – a chase down Toorak Road, which only ended when Jimmy turned and decked the store dick.

Then word came back from Stan's underworld pals that detectives had been asking around about the new gang on the scene. The cops knew the thefts were the work of experts, and – worst of all – they, the cops, weren't getting a piece of the action. If you wanted to operate professionally – and long-term – Russell Street had to get its due. So things went quiet on the hoisting front.

In early December Denise threw a big party at her parents' holiday house on the Mornington Peninsula. The oldies were interstate. The slather was open.

The party started Friday night, and over a hundred people turned up, mostly the Barrel crowd. We set up our instruments in a big shed out the back. The house was well hidden from the road and from neighbours, so we cranked the music up loud. It was more like our own little Woodstock festival than a party. People camped around the property, lit fires, smoked grass, dropped acid. Vic's friends were roasting a lamb on a spit. They had their own keg.

Clive the foppish journo was there, crapping on again about 'the underground.' The Captain was wearing a velvet jacket, drinking cognac, smoking joints, taking lines of this and that.

Oracle – man, I just couldn't get hip to that name – played all that first night. We played pretty well, too – I really *felt* the music, we all did. We tried new things, outlandish changes, and they would always work. Bobby sang a song we'd written together called 'Superman on Dope' – I'll tell you all about that a little later – and the party crowd loved it. We took a break around eleven.

Then Cathy wandered into the shed and back into my life. Her hair was cut short. She looked good in tight jeans and a suede jacket with little coloured beads sewn into it. Cowgirl-hippie-American Indian shaman style, I guess you'd call it. She stopped at the door and slowly looked around the room. She waved to me, or maybe to the room, I couldn't tell. Then she came over and kissed me, smiling like nothing had happened, no story, no explanation required. She took a step back and said, "Mel!"

"Hi," I said, like I was the Duke of Detachment, the Count of Unearthly Cool.

I mean, after all, what was I to say? The Sydney rip, the mad escape down the Hume, her disappearance – that was history. So we chatted. She'd been travelling, she said, had

been to Adelaide, Perth, driven up the West Australian coast
to Darwin, hooked up with a yachting beachcomber crowd,
kicked around Torres Strait, Bali, Java. Now she was back.

Looking at her up close, there were signs of a change
even then, a change I didn't get right away. She was kind
of dreamy, distracted, like none of the stuff we were talking
about mattered. Like it was this, but could have been that,
and if it had been that, so what?

We did a couple of lines, smoked a joint. Denise appeared from somewhere, and it was obvious she and Cathy
had already palled up. Later I saw Stan outside, standing
near the bonfire, drinking a bottle of beer. I asked him if he'd
seen Cathy.

"Oh yeah," he said, in a way that told me something had
gone down, but there was no way of knowing from his tone
whether it was a good something or a bad something. I waited for him to say more, but he just bobbed his head to the
music playing inside.

We played another set, another good one. People were
dancing, and Bobby kept it funky – no endless stoned im-
provisations. It was one of those good times for a rocking
musician – you look out, everyone's dancing, having fun,
you're giving them the music, they're giving you their joy.

It went on for a long time. The lights were low. Plenty of
people tripping, everyone was stoned on something. Across
the room I saw Cathy and Denise dancing together, laughing, waving their arms in the air. Cathy leaned over, slowly,
and kissed Denise on the lips. A long kiss. Denise pulled
back, looked at Cathy, then leaned into the clinch.

We played till late. At three or four in the morning, the
speed was burning out of me and I went looking for somewhere to sleep. I wandered into the main house, pushed on a
random door. A weak beam of light was falling across a bed.
There were people in it. I saw a smooth shoulder, glistening
hair fanning out. A sleepy movement, Denise's face. Another
movement, her breast caught in the shaft of light. Slender

fingers stroked the nipple. Then Cathy's face in the light, smiling. Cathy looked at me then and held the look.

A moment at the crossroads for your faithful correspondent. Cathy, garden of athletic delights. Cathy, goddess of fire. Cathy, pure trouble. Denise, warm and good-hearted, fleshy and substantial. Cathy, and Denise.

Denise's voice, husky. "That you, Mel?"

"Sweet ladies!" I shut the door behind me. But that's enough for you, my filthy-minded little friends. Just take this tip from your old uncle: should such a circumstance befall you – I'm talking to the boys *and* the girls now – don't dilly-dally or shilly-shally. Pick that low-hanging fruit, you hear!

Next morning I awoke alone. I stumbled over to the window. Tents were dotted around the paddock. A couple of campfires were still going, smoke hung in the cool air. The bikey crowd were still carousing in the distance. The wooden rail around the old veranda had been pulled down, and two big ceramic pots either side of the front path had been smashed. Someone was cooking bacon.

I chopped up a line on the bedside table, horned it, got back into bed. Then a couple of Valiums to cool out a little. A flagon stood next to the bed – I took a big draft. Another minute. Better now. I went downstairs.

No sign of the girls. I went outside. The day was warming up, and the music had started again. People were swimming naked in the dam. A couple of nearby partyers, a boy and a girl, were sharing a joint. A bloke lay on the path, drinking from a bottle of beer, singing to himself. A girl was on the grass in front, sunbaking with her top off.

I looked towards the line of thick eucalyptus that surrounded the main paddock. Something going on over there. I watched more closely. Darting movements, flashes of blue – hard to get a fix on, though.

Then a glimpse of a uniform. Police. More than one. A *lot* more than one. Flitting, bobbing, hiding. I'd look one way, and see a flash of movement, then nothing. Looked the other way, same thing. They were fast, those fuckers. There were trees along three sides of the paddock, cops on every side. Watching us. Somewhere the squawk of a walkie-talkie.

This was it. The thing every dope fiend in all of history has known is coming, is always coming. The big showdown, the reckoning. The shit which doth hit the fan. Must bust in early May. Oh holy creeping Jesus, I thought. A fucking army of drug-squad jacks. I looked left and right. Those about me were oblivious.

I froze, unsure whether to scream blue murder, urge all zonked-out heedless heads to ditch their stash and take to the hills post haste, or just get up and make a run for it myself. I cogitated for a minute. Maybe it was more than a minute.

I stood up slowly, ambled over to the elf-like couple on the veranda, being cool, careful not to tip my hand to the watching Man. "Hey," I whispered.

The girl turned to me, smiling. "Want some?" she said, and held out the joint.

I shook my head. "Don't turn around quickly. But check it out. Over there. In the trees."

She looked confused.

"We're being watched. Cops," I said.

Her smile cooled. She turned casually and glanced across the paddock, then back to me.

"Where?"

I looked myself. Nothing. They'd hidden themselves. Or maybe gone. Cunts.

The boy on the veranda whispered something and the girl giggled.

I went inside, mooched around for a while. Still no sign of the girls. Nor Stan, nor Jimmy the Thug. I thought, fuck it. I'd had enough. The sylvan setting was giving me the shits now. I went to the shed and packed my equipment, feeling sourer by the minute. It was hot outside. The trees were still. No movement at all. No jacks.

By the time I drove out, the bikeys had set fire to the paddock and the line of flame was moving slowly towards the house. No one seemed to give a shit.

I was nearly back to the highway when Stan's Fairlane came skittering around the bend and skidded to a stop in front of me, gravel flying. Cathy, Denise, Jimmy, Stan, and Clive the journo.

They tumbled out of the Fairlane. Amped. Laughing. Jimmy had a big paper bag. A couple of twenties fell out of it, he scooped them up, stuck them back in the bag. Cathy clutched a gun. Denise was wide-eyed. Clive scared shitless. Stan calm as ever, moving slow and easy.

"Can you take the girls with you, Mel?" He glanced sideways. "Clive too."

"What's happened?"

He looked down the track towards the house. "What's with that smoke back there?"

"The bikeys started a scrub fire. Maybe the house is going up by now."

He thought for a second. "Cops could be along soon."

"They've already been," I said.

He looked at me strangely. I should've kept my trap shut. "They were hiding in the scrub this morning, watching the house."

A searching look from young Stanley. All right, young'uns, I know what you're thinking – amphetamine psychosis, right? Well fuck that, is all I have to say. I saw what I saw.

In any case, Stanley chose not to pursue that particular line of enquiry right then. "Get going right now," he said. "Jimmy and me'll get another car after we hide the Fairlane up in the scrub."

Denise was looking back towards the house at the column of smoke. She shook her head, then got in my car. "Let's get out of here," she said. So much for the parental pad.

Stan said, "See you back in Melbourne."

SOLID GONE

We drove back to the city, me and the two girls sitting across the front bench seat of my car, Clive in the back. The girls excited and babbling, me shitting blue lights, eyeballing the rearview mirror, driving like your grandmother. I didn't know what had gone down, but wigged that it was something serious, that the ante had been well upped. Pay attention to me, my tender young desolation angels, and dig the truth. The tide had turned, the pressure was on, and the shit was deep.

Eventually I got the story. They'd driven out that morning to get cigarettes, the girls, Stan, Jimmy, the useless Clive. The lasses had tried to wake me before they left, they said, but no luck. Anyway, they had no particular criminal intentions, though they were in a reckless mood, still drunk and stoned.

They'd got the cigs, but the bloke behind the counter had sneered at them – so Cathy reckoned. More likely he had *leered* at them, I thought. Cathy was wearing that old army shirt, only one button done up, her shapely right tit more out than in. Denise was similarly bed-dishevelled. The hodad at the petrol station must've thought he was in a hippie-chick dirty picture. Anyway, some kind of uncalled-for remark was made. Cathy goes back to the car, gets the gun, marches back in and makes him open the safe. Just like that.

Now, it so happens your hardboiled narrator knows a bit about waving guns about, extracting money from safes and whatnot – don't ask, just take my word for it. The musician's life is a motley business, feast or famine, so it pays to have a sideline, and brother, I've tried them all. Anyway, the one thing you never ever do, obviously, is pull a job using a car registered in your name, or the name of anyone who knows you. But that's what Cathy was doing, just because some jerk had given her the shits.

To their credit, Stan and Jimmy swung into action without a moment's hez. They gave the dag a touching up and emptied the safe. Bingo. Clearly the owner had not made it to the bank the previous week.

Did he get their number plate? The girls didn't know. He'd gone numb with fear, they said, and I could see they were digging that idea, the squarehead having the daylights scared out of him.

There would be serious heat from all this, but the funny thing was, as the heedless lassies told me of their bushranger-like deeds of derring-fucking-do, I sort of caught their bug. The fool at the garage – fuck him if he couldn't take a joke.

All the way back to Melbourne, the fearless damsel duo told and retold the story and I picked up more of their couldn't-give-a-flying-fuck mood. I was thinking, fucking-A. Stick it to 'em. I felt better and better, like it was a win for my side, for our side, whatever that was. I mean, I'd long ago made a decision to follow the crooked path. Otherwise, I wouldn't have been where I was, right? I'd be working with the old man in the family newsagency, or clocking on every day at Arsefuck and Sons Pty Ltd, measuring my life out in teaspoons and all that sorry shit.

By late afternoon we'd reached the outskirts of Melbourne and hadn't so much as seen a cop. Yeah, a sign, I thought. I'll tell you something, my dear demimondaines, note it down for later: my earlier, er, anxieties, shall we say, notwithstanding, it is a fact universally acknowledged among the rebellious element that in most places, most of the time, you can do whatever the hell you want. Light up that dooby, hop through that window, pinch that car – odds are you'll be all right. Ol' plod will be back at the station doing the crossword. Anarchy *now*, baby!

We pulled over in the burbs somewhere, did a line of go-go, smoked a joint and glided home. There was a whack-up later that night at my pad, and a nice earn for Mel for being wheelman (you see, my innocent baby sparrows, I was already hip to the underworld patois). Funny thing, we never ever heard or read a single word about the hold-up. All I could figure was the servo geezer had kept his trap shut.

The speed ran out on Wednesday. Just like that. I called Stan that morning. "Need another ounce," I said.

"Can't do, Mel. It's gone."

"What do you mean, gone?"

"We sniffed it all."

The light shifted. The air chilled. The floor dropped away. Everything changed. The abyss.

"I . . . Can you get more?"

"That's it. The end of it. All there ever was."

I had nothing to say. But I spoke anyway.

"I'm going to miss it."

Stan laughed. "Me too. But there you go."

I felt listless, off-tap. Kicked around the house, uninterested in everything. Except more drugs. I smoked some gear, but it just made me edgy. A generally fucked-up day.

Denise came by that night. She was sweet. She brought some cocaine from a medical friend, put out a couple of lines. It did the trick. I jollied up. We smoked some gear, had a laugh and a bit of a cuddle. Then she went out, bought some fish and chips. We drank flagon wine.

I was moved, pilgrims. Later that night, settled back, feeling mellow, I said to her, "You're an A-grade, first-rate, top-of-the-range chick, my sweet Denise" – I was only half joking – "and I could do far worse than throw my lot in with you. But baby," I said, "this thing with the petty crime?"

"What do you mean, 'this thing'?"

"You signing on with the crims. It's just playing around, right?"

I'd meant it as a joke, but it came across as an accusation.

Denise had been sprawled on the couch, but she sat up

straight then. "I'm not playing," she said.

"Petrol station busts? Oh, come on, sweetheart."

"That's worse than drug dealing?"

She stood up, full of girlish fire. Gave me the spiel. I'll spare you the details, but the gist was, Stan and Jimmy were 'existentialist heroes.' They were practising an 'aesthetic of crime.' Something about 'the grace of the deed' and 'the poetry of the act.' There was mention of Burroughs, Genet, Kerouac, Camus, Bowles and Sartre. Even old Ned Kelly got a look-in.

I kept my mouth shut long as I could, nodding pleasantly (dig, I was still hoping to get laid) but when she said, all full of schoolgirl wonderment, that their lives were a kind of art, that their art was in their life, I blew my top.

"That's such bullshit," I said. "Middle-class bullshit." I was standing now too.

Denise looked at me pityingly.

"*You* might not get it, Mel, being from Sydney or whatever, but it *is* art. Of a kind. Or so like art that it doesn't matter," she said quietly. "Clive is writing a magazine piece about us."

"Madness!"

"Yeah? How about this?" She dived into her embroidered shoulder bag, pulled out an eight-by-ten print. Cathy in her army shirt, grinning, holding a pistol in the air, like a guerrilla. Outside an Esso service station.

"You took this?"

She nodded.

"This is the place you robbed?"

She nodded again, chin thrust out a little.

"Oh, my sweet child," I said. "Listen to me. Burn this print. Now. Then go home and burn the negative. Tonight."

I collapsed onto the chair, shaking my head.

Denise smiled with an air of superiority I didn't care for. "It might not make sense to someone of your generation, Mel."

Oh, the viper!

"Or maybe it's because you're not in control of this. God knows, I've heard *you* crap on about Burroughs and Kerouac and Charlie Parker often enough." She struck a defiant pose, daring me to contradict her.

But I had nothing more to say.

"Anyway," she said, "things have gone way past the petrol station bust."

"How so?"

She went all mysterious, but could only hold back for about three seconds.

"We robbed a bank yesterday."

I stared.

"It was on the telly. It's in the papers today."

She tossed her head. Flicked her hair. A good gesture, I thought, even while I was thinking, Oh holy mother of fuck.

"Bank robbery is not for dilettantes," I said quietly – calmly, I hoped. Dig, I probably sounded like her old dad.

"What makes you think that's what we are?"

That was pretty much it as far as any possible romantic developments were concerned. Denise chopped out a pile of coke on the kitchen table – very generously, I'd have to say, under the circumstances –and left.

Bikey Vic came to my pad the next day, Thursday morning. I told him straight up, the go-fast had gone.

But Vic grinned and shook his head at me, then did a little tap dance. "Well, well, well, Mr Speed Daddy Mel, I might just have some good news for you."

"Huh?"

"Come with me."

He led me around the corner and down the road. We stopped a hundred yards from his car, which was parked, in accordance with all agreed protocols, well away from my flat.

"I want you to meet someone," he said.

"Who?"

"A kid. Junior scientist of the year or something."

"So?"

"Also a drug fiend."

"Yeah?"

"Let's go and chat to him." Vic grinning.

What had I to lose?

A blond-haired young man was sitting in the car. Looked harmless enough, like a surfer or uni student. He got out as we approached.

"Mel, this is Mark, alias 'the Boy Wonder.' Mark, meet the Man."

The kid's pupils were as big as marbles.

We shook.

"So what have you got?" I said.

Vic shook his head. "Let's go for a walk."

We strolled down the road towards the milk bar. A hot, humid Melbourne summer's day.

"Mark, tell Mr P. how you got interested in drugs."

"How I got started, you mean?"

"Yeah, all that. Mel, you'll love this."

The kid smiled shyly. "Well, a few years ago, when I was fifteen, I read an article in the Sunday paper. About pot."

"And?"

"And it was interesting. It said that when smoked in a cigarette, it produces a sense of euphoria in the user."

"So?"

"So I looked up 'euphoria' in the dictionary – 'a feeling or state of intense excitement or happiness.'" He paused, looked from Vic to me. "I *knew* I wanted that."

"Who wouldn't?" said Vic. He turned to me. "Who said the education system was up to shit?" To the kid he said, "Go on."

"Well, I found out," he said, looking from Vic to me, "euphoria is produced by a number of substances besides pot – like opium, heroin, cocaine, amphetamine sulphate."

"True enough," I said.

"I set about trying them all. A psych nurse got me the cocaine. That was pretty good. She got me some amphetamine sulphate, too. Also good. Then I tried heroin. *Really* liked that one. And then someone brought back a little opium from Penang. It was okay, but I liked the others better."

"Tell him about your troubles," said Vic.

"Well," he said earnestly. "I found I wanted to get high regularly and often. But it was no good having to depend on others."

"True," I said.

"So I started breaking into chemist shops, raiding their drugs cabinets."

"Uh huh."

"It's quite easy. I did it many times, and there were no repercussions. At first. But then I had a bit of bad luck and was busted."

"Right."

"More than once. I was sent to jail."

I shook my head.

"I did three months. It wasn't so bad. Plenty of time to consider things. I decided I would have to change my ways. I realised that if I kept doing chemist jobs, I'd get caught again sooner or later. So I availed myself of one of the training programs in jail. I did the Higher School Certificate."

I looked at my watch. "Get to the point, kid."

"I did first level science—" he paused, looked at Vic, then back to me, with a shy smile, "Chemistry, actually."

Vic looked at me, grinning hugely.

I turned to the kid.

"Young feller, you have my full attention," I said.

"I found out quite a bit about organic chemistry. Especially in regard to what are called psychoactive substances. I found out cocaine and heroin are made from organic substances which are not that easy to get. But amphetamine sulphate – shit, I could make that myself."

Vic looked at the boy proudly then turned to me. "You see where this is heading?"

"You got a taste for me?" I said.

The kid looked uncomfortable. "I've only made one test batch so far."

We were outside the milk bar. Vic said, "Let's go in and get a milkshake."

We took a booth in the semi-dark at the back of the shop, ordered cappuccinos. There was no one else in the place.

"So, show me," I said.

The kid pulled a double-O cap from his pocket, tipped a little powder onto the glass tabletop. It had a weird glow to it.

"It's yellow!"

"It's not perfect. The next batch will be better."

Vic said, "Just give it a go, Mel, for Christ's sake."

I rolled up a dollar note, sniffed it up.

Vic put his hand on my arm. "Still a few bugs. It gives some people a headache. It goes away. Excellent piss after that."

My head started thumping. Every heartbeat was like a biff in the skull. Serious pain. Aneurism, haemorrhage territory. I reeled back, clutching my head. "You cunts have poisoned me."

"Just give it a moment."

Seconds later the headache stopped. My scalp contracted. I shivered. It was good. It was *very* good.

The kid said, "I know precisely what the problem was. Next lot will be even stronger but no side effects. I guarantee it."

They were both looking at me, waiting.

"What do you need? And how long will it take?"

Within a week we had the Boy Wonder installed in a laboratory – by which I mean a tin shed way out back of a deserted farmhouse, hidden behind trees, on a dead end road, out Echuca way. The kid was very thorough, clean and careful. And he knew his science. Gave me hope for the coming generation.

The makings had been easy enough to get, and sure enough, the next batch was sweet – no cranium-busting, just a good clean speed buzz.

By the new year Vic had started selling the shit to his bikey mates, who by all reports were taking to powder drugs with great enthusiasm. Some of them were selling it on to interstate truckies and the like, footballers even. The brawling and troublemaking routinely instigated by those various chaps changed somewhat in character, but what the hell, life is change, is it not, my jaded little nihilists?

I was moving respectable quantities of the powdery stuff to the Carlton heads, extracting a few spondulicks here and there. By now I'd rounded up a crew of serious speed freaks, boys and girls who liked good shit and knew they liked good shit and didn't fuck around.

The Boy Wonder made himself useful in his off-hours by helping me with my music gear. Soon he was setting up the stage for the whole band, handling the PA and so on – he was good with electrics – brilliant, actually. Hotted up my amp, worked on Bobby's PA.

When the next batch of sulphate came in I took a bag of it to show Stan. It was six weeks since the weekend house party. He and Jimmy were staying in a big old terrace house in East Melbourne. Good pad, full of dark Victorian furniture, Persian rugs and whatnot. Denise and Cathy had moved in too. Cosy.

I banged on the door, waited a while. A movement of the curtain, then Stan opened up. Jimmy the Thug was in the kitchen, reading a Phantom comic. The girls were off somewhere.

I chopped up a couple of lines right there on the kitchen table, stood aside and bid Stan and Jimmy to go for it. They did just that.

"Well," I said, "you want?"

Stan glanced at Jimmy. Jimmy said nothing, but then he moved his head in the shiftiest, most minimal nod you've ever seen.

Hello, I thought, who's in charge here?

"Where's it from?" said Jimmy.

"I made it. I mean, I had someone make it. A chemist."

Jimmy went back to his comic.

"All right Mel," said Stan after a few seconds, "leave us an ounce."

I could sense Jimmy to the side, watching.

I'd hoped, expected, Stan would want an ounce, and had one already weighed out. I dropped it down in front of him.

"You haven't asked me the price," I said.

Stan looked at me lazily. "No."

"All right, no need to go strange. I'm hip. This one's on the house. But then we're square, agreed?"

Stan smiled. "Sure thing, Mel."

I took my leave. I had calls to make. As I got in my car and pulled out, a bloke was walking stiffly down the street. Young and bulky, Leisuremaster slacks and brown shoes. Bad haircut. A cop? Could be.

I drove on at moderate speed, careful not to look at him. In the rear view mirror I saw him turn into Stan's gate. I pulled around the corner and walked back just in time to see the door open. Stan shook hands with the squarehead and invited him in.

I drove home rattled. Maybe it wasn't the Man. Maybe it was just some guy, some underworld cat. Yeah, and maybe I was King Zog of Albania. Old Mel's radar does not lie. What did it mean? A bust? Didn't figure.

As I parked and walked towards my flat, I was still distracted. So distracted I didn't see the two men in the lobby waiting for me until one of them had belted me a beauty, twisted my arm behind me and pushed me to the floor, his knee rammed into the middle of my back.

ICEBERG MEL

"Señor Parker."

I craned my head up off the tiles.

"Oh, Alex. Hi," I said, cool as I could manage. "Get this cunt off me, will you?"

Which earned me a sharp punch in the kidneys.

A long pause. Then a sigh.

"All right, Barry, let him up. Open the door, Mel."

I got up slowly, looked around. The heavy was an ape-like young fellow, easy six and a half feet tall. Sweaty, with a deranged look in his eyes. Watching me with a half-grin, itching for me to make a move. Not without my trusty .38, boyo! Which was inside.

I dusted off my threads and fished for my front door key. The goon grabbed my wrist and twisted my arm again.

"Relax, Igor," I said. "If I make a play, you'll be the first to know."

He laughed, but not in a pleasant way.

Alex slowly shook his head. "If only you knew." To the ape he said, "Get him inside, and we'll get this over with."

Not a good thing to hear, my young dharma bums.

Five minutes later we were sitting around my kitchen table. They hadn't found my gun, which was well stashed, but they'd found my money and the speed – half a pound of it in a plastic bag, now sitting between us on the table.

My faithful readers, you'll remember Alex, aka 'the Greek.' Let me tell you a little more about him. He came from a true gangster family. Hard bastards. No peace and love and kindness at all. Very big on the vendetta. Knives. Blood oaths. Alex himself was more into hanging out at Push pubs, taking drugs, listening to rock music, getting laid. A short, slightly rotund bloke with olive skin and curly hair, still sporting that bushy hippie beard. A jolly fellow at heart, not cut out for high-stakes crime.

But I was digging a different Alex now. Not interested in getting anything from me. No questions, no demands, like that I maybe should make some sort of restitution. Which meant he was here to kill me. Then find Cathy and kill her.

"What's that?" said Alex, nodding at the bag of speed on the table.

The only card I had to play, is what it was.

"Speed." I said it casually, but watched him closely. A flicker of interest there. "Pure. Laboratory-made," I said. "It's the new thing."

He nodded, but didn't make eye contact.

I had to use the pause. "So now that you're here, Alex," I said, "obviously there are things to discuss. There's the question of what I owe you for that hash—"

"Shut up. Where's the rest of your money?"

"—and perhaps the question of whether you want to be part of this new speed thing—"

Barry stood up, took a step towards me, and gave me a backhander that sent me sprawling off the chair and against the wall.

I got half-upright, put my hands up. "There is no other money."

Silence.

I looked at Alex. "Have you ever known me to hang on to bread? You know that's not me, Al."

More silence. Try another play.

I stood up carefully. "So normally the next step would be, you guys kill me, right?"

Alex looked at me a while, but said nothing.

"But that'd be exactly the wrong move."

Still nothing.

"For you. Because you'd be shorting yourself." I sat down at the table again.

"How so?"

"That money right there is all I have . . . for now. But there's more money to be had. A lot of it. I can let you in."

"Selling speed? I *hate* speed."

"Something else."

"*What* else?"

"The biggest robbery ever committed in this state. Fuck that, in the whole country."

"And what exactly would that be?"

"Tattersall's Lottery. We're going to take the whole lot."

I'll spare you the sordid details, young seekers, but over the next hour your silver-tongued correspondent managed to stave off his own homicide by offering Alex a piece of the speed action *and* a percentage of the forthcoming Tatts robbery.

What robbery? I hear you yodel. Well, that was it – I was improvising, jamming on a crazy speed riff, a long, twisting tale about a super-heist involving some expert break-and-enter men, with big paydays for all players. Alex listened. Fact was, I'd bought a lottery ticket just the day before, and that's what popped into my head.

I went on, stitching together bits and pieces of every cheap detective book I'd ever read, turning it into some kind of Ben Hall-Ned Kelly-Darcy Duggan-Scarlet Pimpernel adventure, decorated with cries of "Bail up, you bastards, or we'll ventilate your scurvy spleen!", high-speed geta-ways, complex switches and costume changes, secret codes, hideouts and whatnot, ending up with our band of urban bushrangers having foiled the traps yet again, sharing a tankard or two of rum. What ho, me lads!

I kept spieling. I threw in a bit of technical talk. Offhand-sounding, professional. Couldn't name the other players, of course.

Alex, good-hearted simpleton and comic-book reader that he was, wanted to believe it all. I almost had him, I could see that.

The other bloke, Barry, was a different story. He said nothing the whole time. But I could *feel* him there, and the more I tried not to look his way, the more I sensed his presence.

And all the while I was laying out the plans, strange and freaky images kept forming in my head. Many faces. A cowering dog. A frightened child. A sense of prolonged pain. All emanating from Barry.

At one point I paused and let myself glance his way. He was smiling at me.

"You get it, don't you?" he said brightly.

"Don't know what you're talking about," I said, but my voice was shaky and hollow. The psychotic cunt was reading my mind. At least, he knew I was picking up bits of telepathic static from *his* fucked-up consciousness.

Barry smiled, almost amiably, and it wasn't nice.

Alex glanced at him, confused, then back at me. He cleared his throat. "Mel, you're a dead cunt. You know that. You're full of shit. You always were. And you are now."

"Harsh words for an old friend, Alex."

"But irregardless, I'm going to give you the benefit of the doubt. We'll wait a little. Get this straight, though, Mel – if your story turns out to be bullshit, which it probably is, but just might not be, then every day that you made us wait will be another day Barry will keep you . . . under his care, if you get me. And you don't want that."

Until this point, Barry's gaze had been fixed on me, without so much as a blink, but now he turned and stared at Alex. I was relieved, I can tell you, my delicate ones. Alex was struggling to keep his cool.

After a long, uncomfortable silence, Barry slowly turned back to me and prodded the bag of dope on the table. "Is that any good?"

"It's pure."

He looked at Alex again. "Aren't you going to try it?"

Alex, more wretched than ever, took the bag, opened it. And tipped out some powder. "I suppose I better test it, eh?" A nervous laugh. "Bloody speed."

He took out a penknife, started working the powder into a couple of lines. Jesus H, I was thinking, *please* don't give any to your mate.

Alex pointed at me. "You first."

I leaned over and snarfed up a line. Alex watched me a moment then did likewise.

Barry looked from me to Alex, then back to me. The shit kicked in, my scalp crawled.

Without taking his eyes off me, Barry slowly picked up Alex's penknife, felt the edge. Then he rolled up his left sleeve and carefully cut a two-inch line across his forearm. Deep. Blood dribbled out onto the table. Then he cut another line, same length, perpendicular to the first one. Then another two, across those. Like he was about to play noughts and crosses. Smiling at me the whole time.

Then he stood up and walked to the door, went out leaving a trail of blood.

I looked at Alex, who was very pale. We sat in silence a few moments.

"He gone?" I said.

Alex shook his head, then sighed deeply. "Fuck knows."

A pause. That dragged on.

"How did you get mixed up with *him*?" I said.

"The family," he said. "It's their idea."

"*Jesus*, Alex."

He shook his head. Ruefully, I guess you'd have to say.

"This is way out of my hands. If they had their way, we wouldn't even have talked. Barry would have just done his thing. Where's Cathy, by the way?"

"Western Australia. Last heard."

"Well, you're it then, Mel. That story you told, the lottery office? Jeez, I hope for your sake there's something in it."

"How did you find me?"

"I saw you on telly last week."

"What happened with Drew?"

Alex put his hand up. "Don't. Better not to talk about that shit. Now or ever." Alex was shaking his head.

"Yeah, it was wrong, in every way. I know, I know."

Alex leaned forward and jabbed his finger at me. "I set that whole thing up, and let you in as a favour. So after you pulled that fucking stunt, it was *me* in the hot seat."

"I didn't think," I said. "Those bikey blokes were obviously arseholes. And Drew, a useless piece of work. Not that I endorse homicide."

Alex shook his head slowly. "The bikeys complained to my uncle. He pays them to keep an eye on that pub of his at Botany."

"Oh fuck."

"Yeah. And then it was really on. My uncle made good, so that put you and Cathy in his sights."

"What do I have to do?"

"You were supposed to die. Today. There never really was any other plan."

"How about I pay you back? Double?"

He shrugged, without much enthusiasm. "I can put it to the old man. Wouldn't hope for too much, though. For chrissake, give me some more of that fucking goey."

"You said you hated speed."

"I do. Give it here."

Alex left a few hours later. Then I paced. The outlaw-type shenanigans was something I'd made up on the fly, but the more I talked it up, the more convinced I had become that it was my best way out. I had no objections to robbery per se. Hadn't Johnny and I once cut a dashing swathe through Sydney's underworld, robbing evildoers, defending our swag from bent coppers, fascist thugs and assorted villains? Johnny? You out there? *You* remember, right?

No, my dears, stealing from the wicked was no crime in Mel Parker's book. Property being theft and what have you. But running into a bank waving firearms about – goodness, there must be an easier way.

On the other hand, your armed robbery is quick. Bang. You make a noisy entrance. Hands up, you cunts. Give us the money. In the bag there. Thank you. Goodbye. In and out. If you get away clean, that's it. Your work is done. Let's have a party.

And didn't I have a direct line to my very own band of bold bank robbers? Oh yeah, I know, I'd shitbagged armed rob to Denise. And, yeah, Denise was in way over her head there. But Stan and Jimmy were seasoned crims. And Cathy – holy Jesus shit, she handled a gun with more panache than anyone I'd ever seen.

There were problems, admittedly. The mysterious cop-like bloke I'd seen visiting the robbers, and the strange off-handedness I was digging from that whole crew – which by now I was getting a pretty good idea about. Not to mention Denise's naiveté. But nothing's perfect in this world, right, my little jaundiced ones?

Anyway, my musings didn't have much bearing on how things turned out. Fuck me if Fate hadn't chosen just a little while before to stick its fickle finger right up my date. Yeah, that's right – after a lifetime of strumming ukuleles, pawing pianos and flailing at guitars, dressing up variously as a cowboy, gypsy, beatnik, juvenile delinquent, beach-bum, lounge lizard or whatever the fuck, suddenly it had all come to fruition. Kind of. Up to a point. But as old Carl Jung once said: Beware the gifts of the gods, 'cause they mean to fuck you up if they can. So gather round me, earnest young seekers and listen closely. It happened like this.

First, let us wind the clock back to the previous winter. We – that is, Bobby Boyd and the Oracles, recently (sorrow-fully) renamed "Oracle" – had been playing our busy round of dances and discos and one-off events. Like I told you, the inner-city crowd had long since stopped dancing, except for a little free-form hippie arm-waving. It was the pot, dig? And the acid.

But the suburbs still floated on an ocean of beer. Beer and hot cars, brawls out the front, sex out the back. Just like always.

And then it changed. One week it was booze and knuckles. Next week it was peace and love. Knowing looks and nods, secret knowledge. Everyone was in the club. The suburbs had discovered marijuana.

The penny dropped at a dance in West Heidelberg, which used to be one of the rougher places in Melbourne, a hard-bitten Housing Commission burb, to which I always took a shiv and an iron bar, at the very least. This one week it was suddenly different. Smiles, nods, much digging of the music.

A bunch of kids came up to me during a break and invited me out back for a puff. And they had good gear. A blond girl told me she was reading Meher Baba. Another was into some Buddhist, *Cuckoo's Nest*, *On the Road* kind of thing. Yet another wanted to talk about William Burroughs and the Incredible String Band.

Back in Melbourne the next day, Bobby Boyd and I knocked out a song about all this. Him strumming chords, me tapping out words on my Olympia portable.

We started with the line "The Phantom's shooting dope!", which led us to "Boofhead's dealing coke!" and then "Superman is stoned off of his dial." On it went, for many verses. "Clark Kent just robbed a bank," we wrote, "Mandrake's got a shank." And so on. We had Ginger Meggs on the nod, Dagwood fiddling the books, old Dick Tracy taking orders from the mob, Batman and Robin . . . that's right, you guessed it.

Bobby had backed away from the space-cadet hippie thing by now; he was looking and sounding more John Lennon-John Sebastian-Grateful Dead these days. He sang this new song Dylan-style, spitting out the lines, all on one note, kind of an "It's All Right, Ma" rip, but with a funk beat.

In one hour, zap, we had our song. This was the one that had gone over so well at Denise's house party in December.

The ditty had its first truly public airing at a weekend music festival just before Christmas. It was one of those half-arsed Woodstock-type get-togethers which had suddenly become the big thing. You know the drill: you get a horde of hippies and psychos hopped up on grass and flagon wine, feed them kebabs and macrobiotic food. You *claim* to have booked some renowned international rock act, who for some reason always cancels at the last minute, but the punters don't find out until they've already handed over their hard-earneds and are sitting in a paddock somewhere.

So there we were. John Lennon hadn't shown up. Big fucking surprise, huh? Billy Thorpe was supposed to play, but he'd cancelled too. So we were put on stage at ten o'clock on the Saturday night. Perfect timing. It was a warm night, but camp fires were burning. Hash and grass and wood smoke wafted out of the crowd. The lushes were nicely lit up, but not yet drunk and ugly. Bobby went to the microphone and just stood there. He was good with the patter and people knew that. So he's standing looking out at the crowd, while the rest of us are poised, waiting to be counted in. The crowd is silent, patient, expecting something funny.

"Batman's shooting dope . . ." Bobby shouted, then paused. The crowd cheered. "Boofhead's dealing coke!" More cheers. "And Superman is stoned off of his diiii-iiiaaaaaaaaaaaaalllllll!" Then the old "One, two, three, FOUR!!!" and away we went.

It was the hit of the festival. We did encores. Later a bloke from the ABC approached us, arranged for us to go into the studio the next week and film the song for broadcast. We had that effer properly recorded within a week, were on TV with it a week later, and bingo – by New Year we were the fastest rising act in the business. Got an album recorded quick smart: *Deeply Disturbed*, it was called.

So that's how Alex had found me. Saw me on the idiot box.

SOMEBODY DONE HOODOOED
THE HOODOO MAN

It wasn't that hard to muscle in on the robbery caper. The day after my visit from Alex and the self-lacerating fruitcake, I went to see Stan and Jimmy. Didn't tell them too much, just said I wanted in. They were surprised, but cool with it. I had come through all right on the Mornington Peninsula getaway. So I was to be wheelman on an upcoming job. Out of town. Fat little post office in the boondocks. Cathy and Denise weren't part of it. Just us. This was one for the boys.

It went like this: we drove up first thing on pension day. Plenty of money there waiting. We timed it for right on the knocker, nine a.m. Door opened, oldies wandered in. And we bold Knights of the High Toby barrelled in behind them. Well, Stan and Jimmy did. Me, I waited in the car, right outside the door. After a little bit of dramatic carry-on, the tellers handed over the bread. No heroes – this was the post office, after all. No one was hurt. Less than a minute later the boys were back, and I was driving off, taking it slow. We switched cars around the corner, less than two hundred yards away, and motored off again. I dropped the boys at a rented fishos' cottage down by the river, then took the second car back into town, left it near the railway station. Stan followed me in a third car, a clean one which we'd parked back at the cottage. He picked me up, we returned to the cottage.

We spent the next three days fishing, playing cards, relaxing, then drove calmly out of the area. By then the heat was off. Cops might've assumed we'd left by train days ago, or that we'd somehow dodged the roadblocks and driven back to Melbourne, the nearest big city. By the time we mosied down the highway, there were no cops around.

Sounds easy, muchachos, right? Truth is, I was shitting bricks. At least in the lead-up I was. Right through the careful setting-up of getaway cars, hideouts and such – rising fucking panic. When we did our practice run, I was all a shit and a shiver. Kangarooed the car, then stalled it. Nearer the job got, the worse I got.

A day out from the job, Jimmy the Thug got cold feet. We were staying at a cabin in the Dandenongs, halfway between the job and Melbourne. It was morning. Stan was frying eggs and bacon. I hadn't slept for two nights. Which was nothing unusual. Jimmy came into the kitchen, took a glance at me, shook his head.

"Can't do it with him like this," he said, nodding my way.

"I'm absolutely a hundred percent fine," I said.

Stan turned around, looked at me.

"I'll drop some Mandrax, get a little shut-eye. I'll be right then."

"It's more than that," he said.

They ate their breakfast. I stuck with coffee. My hands were shaking so much it slopped out of the cup. Stan finished up, left the room, came back with a cap of white powder, a teaspoon and a fit. Cooked up right there on the table. Loaded the fit, and held it out to me. Didn't say anything.

I looked at him. I didn't say no, didn't say yes. Now, my little dumbsaints, I was no stranger to the narcotic class of drugs. I'd had the odd sniff here and there over the years – pills on occasion, when someone had visited a chemist's after hours, gifts from lovely ladies in the psychiatric nursing profession and so on. But the strong opiates had never done much for me.

A couple of seconds passed. Stan said, "It's up to you."

"I figured you lot were into the gear," I said. "That's why you've been so, whatever, laid back. Right?"

Stan still said nothing. So, I picked up the fit. Bang, I whacked that shit. Tasted it back of my throat. My hands stopped shaking. I felt calm. I felt alert. The speed buzz didn't go away, but somehow the skag cleansed and refined it. I'll spare you any description beyond that, my little subterraneans – I never read a believable account of a smack stone, and I won't try now.

We went ahead and did the robbery. I was right there, all present and correct. In the pocket. On the wavelength. And everything went perfectly. Had another taste after the job. And another one after that, for reasons that now elude me.

A week after getting back to Melbourne I met up with Cathy in a Carlton pub. Dig, my young pistoleros, Cathy and I hadn't so much as *mentioned* the Sydney shootery since she'd reappeared. Water under the bridge. Too complicated. Too scary. Whatever. But she needed to be told of recent shit. All I had to do was tell her. Like that. Easy. Cathy, a couple of killers would like a word with you. Just letting you know.

Mid afternoon. Cathy was in the ladies lounge, sitting at a table on her own. She glanced at me as I sat down. "You're pinned," she said.

"The last one on the bus, it seems."

"And you're working hot with Stan and Jimmy?"

"Yeah, that too. But I have a reason, a good reason. So listen to me."

"Yeah?"

"There's trouble."

She waited.

"*Sydney* trouble."

She nodded, still waiting.

"The Greek. He came by. With a heavy. To square up."

"What did you do?"

"Spun them a yarn. Bought some time."

"What yarn?"

"I said there was a job in the offing. A big one. They hold fire and they'll get a cut, I said. Square up for Sydney plus a bit more for their trouble."

"There's other trouble. *Melbourne* trouble," she said, pulling a folded *Daily Earth News* – a hippie rag out of Carlton – from her shoulder bag. She passed it over. "Second page."

I opened it up. There at the top was Denise's photo of Cathy at the service station on Mornington, holding the gun. Blown up big, but with a black bar across Cathy's eyes. The headline next to it said, "Fall Among Thieves – My Night with the Hippie Robbers." It was by Clive the Fop.

"Uncool as hell. But that's a great shot of you."

"That was Denise's idea. She's a fool. And Clive's an idiot. She passed that photo to him. I'm dumping them. You should too."

Then Cathy bit her nail and looked away, thoughtful. Or preoccupied.

Something else not right.

"Hang on," I said. "At this stage, you should be plying me with questions about the Greek and his mate."

She looked at me, waiting.

"You know all about it."

Nothing. Meant yes.

"You've seen them already?"

"Two nights ago. I saw Alex at the T. F. Much."

"You talk to him?"

"Yeah." Cathy looked at the door. She sat up straight, suddenly looked bright and on it. "Anyway, I want you to meet someone. Now keep a cool head, Mel." At that she stood up and smiled big, ready for a greeting. I turned around to see who was on the receiving end.

A tall, thickset bloke in ill-fitting flairs was striding towards us. The palooka I'd seen outside Stan's digs. The copper. The fucking copper. Right here, grinning at Cathy.

"Craig. Hi, darl." When he got to our table she stood up and gave him a peck. "Craig, this is Mel Parker."

We shook. My hand grip was weak, meant to convey indifference. His was a bone-crusher, meant to convey he was a complete arsehole.

I was playing it cool but I was wired. Fight, flight, freak? The hell was the crazy bitch up to?

The copper gave me the lingering stare. Meant to

remind you of every time you'd ever got in the shit, since you were three years old, give you that squirmy feeling again. I was having none of it. I stood up. Cathy grabbed my hand, called out "Craig!" – and waited until the copper looked at her. She said nothing more, just gave *him* the look, and fuck me if he didn't lower his eyes like a chastened schoolboy.

Then back to me. "Sit down, Mel. Craig's with us." Pause, then to him. "Aren't you, sweetie?" He grinned, shrugged.

"Get us a gin and tonic, will you, Craig?" she said, and off he trotted.

I sat down again.

Out of earshot, Cathy said, quickly, "You know him, then?"

"I saw him outside Stan's the other day."

"He's covering for us at Russell Street. We need him."

"Who's he with?"

"Armed Robbery Squad."

"Jesus, Cathy, you crazy fucking idiot. They're assassins, every one of them."

"Well, he's *our* assassin."

She let that sit there, while I caught up with her twisted but – I had to admit – in its own way brilliant thinking.

The cop came back.

"So," he said. "Cathy tells me you got a visit from Barry." I shrugged.

"A very bad man is our Barry."

"Tsk, tsk."

The cop's superior little smile faded. He turned to Cathy. "Your mate going to play the smart prick?"

"Don't worry about it, Craig. Just tell us what you know."

"All right." Turning to me, "Barry is a first division Sydney maggot." He paused, looked from Cathy to me, back to Cathy. He leaned forward, dropped his voice. "Kiddies, you know?" He straightened up. "Barry's presence in Melbourne isn't appreciated. By *anyone*." Significant stress on the last word. Meant Russell Street, I supposed. "Barry will be made aware of that shortly." Another meaningful pause. "What *you* need to do is let me know if you see him or hear from him again. Or tell Cathy. Without delay."

"Oh yeah," I said. "And what good does that do us?"

"That's obvious, isn't it?"

Cathy said to me: "I told you. Craig's on our side, Mel."

I stood up. "Your side maybe, not mine," and with that parting riposte, I fucked off.

You think me hasty? Well pay attention, young hooligans, I happen to know a bit about dealings with the morally flexible elements of the constabulary, and this much is true: you deal with crooked coppers only when you need to. A payment here or there, to get a certain matter overlooked, or see a vital piece of evidence go missing – sure. *When there's no other way.* But up front, let's all be chums, and venture forth to have some spiffing Famous Five–type adventures together? Fuck that shit. A bent copper will rat on anyone and everyone. Plus, they're coppers. We're on one side, they're on the other. They've already proven their bad faith by becoming coppers in the first place. This is Australia, after all.

So I was out of there. No one came running after me.

I stopped into a record shop in Lygon Street and bought a *Daily Earth News*, read it when I got home. The Fop hadn't given all that much away. Wrote about how he had managed to crack an interview with a gang of robbers. But they were not like your regular members of the criminal classes. This gang was "political," he said, against the war in Vietnam, opposed to conscription, in favour of the legalization of grass. They listened to Hendrix and Dylan. He had one of them – one of us – quoting Bob, in fact, to the effect that to live outside the law you must be honest. Maybe Stan had said that, more likely Denise, but most likely Clive just whacked it in because it sounded cool. This was some sorry journalistic carry-on, my young seekers, and you can take that from a cat who has earned a dollar or two over the years as a penny-a-liner. I even spotted right away that the Fop had lifted his style from Hunter Thompson's book on the Hells Angels, which had been doing the rounds that year.

After I'd read the piece a couple of times, I calmed down a little. There wasn't too much in it. Clive had spent a night talking to people who'd told him they were robbers. No proof, nothing concrete. That was about it. With luck it'd die a natural death.

Next morning the photo was on the front page of the *Sun*. "HIPPIE ROBBERS" said the headline. The story puffed up the thin stuff from the Fop's article, added a bit of spice – Cathy's shirt in the photo was open at the top, show-ing, as I may have mentioned already, a partial glimpse of pleasantly curving bra-less tit.

The story speculated a bit about pot and free love among the criminal classes. Also quoted some unnamed old lag who said he would never ever, in his day, have done a robbery with a sheila. Added that druggies in his opinion had no place in the criminal world. There was no comment from the Armed Robbery Squad.

I went to Stan's place in a state of high alarm. He and Jimmy were putting bags in their car when I got there. "We're fucking off," Stan said. "Queensland. Come along if you want."

"The bullshit in the paper?" I said.

Slinging a bag in the back of the wagon – Jesus, I could see the barrel of a pistol right there – Jimmy said, "Can't work with that going on. We let it die down. Start again when the dust has settled."

For a moment I was tempted. Make a new start. Would Alex and his mate find me? Not for a while. But yeah, even-tually. My name was shit in Sydney, so that was out. And what would I do in Queensland, *water ski*?

Plus, although I wasn't quite admitting it to myself yet, I had become just a wee little bit accustomed to the smack. It cooled me out nicely after the speed. And I had to admit, since I'd been indulging, there'd been no more visions of creeping tree-coppers and such.

The station wagon was packed and they were ready to hit the road. We stood around for a moment. A strange moment. Like we were reluctant to break the connection or something.

Stan reached into his pocket, glanced around, and handed me a couple of packets of powder. I gave him all the speed I had with me.

"If you want any more of that," he said, nodding at my pocket where I'd stashed the bindles of smack, "go see the Captain."

I was surprised at this, but made no comment.

We all shook and off they went. Cheerio lads. Send us a postcard.

Cathy stayed in town, even though it was her picture on the front page of the daily paper. Her reasoning: a slightly soft-focus photo of a tall, slim chick with straight brown hair, smiling, holding a gun, *maybe* after having just robbed a service station? Could've been anyone. That photo on its own wasn't going to put her in jail. More than a few heads knew it was her, but so what?

HOW HIGH THE MOON?

Things settled down, or seemed to. One more story ran in the *Sun*, page five, about the revolutionary hippie armed robbers, but there was no real heart in it. A statement from some detective saying there'd been no reports of the so-called hippie gang. Nothing after that.

Stan's dope lasted me a week, then zilcho. I knew I was going to run out, obviously. While I was stoned, my plan was to just cop it sweet, get the shit out of my system, carry on without. But day one with no heroin was a drag. No man with the golden arm stuff, understand, just aches and pains, sniffles and deeeeeeep fucking dreariness. Mid-morning I'd more or less decided to go and score. Yeah, yeah I know what you're thinking – disgusting. Just telling the truth here, little ones. Take it or leave it.

I knew the Captain lived somewhere in Albert Park, but had no idea of his actual address, and no phone number. I rang a couple of people. They didn't know either. Sooner or later I'd see him, no doubt, but for now . . . I went to a house in Prahran whose inhabitants, I knew, sometimes used a little skag. No go. Another in St Kilda. Same. Then I thought, fuck it. That's how it is. Comme ci, comme ça, c'est la vie, semper fidem, and a bunch of other bullshit foreign phrases whose meaning I don't know. It all added up to no hard drugs for Mel.

Something odd happened then. I started thinking it wasn't a big deal, really. Maybe a godsend. I'd been to this point before, and knew I was still well short of a real habit, and I could keep chipping a while longer, but . . . You get my drift. Accept it, move on, go with the flow. Yeah, I could do that. I really could do that.

This was going through my head as I walked down Fitzroy Street, not sure what to do next. Then up ahead I saw Alex the Greek. With Cathy. Standing, talking. Fifty yards away, at the next corner, a ratty looking couple waited, eyes on Cathy. What strange craziness was this? The answer was apparent even from a distance: drug business was being conducted.

Cathy saw me, signalled me over. As soon as I got within earshot and without even a greeting, let alone a word of explanation as to how such an unlikely alliance should have come about, Cathy said, "Got any money?"

I looked from her to Alex, who was looking – fuck me if it wasn't true – ragged and strung out, but at the same time kind of hopeful.

"For what?"

"You know what," she said.

And in that moment the way forward became absolutely crystal fucking clear. I gerried: Alex was on the spike. Probably had been in Sydney. Family had sent him down here as his last chance to show them he wasn't a complete fuck-up. Get the money from Mel, settle the vendetta with blood, whatever. Come back with honour. Might have happened, but Alex hadn't quite had the stomach for murder, had given me the benefit of the doubt, and decided to wait for my pipe-dream big score. His offsider Barry had left disgusted – no doubt to report Alex's dereliction to the family. And waiting around Melbourne had been too much for drug-hungry Alex. Cathy had spotted him at the T. F. Much – she'd told me that, but obviously she'd made contact, and quickly dug what was going on.

My guess – keerect as it turned out – was she'd been supplying him with skag. And no doubt levying a good tax for herself. The couple waiting at the corner would be part of it too. Cathy had been getting the stuff from Stan, but now Stan was gone, and she was scrabbling around to buy a cap of powder. Small time. Which meant she didn't know the Captain was the man. Interesting.

"You can score around here?" I said.

"We need some more dough."

"How much you got?"

"How much have *you* got?"

Fact was, I had plenty. I still had my whack of the post office robbery, most of it. And speed money had been coming in faster than it was going out.

"You're going to score some crappy deal around here? Go ahead." I shook my head. "I can do *way* better."

That got their attention.

"Do what you have to do," I said. "But when you're ready to get serious, come see me."

Open-mouthed.

"Not today though." I turned around and sloped off.

I wasn't planning on being the man, exactly. But dig, if there are drug fiends to your left and a drug supplier to your right, what is to be done? Obvious, right? Oh, don't give me that "God damn the pusher man" bullshit. When it comes to drugs, no one makes no one do nothing, if you catch my drift. There's been more hypocritical crap spoken about "drug peddlers" trading in misery and death, perverting young whatevers, renarda, renarda, renarda, than any topic in the history of the world. Sorry my earnest young truth seekers, but things aren't that simple. They never were.

But I digress. Let me tell you how Mel became the king of the Melbourne pushers.

After a bit more sniffing around Albert Park, I found the Captain living in a semi-swank private hotel. I didn't mention it before, but our paths had crossed many years earlier, in Sydney. Long story, no need to go into it here. Let's just say I knew the Captain was an operator with many a crooked card up his sleeve. And not to be underestimated.

So I simply rolled up unannounced and banged on his door. He was a big fellow in his late 40s, maybe 50s, with a Captain Beefheart moustache. Lank, longish hair. Well dressed – tweeds and bespoke what-have-yous, sometimes a velvet smoking jacket. Soft-spoken, educated accent.

If he was surprised to see me he didn't let on. "Mel, dear fellow," he said. "Come in and join me in a vodka." It was two in the afternoon. His flat was okay – leather-covered armchair, Persian rugs, that sort of thing. He lived alone by the look of it.

Straight out with it. "Stan has shot through," I said. "Jimmy too. This bullshit in the papers. You probably know that already." No response, yea or nay. "Anyway, Stan told me to get in touch with you if I needed . . . anything."

"Anything?"

"Well, the Robert Stack, in particular."

He raised his eyebrows.

"The s*mack*, for chrissake."

He thought about it a bit.

"How much?"

Quick thinking from your doughty correspondent.

"As much as you can get."

A slight snicker from the Captain. Meaning either, you're having yourself on. Or, that's *so* much dope, you have no idea what you're asking.

"You've got people who can take it, I gather."

"Perzackly."

He considered me for a moment. "None of my business, I realise, and I don't wish to pry, but you, Mel – do you yourself indulge?"

I shook my head. "Have done, but no, this is business."

He simply said, "All right," left the room and came back with a tobacco tin. Put it down on the table in front of me.

I opened it. Inside, four neat packages wrapped in clear plastic. Yellowy-beige powder, a little lumpy. Number three heroin, as it was known in the trade (I found out later).

"This isn't the same stuff you've been selling to Stan, is it?"

"Not quite. This is new. Better. Why don't you take one package for now. See how you go with that," said the Captain.

I picked up a packet.

"Sorry to be the censorious old school marm, Mel, but you must understand, if *you* start using the stuff all bets are off."

"I dig it."

I met up with Cathy and Alex the next day. Cathy was very curious about the dope: where I'd got it, *how* I'd got it. She cooked up a taste right in front of me. Added a few drops of vinegar to help break it down. She peered closely at it as the pale powder dissolved. Did the business. Sat back. Sighed. Then she asked me again where I'd got it, very sweetly. But no deal.

I left the package with them. They broke the stuff up into smaller denominations – no doubt diluted somewhat

– and took it onto the highways and byways of Melbourne, sold it to a bunch of people I didn't know. And no doubt some of those people sold it on again, in even more diluted form. So there you have it, my young psychonautical entrepreneurs: heroin dealing. Capitalism in microcosm. Big dividing line there: I didn't use any of the dope. I'd put it behind me. I paid the Captain first thing the following day. He gave me another package.

A few weeks passed like that. With Alex and me, the way it was supposed to be working, we'd keep doing business. I'd get some serious bugs together, enough to clear the debt between us. Meanwhile Alex would earn some bread for himself selling the drugs I was slinging him. What we knew, deep down, but didn't say, was Alex probably wouldn't save a sixpence, because he was a drug fiend. Seems obvious now, but dig, anything to do with drugs is shot through with self-deception and make-believe, and none of the big dreams come true in the end. Almost none. There may be exceptions. I'm just saying.

The summer burned out. Leaves turned from green to brown – no pleasant autumnal jive along the way, just a dusty exhaustion. But my money was piling up, so I was getting Alex paid off. And I still had a sacred duty to perform. A setting-to-rights with my erstwhile business partner. The cat I left in Sydney holding the baby, right? You think I'd forgotten? I knew that sooner or later I'd have to return to Sydney. And there was only one way to do it – with a shitload of money. Pay off, buy off all naysayers and backbiters. Get Johnny out of whatever hole he was in. Hence the nest egg.

Meanwhile, back on the rock'n'roll front, Oracle were kind of successful. Selling a few records. You'd see the name around the place, on posters. Sometimes we were on telly. The big time, right? Forget it. We were barely making a living. From the music, I mean. But dig, music is its own reward right? And the life of the working musician is not a bad way to sell drugs either.

Getting a wider audience meant Oracle lost some of its old inner-city crowd. People around Carlton had started calling the band "Orifice" – how do you like that? I still did the occasional job with the suburban rock'n'roll fossils, even the odd jazz date too. Kept writing, arranging. Started thinking about writing a jazz-rock opera. Dreaming big dreams, my little ones.

Shit was going swimmingly. Kind of. In a fool's paradise sort of way. But there were hints and forebodings, clouds on the horizon. Certain whispers, foreshadowings. Quite a few, actually. Here's one:

It was a day in late April. A cold wind was blowing off Bass Strait. I was meeting Vic in a Carlton coffee shop, to do a routine drug swap (speed and grass, if you were wondering). We sipped our coffees. A bedraggled kid in a frayed sweater was hanging about outside, glancing back down the street every few moments. A girl there, with a gone-to-seed hippie look. She was, pushing a pram. Dopers. Across the street, someone else was hanging about, not related to them as far as I could tell, but also obviously a doper. Strung out.

Vic and I wandered out of the café, down Lygon Street. We saw more junkies down the block a way. "Is it just this morning," I asked Vic, "or is *everyone* on the gear?" He shrugged. We did our business, then went our separate ways.

I went home. Let me tell you, little ones, those wall-to-wall drug fiends worried me. I'd always figured that drugs were the keys to the otherwise mostly locked, barred and chained-shut doors of perception. Giving drugs to someone who wanted them was a good and kind act. Everyone thought that. No one begrudged the small earn you might make. But the girl with the pram . . . Led to some deep cogitating by your doughty scribe.

That night I met up with Cathy at the Waiters Club. I aired my thoughts. As usual she was way ahead.

As I told her about the marauding hordes of junkies on Lygon Street, she shook her head impatiently. "*Yeah*," she said, "what did you expect?"

I looked at her, waiting.

"It's not what it was, Mel. Maybe it never *was* what it was."

"What would that be exactly, dear lady, that isn't what it was, exactly?"

"Oh, you and your fifties beatnik thing," she muttered, with an impatient wave of the hand.

"Steady on, lassie," I said. "You're waving my whole goddamn life away there."

She looked at me, smiling and curling her lip at the same time. "Getting *high* on a *reefer*, smoking a little of that *mellow gage*." She started laughing. "Like crazy, pops! What all the cool *hepcats* are doing."

"I never—."

She looked at me levelly. "How many people in Melbourne do you reckon use smack?"

I thought about it. Not long before I'd have said, maybe ten, twenty.

"A hundred? Two?"

She slowly shook her head. "Multiply that by twenty. At least. And it's only just starting."

"Jesus."

"Not so hip once everyone's doing it, right?" She grinned. "What's happening now, everyone who comes across the stuff either says, Whoa, and backs the fuck right off. Or else they dive on in. Not that many back off. It's a virus most people catch." She took a swig of her red wine. "Has a long way to run yet." She looked away, tilted her head.

"Where does it end?" I asked.

"You tell me."

"People start getting off the shit. Move to a higher plane. Like Aleistair Crowley says."

"He died a junkie, didn't he?"

MEL SHALL OVERCOME!

Melbourne that autumn was aflame with anti-war carryings-on.

The Vietnam War, conscription, a shit-for-brains government. And other very uncool goings-on, of a fascist police-state military-industrial-complex-type nature. So plenty of fomenting, anywhere you looked. There were factions and groups and cells. Old lefties. Young lefties. Old centrists. Young centrists. Sweet old ladies from Duckberg. Quakers and liberal church types, school kids, squareheads. Uni students, old-school trade unionists. Fired up with anti-war zeal. And the rest of the country fired up about *them* being fired up. Which was one reason the Man hadn't noticed the hard drug scene growing right there under his snout: he had his eye on the militants.

The big event on the calendar that year was the so-called Vietnam Moratorium. Dig: I was onside with all that, even played a couple of benefits and whatnot. Bobby Boyd was vocally anti-war, and the rest of the Oracles went along, except for the drummer, who was a crypto law-and-order freak, into war history, collected Nazi weaponry.

Not that your old Mel was *that* much of a political head – please don't send me off to a collective cabbage farm or whatever. And as for socialism – well yeah, that's cool, but maybe it's like my old pal Lenny Bruce said, socialism's just one big phone company, right? One for you to ponder, my earnest young guerrillas. But anyway, I was more or less hip to the workings of your repressive capitalist state, renarda renarda (some family history there, generally of a reddish hue, enough said).

I hadn't paid too much attention to the big Moratorium rally coming up, though. My position was: good for you, boys and girls, I'm with you all the way, but I must proffer my apologies. Toodle-oo! Don't forget to smash the state!

Others saw it differently. Like Stan, for instance. Oh yeah, he saw it with fresh eyes - with *I Ching,* "crisis equals opportunity"–type eyes. He turned up unannounced from North Queensland a month before the march. He scrubbed up well: tanned, fit, healthy, no hard drugs. Dressing now in the style of your Melbourne sharpie. Jimmy and Denise showed up a few days later.

We had a big jolly reunion party at East Melbourne. Cathy, Denise, even Clive the Fop was there, plus a whole bunch of others – hard types, mostly.

Late afternoon in the backyard, Stan sidled up to me holding out a joint. I took it from him, passed it back. Minor chit chat ensued. Then with elaborate casualness he said, "I hear you've been doing good business with the Captain. I'm guessing you'd have a bit of a bank by now. A little something that's . . . not really doing anything for you?"

Fact was, I *did* have a few parcels of money stuck away, here and there, the beginnings of a sweet nest egg. My re-entry ticket to Sydney.

"Hmm, maybe," I said.

Stan looked around – no one nearby. Moved closer. Lowered his voice. "I'm ready to work," he said. Dig that word, seekers: "Work." Underworld argot for any and all forms of breaking, entering, ripping, running, looting, shooting and derring-do criminality.

He went on, so softly I had to lean in further to hear him.

"Wanted to let you know. There's something coming up. It's big."

"Yeah? How big?"

"The biggest."

He looked at me. At that point I could have said: Spiffing. Wonderful. Hope it goes well. Bye bye. That would have been the shrewd, level-headed response. I flashed on that, for maybe a millisecond. Thing is, I was dead curious. Hungry too, I'll admit it. So I asked him, just as he knew I would, "What?"

He leaned right in close and whispered, "The ANZ Bank in the city."

"Yep, that is big."

He waited a moment, then said, "And the Colonial Permanent Building Society at St Kilda."

I said nothing.

"And last but not least, the payroll at Sunshine Pipefitters. It'll be a big one."

Mel was flabbergasted.

"Get it?"

"Like a crime spree?" I said.

"Right, but we hit them all on the same day at the same time."

Mel, the Dumbfounded Kid.

"There's one more thing. A little earlier in the day. A diversion. We'll blow up the King's Bridge."

"I . . . It's . . . But . . . How . . . Wha—?"

"We've been working up to this for a while. It *was* meant to happen later in the year, maybe spring. But now there's this other business. It's just too good a chance to pass up."

The guy's barmy, right? I knew that. But I asked, in my dazed, stupefied state, "What other business?"

"The Moratorium." He let that sink in.

"You . . . do it on the day of the march? While the march is going on. When the police are busy."

"Got it. Every cop in the fucking state will be at the march." He smiled. Proud as you please. Preparing to paint his masterpiece.

Ooh, yes, my young scoundrels. This was serious A-grade, first-division, top-rank, move-over-Ned-Kelly-type criminal enterprise.

"Thing is, Mel, for something this big, we need a good bank just to get the thing organised. I'm looking for a financial backer."

"Me?"

He smiled.

"How much?"

"There's a lot to set up. It'll take at least four cars and a truck. Some advance pay-offs and hush money. And we need to tool up."

"Yeah. So how much?"

"We still need ten thousand to do it right." He let that hang there. "You'll get two hundred percent back on any money you put in."

"All these people here today, they're part of it?"

He didn't say anything to that.

"All right, just hypothetically," I said, "I put the money up, it all goes to plan. I get my payoff. Wonderful. But what if it goes bad?"

"You'd still get your two hundred percent back." Looking me right in the eye. "You'd have my guarantee."

"Let me think about it."

Think about it I did, my larcenous young friends. It was a good investment, any way you stacked it. If it worked, I'd get my money. It went bad, sooner or later I'd still get my money. How so, I hear you politely enquire. I'll tell you: Stan and Jimmy were old-school, my-word-is-my-bond-type brigands. A handshake deal with them was rock solid. That's how their lot operated. Only a loser or a lagging dog would renege on a debt. It was all about reputation. So that money would be mine, sooner or later. Even if it turned to shit and they all went to jail, eventually they would make good.

But elsewhere another stew was cooking. Next day, I was mugged. In the middle of a drug deal. How do you like that? Happened like this. Late afternoon. I was waiting for Alex and Cathy in a little park in Carlton called Murchison Square. Not quite dark. A chilly breeze blowing. I had the drugs in my car, a block away.

A couple of young blokes came walking up to me quickly. Leather jackets, hunched over. One of them in grubby white jeans. I could see they were nervous and I didn't like it. I started away. "Mel! Wait." They knew my name.

I paused. Shouldn't have.

"I've got a message from Alex," one of them was saying, closing the distance between us. That was it. Too late now. The other had circled around, and I saw the kid in the white jeans was holding a knife. I stopped. The other said "Jesus, put it away!" to his mate, then to me, "Sorry Mel, we just wanted to get, you know, a taste from you."

"Fuck off!"

"Come on, Mel. Just give us what you've got and we'll piss off."

Another figure approached through the gloom. A big, rangy character striding towards us. Unseen by the punks. Psycho Barry. He walked straight into the one who was doing the talking with enough force to knock him flying. The one with the knife froze. Barry was grinning. He walked up to the kid, took his forearm, held it in two places, and carefully, effortlessly, broke it over his own knee. I heard it. The kid screamed and collapsed. Barry turned to the other, who was on his feet, already limping away. He turned back to the kid on the ground, now holding his arm and sobbing, and kicked him in the stomach. He picked up the knife and leaned over the kid. He was breathing fast, staring hard at the writhing kid.

A voice out of the gloom shouted "Barry!"

Alex was approaching briskly. "Barry! We've got to get out of here."

"You set this up, you dog!" I said, as Alex got closer.

"I swear, Mel, I fucking swear I didn't. They must have overheard me on the phone. They were probably planning to jump *me*, but I got caught up on Punt Road." He looked around. "Barry, we've got to get out of here."

Barry straightened up, then looked around. With obvious reluctance, he dropped the knife, kicked the kid once more, looked at Alex, then at me. He tapped Alex's shoulder, none too gently. "Come over to my car." To me, "You too. Quick." I could hear the kid groaning as we left the park.

We walked in silence around the corner, a couple of hundred yards along Faraday Street. Barry stopped at a new-looking yellow Charger and said, "Get in."

Alex was shivering – from fear or dope sickness, I couldn't tell. Barry walked around the car and got in the back next to Alex, gestured for me to get in the front. As soon as Alex settled himself, Barry hit him hard on the side of the face.

Alex's head bounced around a bit, then he put his hand to his smarting cheek and said, "Barrrry! Fuckin' hell, man!"

Barry pulled Alex's hand away and hit him again. "Shut up."

He chucked his car keys to me. "Drive away," he said.

Ten minutes later he told me to stop on a dark stretch behind a factory in North Melbourne.

I thought it best to start the conversation. "There's been business between Alex and me," I said to Barry. "I've been steadily paying him back that outstanding debt. I have the paperwork to prove it."

Barry shook Alex, who was shivering worse than ever. "Is that right?"

Alex nodded, but without much enthusiasm.

To me Barry said, "How much have you given him?"

"Three thousand," I said.

To Alex, "True?"

"Round about, yeah, something like that."

"And how much have you still got?"

Alex opened his mouth to speak, but Barry cut him off, "Don't shit me."

Alex paused, then said quietly, "A few hundred."

"You," he said poking my shoulder, "you're in the shit." He nodded towards Alex. "This one is the big bloke's nephew. But you, you're just some cunt."

"Some cunt who has made partial restitution in good faith."

Barry shook his head. "You *knew* he'd give the money straight back to you to buy gear. Any fool could see that. The boss will see that." He let that hang there a few seconds. "He told me to tell you that whatever money you've already given Alex doesn't count."

"Hardly fair."

"You and your slut *robbed* the big man's nephew. Haven't you wondered how come you're not dead yet?"

I said nothing.

"Well, I'm waiting." Barry was smiling.

"He wants money?" I said.

Still smiling, no answer.

"He wants smack?"

A slight tilt of the head.

"He wants money and smack?"

"You're not just an ugly face, are you?"

PANIC IN ALBERT PARK

Barry dropped me back in Carlton, took Alex with him. I rang Cathy from a public phone, told her the news.

"Don't freak, Mel. I'll come over to your place. We can use this."

She arrived twenty minutes later. I banged up some speed mixed with the teensiest, weensiest little smidgin of smack, just this once, to help cool me out. Cathy had her regular blast.

We talked through the angles late into the night. The gist of what I'd gleaned from the psycho messenger was, the Greeks wanted to try their hand at heroin selling. Probably reasoned if grass and hashish were such good products, how much better would skag be? Except they didn't know how to get started. I could help with that.

From my point of view it was a complete catastrophe. Or else it was the best thing to happen in a year. One of them.

Get a fucking huge pile of smack and a pile of money, give it to the big man. If all went well, and the Greeks decided they wanted more, I would put them in touch with the Captain. Together they would then proceed to deliver narcotics to the people of Australia. And I would quietly slip out of it all, maybe with a little see-you-later bonus.

Of course the wily Greeks hadn't specified exactly how much money and drugs they judged to be an appropriate square-up. Leaving that to me.

Cathy and I talked about possible ounces, even pounds, of heroin and whatnot, speculated as to how much money might be reasonable under the circumstances. We kicked around the other questions: should we let Craig the copper know that Barry was back? What would happen if we kept mum? Should we pull Stan and Jimmy in on this?

All through our discussion, I knew Cathy was itching to find out where I was getting the skag, but I wasn't letting on. Finally she asked me outright. No way. Dig: I wasn't going to give away the only bit of an edge I had in this whole sorry business.

We went to bed. It was sweet. United in adversity. I didn't query the status of her and Stan, or her and Jimmy for that matter, or her and anybody. Tonight was cool.

She left in the morning.

That afternoon I went to see Jimmy and Stan and told them to count me in for the big knockover. I gave Stan a couple of thousand bucks right then. Didn't leave me with much, but I was square with the Captain and could no doubt get the next package on tick.

Something else I should mention here: a regrettable disagreement with Bobby Boyd, who remains a good cat to this day but who took an uncharacteristically narrow and unforgiving attitude to my venture into the heroin business. He hadn't minded the go-fast – hell, he'd been a major beneficiary – but he would have no truck with skag. Upshot was, my young troubadours, by the end of that week I was no longer an Oracle.

I didn't mind too much. Had a good experience that Friday night playing with the Rods, the bequiffed and greasy-haired rock'n'roll diehards with whom I'd never stopped moonlighting. It was a dance in Geelong. The nineteen fifties all over again. People were dancing. With one another. Looking out from behind the piano, watching the smiling dancers, the ladies' eyes closed as they whirled around the floor, I felt more a part of the music than I had in an age, like I was back in the game in some way. Even though your Carlton hipsters would've viewed this as some sorrowful, old-timey stuff, I knew it was the real, no bullshit, be-here-now thing. Hearken unto me, my little hepcats!

Next Monday there was a story in the *Daily Earth News*: "The New Heroin Plague." By Clive the Fop. I'll spare you the details – suffice to say, the Fop took a dim view. At least, pretended to. There was no mention of the many free lines, tokes, hits, tastes, blasts, etc. he'd copped from the evil drug sellers of Melbourne. Second column half way down, he claimed that smack was even making inroads into the traditional underworld, citing rumours that members of a certain gang of armed robbers were dabbling in it, maybe even running habits, and likely putting the proceeds of their robbery up their arms.

Then he quoted some Carlton idiot saying that heroin was the "existential drug" – the only drug, really, that's why it was "favoured by poets, musicians, writers, dreamers and outlaws." It finished with the Fop wondering aloud where all this high-quality gear was coming from. Over and out.

A potted version of the story turned up a couple of days later on page three of the *Sun*. All this and less than a week to go before the Moratorium and the big knockover.

I went to see Stan, half intending to get my money back. Found him at the East Melbourne house. He wasn't interested in the Fop's exposé, though. Right there at the front door, he hit me with, "Bloke named Barry. Bad bastard. From Sydney. What do you know about that?"

I stepped inside and Stan closed the door. Jimmy came out of the kitchen. I could see there were three or four blokes in there; smoke, beer bottles, fish and chips. Jimmy pulled the door closed

Stan and Jimmy were waiting for my answer. I wasn't sure how much Stan knew about the messy events in the house at Bondi the night of his escape from Goulburn Jail. Cathy *should* have told him, but she always had her own ways of doing things. He looked at me, gerried that I was hesitating.

"I know about the rip. Cathy told me. And we know Barry is in with the Sydney Greeks. We need to know if he knows about *our* job."

"How could he? No, of course not."

Jimmy said, "The cunt knows *something.*" Looking hard at me now, jerking his head up aggressively. "Well?"

"Barry and Greek Alex fronted me a few months ago. Tracked me down to my place. I bullshitted them. Barry left. The Greek stayed in town. Then Barry turned up again last week."

Stan and Jimmy looking very serious now.

"But it's not about, all *this* . . ." I gestured around the room. "It's about the Sydney rip. Really, it's about the Greeks wanting a smack supply. Nothing to do with your job."

"How do you mean, you bullshitted them?" Jimmy, sceptical.

Oh, Jesus H. Christ on a bike, I thought. My desperate gobbing off back then, my heist-novel riffing about robbing the lottery office. So obviously far-fetched that Alex had politely not mentioned it in our subsequent dealings. I'd thought it was forgotten. But maybe Barry had got a whiff from somewhere else that made him think again about my tall tale, put two and two together.

So I told them. When I finished, Jimmy sighed, long and deep, looked at Stan, who was deep in thought.

"I did jail with Barry," Stan said, "Parramatta. Years ago." I waited for the explanation, but none was forthcoming.

After a few more seconds Stan said to Jimmy. "We can't do anything now, too near the job. We just play it by ear. Cut him in if we need to. Deal with him later." Something else unspoken passed between the two of them – oh, my little peaceniks, you don't want to know!

Astute observers of human behaviour among you might be wondering just how well your trusty correspondent was dealing with all this aggravation. Truth is, not well. I'd never stopped taking speed, and I couldn't remember the last proper night's sleep I'd had. Despite what I'd resolved earlier, I was using the smack now, too. Mixing it with the accelerant. The term "emotional roller-coaster" comes to mind. But I wasn't paying for any of the dope, and I had access to so much of both varieties, my own chipping wasn't making any real difference to the profits.

Day to day, I was still doing plenty of goey biz. With Bikey Vic. Who was also part of the team on the big knockover. Yeah, I haven't mentioned that yet. Well, like me, Vic had been brought in as an investor. He and his bikey gang mates had a pretty good bank by then. But Vic was itching to get actively involved in the armed robbery caper. Jimmy and Stan had come to trust him, even like him, tough little bastard that he was, so they'd let him in.

I'd made a point of *not* asking questions, but Vic had let it drop that he and a couple of mates had been assigned a task that was very near to their nihilistic hearts: they were to handle the explosion on the King's Bridge. They could get hold of explosives – Vic hadn't said how, but I guessed the Boy Wonder might have something to do with that.

Vic had also taken to horning the odd line of hammer and tack, which was strictly non-U for your bikey brigade, but we're only human, right?

Anyway, Vic was a reliable cat, and I'd always liked his company. So when he came to my flat one night after dark, highly agitated, and said, "There are two blokes sitting in a car outside," I took notice. After turning the lights out, I drew the curtain and peeked through the window. The street was quiet. A plain Holden was parked back a bit from the street light. I couldn't see shit.

"Did you come in the front?"

Vic shook his head. "Round the back. Seen them before?"

In truth, my little scoundrels, for some time now I *had* been seeing suspicious loiterers, and more than once had the feeling cars were following me – I'd put it down to a return of my drug-induced discombobulation. A grain of salt, renarda renarda. Fact was, I'd spotted that same car outside twice in the past week, but my cooler-headed self had prevailed, reasoning, why the fuck would they be looking at old Mel, really?

"Could be nothing," I said.

Vic was already dialling a number on my phone.

"This is the Reverend Edward Entwhistle here, and I wish to report grossly indecent acts taking place right now, in a car, in my very street, between two male persons." Pause. "Yes." Another pause. "Sodomy, I believe." He described the green Holden, where it was, gave a bodgey address as his own, a few doors down from my real address, demanded a peeler come around and investigate, and hung up.

We kept the lights off. A quarter of an hour later a cop car cruised down the street and stopped. Two uniformed blokes got out and approached the parked car, one either side. There was some talk through the window. Whoever was in the car didn't get out. Then one of the uniformed men looked at his book, went off to find the Reverend Entwhistle. He came back a minute later, and both cars drove off.

Next morning it was cold. I went out early to the Captain's for a restock.

He was bleary-eyed, wearing a heavy sweater. He led me

into his lounge room, left me for a moment, then came back with a tray – teapot, cups, saucers, cigar box. He poured tea for us both, then opened the box, brought out a large plastic bag, put it on the coffee table.

The stuff was white – not sparkly like speed, but pure, matte white. And fine-grained, no lumps at all.

"This lot is different," he said. "Stronger. You'll need to be a bit careful with it."

It was the same price as before, though. I paid him for the last load, then left with the bag of new stuff, went over to Vic's place to repack it. He cooked up a taste.

Some drug lore here, young seekers. The stuff we'd been getting till now needed to be mixed with a little vinegar or lemon and cooked up in a spoon. Whereas this stuff dissolved easily, no acid needed. Vic looked at the spoon closely. "Interesting," he said. He drew it up into his fit, banged it away, and promptly went on the nod. He came around twenty minutes later and said, "That was like a train going through my brain."

Met Cathy later on at my place. We were sitting at my kitchen table. She'd brought falafels. I dropped a little folded-up package in front of her. She opened it up, stared at it up close, like a scientist, prodded it with her fingernail. "This is different dope."

"It's good piss."

She tipped it around in the open package, nodding. "This looks like number four."

She looked at me searchingly. "You getting this from the same source?"

"Never mind." I picked up a falafel, and started in on it. Mainly to avoid her gaze. Cathy cooked a taste, hit it up. Went pale, closed her eyes for a minute. She breathed deep. "Yep, number four," she said, then got up, put the dope in her pocket and left.

Two days later Cathy came back needing more. She was selling to Alex's people now too, which meant her business had nearly doubled. I had none left – I'd taken the last sker-rick twenty minutes before. So I bundled up the money I had, told Cathy to sit tight, left her at my flat while I went to see the man.

I rang the Captain from a public phone down the street – I didn't want Cathy eavesdropping – then drove to Albert Park. An hour later, deal done, I walked back to my car, which I'd left parked around the corner. Soon as I got in, the passenger door opened and Cathy hopped in smartly.

"You're getting the dope from *him*?" She nodded in the direction of the flat.

"Who? No. Jesus, Cathy, I told you to wait at the flat."

"There's something you need to know. Let's get out of here."

MEL'S HISTORY LESSON

Back at my place Cathy put a hit away, got up quickly, went to the bathroom. She came back a minute later and sat down at my kitchen table.

"Remind me," she said. "When were you last in Vietnam?"

"Early sixty-seven," I said.

She didn't say anything more for a while. Taking a little wander down memory lane, I guessed.

I'd first met Cathy in Vietnam. Did I tell you that already? At an army base in Phuoc Tuy. I was on tour, playing piano with Ray Rock and the Rockbeats. War is hell, baby, it's true, but that was a good gig. Cathy was one of a group of New Zealand dancers. They were doing their thing on stage that day, really shaking it. Went over big with the boys.

We smoked some ganja together afterwards – strong smokables in that part of the world, my young tea-heads. Cathy had been in Vietnam for over a year. Went as a nurse but was drawn into the entertainment scene. Good life for a party girl.

Next time I saw her she'd stopped dancing, was co-running an agency booking Filipino soul bands, Maori groups, Aussie country and western acts – anything, really – into military bases. South Vietnam was the show-biz capital of the earth for a while there: the chitlin' circuit, Broadway, Nashville, Hollywood, Kings Cross and Jimmy Sharman's tent show all rolled into one.

We met up once or twice again at different stops along the circuit. Then she disappeared. I didn't see her again until she turned up at the Joker looking for work. That's when she and Johnny had fallen in with one another, even though he already had complicated domestic arrangements. She became part of the Joker R&R scene, but we'd never really talked about our Vietnam days.

I looked across at Cathy, still deep in thought. I got up, put the kettle on for a cup of tea.

She snapped out of it. "Last time I saw you over there. Where was that, Saigon?"

"Yeah, I guess so. You had that office. In the Continental Hotel, right? Haven for assorted hoofers, guitar-slingers, urgers and no-hopers."

"You were one of them."

"Unkind."

"Anyway, you'd better listen to this, Mel. I've got some shit to tell you, goes back to then."

"Go for it."

"One time there was this big fuck-up with the booking business. We had this guy in Manila used to send us soul and rock groups. They were good bands too, only one drawback: they played all the songs off a single album, nothing else."

I brought the teapot and cups over to the table. "I remember seeing one of your groups," I said. "The Saints. They played all of *Rubber Soul,* note for note, but that was it. If someone requested 'Happy Birthday,' they were fucked."

"Exactly," she said. "But they cost way less than Australian or American outfits. Anyway, this trouble with our Manila connection. We'd sent him money to kit out three new bands, and he'd gone quiet on us. I was in the hotel bar, telling this fellow I knew, a correspondent, about it. How I needed to get over to Manila to sort it out. Out of the blue he says, 'I'm going there in two days time. Come with me.' Sure enough, on the day he picks me up in a cab, we head off to the airport. But it's not a regular flight. It's a US Air Force transport. One of those C47s."

I poured the tea and pushed a cup over to her. "He's a spook, right?"

She took a sip. "We get to Manila. He trots off to do whatever. I go see my guy. He's shamefaced. He'd blown the money we'd sent him on cards and hookers, and his wife had booted him out. It was obvious she had the brains, so I got *her* to take over the business. Even got our money back, in time. After three days in Manila, I meet up with my Saigon friend again. He's done what he needed, everything is hunky dory. We fly back to Saigon."

"Who is this guy?"

She took another sip, lit a cigarette.

"Monty. Shit name, huh? We meet up for a drink from time to time in Saigon. He's a regular at the Continental. Then a month after the Manila jaunt he tells me he has to go to Laos for a couple of days, would I like to tag along? Same deal, American plane. We end up in some town where Monty's doing something with the local mayor, a hill tribe guy. We're at a hotel. Everything's going on in French, which I can't follow, but I can tell things aren't going as planned. The mayor guy is being cranky and difficult. I'm hanging about, pouring drinks, being sweet. So I make a big fuss over the mayor – it's no skin off my nose, right? I lean over to pour his drink, give him a bit of a look-see down my front. The old goat loosens up a bit, starts smiling. Everything ends up good. Monty is very happy.

"We hung out together a lot after that. With correspondents, diplomatic staff. Hustlers and scammers. Military people too. He was welcomed *anywhere*."

"Is this guy military?"

"He was *supposed* to be a correspondent for something called the *Far Eastern Affairs Bulletin*. Might have even been a grain of truth in that, though it would've been a CIA front, of course."

"Of course. Need I point out, my dear Cathy, that they're the evil fucking enemy?"

"Yeah, I know, I know. But it was an education. Amazing. One day we're in Saigon palling around with the foreign correspondents, politicians, military. Next day we're knocking back the cognac poolside with the Lao royal family – who are pretty good fun, by the way. Day after that we're helicoptering off to some mountain village. We went to Thailand and Cambodia too. US Air Force planes mostly. Sometimes South Vietnamese Air Force."

"Doing *what* exactly?"

"There was business everywhere we went. Wherever we happened to be. Monty would meet local honcho types – lawyers, mayors, doctors, fixers. Priests, too. Anti-communists. Crooks, most of them. Anyone could see that."

"And you were, what, along for the ride?" I said.

"No need for that judgemental tone. Monty was meeting up with people from the *other* side too: Pathet Lao, even North Viets. Spies and double agents, whoever. Trying to figure out whose side they were really on. And it served his purposes to have me along. He let the cronies and fixers think I was his piece of tail. Maybe he figured they'd respect him more having, let's face it, a spunk like me along. Pouring drinks, lighting ciggies."

"Doesn't sound like you."

"Obviously I was just playing along. Thing is, something else was cooking. As well as the spy business, I mean."

"Meaning?"

"Remember the dope over there?"

"Sure. Best ganja in the world."

"And . . ." She waited.

"Well, opium of course."

"That was Monty's real business. Thieu and Ky and the rest – they're all in the opium trade. Have been for years. The Yanks are helping ship the raw opium from the hill plantations to the cities. Monty was helping set up the air transport." She stopped.

I shook my head. "The Americans flying opium? I don't believe it."

She shrugged. "The hill tribes are diehard anti-com, and their only way of turning a dollar is growing O. The Yanks figured, help them out, they'd return the favour. Made sense. They built landing strips all through the hills of Laos. Take military hardware in, bring opium out. There are opium poppies growing right there on the hillsides. You see the women and kids doing the weeding, watering. The blokes resting up back at the hut. Then harvest time, tons and tons of the stuff to be got out. There's a whole city up there that's not even on the maps. Has the busiest airport in the world. They were slipping the opium in with the official cargo. Shit, half the time it *was* the official cargo. The CIA didn't care – a bunch of gooks smoking their faces off."

"Still . . ."

"I saw the opium, Mel. I saw it on the planes. On US planes."

"You were getting into it too, right?"

"Yeah, but I knew what was what. Monty was into it as well. Our little secret. For him it was a private state-ment. About not really being part of the establishment. Or something. I forget now. We started doing little bits of skag – chasing the dragon."

She got up and went to the bathroom, came back a min-ute later.

"Thing was, the hill tribes were getting hip. For decades they'd been selling their opium harvest to Hong Kong gang-sters, who turned it into heroin. Then some of the hill-tribe hardheads learned how to refine the raw O into morphine base. From there it was no big deal to cook it into number three skag. The crude stuff. The rocks. Once you know how, you can do that in a shed or a lean-to. Easier to transport, obviously, plus a much much better price for the grower. The CIA didn't raise any objections."

"This is so far-fetched."

"True, nonetheless. Anyway, the next stage is turning number three into number four. White powder. Twenty times stronger. Maximum value. But not so easy. Takes a proper laboratory, good technicians, the right chemicals. There's a risk of explosion. The Chinese chemists are the best anywhere. They work for the gangs, mostly based in Hong Kong. If the interested parties were going to refine number four, they'd need the Chinese in on the deal."

"This is Disneyland."

"Monty's big project was helping set up the first Chinese laboratory. Right there in the Golden Triangle, within cooee of the poppy fields."

I shook my head. But – dig, chillen – despite my protestations, Cathy's mad rave was making a kind of ghastly sense to your worldly-wise correspondent.

"A few of the spooks were in on it. Some because they were old-school idiot flag-waving patriots, who thought anything was justified in defence of the great blah blah. Others were straight-up crooks who saw big money. With a perfect US government cover."

"And what did *you* see?"

"I'll tell you what I saw: an earn for myself. I won't deny it. But also for our side. You know – the good side? A big pile of money."

She went quiet for a moment. "And I was in love," she said.

She said it so plainly, I held off with any smart remarks. "With Monty?"

"Yeah. He was in love with me, too."

She was quiet again, for a whole minute, then went on in a small voice. "Early in the piece, we were in Vientiane, supposed to be meeting a Lao official. Monty had this funny turn, an 'episode.' Wouldn't come out of his room, wouldn't talk to anyone. *Couldn't.* This went on for three days. He was completely off-tap. I knew what had to be done. So I met the official on my own. Just winged it. It went fine. Next day Monty snapped out of it, but the business was already done. He knew what had happened.

"After that we were in it together. Then the deal with the Chinese came up. If we pulled it off, we stood to make a fortune."

"Yeah?"

A big sigh from Cathy. "It went sour. The Chinese. Their main guy came up to the air base in Laos. The secret one? Monty was to go with him up into the hills, a helicopter trip away. All the spadework had been done. The big boss just had to put the final seal on it.

"We were all staying in a hotel in Luang Prabang, way up north, the swishest place Monty could find. The lab was to be set up near there. The deal was nearly done. But it didn't go well. The guy took exception to me. Some instinctive, gut-feeling thing. He was a little, round, smiling guy, cruellest eyes you ever saw. I was doing my hostess bit, being nice. But he was watching me. At one point he said very simply to Monty, 'This one listen too much.' He pointed at me as he said it. No attempt to be polite or subtle. Monty didn't try to shit him, or smooth it over, he just went quiet.

"A little later I looked across at Monty. He looked sad. I knew I was in the shit. He saw me looking at him, and he knew that I knew.

"I was bundled out of there the next day. Escorted back to the air base, given sleepers and put on a plane. I woke up in a hotel room in Saigon. An old Viet woman keeping an eye on me. She spoke no English. She didn't know who I was anyway. I figured I'd been out of it for forty-eight hours.

Police came the next day and said my visa was revoked, I'd better get on a plane out of there pronto.

"I went to Darwin, then on to Sydney. Stayed in a share house up on the Peninsula. Didn't tell anyone what had happened. Too weird. Then I heard you and Johnny were running the disco."

"And what became of Monty?"

"Haven't you worked it out yet?"

"Monty is the Captain."

She nodded slowly.

"What did he say when he saw you down here?"

"He doesn't know I'm here."

"How could that be?"

She shook her head.

I thought about it. The Captain had been in the thick of the party scene last year, but Cathy had been away travelling. And he'd been lying low since then. If Stan hadn't mentioned Cathy – and why would he? – then there was no reason their paths would have crossed.

She stood up, started walking around the room. "That white powder . . . it can only mean the lab deal finally came through. Monty would've got a commission for his part."

She turned to me. "I had a feeling. Remember when all those strung-out Yanks started turning up at the Cross last year?"

"Of course."

"The white powder has hit Vietnam." She pointed at the foil package on the table. "And now it's here."

She looked at me, waiting like a teacher with a dimwit pupil.

"Tomorrow the world," I said.

"A shitload of number four," she said, "can only mean Monty did the deal, got the refinery set up – maybe a string of refineries."

"So he's the dope czar now?"

"Can't see that, somehow. He's too erratic. Maybe he

gets a commission. Or if he got a one-off payment, maybe part of it was in smack. Who knows? But he's holding right now. That's what's important."

She turned to me with a smile.

"What?"

She shook her head, as if to say, need I spell it out? Then finally leaned over, took my hand, looked me in the eye.

"We rob him."

The floor fell away beneath me.

"We rob him then get out of here. Take the white powder to Sydney. Give it to the Greeks as a peace offering. Keep a little back to sell, build up a bank. Square up with Johnny.

"Come to think of it," she said, looking out the window, "I could probably put the Greeks in touch with one of the CIA crooks, which would mean a connection to the Chinese. If that's what they want.

"Holy Jesus fuck!" I said.

Cathy's smile disappeared. She turned back to me, very grave.

"Half of that payoff is mine, Mel. The maggot owes me." She smiled again and tossed her head slightly.

"I believe you have a gun."

I, BANDIT

We were in a motel on Sydney Road. Rough piles of paper money spread out across the table. Next to one of the piles was my .38. I hadn't slept for four nights. Cathy was at the sink, cooking up a hit of smack. Jimmy was at the window, watching out for the Armed Robbery Squad. Stan and Denise were sitting in the lounge room, drinking gin straight from the bottle, listening to the radio, waiting for a news bulletin to find out whether the bloke I'd shot was dead.

Oh, let me tell you, my little dharma bums, there'd been many a sudden shift in tempo and some wild improvising to bring us to this crazy and generally fucked-up point in the proceedings. Let me tell you about it.

Second thoughts, fuck that. Everyone *knows* the story. The Moratorium. Big thrill, right? We the People, boring it up the Man. Dr Jim spruiking peace in Bourke Street. A hundred thousand people marching.

Meanwhile, we the *other* people were taking even more direct action – setting charges, brandishing firearms, robbing banks. Bail up you bastards, your money or your life, look smart there, you rotten sons of trollops, and what ho, off we ride!

Oh yeah, my pets, much of our meticulously and marvellously planned brigandage worked perfectly. Banks were indeed robbed, bags filled with armfuls of money, speedy getaways effected. There was just the teensiest bit which didn't go so well, and thereby were we fucked. Royally. But that's pretty much public knowledge too, right? Given what happened afterwards.

So I'll spare you an account of every single hiccup, cough, sneeze, snort, and beg your pardon. There's some stuff the newspapers *didn't* tell you, though, so pay attention now, and learn from the mistakes of one sadder and wiser than you, my young outlaws.

It all came down to Denise. Denise, the sweet and lubricious upper-crust slummer, sometime love partner of my good self and of polymorphous Cathy, of the silent robber Stan and Jesus knows who else. Well, that same Denise, long-time devoted amateur photographer, had recently acquired a handy Bolex 16-millimetre movie camera, and without letting on to her fellow bandits, decided that our gun-toting revolutionary proceedings would make for a spiffing cinematographic assemblage. To be shown to like-minded outlaws, anarchists, narodniks, heads, hippies and no-goodniks at secret late-night underground screenings around the world.

Seasoned crooks like Stan and Jimmy, edgy new robbers like Bikey Vic, and jaded yours truly would naturally have no truck with such suicidal carryings-on, so Denise had decided to keep her plans to herself.

So there we were, at the site of robbery number one, the Australia and New Zealand Bank in Exhibition Street. At the prearranged moment, bold robbers Stan, Jimmy, Cathy and Denise tumbled in, brandishing firearms. They'd brought those big, tough postal sacks with them to transport the booty out of there. And Denise had brought her camera, unbeknownst to her fellow bandits. A minute into proceedings she had the thing out and running, happily producing some highly verité observational agitprop revolutionary cinema which would no doubt elicit some active dialectical-type discussions in Berlin or Berkeley or Bolivia.

Stan, Jimmy and Cathy were doing the business – making the withdrawals, scaring the shitter out of bank staff and assorted customers. They realised what was happening on the cinematographic front, but it was too late now to stop the fair camerawoman.

Thing is, this wasn't your run of the mill, roscoe in the teller's face, empty the money tray bank robbery. This was your once in a lifetime, methodically clean out the whole fucking vault, cast of thousands, Cecil B whatever the fuck, Guinness Book of Records hoist. Because the lads had the mail that right then, on that day, at that time, the virtually impregnable vault would in fact be wide fucking open, as per the secret schedule, with no more than a couple of jobsworths overseeing it, and – tra-la-la – suitably armed and masked robbers, if they happened to be hip, might just swan in and have their wicked way with it.

Which is exactly what they did. They filled their postal bags with mucho big denom currency.

Cathy cut a fine figure as usual, holding a sawn-off article, a beret on her shapely noggin. Jimmy and Stan, both dressed in black jeans and black t-shirts, looked hip and existential, like they'd strolled out of a Froggy film. The two other men on the job were speedy young sharpie types, and didn't let the side down in the edgy good looks department. Too good not to catch on film, right?

According to the plan, Vic and his incendiary comrades should be detonating a charge on the King's Bridge at that very moment – which would provide a further distraction for any police who weren't already on crowd-control duty in Bourke Street.

And sure enough, at a little after one p.m. there was a big, deep, window-rattling boom in the distance. At which bank staff and customers shat themselves. The Viet Cong had arrived. The end of the world.

The robbers were happy. No police had shown up.

Outside the bank a car was waiting, at the wheel of which sat your trusty correspondent, drafted in at the last moment because the professional driver had pulled out due to a sick mum or some such. So there I was, right across the road, propped in a loading zone, motor running. Patiently waiting for my muchachos to emerge.

I had freely partaken of the powdered relaxants, a couple of hefty packages of which were stashed under the driver's seat. Oh yeah, I didn't tell you – Cathy and I had robbed the Captain that very morning. It was easy enough. We knocked on his door, put the gun in his face. Give us your drugs. We extracted the dope, not even properly hidden, from a cupboard in the kitchen. The Captain said very little, staring at Cathy the whole time. She was quiet, efficient, no bullshit, thank you very much. The shit between those two, dig, I did *not* want to know. We left the flat with two housebricks of tightly compressed white powder.

Again with the Cathy, the gun, the drug ripping and running thing. Some cats never learn, dig? Anyway, that was that. We stopped at my pad to sample the goods, then off we fucked, to rob banks and support the revolution.

First robber to come out of the bank was Jimmy, holding a big swag. He looked around. No wallopers. He nodded to the crew inside. Next came Denise, bum first, pointing her camera back inside. At Cathy, in fact, who stepped out into the sunlight a second later, a big bag in one mitt, the sawn-off in the other. She stopped, smiled at the camera, raised the weapon, Black Power salute style. Good footage, no doubt. Then came Stan carrying a swollen bag of booty. Camera-shy, he dodged around Cathy, looked left and right, started towards the car. After him came the sharpie lads. Each of them detouring around Cathy, the laughing show-off, but everyone too busy to take in what was happening behind them. The four boys were already halfway across the road when the bank clerk appeared in the doorway. Young verging on middle-aged. White shirt, tie, sleeves rolled up.

Gun in his hand.

He's right behind Cathy, who's blocking Denise's view of him. I can tell he'd had expected to run outside waving his gun only to find the bold bankrobber types had all long since bolted. Which would have left him looking good at zero risk to himself, showing his employers how devoted he is to their cause. But now here they were still, poncing about with revolutionary salutes and whatnot.

He stopped in the bank's doorway, uncertain what to do. Then, rather than demand a laying down of arms, a return of purloined cash, he shakily raised his gun until it pointed at Cathy's back. Blind confusion on his face.

Not sure how it happened, but a second or two later, there was I, trusty .38 in hand, standing in the middle of Exhibition Street and firing past Cathy and Denise into the bank, in the general direction of the clerk. Don't know how many shots I fired, but the plate-glass door shattered, and there were screams.

I became aware of Stan and Jimmy yelling. The girls were running like billy-o towards the car. I could hear sirens.

I got back in the driver's seat and off we went. Passed a fire engine on Nicholson Street, going the other way.

We stopped behind a factory in Richmond, where three cars were waiting for us. The sharps took off in one, with a single bag of loot. Jimmy and I put the rest of the loot, another two big bags, into the second car. Stan and the girls headed off in the third car to the Moratorium.

Twenty minutes later Jimmy and I pulled up outside a motel on Sydney Road, booked the night before, two rooms for the lot of us. We'd hardly said a word the whole time.

We jammed the swag into a closet. No need for high security now. Then we stood back, the door still open, and just stared at the bags.

"For some reason," I said, "I can't see that as actual money. Money you'd spend, buy stuff with."

Jimmy glanced my way, his dial almost deadpan, just the tiniest trace of a cold, amused smile.

"Yeah?" he said, in a way that might have been genuinely curious or might've signalled his bemusement at how slow I was at catching up.

"I mean, fuck me. This much . . . it's, like, it's *too* much," I said. "Too much to have, too much to spend." Then I thought some more. "Jeez, come to think of it," I said, "how many coppers will they assign to this?"

Jimmy kept looking at me, his expression unchanged. Waiting for me to catch on. But I didn't, not then. He said, "Better have a quick taste," and proceeded to cook up a blast.

Afterwards, we sat there a while, smoking cigs, digging the stone. In all the time we'd hung out in each other's general vicinity, I had never really talked to Jimmy, one to one. He'd had no cause to start up any sort of chummy old mateyness, and nor had I.

He still had that cool and knowing look on his face.

"You know, Jimmy," I said, "I'd always thought Stan was the boss, and you were sort of the quiet mate."

"The sidekick?" he said.

"I guess. But now I get it. You're like the bass player or the drummer who leads the whole outfit from the backline. The singer and the lead guitarist poncing around for the crowd, but you hold the reins."

He gave me the "you're a slow learner" look again and shrugged. He didn't say me nay.

"When you and Stan first came to me with the speed, last year, that was your operation, right? Not Stan's?"

He smiled, sort of.

"So why come to me?"

"I like you, Mel. You're kind of loose."

I grinned like a fool.

"But underneath all that, what you're really about is looking after number one."

My smile went.

"Means I know which way you're likely to jump. It's a good thing."

And that was that. He stood up. "Better go and find our comrades," he said.

"The black jeans, black t-shirt thing," I said. "Whose idea was that?"

He stopped, grinned again, just the tiniest bit sheepish. "Denise's," he said.

"Ah. You knew about the camera?"

"Not really." The almost-smile said otherwise.

"So you've got a bit of the show-off in you after all," I said.

And off we sloped.

The others were waiting, as per the plan, at the corner of Bourke Street. There was an exchange of hugs and kisses, and off we trotted, part of the great anti-war throng.

Looking back at it all now, I struggle to believe it really happened. Of the great revolutionary-type gestures – your Eureka Stockade, your Jerilderie Letter, your "Such Is Life" and whatnot – the fact of me and Cathy, Stan, Denise, Jimmy, anti-war marching down Collins Street, singing 'The Internationale,' not even an hour after pulling maybe the biggest Melbourne heist ever – *that* particular moment, my ardent little students of history, deserves to be remembered.

Denise was still schlepping her confounded movie camera, which I thought was loony, but by this stage no one else seemed to care. They were ecstatic. Jimmy and Stan, and Cathy, were not giving much away, but despite all the smack they'd hit up, their eyes were bright.

It was dawning on me slowly. For a certain type of armed robber, Jimmy and Stan's type, it wasn't really about the money, about getting it, spending it carefully, making it last, being judicious. It was the act itself. Get caught, go to jail? So be it, just so long as you make a fucking big splash on the way, behave with suitable dash and flash.

Which I could dig, a little – but really, only a little. Mel says, if you want to make a splash, go to the fucking swimming pool. Need to express yourself? Play funky Hammond B3 organ. Make etchings. Grow roses. Do flower-arranging. Whatever. But that afternoon, at the march, holding hands with revolutionary-type brothers and sisters, I wasn't sure whether I wanted to smash the state or go and hide somewhere.

Jimmy disappeared into a phone booth a little after we'd joined the march, came back with the news that the Building Society rip had gone bad. Two blokes had been nabbed, another two got away, but without the money. The Sunshine Pipefitters payroll heist had gone to plan, though. Hadn't counted the take yet, but it looked good. The explosives side of the project had, as we already knew, been more or less successful, in that there had been a fucking big bang on the King's Bridge. No one had been hurt, although it turned out a tram had its undercarriage blown to the shithouse.

There was much excited talk amongst the Moratorium crowd about the bombing. No one knew what it meant: had a breakaway direct action group set the charge? Or was it the cops or ASIO, as a way of discrediting the Moratorium? None of the robberies had made the news yet, but they soon would. Fuck me, would they.

So it was all very jolly and comradely on the march. The others smoked a sly joint, and were getting merrier each step of the way. The crowd stopped at the top of Bourke Street, and the speeches started. All very inspiring and We Shall Overcome. Even old Mel was a bit moved. Some very stirring revolutionary shit, my friends.

We slipped away mid-afternoon, took separate paths back to our motel hideout. The idea was to leave that night for the bush, a cabin in the Dandenongs. Stan and Jimmy would meet up with Vic and his people, and with the other robbery gangs, over the next few weeks and do the final whack-up of the proceeds: an equal share for everyone, regardless of their part. All very fair and honourable.

Now, my alert young readers, I hear your question, and I will answer it fully and frankly. How, you're wondering, was your intrepid but sensitive correspondent coping with all this shootery, rippery and robbery? To tell the truth, I'd felt better. The heroin had long since stopped being an efficacious antidote to the goey, and the latter was having a dramatic effect on my imagination. That's right, the creeping tree-coppers had started to reappear, along with things of an airborne nature. Telecommunications were compromised, I believed. Certain voices were heard from time to time. Vic spotting the two actual rozzers outside my flat had reignited my whatever the fuck you call them. All right, let's not mince words: my *hallucinations*. I had caught a dose of the Big P, as we'd taken to calling it. But dig, my sceptical young ones, the things I saw were as real to me as anything was ever real – and to this day I'm not sure how much we were actually being staked out, and how much I was a watcher of imaginary watchers (Whoa, a little zen-type paradoxical carry-on for you seekers there).

So the Moratorium march had been a tough gig for me, oscillating between revolutionary elation and florid paranoia. Every time some longhaired peacenik or -nikette made eyeball contact, I jumped out of my skin. Stan had to physically restrain me from throttling a gentle Quaker proffering a leaflet – I thought he was aiming a roscoe at me. Office workers leaning out of upstairs windows? CIA informants. Which is how we got to the unhappy state of affairs foreshadowed at the beginning of this chapter. Me pacing up and down, strung out, strung in, strung sideways and strung upside fucking down.

The girls came in from the other room – god knows what they'd been up to, but I could guess (easy there, my little perverts!), and we all had a hit of the Captain's smack. Then we settled down to watch the evening news on telly. Cocoa, anyone?

The Moratorium march was the big news. History in the making. Doc Jim. Linking of arms, singing of folk songs and such. Meanwhile in Canberra, Prime Minister Gorton smiled for the cameras. Premier Bolte thought they were just rabble and commos. Renarda. Then the story we were waiting for: the daring robbery of the ANZ Bank. Plenty of hard-earneds had been removed, the newsreader said. Shots had been fired. The heroic bank clerk who'd given chase had been shot for his pains. The injury was not that serious, apparently, and he was in stable condition (which was more than could be said for the gazabo who'd plugged him).

Across town, the newsreader said, there'd been a robbery at Sunshine Pipefitters Ltd: the payroll had been liberated by a band of heavily armed men. Serious dollars hoisted. Then the failed hold-up of Colonial Building Society. Two men arrested. Could they all be linked? Police had no comment.

Then the bomb blast on the King's Bridge. Cops were saying it was some kind of malfunction of unknown cause, possible a gas main. Which augured badly, because by now they *must* have known it was a set-up. Which meant Russell Street had an angle.

Jimmy stood up, glanced around the room. "I'll make the call now," he said to no one in particular. The others remained slumped around the room watching the television. I continued pacing up and down.

He came back ten minutes later, very serious. Stan looked at him. Jimmy gave a slow shake of the head.

Cathy, onto it. "What?"

"Craig wants two-thirds."

"Of our rip?"

"Of *everything*. Our rip, Sunshine Pipefitters."

"Fuck him."

Stan turned to her and said, "It's not just him. It's the whole Armed Rob Squad."

He stood up, got his pistol from his bag, put it on the table. Jimmy went to the bedroom, came out with three guns and put them on the table with Stan's. They set about carefully checking them.

"They're not coming *here*, are they?" I said.

"We meet Craig in an hour. To talk." Stan didn't look up.

An hour later we're in a back street in Footscray. Yes, *we*. Meaning yours truly. Tooled up, dagger between my bared teeth, ready for rough stuff. Vic too, and a couple of his trusties. And two blokes from the payroll robbery. Our gang. Ready for some OK Corral–type action.

Why was I there? In truth, dear ones, I was making up the numbers. One more desperado with nothing to lose. Denise was back at the motel, minding the loot. Cathy was right there with us. And she was *heavy*.

Stan and Jimmy were up front, next to their car. Vic, me, Cathy, the other roughnecks, were scattered further down the street. Dig, the lads were expecting to meet Craig and another envoy from the Armed Robbery Squad. We were meant to be visible. The cops would see us, the reasoning went, and instantly be persuaded not to try anything flash. We'd negotiate a split, go our separate ways. Nothing unpleasant. Farewell, and give my regards to your mum.

It didn't go down that way. I told you I was – well, cards

on the table, I was in a fucking state. Couldn't tell my arse from my elbow. My vision had gone weirdly, radically double, like two entirely separate views had been superimposed in my brain. And everything was kind of shaking and crawling. I was hearing things too – muffled voices. I was, in a word, agitated.

We heard a car coming around the corner. Craig was at the wheel. He waved to Stan. We're all mates. Going to sort this out, no worries.

But I saw it differently. For the fifteen minutes we'd been waiting, some very weird shit had been going on in my head. Thoughts, feelings . . . fuck it, visions and epiphanies. Voices, murmurs. So I knew – I mean I really knew, no question, as much as I'd ever known anything, that this was a trap.

There was Craig, walking towards Stan and Jimmy. Smiling, saying something. And there was me, blazing away. Second airing of my .38 in one day. Craig went down. Stan and Jimmy were frozen, staring at me.

"It's a trap. Barry is here. We've got to split."

Jimmy stared at me for a second longer, then nudged Stan. "Quick," he said. Then shouting at the rest of us, "Out now!"

We ran to our cars. Right on cue, another two cars came screaming around the corner behind us. A yellow Charger and a light blue Holden. We were already in our cars, moving. And shooting. The drivers of the Charger and the Holden hit their brakes, unsure what was happening. We drove past the latecomers and down the street, jumping kerbs, shooting like crazy.

I looked back when we got to the end of the street. Craig was on the deck, not moving. Their cars were doing three-point turns, trying to get on our tails. A split-second pause. Psycho Barry behind the wheel of the Charger, looking me right in the eye.

BRINGING IN THE SHEAVES

Back at the motel an hour later. Vic and the Boy Wonder there now. Television on, radio in the other room. The violent gunfight in Footscray was all over the airwaves. The gang believed responsible for the Moratorium Day robberies had been cornered, had shot their way out, seriously injuring a detective sergeant from the Armed Robbery Squad.

I turned to Cathy. "I thought your mate Craig's brilliant plan involved running Barry out of town? I don't recall any talk of him joining up with Barry in order to fuck us."

No answer.

Old police photos of Jimmy and Stan flashed on the screen, the announcer saying the robbers were considered extremely dangerous and should not be approached, but that members of the public were asked to look out for them.

"We've got to get out," Jimmy said. He was throwing things in his bag while he spoke. "What we'll do," he said to the room at large, "each crew will hold on to what they've got for now. The final whack-up will have to wait till we can all meet up. *Not* in Melbourne."

He dug into his bag, counted out a big wad of money and handed it to Vic. "In the meantime, this is for your mob, on account." Because Vic and co. hadn't actually robbed anyone, being involved as they were in creating explosive mayhem. So that little payment in advance was fully kosher.

Vic looked at him for a few seconds, then turned to me. "What'll you do?"

"Shoot through. With this lot."

Vic said, "All right. How are you for goey?"

"Could use an ounce or two. Want some hammer?"

Bags of powder were duly swapped. Then everyone present had a hit. Most opted for a cocktail.

We got in our cars. Me in my old Holden with Cathy and Stan. Jimmy and Denise in a VW. There were two other robbers' cars parked nearby. Not wise for us to be all together, but there you go.

Stan was herding everyone along. No more tactics or strategy, now it was simply, run.

So this was it. Leaving Melbourne. My flat full of stuff. Hammond organ, tape recorder, guitar, amp. Too bad. The rest I didn't care about – clothes, a few books, some records.

As we pulled out of the motel car park, the proprietor eyed us through the plastic curtain. Hello, I thought, he'll be on the blower before we've gone a hundred yards. But we got out of Melbourne without incident. Drove almost to Wadonga – the Dandenong hideout plan had been abandoned – and found a shack in the hills where Stan had spent time as a kid.

We broke the padlock on the door and settled in. Guns at the ready. Lit a fire on the wood stove and Stan cooked steak and eggs for all.

After we'd eaten and partaken of drugs, Jimmy leaned back and closed his eyes.

"So, Mel, how did you know it was a trap back there?"

"Fucked if I could tell you. Just did."

Jimmy nodded. "I've seen that happen before. Lucky for us." He smiled at me. "I *knew* you were worth having along. Any more thoughts like that, let us know, eh?"

Next morning I went into town to get supplies. In the newsagent, the *Sun* headline: HIPPIE GANG CRIME WAVE. A large grainy image of Cathy on the steps of the bank, holding her sawn-off in the air. Smaller inset pictures of Stan and Jimmy. Top of the next page a photo of Denise. Next to her, a smaller pic of Cathy, the one from last year outside the Esso service station. She was referred to as "a former striptease artist." Bottom of the page, there's me, right there. Melvin John Parker, legendary Kerouacian hipster, recently known to have tickled the ivories with the pop group Oracle. Now a card-carrying member of the Hippie Gang.

The first three pages were given over entirely to the story. A publicity photo of Oracle. High school photos of Denise. More police photos of Stan and Jimmy. Also a piece by the Fop: "Inside the Hippie Gang."

I paid for the paper and shuffled out of the newsagent. As I got in the car, I could see the shopkeeper peering out at me.

Back at the cabin, Stan had got the ancient television working. Snowy picture, but right there on the screen, shaky footage of people with their hands in the air. Fuck me if it wasn't the inside of a bank. There was a cut, then we were watching Cathy on the steps of the bank. Making revolutionary gestures. A couple of figures darting behind her – Stan and Jimmy. Then a shadowy blur appeared behind the glass. Then the glass explodes and the camera goes spazz.

Stan said to me. "Denise left a film canister in the motel room. The police found it."

Denise said, "Sorry."

I held up the newspaper.

Cathy grabbed it out of my hand, started reading avidly.

"'Former stripper.' How do you like that? Of all the things they could have said."

But I could see she was pleased as punch.

The others crowded around to read the stories. One would read aloud this or that bit, then someone else. Denise loved being referred to as 'the heiress revolutionary.' Even Jimmy was tickled: "Jimmy 'the Thug'," he read, "is a lifelong petty criminal who has recently turned to armed robbery. He is considered by police to be extremely dangerous." Yuk, yuk, yuk.

Denise read a bit that said, "The gang are known to be drug users, addicted to cannabis and harder drugs. The gang members are also believers in 'free love'."

They were all in stitches.

Cathy seized on a paragraph on page three. "Melvin

Parker was described by a source in the entertainment industry," she declaimed, "as 'a half-baked beatnik and failed variety entertainer.' The source went on to say, 'He's tried every gimmick possible. Singing cowboy, Hawaiian entertainer and trad jazzer. He's even posed as a rock musician!'"

She kept reading, with way too much relish for my liking. "'Parker has recently experienced some success in the rock music scene, playing organ with Melbourne pop group Oracle. The group's leader Bobby Boyd commented, "Mel Parker has played a couple of dates with the group. We always thought he was one of the great old characters of the discotheque scene. We had no idea he was involved in crime and drugs."'"

I stood by the sink watching them, noting their childish excitement. There was no pretence that it was about the money any more. It wasn't even about getting away. That's when I knew our paths would diverge. And soon. Knew it for certain. The turning point. For me, for my story. Big changes not far off now. I wanted out.

A couple of hours later we split. We left the stolen VW at the cabin and all crowded into my car. There was a mile of dirt road between the shack and the Hume Highway. Halfway along, we came face to face with another car, a new, dull green Holden. Staring at us from behind the wheel, a uniformed cop.

I reversed back a few yards. Cathy leaned out and took a pot shot. I drove around the car, couldn't see the driver now. I thought maybe she'd hit him, but a minute later I saw him in the rear view mirror, coming up fast.

"Pull up!" said Jimmy.

I did. He and Stan tumbled out of the car and started shooting. The cop skidded to a halt well behind us. The lads started to run towards the cop car, which was now reversing away from them. I heard more gunshots, then saw in the rear view a cloud of steam rising from the bonnet of the police car.

Stan and Jimmy trotted back, hopped into the car. "He's all right," said Stan, puffing. Our reasoning as we drove away, the cop hadn't had any idea we were notorious bank robbers. Maybe investigating a reported break-in at the holiday cabin. Maybe something entirely unrelated. But they'd be on to us now.

We drove for half an hour. Our plan was to get out of the area before we stole another car. The police would assume we were heading north, we hoped, so we headed south instead, back towards Melbourne.

We stopped at Glenrowan and Stan made some calls. We filled up and headed off again. Stan was cagey, but said to keep heading towards Melbourne. An arrangement had been made.

The mood in the car was grim. No chat. Me behind the wheel, thinking. Then a little while later, a strange feeling.

"We can't go on," I said.

"Here we go," said Cathy. "Why not?"

"I . . . I don't know." I turned to Stan. "Who'd you ring back there?"

A long sigh. "Vic. He's bringing us a clean car. We just have to make it to Violet Town."

"Something's not right," I said.

Jimmy, sitting in the front passenger seat, turned to me. "What's not right?"

"Don't know. It's just not right."

Jimmy shook his head. "It's *all* not right. Nothing is right. Our best chance is to make it to Violet Town quick as we can, then lay low until we hook up with Vic." He glanced at me again.

"Drive on," he said. Resigned. Like he knew already it was going to shit.

THE WANGARATTA BOOK OF THE DEAD

A hot day. Blazing sun. I was in the middle of a wide, flat paddock. Driving a tractor (an old Fordson, if you're interested, my eager young collectivists). I was wearing a faded work shirt, dusty trousers, a battered straw hat grubby with sweat. A line of trees way off in the west, some low hills to the south. To the east, a house and shed.

I put the brake on, turned off the engine, got down from the tractor and walked the three hundred yards to the buildings. In an iron shed, a swarthy old man was bent over a bench and vice – a sour, snaggle-toothed old cunt, if ever there was one. He looked my way then scurried to the back of the shed and out the door. I called to him. No answer.

I walked around the property. It was a dump. A couple of tumbledown sheds, rusty water tanks and a small kitchen garden out back of the house. A snarling cur on a chain.

I went to the front of the small house, opened the screen door, poked my head in. Dark and dank inside. I let go of the door, and walked around the side, to a little outbuilding twenty yards away. Unpainted, rundown. An old cloth over a broken windowpane.

Inside, a chair and a little table with a kero lamp on it. A stretcher bed. Next to the bed an upturned packing case with a candle on it, and a copy of the *I Ching*.

Under the bed was my old overnight bag. Inside it was my typewriter and a change of clothes. A wad of money too, bound in rubber bands, stuffed into a manila envelope. Under the money was a gun. And a folded piece of paper. With a diagram on it. Very detailed, in my hand. A scrawly main road. An arrow pointing to the right labelled "W-town approx 35 miles." A little house marked on one side of the road, a spot marked "Black Rock" on the other. A turn-off, a track, a cattle grid. A bridge over "Seven Mile Creek." A bend in the path. A crudely drawn tree ("stand of coolabahs") and a big circled "Dig for H, 3 ft" at the corner where four paddocks met up. I wigged that it was some kind of ye olde buried treasure map.

I returned everything to the bag and slid it back under the bed. Noticed a stack of twenty or thirty yellowing newspapers there too. I pulled out the top one and looked at it. *The Sun*, Melbourne, Thursday, May 21, 1970. I put it back.

I went out to the paddock again, over to the tractor. It was an old crank job, but I knew how to start it. I climbed up behind the wheel and put the thing in gear. I'd been midway through harrowing the paddock prior to sowing the next crop. Dig, I'd never driven a tractor in my life, never had the slightest interest in agriculture. But here I was. And I knew what to do.

I spent the rest of that day on the tractor, going up and down over the same ground, exposing the old growth to the sun to kill it off. When the sun got low I walked back to the sleepout. On the step was a plate with a clean cloth over it. A meal of chops and potatoes.

I had a wash under a bucket suspended from a tree branch, went back inside and lit the kero lamp, picked up the *I Ching*. I cast the coins: *Hexagram 36. Darkening of the light. In adversity it furthers one to be persevering.*

Next morning there was a bowl of porridge outside the door. I ate it, went out to the paddock and continued harrowing.

I didn't catch a glimpse of the old bloke all day, but there was a meal outside the cabin again that night. Again I cast the *I Ching*, as I sensed I had done every night for a long time now. I got another nondescript, business as usual, go with the flow kind of message, something about working within limitations. Turned in, got up the next morning, worked the tractor again all the next day. Finished that paddock and moved onto the next.

It went on like that for a week. I was conscious, fully aware, and I knew my daily routine unerringly. But that was all. The stuff in the bag, the money, the gun, the map – I knew at some deeper level it was mine, but I had no idea what any of it meant. I didn't know my name, or where I was, how I'd got there, how long I'd been there. But that didn't bother me. It was like being in a dream – there's some far-fetched shit going on, but you just cop it sweet, go with it, because that's what the logic of the situation dictates. I'd catch an occasional glimpse of the old troll, but he kept well clear. Which didn't bother me.

So there I was, being the farmhand. At odd moments the big thing, the Great Beast, Me and My History, would loom, but when that happened I'd just get on with the routine, and everything would settle again.

The days blanked themselves out, Each evening I had trouble remembering long parts of the day just completed – but sitting on a tractor in the sun all day will do that to you anyway, I guess.

The fog lifted slowly and unevenly. After about a week I knew I was Mel Parker, long-time ivory tickler and string picker. A day or two after that I remembered I had been a pop star of sorts, if only briefly. The rest was a mess.

I had questions now. I bailed up the old bastard the next morning when he bought the porridge around.

"Who are you?" I said.

He bared his teeth and backed away from me, then hobbled off muttering to himself.

Next night I waited inside my door, and the moment I heard him put my dinner down on the step I jumped him, got him in a headlock. He was a hundred and ten years old but a wiry little bastard. He squirmed and twisted, bit me hard on the wrist, drawing blood. I gave him a good swipe. It took another one to settle him down, but then he went still.

"Who are you?" I shouted at him.

He looked at me, said nothing. I backhanded him. "Who are you?"

He shook his head. I let him go. He stood back a few feet

then spat out a rush of angry, excited words. Guttural, foreign. No lingo I could recognise. He went on and on – much to tell. Kept coming back to the old crazy loco gesture, finger circling at the side of his head, then pointing at me. And the sign to ward off evil. Other gestures indicating crazy behaviour. Sickness. Driving the tractor. Him cooking meals for me. Me digging in the dirt. Work, eat, sleep, time passing.

I got it. I'd been there a while. Following the routine. Working. In a dream. Yeah, *working*. I rubbed my thumb and index finger together and shouted at him, "Pay?"

A look I hadn't seen from him yet: child-like innocence.

"Money?" I said.

A little shake of his head. Hands turned upwards, like, I'm hopelessly in the dark on this.

I grabbed him, locked my hands around his scrawny neck and shook him like a rag doll. "You overplayed that, you miserable old mongrel. Give me my baksheesh. Spondulicks." I pushed him away. "Or else," I said, drawing a finger across my own throat then pointing at him.

He looked at me darkly.

"Yes, you understood *that*, didn't you?" I said, and walked away.

Next morning, under my porridge bowl was an envelope with a bunch of twenty dollar notes in it.

I kept to the work routine. Truth is, I found it reassuring. Chopping wood, drawing water. One foot in front of the other. Out in the blazing sun each day. Feeling nothing much, but soothed by the ceaseless chugging of the Fordson, the orderly criss-crossing of the paddocks. Eating, sleeping. Not dreaming, not much. Dig, my head wasn't right still, obviously, and I knew that. But hey, there are worse things, no?

My memory returned bit by bit. The Moratorium. The blown deal with the Armed Rob boys. The whole Melbourne thing. But the Big One, the minotaur in the labyrinth, the heart of my darkness – whatever it was . . . That was still sleeping, out of reach.

I got in from work one night – it was hot, insects buzzing around. Not unpleasant, though. I sat down to eat and heard a voice say "Mel?"

Cathy. I looked around. No one there. Then the voice again, calling with the same questioning note.

Holy shit, it was Wuthering fucking Heights. I stood up, went out into the twilight. I could smell Cathy. Smell her hair, her skin, her cunt. And then I knew. Knew all of it.

VIOLET TOWN

We were driving back *towards* Melbourne, instead of north, where we'd figured the roadblocks would be. The whole gang crowded into my car. Going to meet Vic in Violet Town. My sense of impending catastrophe getting stronger with every mile.

Somewhere or other, I pulled off the road.

"Fuck it," I said. "I'm not going any further."

Stan leaned forward, put his hand gently on my shoulder. "Just be calm, mate. It's all right. This is the right thing. Get back to Melbourne."

Jimmy said nothing.

Maybe Denise had something to say. I can't remember. She'd gone very quiet.

I sat there, staring straight ahead. Cathy was sitting next to me. She leaned over.

"You're speed crazy." She gave my arm a shake. "Swap places. Give me the keys."

Maybe I was psycho. Hell, I was, no doubt about it. I hadn't slept in a week. I was seeing twitchy, wobbly movements wherever I looked. Faces, eyeballs, cameras, hidden microphones. My vision was maybe thirty percent hallucinated. That's just an estimate. Possibly a conservative one.

Cathy gave my arm another shake. A moment of clarity. I had to go it alone from here.

But dig, it was *my* car, the same old light blue HD Holden station wagon I'd driven out of Sydney the previous year, the one that had spirited Stan away from Goulburn Jail, had shat itself on the Hume all that time ago, had been my Hammond–transporting workhorse this past eight months. Which my bank robber companions – especially Jimmy, who had become the unspoken leader of our doughty band – were convinced was their only means of escape.

I took the keys out of the ignition, removed my lucky tiki from the key ring, turned to Cathy and slapped the car keys into her mitt. Dug into my bag, gave one of the bricks of heroin to her. And got out of the car.

Upshotville: I was left standing by the side of the road, clutching a bag with a change of daks and underwear, a fat wad of money, a typewriter, a heavy load of number four white and my gun. On the outskirts of a town whose name I can't remember. There was a notional understanding that we would all meet up that night at an address in Frankston, Vic's bolthole. Where we would calmly and rationally plan a more orderly escape from Melbourne.

Detailsville: hazy. I guess I just sat there for a while. I *do* know that a little while later I was in a car, which I guess I'd stolen, because I can't remember how I came by it. A green Morris 1100. I was on the highway, driving towards Melbourne, coming up on cop cars and a roadblock.

Except it wasn't a roadblock any more. They were waving us through. Past police and men in dustcoats photographing a smashed up police car, and bits of splintered barrier. Like everyone else, I slowed down to get a better look. A cop gestured impatiently for me to move on.

A massive Hiroshima-like cloud of evil brown smoke rose beyond the next rise. Traffic not going anywhere. Then sirens. A minute later, two fire engines and an ambulance drove around the backed-up cars and trucks.

People were getting out of their cars. Me too. I walked

up to the rise ahead, got to the crest. At the bottom of the slope in front of me, maybe four hundred yards away, was a wooden bridge. Just this side of it, at a ninety-degree angle to the road, surrounded by a huge black circle, a still-blazing oil tanker. And a car, right up against the truck.

The bridge was fucked. And that car wreck was my HD. The remains thereof. I walked further down the hill. The uniformed cops were keeping people well back from the scene. I stopped at the barrier and stared. Bloke next to me shook his head. "My God," he said, "Holy fucking shit."

I kept staring. It was hard to make out what had been what. Best I could figure, the whole top of the HD had been sheared off. I read later that was correct – first the neat shearing off of the top of the car, then the explosion. Nothing left but twisted and melted metal.

Firehoses played on the burning truck. Cops everywhere. Parked haphazardly around the scene, but well away from the blaze, were three fire engines. An ambulance. Five or six police cars. Two tow trucks. And at the back, already hooked up to a tow truck, a car with a smashed-in side door. A yellow Charger.

Across the creek, on the opposite slope, a bunch of five or six grim-faced men in suits, not doing anything, just watching. The Armed Robbery boys. And right there in the middle of them, Barry. From half a mile away I could feel him, probing. He looked in my direction, and I moved behind the gawker next to me. Even at that distance, he sensed my presence as much as I felt his.

I turned the Morris around and drove away. Pulled off the road a little further on, shot up a cocktail. Kept driving north.

I stayed that night in a motel across the border, moved on the next day, stopped at Cootamundra. The day after that I drove to Forbes. From there to Young, then Condobolin.

I never planned it that way, it just happened. Each morning, I'd consider what to do that day. No point hanging

147

around, too risky. So I'd drive off. Couldn't go to Sydney or Melbourne, so I went to whatever bush town was a half day's drive from where I was.

Each day shoot some dope. Drive. Stop. Check in. Shoot more dope. Next morning, drive again. It went like that for a while, a few weeks. Maybe longer. Actually, longer. Much longer.

I got another car, a Valiant, went from central New South Wales out to the north west and back to the north coast. One-night stands. Then into Queensland, criss-crossing the state. Left Queensland, went even further afield. Anonymous motels suited me. When there was no motel I slept rough. Kept away from hotels and small-town stickybeaks.

My money was holding out well enough. So was the dope. I'd run out of speed up in Bourke and that had been a bit rough, but not too bad. Got some pills from a bush doctor to help with that.

The number four was my mainstay. I'd scrape a little bit off the brick every so often, but it was so densely compacted my scratchings didn't seem to make any great difference to the size or weight of the block. I knew I couldn't just keeping banging the shit up forever. Not good for one's health, obviously (though not as bad as you might think). Plus, of course, that brick was my superannuation, my nest egg. My future. Whatever, I tried to keep it under control. I'd have a taste in the morning, a top-up mid-afternoon, and one for beddy-byes. No between-meal snacks.

That was my life. Smack. Road. Sleep. Simple really. Not much fun. But that wasn't the idea anyway. I was David Janssen, the fugitive. Down every road there's always one more city, and so on. A fugitive must be a rolling stone.

Except that no one was looking for me, on account of I'd died in the crash at Violet Town. Too bad about old Mel, but he'd always been a bit of a wrong'un.

THE THREE CHORDS OF WISDOM

I saw enough newspapers and magazines to keep up. The story of the Hippie Gang's demise was told and retold. How the cops had picked up the chase somewhere around Benalla. How the robbers crashed through a road block ten miles south of there. How the car lost control on a bend and hit a petrol tanker. How all its occupants were incinerated. Party girl and former stripper Cathy, socialite Denise, jail escapee Stan, long-time professional crim 'Jimmy the Thug.' And legendary hipster Mel Parker.

A couple of days later it was reported that contrary to earlier reports, one of the outlaws had dodged the fiery Hume inferno. "Heiress revolutionary" Denise had apparently bailed out before the crash and was helping the police with their enquiries. They were understood to be investigating the possibility that she had been kidnapped by the outlaws, or was operating under some form of compulsion. Well, good luck to her, I thought. She'd always been good with a yarn.

A Vietnam Moratorium Committee spokesman was quoted in the *Age* saying the so-called 'Hippie Gang' was not affiliated with them, and that the Committee in no way endorsed the violent and lawless actions they had allegedly perpetrated.

A note in the *Sun* a little later: the detective sergeant from the armed robbery squad was making a slow recovery from gunshot wounds sustained in his heroic shootout with the Hippie Gang. A week after that, a story about him receiving the Queen's Medal for valour.

In Brewarrina I read a Sunday newspaper that claimed the now legendary Hippie Gang had become one of the most sensational news stories in Australian history, up there with Ned Kelly, the death of Pharlap, Harold Holt's big swim.

Over the next few months the events of that day were much retold in magazine articles, and in television documentaries I watched in crappy motel rooms. Discussed, debated, analysed, autopsied. Much talk about Australia's very own branch of the Weather Underground Baader-Meinhof Black September NLF Che Guevara Ned Kelly-type whatever the fuck. Networks of Maoists, Trots, Stalinists, nihilists, terrorists, criminals, anarchists, highwaymen and women.

Denise's film footage was at the heart of it all. Replayed over and over. Shown around the world. Statements from revolutionary groups elsewhere denouncing, applauding or simply acknowledging the actions. Malcolm Muggeridge commented on them. The big etcetera.

As time went by, there was less and less in the papers about the other jobs – the bombing, the Sunshine payroll – but no let up on the Hippie Gang. Clive the Fop wrote pieces in the *Age*, no less, emphasising how close he had got to the robbers. Then, many months later, a small report in the *Sun* that the police now thought it was pure coincidence that armed robbers had hit three separate spots at the same time on the same day – as far as they could tell, the robbers had acted independently of one another, all taking advantage of the disruption and mood of lawlessness fostered by the Vietnam Moratorium campaign, renarda, renarda, renarda.

So the cops were playing down the story, when you'd expect the opposite. Which likely meant they had something going on. An interest. They were on the inside.

The obvious question arose: Did this mean someone had turned dog, thrown in their lot with the peelers? The two robbers pinched back at the building society rip? Or maybe the crew who did the Sunshine Pipefitters. But they had got away clean, and why would the other two talk now, after so long? And how much did any of them know about the whole plan anyway? Sorry my eager young sherlocks, but that just didn't make sense. Apart from yours truly, Bikey Vic was the only one still free who had known the whole deal.

Could Vic have turned bow-wow? I mulled that over for a while. Maybe he'd paid off the Armed Rob boys. If he'd been pressed – maybe under threat of a jail sentence – the Vic I knew would have spun a yarn, minimised the risk, while sounding plausible. That's what I hoped. But you've got to be realistic.

Not that I cared all that much. I was going through the motions. Waiting for Godot. Had time on my hands. Nowhere to be, nowhere to go. I've laid around and played around this ol' town too long, so now I gotta travel on. Have gun, will travel. I was the yodelling bagman. A knight without armour in a savage land. From now on, all my friends are gonna be strangers. Got to keep moving, 'cause blues falling down like hail. Had the key to the highway, booked and bound to go. Looking for me? Then meet me at no particular place and I'll be there at no particular time. Make that the twelfth of never. Beyond the reef. Across the great divide. East of the sun, west of the moon. Relaxing at Camarillo. Cruising around in my automobile.

Oh yes, I was drifting and drifting, like a ship out on the sea. With a low-down aching chill. Another guy on the lost highway. A rolling stone. All alone and lost. With mean things on my mind. A complete unknown. The iceman. The iceman who goeth. On the road. Start spreadin' the news, I'm leaving today. 'Cause I'm the next of kin to the wayward wind. I've been everywhere, man. Crossed the deserts bare, man. Don't bother to write. Don't call. No correspondence will be entered into. No hawkers or canvassers. I was walking with a zombie. I *was* the zombie. Dig, dear friends, I was *shut down*.

The weather got cold, then got warm again. I kept drifting all through the hot inland summer. I scarcely noticed. Town to town. Time passing. Saw some things here and there. Nothing I want to talk about.

Along the way I looked up some folks from the old Sydney days. I saw the Cat, proprietor of a chemist shop, a picture of respectability. The Multi-Grip Kid was running a big garage down south. Molly had a motel. Mr Bones, Brylcreem, Steptoe, the Reverend, the Sexational Gypsy Woman. Yeah, Johnny, you know them, our people – they send their regards. The old crew. They're all out there. There was no "let's reminisce about the grand old days over a glass of port," just a bit of help when needed, usually paid for. Or no more than a sly nod of mutual recognition. Thanks very much. See ya later, like, maybe never. No offence meant. None taken.

That's how it was for me. Apart from them, never saw a friend I knew. They were all rank strangers to me.

Then one day, nothing special about it, I saw a sign in a music shop window: a fifty-fifty dance band needed a guitar player. I bought an old Maton semi-acoustic and a little Moody amp in a junk shop, rang the number. Doris, an older girl with a forty-cigarette-a-day voice. She played the organ, she said, and booked the jobs.

"Can you play fifty-fifty?" she said. I told her yeah.

"Do you know 'I'll Take You Home Again, Kathleen'?"

"Yeah."

"How about 'Giant Steps'?"

I said nothing. She said, "Just kidding you. You'd better come along to the RSL this Friday night, eight o'clock, and we'll see how you go."

I told her okay, and thought, All right then, here we go. How bad could they be?

Oh, my sensitive young music lovers, they were worse than bad. Starts were messy, finishes worse. Middles horrible. Doris pummelled away at a rinky-dink organ like she bore it a grudge. There was an Abo bloke named Dougie on steel guitar who was so faraway he was hardly there at all. The drummer was a middle-aged bloke with a pencil mo and a permanent vacant grin, obviously a wet brain, who insisted on calling me Noel. A younger bloke named Kev on bass stared off into the distance the whole time. Doris's niece

Elaine got up and sang a song with a certain gusto, but with enough dud notes to undo the good. The crowd danced like they were doped. Which in a way they were.

No one in the band listened to anyone else; each of them just ploughed ahead regardless, doing what they did. Which to me summed up the whole life out there – everyone in their own narrow, joyless little world.

The night ground on. The crowd got drunker, the jokes got stupider. My mood sank lower. Not that I minded that much. Dig, this was the fate of the drifting Mel, to wander endlessly between the winds, and so forth, and in a way, the purgatorial bleakness of it all suited me perfectly. To a T. So at the end of the night, when Doris invited me to turn up the following Thursday at some arsehole-of-the-earth bowling club in the next town along the way, I told her sure, I'd be there.

I dutifully turned up at the Arseholeville Bowlo. Strummed the guitar. Same result. Another job the following weekend, a wedding party out on a bush property – I did that one too. So it went. I became part of the group.

They were terrible in every way. "Modern" to them meant a bit of stodgily played forties boogie-woogie. The nearest they got to rock'n'roll was 'Running Bear' and 'Mountain of Love,' which they managed to play with no swing at all. They ritually murdered 'Fly Me to the Moon' and committed nameless atrocities on 'The Girl from Ipanema.' No one seemed to notice.

I played my part, showing up on time, strumming rhythm, pocketing a few quid, then fucking off again. None of them asked me anything about myself, which was a relief. To them I was simply 'Mal Parsons.'

On it went like that for three months. Dances, weddings, clubs, bachelor and spinster balls, whatever came up. In time I got used to their eccentricities. The young bass player, Kev, wasn't *all* bad, and seemed maybe a tiny bit open to new ideas. We killed some downtime one weekend by working out a couple of intros and outros. That worked okay, so we moved on to hooks and fills.

Over time I taught them all how to bring in a song with a proper double count, instead of the Rafferty's rules, Brown's cows 'Here we go, boys' that Doris favoured. The drummer was beyond teaching, but he could play half a dozen feels without fucking up the tempo too royally. Kev's time sense was okay so I suggested he take over the drums for a few numbers, which allowed the drummer to go and prop up the bar, which suited him better anyway. I put young Elaine on the bass – she wasn't great, but if she kept it simple, she could do her bit.

Doris was wary, inclined to do things the way she always had, but I persuaded her to give over the middle set to the new routine, and it got a result, so she went along.

Dougie the steel player – one of the most silent men I'd ever met – turned out to have a good ear. Played old-style country with a swing inflection. He sang an exact quarter semitone flat, which on the right songs – anything by Hank or Lefty – sounded fantastic.

As far as I could tell, Dougie hadn't been in a big city for decades, but somehow he'd heard the Flying Burrito Brothers. So we worked up a blackfella hillbilly version of 'Sin City.' I persuaded Doris to let Dougie have a guest spot, and his 'heart songs' soon became an indispensable part of the show. I don't know what the yokels made of gold-plated doors and the Lord's burnin' rain, but it sure blew *my* mind.

Bit by bit, the combo cleaned up its act, shined its shoes and winked at the world. After a couple of months it had turned into something else.

Dig, my young cosmopolites, it was still squaresville, but that bit of smartening up made all the difference. We started getting more people onto the dancefloor, then we found we were being asked back, and can you make it soon. All because of yours truly.

And I got something back for it. Dig, all my life music had been *the* thing. My grail. The sacred invisible shape after which I had quested. My own kabbalah. Music, there and not there. Ethereal waveforms, imaginary structures, vibrations in the air, tricks played in our heads and in our ears and with our hands. Bits of string and wood and tin and animal skin hit, plucked, stroked or rubbed a certain way, and fucking bingo, you've conjured up something more real than bricks and mortar. It's magic, baby, and your humble correspondent Mel was and is a fully initiated, thirty-third degree member of its priesthood. We didn't give a shit if the squareheads thought us drunks and wasters. We *knew,* baby. We had the knowledge. Fucking shamans, man.

I didn't mind playing those square venues. You hit the rhythm, however unhip, and watch the dancers take to the floor. They shuffle around a bit, but then the music gets into them and they move in a different way. And they can't help but smile. So you in turn play that bit closer to the beat, and they feel that too, and we're all moving closer to something. The holy ghost, baby.

Then it's over. They go home, pissed as newts, so next day they can't even remember that the night before they were fucking well waltzing with the angels. Dig what Mel 'Master of Rhythm' Parker is putting down here, my young boppers: such is the lot of the jobbing musician. Wasn't news to me, I'd been through that my whole life. Pearls before swine and so on. Not swine exactly. You know what I mean.

Doris was grateful for what I'd done for her band. She didn't try to hide it. I mean, she was well advanced in years, but many a good tune et cetera. Not that I was that interested or anything. But I did my bit. She had a hubby in the wings who tagged along some of the time. Jacko had a long lean face, thick tufty hair. A man of few words, but a canny old codger, I guessed.

Doris and Jacko were old-school tent show people. I knew their type. Bush-bashing year in, year out. Could turn their hands to any number of stunts: sing and strum, trick ride a horse, juggle, tumble, deliver a humorous recitation. Run a take-all-comers boxing troupe. Whatever was called for. Doris had been something of a dish back in the old days, I gathered, had looked good in a skimpy bathing suit. In their heyday they'd been top of the travelling show racket. They had a house up on the Gold Coast, which they got to once a year. Mostly they preferred to drag a caravan around.

I need to tell you about this Jacko fellow. Indeterminate age, but he'd been a showie since before the war. Had a rolled ciggy permanently on his lip, which he could fire up by force of will alone. He wore a little pork pie at that particular jaunty angle favoured by people whose business concerns horses. Actually, he did have a sideline – a small livestock transport company, whose business was based mostly out west. He sipped scotch with ginger ale from a small tumbler, starting after lunch, going into the night, every night, but never got sloppy that I saw. Until eight o'clock every night he was on top, after that the best he could manage was a friendly grin.

He spoke quietly and not too much, never looked at people or things too directly, he would take it all in with a quick sideways glance. People we met around the place seemed to like and respect him, but there was something under the surface, too. I noticed that people kept a certain distance.

He busied himself with the trucking business, and I guessed he was doing bush stuff as well, a little real estate and livestock trading. Jacko was altogether too shrewd, and I did my best to keep clear of him.

Not clear enough. One autumn morning, after I'd been with the outfit six months or so, I found myself sharing tea and toast with him in a milk bar in a far west town. We'd driven there, just the two of us – he'd specifically asked me to give him a lift to a wedding job we were booked for.

As we sipped our tea, Jacko started dilating on the different kinds of tent show he'd been involved with over the years. Then out of the blue he said, "We don't pry, you know that, eh?"

I looked at him.

"Our sort of people. Showies. No names, no pack drill. That's our thing." He liked to use those terms: "your thing," "no hang-ups," "a rip-off."

"Is that so?"

"Yeah. *Mal*." Saying my bodgey name like he was picking it up with tweezers.

I took a sip of tea. My hand was trembling.

"Jeez, we've had a few odd bods with us over the years." He shook his head, smiling. "But where they're from and what they've done, the way I see it, that's their business."

"Yeah?"

"So long as they don't bring their shit with them."

"That's the best way," I said.

"But it's part of my job to look out for trouble, too. Head it off."

Dig, people, Jacko's tone was gentle, friendly – the kindly old uncle. A little hypnotic even. Like a snake.

"Of course," I said.

"Doris says I'm just a bloody old stickybeak."

"Yeah?"

"But I like meeting people. Especially people who are a little bit different."

Pause. "Like you."

"I'm different?"

"Yeah, you are. In lots of ways. And I mean *apart* from you being on the gear. And to be honest it made me curious—" He allowed another meaning-laden pause, then smiled, looked at me directly and said, "Mel." With half a question there, still looking at me.

I looked back at him. Man, there was cold steel in those glims.

"It is Mel, isn't it?"

How could he know?

"What makes you say that?" I said.

But I'd waited too long to answer him, and he smiled at me, unable to hide the hint of triumph.

"See, mate, I was sure I knew you from somewhere. Then it hit me. Years ago. You were strumming a guitar. You probably don't remember me." He smiled again, looked away. "Gee, they were great days, weren't they, before the idiot box came and fucked us all."

I looked at him closely. No recollection. But dig, you hip and in-the-know readers, when my detractors in the yellow press had referred to me as a one-time singing cowboy, there'd been a grain of truth in it. I'd played the tent shows, spent many a long day and night on the road, following them dusty old fairgrounds a-calling, and what have you. Long time ago. When I was still a kid.

But Jacko had picked me. Which meant the wily old bastard knew the story. Knew all about the infamous Mel Parker. Knew I hadn't died at Violet Town.

I did some quick reckoning: maybe he'd observed that I didn't give a shit about anything much, was indifferent to the money. That I was supposed to be dead but wasn't. After a series of bank robberies. The best possible conclusion: he'd figured I was lying low, holding folding. And plenty of it. Only reason he could have for bringing it up. He was putting the hard word on me.

I had only one card to play.

"If you want to ask me something, go ahead – ask," I said.

FIRE ON THE MOUNTAIN

He looked at me now, his smile gone. Waiting for me to make my move. All right Jacko, here we go.

"But I know what you're up to, you thieving cunt, so keep that in mind."

He kept looking at me.

"Sheep and cattle duffing, right? How many head a year you moving, Jacko? Fucking plenty, I'll bet. Using your trucks. You want to talk about that too?"

Dig, this was fifty percent guesswork, but it stacked up: the closed meetings with dodgy characters, the fleet of trucks. I'd picked up bits and pieces of news, too – thousands of heads of livestock being stolen from properties out west, some of which were bigger than European principalities, their stock spread out over hundreds of square miles. A poor cocky wouldn't know until days or weeks later, by which time his stock had been sold, maybe more than once.

Jacko held the look for another second or two, then laughed, shook his head and patted my arm in a friendly way. He stood up and said, "Fuck me, I'm worse than an old sheila, eh? No offence meant. I overstepped the mark a little bit there, and I'd be grateful if you put it out of your mind," and went and paid for our tea. He came back, "Well, we better go and see about getting this happy couple properly hitched, eh?" And that was that.

My mind was racing the whole time I played the reception that night. Jacko was running his thieving trade very smoothly, thank you. He had more than a few rough types on the payroll. And he must have had someone in authority onside. A copper, maybe a team of bush coppers. Yeah, there had to be an entire network – otherwise it couldn't be happening on such a scale. We were in New South Wales at the time, but Jacko's business seemed equally at home in Victoria, Queensland, even South Australia. Which meant he'd probably have heavies and crooked cop mates throughout the four states. Fuck me, the guy could be the Little Caesar of the western boondocks.

When the gig finished, I got in my car and drove away – and kept driving. When I became too tired to go on, I pulled into an abandoned quarry, slept in the car. I woke after three or four hours and drove again for another couple of hours. Pulled into some dump of a town and ordered breakfast in a café. The old lady serving me smiled and said, "Oh hullo. You're with Doris's group, aren't you? I saw you at the ball last month. What are doing all the way over here?"

I looked at her open-mouthed, mumbled something. I'd forgotten: out here you can drive a hundred, two hundred miles to the next big town and it's like you've strolled across Oxford Street from Darlo to Surry Hills. They're half a day of high-speed driving apart, but they're neighbours. And don't forget the bush telegraph, so fast that people in those two towns could be a couple of old chooks magging over the back fence.

I finished my breakfast and started driving again. I backtracked for an hour, then took a side road and headed east. This time I kept driving. Out of the district. Slept in the car, drove the next day, halfway across the state.

I drove and drove. Wound up on the coast, which I'd been avoiding in my travels so far. I booked into a scabby motel, pulled the blinds. I set my bag on the bed and went through my possessions, putting everything in neat piles. Some sort of neurotic jag, I guess. My changes of clothes. My music stuff. My big bad brick of heroin. My drug paraphernalia. My gun. My bundle of money. My typewriter.

What had I been thinking? How many people knew me now, and how many of them knew who I really was? Had word got back to Melbourne? Christ, to *Sydney*? Oh children, I'd let my shit get mucho untogether.

I threw the *I Ching*. Came up with: *Fire on the mountain. The Wanderer. Success through smallness. Perseverance brings good fortune to the wanderer.*

I dug that for a long time. On the face of it, it sounded okay. But you've got to get hep to the Ching – there's always a twist, usually a nasty one. Its message this time seemed clear enough: Mel was the wanderer – things would come good somehow. But I wasn't buying that. I sat there, tuning into my feelings, getting deep into it. Strange sensations way down in my stomach. Images in my head. They didn't go away. More I thought, the heavier they got. Fire on the mountain. And a cold wind blowing on my skin. I knew this one. It meant the nearness of enemies. *The* enemy. Barry was out there. Looking for me.

Then I dug the meaning: *Barry* was the Wanderer, who roams around, around, around, around. With his two fists of iron. Whose perseverance would bring him good fortune. Now with the full protection of the Victorian police.

Barry who had driven my comrades into the path of the oncoming oil tanker at Violet Town. Maybe he'd just been trying to force them off the road. Maybe he hadn't meant to kill them all. Or maybe he'd *started* out trying to run them off the road, but his mind changed halfway through, and when the opportunity for mass murder arose, he couldn't resist the urge.

I picked up the bundle of notes from the bed, flipped through it. Not a fortune but still a goodly whack. Checked out the heroin again. The brick was perceptibly smaller now, one entire corner chipped off. But still heavy. Evil and heavy.

I stared at the rest of my stuff, imagined the random sequence was a message, a sentence. Or a hexagram. I kept staring until I got it, until I knew what was to be done. What I'd always known, but had pushed aside, pushed down, too chickenshit to face it.

I woke with a start. It took me a few long moments to place myself.

It was daylight. I was in the Matraville shack, lying on top of the stretcher bed, fully clothed. The book was on the floor next to me. My back felt sore when I got up. I walked outside to lose the stiffness. The sun was well up, the sky was blue, a sea breeze was blowing. I washed, ate a slice of toast, then picked the book up and skimmed through what I'd read last night. I went back outside and lit a smoke. After three puffs I chucked the butt away, thought, I'll have to knock these ciggies on the head.

❖ ❖ ❖

The moment I say "no blue," Fred and Donny exhale slowly and lean back in their seats. Donny says, "It's the right thing, Bill." Fred says nothing, just nods. The three of us leave the espresso bar and go back upstairs. Over the next hour matters are duly stitched up. Abe will compensate Joe Dimitrios. It's a hefty whack by my standards, and will be added to what I already owe Abe.

The Combine will charge no interest on the principal they reckon I owe them, but while it remains unpaid, I have to do work for them. Odd jobs. They put me in touch with one of their people, known as 'the Professor,' a Hungarian migrant with a fleet of cabs. I'm to get one of his cars at a special mates' rate. I can push it around town to my heart's content, do my own rorts on the side, but have to keep myself available for Combine tasks, for Abe, Joe, Phil, whoever.

The House of Cards will be no more. A month after the carve-up Abe rings me. "The poofs are looking for a venue," he says, and within a week he reopens the place under the name Harlequin's, featuring an all-new drag revue.

In 1970 Max Perkal becomes famous, twice. First as the weird-looking beatnik organ player in a film clip that gets played on *GTK*, then as an armed robber. The book has those robberies happening in May, during the first Vietnam Moratorium march, but in fact it all happens in September at the second march, which was nearly as big as the first.

Otherwise the account is true enough, according to the bits and pieces I hear later. The car full of bank robbers hits the oil tanker on the Hume Highway the day after the Moratorium, and that's it. Everyone dies, including the tanker driver. No one can quite work out how it happened – on a straight stretch of road, in broad daylight. Police ask any witnesses to come forward. There's a hint that some third party's bad driving might have forced the robbers' car into the path of the oncoming tanker, but that line of enquiry never gets any further, and there's no mention of any yellow Charger.

Something is scraped up from the wreckage of the incinerated car and brought back to Sydney, and the muso fraternity give Max an old-fashioned New Orleans–style jazz funeral. People in Sydney are shocked to discover Max had become an armed robber.

Meanwhile I've become a taxi driver. I don't hate it, not at first anyway. You drive around until someone sticks their arm out. You stop, they hop in, you take them where they're going, they give you a dollar or two, then they're gone. On a good night it can be exhilarating. But it's no way of earning a living. So I keep my eyes open.

Around Christmas 1970, a bloke called Terry, who I play pool with sometimes at the Forth and Clyde, lets on he has a friend living in the hills back of Byron Bay who has grown a few dope plants. They're ready to go. Just need to go and get them. I've got nothing better to do so we take a drive up to Byron.

Terry's mate turns out to be the surf legend Anthony "Mullet" Jackson. He won a big comp in Hawaii a few years before, started a board manufacturing business, did his back in, lost the business, now writes for surf mags. He lives in a nice farmhouse with his wife Katie.

Mullet is a lair and a risk-taker from way back, noted for hijinks both in the surf and on dry land, and a pioneer LSD user. He's a black-haired, perpetually grinning, fast-moving bloke. Katie keeps her own counsel and, I can't help but think, keeps him more or less half sane. I like them both well enough.

When Terry said Mullet had grown "a few plants," it was an understatement. It's a serious commercial crop. Back then people were still selling dope by the matchbox, but there's enough leaf here for us to go large. So we start selling the stuff by the ounce, packaged in sandwich bags. After that, I'll never see a matchbox deal in Sydney again.

We do a second run, and that sells just as fast. Terry has his friends, I have mine, and that's enough to constitute a market.

Having a neighbourly smoke with the buyers is part of the business. Till one time I find the dope hits me a bit harder than previously. I go home jumpy, can't sleep. Sudden sounds set my heart racing. I get up, lie back down, start stewing on my problems, going over the same shit in my head, again and again.

It gets worse. I start wondering where I stand with things, with people. The word "paranoid" is just coming into use, and I figure that's what I am. It's not pleasant. I try not to smoke so much.

The feeling of being watched stays with me, and I can't tell if it's real or imagined. I start spending more and more time in my old hideaway out by the Chinese market gardens near La Perouse. For no good reason except I feel more comfortable there, because no one knows about it. I fish off the rocks down at Cape Banks sometimes, just me and the La Perouse black-fellas, who keep to themselves even more than I do. We get on just fine.

Next summer Mullet has another dope crop ready for market. Bigger this time. Plus he has a couple of friends up there who now have crops of their own. Terry and I drive north to collect, come back and sell out in quick time.

Early in 1972 I get a call from Fred Slaney. He wants to talk, says it's important. We meet at Bar Reggio in East Sydney.

"Your name has come up," he says.

I don't say anything, wait for him to go on.

"Drug Squad." He waits for my response. I make none.

He goes on. "Something hush-hush they're up to, in league with the Federal boys."

"What do they want with me?" I say.

"They're looking at that surfie feller, Jackson."

I nod. Wait again.

He looks at me, realises I'm not going to offer anything more.

"Who I hear has become a mate of yours," he says. "There are hippies everywhere up the North Coast now, did you know that? On the dole. All of them growing pot. Not just a plant or two out by the chook shed, either. Large scale, some of them.

Drug squad was told to get involved. They've got helicopters and everything."

"Is Mullet in line for a pinch?"

"His name's been mentioned. And yours with it. Someone's gobbing off. Nothing planned, far as I know. But they're watching."

I nod, take a sip of my espresso.

"The Federal blokes do things their own way. If they decide to go for you, they'll prepare a thorough case. If they can't catch you redhanded, they'll look elsewhere. At your bank accounts, for example."

"Yeah?"

"If there's dough there you can't explain, they'll use that as part of their case – it's circumstantial evidence, but juries fucking hate anyone with secret funds. And if that doesn't work, they'll get the tax department to go for you. Who are worse."

So far my share of the proceeds has gone in payments to the Combine, or as support to Eloise and the kids. Plus I've reinvested in the next crop. But I have a modest nest egg – not enough to pay off the gangsters, but too much to lose – sitting in a bank account under a bodgey name. The others I guess would have considerably bigger bank accounts than mine.

Terry and I drive up to Mullet's for a council of war. Anna comes along, and I bring the young bloke for a bit of a holiday. We spend a few days relaxing chez Mullet. Neither Mullet nor Terry is too fussed about the police attention – it's old news up there. There have been cops everywhere for the past year.

But Terry is naturally cautious, and takes the warning seriously. We've covered our tracks well enough as far as the growing and distro goes, but we need to clean our money, he says. Legitimate investment is the way to go, he reckons.

It so happens that Mullet is a more than fair photographer. He's good at capturing those glassy, backlit waves, and his photos help sell his magazine articles. Recently, he's graduated to film, and now he proposes we slide a few dollars into a surfing movie. Always popular, he says, and surfies will back up again and again for their favourite films. With even just so-so luck we'll probably at least get our investment back – as bright, shiny, newly – and legally – earned money. And who knows, we could get lucky. Terry and Anna figure they've nothing much to lose. I'm indifferent, but even the slim chance of a big payday down the track is enough to tip the balance.

So *Surfie Walkabout* gets made. Big waves, small waves. Famous breaks, unknown breaks. Trippy rock music when there's no surf. A little judicious female toplessness. And there's something new in Mullet's film, too –a thinly veiled dope subplot. Drugs are not mentioned explicitly, and never shown outright, but references to "greenery," "vegies of the gods," "heaven's smoko," and so on in the dialogue speak directly to surfer-heads. The smart move is, the film doesn't bother trying to show what it's like to be stoned. But you get the idea that the lads on the walkabout are doing sly business everywhere they go, and that leads to comic situations.

Surfie Walkabout pulls a good house when it opens at the Rose Bay Wintergarden, on a bill with *Reefer Madness* and some old Marx Brothers film. It draws well at university theatres, too, though the Hoyts mob who control most of the country's screens aren't interested.

Audiences like it when they see it, but not enough audiences get to see it, even though Mullet does a lap or two of the entire country, showing it in local theatres, scout halls and surf clubs. In late 1972 Mullet, still hopeful of a breakthrough, takes the film overseas, and that uses up most of our grass profits for that year.

At some later point – I can't for the life of me remember when exactly, most likely early in '71, a few months after Max's death – Barry Geddins makes my acquaintance.

I'm at a barbecue at Tommy's place in Collaroy. Tommy was part of the team on the Alexandria electronics job back in 1968, a driver like me. I'm in the back yard, fishing a beer can out of the Esky, when a lanky, strangely ill-proportioned young man strides over and says, "The famous Mr Billy Glasheen!" His right hand is out, waiting for me to shake. His arms look too long for his body. He's very tall, but he stoops a little, like he's about to fall. Thick short hair. Strange eyes – unfocused, and his gaze suggests he's looking at something off to my left. His clothes are a bit odd, too: a blue sweatshirt, too bright orange jeans.

He says, "My name's Barry, and it's a real pleasure to meet you. I've heard of you, of course. We've just been up the coast. Bloody tremendous part of the world there. You can swim, fish, shoot. I've been to England and Europe and in my opinion they're shitholes. Some people like those places, I know, but right here is the grouse. I've been all over."

He's still holding out his hand, waiting for me to shake it. I find it hard to resist common courtesy, but my reaction to this bloke is strong, and I start to turn away.

"This is Karen," he says, trying to save the moment. He draws to him a blond girl who'd been hovering behind him, late twenties, suntanned, straight hair. She's smiling. My first impression: good-looking, good-natured, not bright. She puts out her hand and we shake. Then Barry shakes my hand before I can retract it.

"Good gathering, isn't it? Tommy's a terrific bloke. Some real Sydney legends here, that's for sure. Including you, of course."

I point vaguely towards the back door of the house and say, "Got to go see—", then nod and mumble, back away. My last glimpse of him, he's looking hurt.

Later I ask Tommy who was the headcase at his barbecue. Tommy gives me a funny look. "He said he was a mate of yours."

Barry keeps turning up. Next he's doing odd jobs for Joe Dimitrios. Then for Phil the developer. Phil tries to team him up with me more than once. My aversion to the bloke only gets stronger. I don't know anything about him – he's just another of the many hangers-on the Combine likes to cultivate: ex-footballers, boxers, karate trainers and so forth. A lot of them have problems – with grog, stupidity, the punt. Barry Geddins isn't obviously any of those. But he's all wrong.

❖ ❖ ❖

I had another cup of tea, then drove to the public phone on Bunnerong Road and rang Eloise. The boy answered.

"Are we still on for this afternoon?" he said.

I paused. Then it came to me. It was Saturday.

"No risk. You and your sister, right?"

"Yes."

"We're on. I'll be there at two. Maybe a little later. Get your mum, would you?"

I could hear Eloise in the background, laughing. She came to the phone and the smile in her voice faded a little.

"Hi Bill, dearest darling. The kids are waiting for you."

"Yeah, soon. I've got a couple of things to do first."

"Not too late, pet. Janice and I are meeting up at the Windsor Castle at three."

"Yeah, all right. Hey, just one thing. Might sound weird, but have you heard anything about Max Perkal?"

A long pause.

"Of course, my darling. Dear Max was the cause of more rumours than anyone I've ever known."

"No, I mean recently."

"Whatever do you mean?"

"I've come across something he wrote. I mean, in the last year or so."

Another long pause, then a sigh. "How absolutely mysterious. You must tell me all about it. But later, pet. The ducklings are so looking forward to their special grown-up outing." And then she was off the line.

I went to Glebe. Barry was in the back bar of the Tocky. He stood up as I approached.

"Late."

"Let's go," I said. "I've got things to do."

Outside he said, "You in a car?"

"We'll take yours."

His P76 was parked outside. An axe handle conspicuous on the back seat. I looked at it, then at him.

"What?"

I said nothing, got in the car.

He drove off. Grinning. Filmed with sweat, as always.

After a minute, "What have you got on after this?"

"Nothing that concerns you."

"Maybe you're seeing that ex of yours, over there in Bondi. Eloise."

I said nothing.

"I was at a party there last week, you know," he said. "Eloise is a really good sort."

"When we get to the house," I said, "you just keep your mouth shut. Phil wants you there, but I don't. So you just stay in the background, keep out of my way."

He grinned and shook his head. "Jeez, you can be a cranky feller. But I don't mind. Part of that famous old-world charm."

It was a quiet street in Annandale. A row of houses on the left, a tidal canal on the right, a timber yard, then a railway viaduct at the dead end.

There were four timber houses in the row, deserted now except for one, which had window coverings and a sprawling front yard filled with tomato plants tied to stakes, other greens in dense rows and a rickety trellis with grape vines growing over it. I could hear kids squealing somewhere.

I knocked on the front door firmly but with what I hoped was a friendly, businesslike tap. The old fellow came to the door. Grey and bristly in a faded work shirt. He looked at me, then at Barry standing on the footpath, couldn't hide a flutter of alarm. Behind him two little girls poked their heads around the door.

The old fellow turned and called out something foreign back into the house. The kids disappeared and the son came out, bringing a smell of garlicky lamb with him. Thirty or so. Also needing a shave. In a singlet and shorts.

The younger Leb lifted his head in a way that could have been a greeting – or a challenge. He eyed Barry darkly.

"How's it going?" I said.

He shrugged.

"Listen, we need you out by the end of this week." I tapped my watch. "Phil says that's it. Next Saturday. Finish."

He shook his head slowly.

"Agreement," he said, miming writing on a bit of paper. "Lease." Held up his fingers. "Three month."

"The lease is bullshit," I said. "You have to go."

Behind me quick footsteps, then a bang and glass shattering.

Barry was standing by the bay window with his axe handle, grinning. Taking a backswing, shaping up to the side windows, looking more ape-like than ever with the axe handle in his too-long arms.

The Leb just stood there staring. I walked over and stood between Barry and the window.

"Get back in the car, you clown."

The two little girls had come around the side of the house, were now peeping over the side fence, a few yards away from Barry. Barry grinned at them, puckered his lips and blew them a kiss. They stared wide-eyed at him. He walked over and picked the smaller one up, the way a dad or uncle might, smiling. He whispered something to her, still smiling, but she looked even more terrified.

A shout from the Leb at the door, and Barry put the kid down, gesturing no harm done, grinning broadly.

He looked back at the door to make sure he was being watched, then turned and headed for his car. He carefully kicked the tomato stakes in his path, gave the grape trellis a good whack with the axe handle, trampled the greens as he sauntered back to his car.

I did what I could to right the trellis, pushed the tomato stakes back into the soft dirt, returned to the front door.

"Sorry," I said, shaking my head.

Two younger brothers appeared at the door. They pushed past us into the garden, looked at the damage, then at Barry sitting in his car. Barry waved and they tensed up, started moving towards him.

The older brother barked out something and they stopped, not happy about it.

"This week," I said to him, spreading my hands, palms down. "Finish. Go."

He looked at me sadly. Pulled out his wallet. Opened it with a theatrical flourish. Look. Nothing there. A hopeless shrug of the shoulders.

"You expect money from Phil?" I said. "Brother, that'll be the day."

He gave me a closer look.

"Greco?" he said.

"Me? No."

"Aussie?"

I nodded.

He pointed at the car, at Barry. "Aussie?"

I nodded.

"Crazy."

"Yeah."

"Why Phil so quick, quick?"

That I didn't know. I shook my head.

"Last week, here—" he pointed to the street, "survey man. Suit man."

"Surveyors?"

"Suit man."

"Council?"

"Big Mr Government Man." He did a mime of a self-important bloke opening a blueprint or plans or something, haughtily looking at the landscape with his nose in the air.

I shook my head again. "News to me, pal."

"Always Phil, slow, slow, no worries. Now Phil, quick, quick, fuck off."

"He didn't tell me why. He says one week. Out. One week."

The bloke glanced at me, but didn't give even the slightest sign that might happen.

On the way back to Glebe, Barry said, "You should've taken a swing back there. Instead of yapping to them."

I said nothing.

"We should go back and burn the cunts out. That'll get 'em moving."

I said nothing.

After a minute he said, "You ever kill anyone?" and looked at me. "I bet you have." He laughed raucously. "I heard you did a bloke in jail. You're in the club, I can tell."

I looked out the window.

"Good feeling, isn't it?"

I said nothing.

"Mind you, there is something that feels even better than that. I'd better not say what it is, 'cause I know you'll go all shitty on me."

"Stop here," I said.

He looked at me, then back at the road, kept driving.

"Don't be so fucking touchy!" he said.

"Stop the car."

"Jesus Christ, I'm just trying to make friendly conversation!"

I leaned across and grabbed the steering wheel and yanked down on it hard. The car slewed left. Barry braked and wrenched the steering wheel back, but the front left of his car clipped the corner of a parked car. The back of his car spun to the right and stopped, across the flow of traffic.

It shook me around, but no damage done. Barry just sat there, maybe a little stunned.

"Keep away from Eloise's place," I said, and knew I'd made a mistake. I got out.

Traffic had stopped. People were staring. I walked away, kept walking.

I rang Phil an hour later. "This is Bill," I said. "The Lebs are doing a go-slow. If you want them out in a hurry, you going to have to pay them off."

"What the hell happened with Barry?" He was almost shouting.

I said nothing.

"Bill? You there?"

"I'm here."

"Barry's spewing. What happened?"

"He made an arse of himself."

"That's his job, for Christ's fucking sake. He says you smashed his car."

"He's overstating it. A ding in the front mudguard. I told you I wanted nothing to do with him."

"Jesus, he loves that car."

"Then he's even more of an idiot. The P76 is shit. It's Australia's Edsel."

"You're being funny?" Phil sighed on the other end. "Well, you better keep out of his way for a while."

"That's always my intention."

"I mean, *really*."

"Is that a warning?"

"He can be a strange bloke, as well you know. Anyway, tell me what happened with the Lebs?"

"Barry fucked it up," I said. "He tried to frighten them. They're digging their heels in now."

"Are they just? Your job was to get the cunts out."

"Why's it so urgent all of a sudden? You never gave a shit about those dumps till recently."

He paused. "I just want things straightened out. We all do." He sounded weaselly, defensive.

"We?"

"Me. *I* want things sorted out."

"You said we."

"Listen. Don't fucking push me, all right? You're on very thin ice, pal." He drew a deep breath, let it out slowly, then went on. "Yes, we. Joe Dimitrios is involved. And he knows you fucked up. So he's spewing too, and if I hadn't calmed him down he'd have called the whole deal off, and his blokes would've been round to see you already."

"What's Joe's interest?" I said.

Another sigh. "You won't fucking listen, will you. All right, so be it. I've done my best for you. Out of respect for your father-in-law. Seriously, Bill, sometimes I think you're one of those cunts that don't want to be helped."

I said nothing.

"All right. So how do I get the fucking falafels out of the house?"

"Give them money," I said.

I rang Terry and Anna's place at Balmain. Anna answered.

"Listen," I said. "I might have brought some trouble your way. Barry Geddins – you know him?"

"Not really," she said. "Heard the name."

"He's bad news," I said. "Very bad. *Not* a lovable rogue. He knows I live in Duke Street, but doesn't know which house. He was there yesterday snooping around. It's possible he'll come looking for me again."

"You said that before."

"Yeah, but things have happened since then. I put him offside. Thing is, Anna, he tries to come across as a nice enough sort of bloke. Smiles all the time. Sharing joints and so on. Might seem friendly. But he's not."

Anna said nothing for a second or two, then, "All right, I get it. There's an overseas telegram here for you. Arrived yesterday afternoon. From Mullet, I guess."

"Can you read it out to me?"

"Hang on."

She came back a few seconds later. I heard her tearing open the envelope.

"Okay," she said. "Here goes: HAVE SHOWN FILM HERE STOP GREAT REACTION STOP CALIFORNIANS LIKE AUSSIE ACCENT AND WEED SUBPLOT STOP DENNY WILSON OF BEACH BOYS INTERESTED IN PROMOTING STOP WILL KEEP YOU POSTED STOP MEANWHILE URGENT NEED MORE FUNDS KEEP WHEELS OILED STOP CONSIDER MAKING NEW PRINT STOP ALSO SUGGEST CHANGE NAME STOP SURFIE WALKABOUT WONT CUT IT STOP PREFER CRYSTAL DREAMS STOP WHAT DO YOU THINK STOP REGARDS MULLET. Get that?"

"Yeah. Mullet wants more money."

"You want Terry to take care of this one?"

"Don't bother for now. I'll send him something on Monday. Is *Crystal Dreams* a better name than *Surfie Walkabout*, do you think?"

"Search me. You're keeping track of these payments?"

"Of course."

I got to Eloise's mid afternoon, let myself in and walked through the house. A radio was on upstairs. Kids' voices coming from somewhere.

Eloise was sitting on the deck out the back. She had a drink going. Janice was there too, also on her way. A strip of blue ocean was visible in the distance. Wind chimes sounded softly in the breeze.

Eloise turned in her slightly overdone languid way. "Oh, Bill darling, the children are *beside* themselves. Do take the dear pitiful wretches away, for god's sake."

I kissed her, waved to Janice. "You two still going to the Windsor Castle?"

Eloise shrugged. "I suppose. Jules is coming around later to cook a curry. You must stay and have some, pet." She looked at me more closely. "Anna says you've gone incognito again."

"Does she?"

"She said you've taken to your secret mountain redoubt."

"I'm here now, aren't I? Listen to me, Eloise," I moved directly in front of her, crouching so we were eye to eye, "has that Geddins bloke been here?"

"Who?"

"Barry Geddins. Tall bloke, thirty-something. Dark hair. Smiles too much. Stands too close. A thug."

Eloise looked genuinely confused.

"Don't let him in the door, even if he says he's a mate of mine. Don't let him anywhere near this place. *Ever*."

"Darling, you're being so dramatic. But of course, I will obey you without question."

Janice snorted into her drink.

Eloise said, "And what *is* this news about Max?"

I stood up. "He didn't die in that crash."

"But really, dear one, how could that be?" said Eloise. "We *buried* him. Rather splendidly, I thought."

"It was a good send-off. But he wasn't there. If what they scraped out of the wreckage was human remains, they weren't Max's."

"So the rumours are true, after all?' Janice said.

We turned to face her. She looked from me to Eloise, back to me. "You never heard them?" No response, so she went on, "That he was working in the bush." She started counting on her fingers. "That he was in New Zealand. That he was in England. That he was in Sydney, for God's sake, living under a new identity."

"Who told you that?" I said.

She shook her head, playing the dizzy bird now. "Oh, I don't know. Various people. Musicians, I suppose. How on earth did you *not* hear them?"

Eloise tapped Janice's knee confidentially. "Oh, Billy doesn't talk to *anyone* if he can help it—". She turned to me. "Do you dear?"

"I do, in fact. It's just *I* like to be the one who chooses where and when."

The girl came running out, squealing, and hugged me. Her brother followed, acting the cool grown-up.

"All right you two," I said. "We'd better clear out while there's still time. Put your shoes on and we'll shoot through."

They ran off.

I waved goodbye to Janice, and signalled Eloise that I wanted to talk to her privately, then headed towards the front door.

She joined me in the hallway.

"There's something else," I said.

She gave me a long look before saying, "Yes?" Picking up on something in my voice, she was more down to earth now.

"Phil has some houses in Annandale. Guilliat Street. Four in a row. Numbers 15, 17, 19, 21. You heard anything about them?"

"Not a thing. Why would I?"

"There's a Leb family in one. The others are empty. Now Phil suddenly wants the tenants out. Joe Dimitrios is involved as well. One of the Leb blokes reckons people in suits have been around stickybeaking. Surveyors, too. So something's going on."

"And you want to know what." She brightened. "Dad might know."

"No, you have to leave Donny out of it."

An appraising look. "All right, give me a couple of days." she said, picking up a pad next to the phone in the hallway, writing down the addresses. A different person now. She tapped the pad with the biro and smiled. "I'll see what I can find out."

The kids came running into the hallway, eager to get going.

We went to the city. They dropped a few dollars in the machines at Playland. The boy liked the pinballs, the little girl the pincers. After that I took them to the Minerva in Elizabeth Street. I had a coffee, they had milkshakes and crème caramel.

"How's school going?" I said to the young bloke.

He looked seriously at his milkshake for a few seconds then said, "All right."

"That took you a while."

He glanced at me. His light brown hair was getting long, and sun-bleached. Covered half his face. "I got into trouble last week," he said, and looked down again.

"Yeah?"

A pause. "For being late."

"You shouldn't be late," I said.

He grinned at me, assuming I was being sarcastic.

"I mean it," I said.

He looked back down at his milkshake.

The little girl piped up: "Eloise *makes* him late."

"Don't tell tales," I said. Asked the boy, "How?"

"She makes me miss the bus, even when I've got time to catch it."

"Yeah?"

"She says punctuality is bourgeois."

The girl said, "She says it's middle class."

"Fuck me. Sorry. Ignore that. I don't want to hear either of you swearing, by the way. Did you tell the brothers the reason you're late?"

"No!"

"Good. Don't be a give-up. Well, that's your mother for you. She's one of a kind, that's for sure."

The boy stared gloomily at his drink.

"One day you'll appreciate her for the way she is," I said.

He nodded again, unconvinced.

"All right, I've got an errand to run. You two okay with tagging along?"

Eager nods from both.

It was a five-minute walk down to the Third World Bookshop in Chinatown. We were greeted with a musty smell partly masked with incense. Some kind of blues record playing, with wonky electric guitar. Maurie was at the shelves, rearranging books, a cranky expression on his dial. Bob Gould, roundish, of indeterminate age, bearded, thick hair sticking straight up, bib and brace overalls, was sitting on the elevated platform behind the till like some minor potentate. A chubby hippie girl sat next to him, sipping a cup of tea, smoking a Drum.

I said to the kids, "Have a look around but keep away from the dirty books." Waved to Maurie, then to Bob. The hippie girl smiled.

"Ah, it's that colourful Sydney identity, Brother Glasheen," Bob announced, "of the Miscellaneous Workers' Union, I believe."

"Comrade Robert," I said.

"What can I do for you?" he asked, in a tone that could be taken as either friendly or contemptuous.

I pulled *Lost Highway to Hell* from my back pocket and handed it to him.

He looked at the cover, the back page, flipped through it. "We're not taking any second-hand books today," he said, "unless you've got some rare labour history." He passed the book back to me.

"But you must know it?" I said.

"Trash paperback. Not terrific." He smiled and went on in a fast, quiet voice. "Could use a little more lesbian sex. Or a better critique of counter-cultural opportunism masquerading as direct action. Preferably both."

"So you *do* know it?"

He shrugged dismissively. "There's a whole *type*," he said, pointing behind me.

I turned and looked at a shelf with multiple copies, face out, of *The Last Whole Earth Catalogue, Ringolevio, Trout Fishing in America, One Flew Over the Cuckoo's Nest.*

"Lower down," he said.

Next row, slimmer paperbacks with lurid covers. Hippie chicks with bandanas and machine guns, half-exposed tits. Gun-toting lads with bandit moustaches. Burning cars, joints, hypodermics, bullets, peace symbols. The titles: *Dangerous Generation, Highway Blues, The Peacenick Gang, The Red Kill, The Bombshell Heiress.*

"They're *all* based on that business," Gould said. "Loosely. Mate of yours, wasn't he?"

I looked at him.

"Max Perkal," he said.

I didn't say anything.

"Never cared for the bloke myself," he said. "Anyway, there's a slew of books about him and the others now. Nothing in them, but we move a few. For a while they were the most stolen books in the shop."

He turned to his side, took a black-covered hardback from a box at his feet. "What I *do* have is this fantastic but hard-to-come-by account of the New South Wales bank nationalization crisis of the thirties." He looked at me, smiling. Genuine pleasure there. "I can do a good price for you."

"How is it for lesbian sex?"

"Not so good," he said, "but the analysis is excellent."

"This is the one I'm interested in, Bob." I held up Max's book. "Where did it come from? There's no publisher's name on the back, and the title page is missing. Nothing even on the spine except for this, what is it, a flag? A map? Any ideas?"

He shook his head and said, "Can't help you, comrade," then walked away to the back of the shop.

Maurie glanced at Bob, at me, then turned back to his shelf tidying.

"Come on kids," I said.

Back at Eloise's there was a gathering. Rich, spicy smells came from the kitchen. A J.J. Cale record was playing. People inside and out drinking wine. Eloise's trendy east-of-centre friends: advertising people, groovy clothiers, art directors, so-called "*Nation Review* types." The kids disappeared into their rooms. I drifted into the kitchen and ate some curry, which was good. A woman in a red scarf, a stallholder at Paddo markets, came over and said hello. She told me she'd just seen a film called *American Graffiti*.

"Have you seen it? It's *great* fun," she said. Then confidentially, resting her hand on my arm, "Fifties nostalgia is *definitely* going to be the new thing. I'm getting rid of my Gatsby stuff and stocking up on fifties tat."

I slipped away at eight, took a cab to Taylor Square. When I stepped into French's, a blues band had just started playing. A very un-blues-looking guy – fresh-faced, pressed jeans, short hair – was blowing harp. It was crisp and swinging just the same. No one much there yet.

Maurie from the Third World Bookshop was at the bar, already looking a bit dissolved. I joined him and ordered drinks.

I took a sip. "This cider tastes of iron filings," I said.

Maurie took a long swig. "You did no good with Bob, then."

"Nah. But it was like he knew *something*," I said.

Maurie barked out a quick laugh. "He *should*. He published that book himself!"

I looked at him.

"Published it then pulped it. Too libellous, I guess. Even for him."

"So why didn't he tell me that?"

Maurie shrugged. "Nothing for nothing."

"Where did he get it from?" I said.

"I always thought he'd paid some hack to write it. One of the Balmain poets maybe." He looked at me quickly. "Why do you ask?"

I shook my head. "Just curious. Never mind."

"I mean," said Maurie, "I know you and Max Perkal used to run that club up the street. Hazyland, wasn't it?"

"Not that, but similar. I'd prefer not to talk about it. Hey, you know anything about fifties nostalgia?"

He pulled a face. "Nostalgia's bullshit."

I drank up and wandered a block along Oxford Street and into a phone booth. After I dialled, it rang a long time, then a husky, unencouraging "Yes?"

"Fred, it's Bill."

"Ah. Himself."

"Got a question for you."

"Of course you have."

"You ever see any of the books that came out about those bank robberies Max Perkal was involved in? The Hippie Gang and all that."

"Never paid any attention."

"Did you ever hear any police gossip about Barry Geddins being involved?"

A long pause. "Involved in what?"

"In the robberies. In the Footscray shootout. In the car crash."

Another long pause. "I believe he *was* involved. I don't know how much. His name never came up officially because he was in thick with Russell Street."

"Is he still?"

A long sigh. "You don't know about Noelene Gray and her kid?"

"No."

181

"She was a Melbourne moll. Had a son, twelve or so. Not quite right. Sub-normal or something. Well, Geddins was keeping company with Noelene, and one weekend he took the kid for a fishing and camping trip, while she stayed in town working. The kid never came back. No explanation given. That was too much, even for Russell Street. Wasn't the first such incident, either."

"So why don't you lot do something about him?"

"She never put in a complaint. Too scared, I suppose."

"Get him for something else then."

"Like doing standover work for Phil?"

"What if I gave you something you *could* act on? Something solid."

"Bill, these things aren't as straightforward as you might think."

"That's what I pay you for. You're what's known as a corrupt cop, Fred. It's quid pro quo. That's how it works."

"How it works, son, is you do whatever it is you need to do, *then* your corrupt cop looks after you. But I wouldn't advise anyone to go up against Geddins. Not without a team." Another long sigh. "Anyway," he said, "you're going to need another mate in the force soon enough. My days are numbered."

"Really?"

"There's no one going in to bat for me. Not any more. After all this time, after all the looking after and fixing up, and all the money that's been kicked in, suddenly, *now*, the New South Wales government is developing scruples. They've watched the Labor boys take over the federal government, they know their run here can't last much longer, and now – fucking *now* – they want to clean house. Which means get rid of old Fred Slaney, or else."

"Or else what?"

"They all end up in the shit."

"Life's so unfair," I said.

"What they don't realise, they're in the shit anyway. That new state Labor bloke, Wran. He's going to win next time. Anyone can see that. Wran's a mate of yours, isn't he?"

"I knew him a bit, years ago. I'd have no influence there now, if that's what you're thinking."

"Ah, well. We must strive to accept the things we cannot change."

"Fred, you know that place, the Third World Bookshop. Down there off George Street??"

"The commos? What about them?"

"I could use some leverage with the proprietor, bloke named Gould. You got anything?"

"I'll ask around."

I strolled back to French's. A group of Maori female impersonators had stationed themselves in front of the band. They were all Mandraxed-up, and there was much whooping and calling out, some falling over. The place had filled up with junkies and longhairs, getting rowdier by the minute. Maurie was at the bar, swaying, well on his way. I listened to another song then left.

I had the cab drop me a mile from the secret redoubt, got back there just before midnight. Everything undisturbed. I cranked up the pressure lamp, lit a coil, sat down with the book.

SATORI OUT THE BACK OF FUCKING NOWHERE

I tracked down the Croaker. He'd been known years ago as 'the Doctor,' as in, "send for the doctor," as in, make that horse go faster. Or slower. Make that athlete jump higher. Or not. Fix that injured bloke who'd rather not go to Saint Vincent's casualty department. The Croaker was a decrepit old fucker you wouldn't trust with a knife and fork let alone a scalpel. Hence the change of nickname. But his writing hand worked well enough, and after a bit of bullshit from me he duly gave me the scripts I needed.

There's been a lot written, proclaimed, and gobbed-off

about the various methods of self-managed drug withdrawal and their relative merits. One authority will favour slow reduction, another the Chinese water torture. One fiend will swear by methadone substitution, another speak up for straight-out cold turkey. Some junkies just drink their way through the worst of it. But your old uncle has the mail on this, learned under the tutelage of Harry 'Big Sleep' Bailey, the crazy Sydney shrink, so pay attention, my young psychic buccaneers. It's as simple as this: you take enough stoppers to snooze your way through the whole thing. However long it takes. Harry keeps his patients unconscious for a whole fortnight, but that's not practical when you're self-managing. Four or five days is the recommended snooze. Wake up when all the shit is out of your system. There you go. New life, blank slate. Bye bye now. Go thou, and fuck up no more. That's what I had in mind.

I carefully chopped a small piece off the heroin brick, rewrapped it and put it inside a poly bag, wrapped that in oilskins and gaffer tape, then bagged it up in a heavy-duty fertilizer bag. Packages within packages, until I was sure the precious stuff inside was super watertight. I drove into the ranges, up through the tall timbers, onto the high country, further west to the slopes, and kept driving until I was well west, way out in the flat, low, miserable landscape of inland New South Wales. When I reached a certain town I knew – never mind the name, my little snoopsters – I took a turn down a dirt road. Drove a long way, then took another turnoff. Found the place. It was just *a* place, kind of random, me following my instincts. But I felt in some way I was being guided there – dig, I wasn't the most rational gazabo in the country at that point. Anyway, I found the spot, dug the hole, buried the H. Drew my map. Work done. Quick blast, back into the car, drive out. I slept by the side of the road for a few hours, took all but the last skerrick of dope, started driving again before dawn. Back east, the long way round, across the border, over the hills and far away.

I came to a rundown tropical town. It was a dump. There was no surf, just shitty farm land round about. No natural features to speak of. No hippies, no trendies. Just white trash and blackfellas. It would do nicely: all I wanted was a place warm enough for a detox. Trust me, young ones, you do *not* want to do your hanging out in a cold climate. I spotted a motel on the edge of town called the Weary Swaggie and checked in. Blowsy old sheila behind the desk barely registered my presence through her Valium haze.

Back in town, I presented the Croaker's scripts at the chemist shop. Which just happened to be Cat's place of business. Yes, I had another reason for choosing this particular dump of a town. I let the Cat know what I intended, told him where I'd be. He did the right thing – threw a few more pills into the bag for good measure, wished me well. I was ready for lift-off. Or splash down. Whatever.

I'll spare you the details, my delicate ones. It's kind of messy. Thumbnail sketch: draw the blinds. Turn on the telly. Lay out the various preparations. Stuff to slow down bodily functions, especially those of the more liquid sort. Opiate substitutes. Muscle relaxants. And sleepers. Plan was, I'd be in la-la land while my body detoxified without me. Surface after twenty-four hours, drop enough stuff to go out for another twenty-four. Until I woke up clean.

It would all have worked fine, but as the stuff was starting to take hold, the dope draining from the bloodstream, a surprise turn of events. I started shaking. Couldn't stop. It got worse. I was fitting. Oh shit. I'd heard cold turkey could do that to some people. Never thought I was one of them. I was.

The fit subsided, but by now Mr Sandman was doing his thing. I was off to the land of Nod, no turning back, with full withdrawal still a little way down the track. And the likelihood of some serious fitting before then. Last thing I remember thinking: I'm going to die.

I didn't die, obviously. But plenty happened. The Cat

found me on day three, in poor shape. He helped me with a few matters.

Now, as I write this, tapping away on my old Olympia by the light of my kero lamp, crickets clicking away outside in the dark, mossies hovering around me, I recall only bits and pieces of what went down the next few months. As time passes, more comes back.

I came through the detoxification. Haven't used any smack since. Haven't been back to the buried treasure. I know that for sure. But I don't know how I got here. I must have fitted some more during the hanging out. And it fucked with my head. Yeah, my children, there's brain damage. Terrible, right? But maybe it's a blessing, too. Forgetting.

This much I know: I split from the motel. Kept my few possessions. Drove inland again. Headed south, baby, behind the sun. I drove, and kept driving.

At some point I doubled back, then criss-crossed further inland, then back again. Quite unintentionally I described a big hexagram. Or maybe a pentagram. Whatever the fuck. But in that way, without meaning to, I worked up some bad hoodoo, because right there by the highway outside West Wylaong, I came upon the Devil. Standing at the crossroads. Thumbing a ride.

He was waiting for me, and he knew I'd stop for him, because he picked up his bag, ready to climb aboard, before I even touched the brakes. I stopped, he jumped in. A clear-eyed, fresh-faced young guy, with a pleasant manner, a nice haircut. The face was familiar. Pressed shirt, well-shined shoes. He didn't fool me.

"I'll beat you yet, you craven swine," I said.

He chuckled merrily, started whistling a show tune I couldn't quite place.

"For all that fancy get-up, you smell like what you are," I said.

He stopped whistling.

I said "Tell Barry . . ." But I didn't know how to finish

the sentence. "Tell him whatever you like," I muttered.

We drove on for a while in silence, then I pulled up at the next crossroads. He turned to me and smiled. He had no eyes, just cold empty space in there. He nodded and got out.

I said it was the Devil, but I realised then it wasn't the Man himself, just an emissary. The Devil's flunky. The Devil's roadie. The Devil's booking agent. Something like that.

Kept driving, it felt like a long time. Wandering Aengus, Flying Dutchman, Ghost Rider in the Sky kind of thing. But maybe it was just a few days.

Driving along out there one night, Nat King Cole came on the radio, slow and sad, crooning about what a mess he'd made of things, how wrong he'd been. How his heart had gone bad. He'd forgotten to eat and sleep and pray. The road sped beneath me, the headlights opening up a circus tent out front as Nat just kept it coming. He cried a little bit, when first he learned the truth. But don't blame it on his heart, just blame it on his youth. A bit of static and the radio went off again, the little light behind the panel faded out. Dig, my young seers, that old beast hadn't worked in forever. Had come good for that one song. I pulled the car over, got out. Big empty sky. Big empty everything. I'd been listening to heaven's radio. I knew I'd be forgiven. Not yet, quite, but sometime.

I don't know how I came across the Old Cunt. These bush towns and dusty farms are riddled with weirdos, fugitives, perverts, vagabonds, wetbrains and the like. If they keep to themselves and stay out of sight, no one worries too much. And to tell the truth, there's not that much difference between them and the supposedly upright ruddy-faced squarehead country party squatter baron chamber of commerce country women's association stock and station moleskin-wearing Cessna-flying polo-playing moron fucks who run things out here. It's just a matter of who's in control and who isn't.

My guess is, I knocked on the Old Cunt's door and he picked me as a walking numbskull. Thought to himself, he'll do nicely as a Man Friday. I'm not sure what me getting my marbles back will do for our employer-employee relationship. Him having to pay me and all. We'll see.

Since I snapped out of it, I've had a look around the district. Even during my long blackout there must've been *some* sort of reasoning going on: because I *know* this place. I've got history here. Way back. You know the place I mean, Johnny? I told you all about it. Remember? When I was a cowboy out on the western plains? The dwarfs? The cowgirls? Come-a cow cow yippee! Mel the Geek? Relax and don't pry, little ones – a secret authorial message to my old compadre there.

It's flat nothing out here. Flies and crows, cow shit and dead ground. Grey trees, dry river beds. Squawking cockatoos. Buildings falling down. There's a dopey bush town not that far away, with an ugly Catholic church (what is it with the Micks and their fucking architecture?), a Masonic hall, a few stupid shops, and a boredom that's palpable. Also a few retard locals, given to drinking and shooting roos, and touching up their kids, probably. The blackfellas have their knowledge and their magic, but they've been hounded to the edges and beyond, and they're keeping it to themselves.

It's the bardo out here. But it's right for me. I had some dues to pay, and I'm paying them.

It's been maybe six months since I came off the shit in the rat motel. I began writing this the day after my memory started coming back, and I've been working on it three solid months.

Everything I've written here is true. More or less. Allowing for a certain poetic license, you understand. You've got to do that. But it's true in the important sense.

Some of what's here you alert students of villainy will already know from news stories, magazine articles, TV shows, even perhaps that shitty series the Fop eventually wrote in the *Daily Earth News*. But hearken, my young seekers, there's plenty here that is not known to a living soul but me.

And now you, of course. As for the places and dates, they're mostly accurate. And the characters are all real, even if I had to rearrange their faces, give them all another name. Well, rearrange *some* faces, give *some* of them a new name. Maybe not all. License, dig?

Cathy. Oh, brother. Cathy. Everything I said about her is true. But there was more to her, more than I could write, and no one has aired it. When Cathy said she was doing the dope thing for "our side," that wasn't shit. She bankrolled a string of child-minding co-ops in inner Melbourne, set up a refuge for runaway kids too, got guitar players to come down, teach the kids to strum and pick. Got Denise and her mates to run writing classes. Introduced a bunch of people to one another, set up a newsletter for down and outs. Her politics were genuine, and whatever she did, however fucked-up, there was always an element of higher purpose in it. No one knew how much useful stuff she was behind, because she didn't broadcast her involvement.

I could go on. No one in that scene had the vision or drive or ambition that she had. She was a crazy chick all right, was Cathy. A *true* revolutionary. Nothing that's been written has given her the credit she deserves. Denise, the 'heiress revolutionary,' was a sweet chick, sure. But Cathy was the real Ned Kelly, Frankie Gardiner, Jesse James and Che Guevara of our push. And, facing facts, maybe the love of my life. But she's gone, comrades.

Johnny Malone. Billy. Whatever. Old comrade. I left you in the lurch. In hock to the Big Man, the Greeks, some crime czar creep or other. I hope this tale reaches you. If so, I know the question you're asking. Answer: Yeah, this is me, right enough. Brother, you want proof that this is good old you-know-who? All right then: *I know about the Skull Cave.* Maybe you're there right now.

A quick explanation, my rabidly curious young hepcats. My old comrade "Johnny Malone" has a secret hideaway right in the guts of Sydney. No one knows where, not even me.

It's his own personal Batcave, Weddin Mountains, Sherwood Forest, Hole in the Wall, Mount Olympus, bunker beneath the chancellery. All I know is a Chinaman is involved. He's always been pally with the celestials. That good enough for you, "Johnny"?

Me, I'm here in *my* hideout. Hiding in plain view, you might say. I'm not going anywhere. It's late. Very still outside. I'm all alone at midnight, when the lamps are burning low. I can hear a mutt barking somewhere miles away. I listen hard, I pay attention, I keep a close watch on this heart of mine. I'm developing my pictures. My mind a dark room.

So dig, brother, I want to make it right between us. I've done my time, and I want out of here.

But Barry is out there somewhere too. I can feel him. Circling.

So I'm here. I'm holding. Waiting. Got my treasure map. Got some money. Got my gun. Come and get me, Billy. We have business to conclude.

I drove a semi-double that Sunday. You get the cab for 24 hours, but only pay in for a single shift. The low pay-in is supposed to compensate for Sundays being so quiet. A little known fact about Sydney taxi driving: Sundays are a motza. No drunks. Little traffic. So more than half the Sydney cab fleet was off the road that day, and my competition was mainly students and new drivers. Plus Steve was radio operating. It should've been a good one.

But I was too restless to get on the wavelength. I didn't bother calling on radio jobs I could've won, drove past street hails without stopping. I was thinking about the book. And what it meant. Or what it *maybe* meant. I'd pull over and flick through it, then drive off again.

After a while things picked up. Woollahra to Balmain, Balmain to Paddo, Paddo to Kirribilli, North Sydney to Randwick

– most of the trips were like that, along contour lines of roughly equal income. Every half-good cabbie becomes an expert on how the different bits of Sydney fit together, and if you hit the right currents, you're laughing. By midday I was on one of those magic chains, each job bringing me perfectly to where the next was waiting, another fare on board before you've finished handing the change to the last. You see a hail standing on the corner, you know exactly where they're going, sometimes even the street, the building, before they've opened their mouth. Occasionally – it doesn't seem possible, but it happens – you know exactly what they're going to say: you recite it in your head before they speak, then nod to yourself when they say it.

Most regular drivers are doing their one trip, going from A to B, but you've been pushing it for five or six hours and by then it's like the other cars are going at half speed. You slide into gaps in traffic before they've fully opened up. You don't need to look in the rearview half the time because you *know* where every car is and where they're going to be next. You have this larger sense of how the whole city is, where people are headed, where they're bunched up or thinned out. And even if you end up somewhere thin, the thread doesn't break – you'll find the one stray fare, or snag the only radio job to come out of that area the whole day, the magic one which takes you right back into the thick of it. Everything is moving in a huge swirl, and you're just riding the currents, following invisible pathways. The passengers sense it too, know you're going to get them there fast and safe. More tips, fewer grumps.

In the taxi game it's called "running hot," and when it's like that you don't stop for a drink or a stretch for fear of breaking the thread. But at one thirty Steve called me in. "Car 370 still on this channel?"

"Here basey."

"Message for you. Says, 'Ring Fred.' Got it, drive?"

"Yeah, roger."

I stopped at a public phone. Slaney picked up after two rings. "Thought you might be still at mass," he said.

"What have you got?"

"Mister sociable. Your commo mate."

"Yeah?"

"The Vice Squad have an interest."

"Old news."

"Wait a bit. So does the Drug Squad. Your mate's selling a pamphlet about how to grow pot."

"It's a free country," I said.

"Newest agricultural science, apparently. Explains in easy-to-follow steps how you can cross-breed a better strain, then re-move the male seedlings so the females try extra hard. Produces a stronger drug. The superintendent found a copy in his daughter's bedroom. She's a schoolkid. So they're planning on popping in there very soon. Tomorrow even. Druggies and vice together. They seem to think they can nail him over this one.

"Okay. Not sure what I can do with that."

"This is where you having the right contacts pays off. The drug boys are still mates of mine. North Bondi Surf Club. They'll hold off if I ask them nicely. So what do you want? Do I ask them?"

"Hell, let me think. I'll ring you back."

A girl I didn't recognise behind the counter. The R. Crumb hippie girl called out from the rear of the shop, "He's at lunch."

"Where?"

"The Tai Yuen, probably."

I headed for the door, stopped, then went back to the counter.

"You got a pamphlet about dope growing? Something about cross-breeding, removing the males?"

She looked at me warily. "You're Bill, right?"

My turn to be wary. "Yeah."

"I know you." She smiled. Leaned forward and pointed to her left. "That'd be the sensimilla book. Very popular. Back of that stand over there, in the Drugs and Counterculture section."

I went to where she'd pointed, scanned the shelf. William Burroughs, Carlos Castenada, Thomas De Quincey, something called *Opium and the Romantic Imagination*, a book on Keyline farming. At the end, a big stack of booklets. *Grow Your Own.*

I picked up a copy. The girl was watching me. I held it up to her. She gave a thumbs-up and I took it to the counter.

"How do you know me?" I asked.

"I'm a friend of Terry and Anna's."

A head. She'd figured – guessed or been told – I was in the business.

I pulled out two bucks to pay, but she shook her head with a knowing smile. "On the house."

Gould was sitting alone at a table in a dark, chintzy corner of the Tai Yuen. He had a foreign newspaper, Italian, open in front of him, and was eating short soup. Mostly with his fingers.

"They'll give you a spoon if you ask nicely," I said as I sat down opposite him.

He grunted and continued eating.

"About that book," I said.

He shrugged.

"I know you published it. I need to know how you got hold of it."

He looked up at me. "How did *you* get it?"

A question I'd been asking myself. "Never mind. I got it, that's all that matters. So?"

"So what?" Barely hiding the sneer now.

"I can help you, Bob. But first you've got to help me."

"How would *you* help *me*?" With a slight emphasis that said it all.

I shrugged. "Find out."

He looked at me for a few seconds. "All right. What's the news?"

"Nope. You first."

He sighed. "A kid came to the shop a year ago. Skinny, long-haired, a bit druggy-looking. He gave me the typed manuscript to read."

"Why you?"

"He said because I publish *Zap Comix*."

"Publish?"

"*Re*-appropriate. Bootleg. Whatever. The kid said the manuscript might be in my line. I had a look. There was something there, but it needed editing, some rewriting."

"More lesbian sex?"

"Among other things. I gave it to Stephanie to work on."

"The girl at the shop?"

He shook his head. "Different one. She was doing English at uni. Wanted to try her hand at book editing. Steph's long gone."

"So what did you make of it, the story itself?"

"What I told you. It's shit. Exploits genuine direct action for outlandish and sensationalistic effects."

"I mean, who did you think wrote it?"

"I assumed your mate Perkal. I'd heard the rumours."

"Right. The rumours. Rumours that . . ."

"He was still alive."

"So who was the kid?" I said.

"Never knew his name. He came back once or twice, then I never saw him again."

"So you printed the book but then you pulped it?"

He shook his head, closed his eyes. "I should've kept a closer eye on Steph. She was supposed to change some things. I was busy, didn't read it until it been printed. A thousand copies. Too hot for me to sell it. For all I know, it could be true, but you can't just say outright that the Victorian Police Armed Robbery Squad were complicit in the Moratorium robberies. I'd need a fighting fund if I went with that, and what for? I'd take up the cause against police corruption, but it's Victorian state politics, which would never be such a big deal in Sydney anyway. Plus the swearing, the druggy stuff. Too much trouble, and for what? Opportunistic bullshit. And for all that, Steph still didn't load up the lezzo sex like I told her to. Which is funny, because she's a bit that way herself. So yeah, I dumped the copies. I didn't know then, but Stephanie kept a few and gave them to her friends. She ripped out the title page with our name on it, the printer's address and all that. So no one knew where it came from."

"Except for that symbol on the spine."

"Supposed to represent a tractor and a pen. Intellectuals and workers. Steph got it from an early Bolshevik poster."

He vacuumed up a wonton. Bits dribbled down into his beard.

"So, Brother Glasheen, what have you got for me?"

"The police are going to raid you."

He laughed noisily. "That's not news," he said.

"I know exactly when," I said.

"How?"

"Never mind. But the Vice Squad *and* the Drug Squad have you down for a visit. Looking for drug literature, mainly. Filth, too, if they can find it."

His face went dark. "You fucking opportunist scumbag. That's criminal extortion. Just what I'd expect from you." He said it without any bitterness.

"It's not my doing," I said, but I could see he didn't believe me. "What became of Stephanie?"

"Don't know. She raised objections to some of the material in the shop. The porn. I heard she went to London, was going hitchhiking around Europe. How sure are you about this raid?"

"The word came from a cop."

I had his attention. "When's it planned for?" he said.

"When would suit you?"

He barked out another laugh. This time it *was* bitter. "It's a shame you're nothing more than a self-serving apolitical petty crook. Day after tomorrow would be best."

"Is that enough time for you to clear out the filth and drug literature?"

"Clear out nothing. I'll get more in, if I can. All I need is time to tip off the press."

"You *want* this to happen?" I said.

"A bit of press never hurts."

I left him to his lunch and went back to the cab, started the engine then turned it off again. I sat there for a minute, then went back to the restaurant. Bob looked up from his paper.

"You're shitting me. Bad language and a bit of drug use couldn't get a book banned anywhere in Australia these days."

"As I said, it was defamatory!" He was trying to sound outraged.

"But it's fiction. At least half made-up. Easy enough to defend, I would've thought."

He waved that away. "But too much trouble."

"I don't buy it. Politics, drugs, hippies – that's right up your alley."

He mumbled something and looked away for a moment, then back at me. "The reasons I gave are true ones. But it was also a favour. For a friend."

"Who?"

"The one who got away. Denise."

"I thought she was in jail."

"She only did a few months. She's been out for a while now, on a good behaviour bond. Does a little community service, sees a psych."

"After a string of armed robberies? How does that work?"

"Establishment family. They pulled strings. The police didn't have that much on her anyway. Frank Galbally represented her. Made a strong case that she'd been temporarily under the sway of charismatic outlaws. Misguided idealism. She'd bailed out voluntarily as soon as she had the chance."

"She a friend of yours?"

"She's . . . politically sophisticated."

"Good for her. So why did she want the book pulped?"

"Competition. She might have ambitions in that field herself."

"She pay you?"

"No. And I've given you more than enough to pay for that tip-off."

The waitress approached and noisily put a teapot down in front of him.

"Do you have a phone number for Denise?"

He shook his head. "She's back in Melbourne now anyway."

End of interview. I stood up.

Gould smiled. "Day after tomorrow for the bust. You sure of that?" he said.

"It's a date."

He was pleased now that he'd thought it through, figured out a press angle.

"Anything else you happen to hear, Brother Glasheen, let me know. There'll always be a quid pro quo."

I drove for another hour, but I couldn't get back into the flow. I couldn't shake the feeling I needed to do *something*, but had no idea what.

I kept going over the events of the previous day, the situation with Barry, couldn't make any proper sense of it. Likewise the Annandale houses, and Phil's sudden need to get the Lebs out. Maybe there was something there. I pulled up at a phone booth in Bondi and rang Terry.

"You know of anyone in your circle who might need a temporary roof over their heads?" I said.

"What sort of roof?"

"There's a row of cottages in Annandale. Pretty run-down. Need some fixing up, but someone who was a bit handy could squat."

He paused for a second. "There's this women's co-op in Glebe looking for somewhere to camp. Want to set up a refuge for battered wives."

"No good. There's a chance it could get rough."

"You know, they'd probably be up to it."

"They'd have to occupy all three houses at once."

"What's your interest?"

"It's complicated. There's a developer bloke who's got plans for them. I might want a bit of, you know, leverage."

A significant pause from Terry. "Yeah? Why?"

My turn to pause. I wasn't quite sure why. "Never mind that. The houses aren't that bad. If someone wants them, they'd be fine."

"Okay, I'll see."

Then I did have a hunch. "Listen Terry, here's the catch: There'd be a time limit. I could promise a minimum crash of two months, maybe longer. But they'd have to agree to get out when I give the signal. Whenever that might be."

"Once they're in—"

"So they'd have to agree not to pass the squat on to their mates. When I say it's over, it's everyone out."

"I'll ask around."

Then I had a thought. "One more thing. Can I get a car from you?"

Another pause, then he said, "I've got a Rover. Brakes aren't great, but it's all right for local."

"No, something for the open road."

A longer pause. "I'm picking up an EK in a couple of days. Panel van. Got a 186 motor in it. You'd have to look after it, though."

Terry's tone told me he was curious as hell what I was up to, but leaving it to me to spill it or not. In fact, I had only the sketchiest notion what I was doing, except that I was taking the time-honoured cure for everything: if you can, get an okay car and just *go* somewhere. Anywhere, so long as it's far.

I finished the shift, made my way back to the shack around midnight. I skim-read the book again, then turned in.

I was exhausted, but slept badly. I had a long, tiring dream. I was leading a gang who were doing some ceaseless but pointless labour, part of which involved trying to trick another mob out of a bag of something or other, but, throughout it all I knew it was hopeless.

I woke up sweating. It was dark and very still. I lay there for a while listening to the low industrial hum in the far distance.

I got up, drank some water. Somewhere a car was driving slowly. Not far away. Then I heard it stop. A door slammed.

I stepped outside. To the west the sky glowed a flickering orange, lit up by the eternal flame from the Boral chimney. The Chinaman's dog started barking. A moment later there was a shout. Then another. Some quick chatter. Then silence. Another door slammed, then came the sounds of a car leaving. The dog kept barking for a quarter of an hour, then all was quiet.

Next morning I dug up the emergency package I had buried in the sand fifty yards behind the Batcave. I took out the bank-book and the bundle of twenty-dollar notes, buried everything else again, deeper than before.

I was at the counter of the Randwick Commonwealth Bank when it opened at ten. Took all the money out of the bodgey account. From there I went to the post office to arrange an overseas money transfer to Mullet. I spent the rest of the afternoon around Randwick, making calls and shopping for the bits and pieces I'd need. I had enough money for now, barely, but nothing in reserve.

Late afternoon I took a cab back to Matraville, stopped a quarter of a mile from the market gardens and walked the roundabout way back to where the track began. Four or five people were working in the market gardens on my left. No greetings were exchanged, but one of the workers straightened up and called out something in the direction of the shed. An old-ish Chinese guy in crumpled grey trousers, white shirt and tie stepped out and waved, signalling for me to wait up. He came hurrying across the paddock, shaking his head.

When he was within earshot he called out, "Not rubber! Not rubber!" Smiling, but agitated.

Jimmy Long was of a certain age, and had been in Australia a good while, but he'd never bothered expanding his English beyond a few a basic phrases. "No trouble" was one of them, and for him it could mean nearly anything.

"*What* trouble?" I said.

He waved vaguely over his shoulder. Over there. Or long gone. Or yesterday.

"Last night?" I said.

He nodded quickly.

"Who?"

"Some cunt, big car," he said. "Not rubber! Not rubber!"

199

I was being put on notice. Keep my problems away from here or our deal was off.

"What car?" I said.

"Ya-ow car." Yellow.

"Okay, Jimmy. Not rubber."

Absolutely no one knew where my shack was. But it was mentioned in the book. So were the Chinese market gardens. And how many such places were there in Sydney? I could think of similar gardens at Mascot, Botany, Kogarah, and maybe there were others out west. But if you were looking, you'd check the ones nearer the city first. It wouldn't take too long to find me.

Jimmy and his mates had chased Barry Geddins off, which was as much as I could expect. Next time they'd chase me off.

The panel van was parked outside Terry and Anna's. It was a faded and nondescript light blue-green, which was good. There was no trade name on it, also good. It was the kind with no windows in the back, so you could sleep in it. The key was inside the front mudguard, on top of the shocky. The engine made a rich throaty sound, but not too unlike the standard old EK motor. I drove it back to Matraville, loaded my stuff and left at midnight.

I took it slow up the Pacific Highway. It was quiet. A few vacant cabs, trucks coming in or heading out. A cruising cop car. I puttered carefully on through Chatswood, Turra, Hornsby. Then the bush. Crossed the river, kept going.

I pushed on for another two hours, then stopped a mile up a dead-end dirt track somewhere past Wyong, unrolled my sleeping bag, and was out in minutes. Four hours shut-eye – not deep, but just enough – and I was driving again. A quick breakfast at Kurri Kurri – not good – and another three hours driving got me over the ranges.

It was a warmer inland, and I was driving into the sun. The undulations gradually flattened, and the road became a series of long straight stretches, separated every half hour by a range of low wooded hills. I had the radio off and the windows open, wind swirling hard inside the car.

By mid afternoon I was tired and sweaty. I stopped at a motel called the Rest Ezy on the outskirts of a wheat town. Not flash, but not too rough either. The woman behind the counter scarcely laid eyes on me as she handed me the key.

A shower, an indifferent meal and another sleep, and I was on the road again at seven the next morning. Just before eight I passed a sign announcing the town of Wee Waa sixty miles further on.

Then droplets on the windscreen, the smell of Bars-Leaks, and a plume of steam from under the hood. I pulled up and opened the bonnet, stood back from the exploding cloud of steam, went and stood under a tree and waited for it to cool.

The radiator water was only moderately rusty, and I couldn't see a leak in any of the hoses. Since the van was a Holden, and knowing that the first time you take *any* Holden on a long run, the water pump will fuck up by way of an introduction, I guessed that's what it was.

I nursed it along the road for the next two hours, hit Wee Waa at lunch time. An average drab western town. People on the street were that typical far-west mixture of prosperous looking farmers and their florally dressed wives, young blackfellas in cowboy hats and Cuban heels, and dusty old codgers who might've been metho-drinking alkies or maybe old-time swaggies. Or maybe just farmers.

I found a wrecker's yard about the size of a football field on the far side of town. The kid near the gate pointed to a large shed, told me I'd find a dozen or more EK water pumps in there, including a couple of recon jobs.

I found the right aisle, heard someone shuffling nearby, muttering angrily what sounded like "Fuck off, fuckya! Fuck off, fuckya," over and over. I peered across the shelf. A crooked old gnome with straggly grey hair was rooting about a couple of rows away. He turned around jerkily, stared at me in a hollow yet somehow hostile way, turned away again.

As promised, there were plenty of water pumps that would fit an EK. I picked what seemed to be the best of the bunch, carried it to the front, paid the kid and left.

I drove slowly back to the main street, then stopped, thinking about the mad old bloke at the wreckers. So I doubled back and returned to the shed where I'd got the water pump. It was empty.

The bored kid was still at the counter.

"Just now, there was an old bloke out in that shed," I said.

The kid looked blank.

"Where the water pumps are. A mumbling old guy. Like a derro. Grey hair, a bit long. Foreign-sounding."

"Oh yeah. *Him.*"

"You know his name?"

The kid shook his head slowly. "He's come in here once or twice."

"This might sound odd, but I'm looking for someone who might be known to his friends as the Old Cunt."

The kid grinned at me, thinking I was making a joke, waiting for the punchline.

"That guy," I said, "could it be him? Anyone ever call him the Old Cunt?"

"He *is* an old cunt, that's for sure," said the kid, "but I've never heard him called that. Never heard him called anything."

"Would he have a property somewhere around the district? Maybe have another feller staying with him, a bloke maybe called Max. Black hair, goatee, skinny."

He shook his head again. "Wouldn't know." It was obviously genuine.

I took the car to the garage the kid had recommended. The mechanic looked at the radiator, the rusty water stains, the water pump I'd bought, and shook his head doubtfully, like I was asking him to find a cure for cancer by this afternoon. Said he was that busy, gestured to various cars about the place, on hoists, on blocks, bonnets up, wheels off, entrails pulled out. Couldn't look at it till this afternoon at the earliest, more likely tomorrow. I said, Sorry, I'd obviously misread the sign out front which said

'Mechanical Repairs.' He said I could suit myself. I got my bag out of the back, left the car with him, and we parted, both of us with the shits.

I found a motel. Spent the rest of the afternoon rereading Max's book. Ate a counter meal at the pub recommended by the old girl at the motel desk, then back to my room, spent the rest of the night reading.

I was sure this was the right town. That stuff at the end of the book about the dwarfs and the dancing cowgirls, that was true. Max had told me about it more than once. How he'd been out here with a tent show in the fifties, and they'd got themselves marooned when the entire district flooded. How they'd been bailed up for a week in a shearers hut, got up to all sorts of hijinks. The hut was on an old cattle station called Native Dog Creek, I remembered.

Next morning I ambled up the main street, went into the first Greek cafe I came to, ordered a grill. And thought about my next move.

I needed to ask a few questions, discreetly. I'd dressed as inconspicuously as I could: pale open-neck shirt, sleeves rolled up to the elbow, nondescript brown strides and brown shoes. A middle-of-the-road bloke with some bit of minor business in town, maybe a tradesman or a cocky. Or a family man with wife, kids and caravan in tow. But you wouldn't care who he was, and you wouldn't look twice.

I finished the breakfast – not bad – and went to the hardware, which had just opened for the day. I bought a can of WD40 and some insulating tape, the most neutral items I could think of. I was served by a genial, round-headed, middle-aged Lions Club type. I offered that it looked as though they could use some rain in the district. They certainly could, he said. It'd been a dry season, and they were overdue. We touched on the price of wheat and wool, whether or not it was time to devalue the dollar again. The conversation rolled on. He held Gough and the Labor mob in low regard, especially Jim Cairns, to all of which I murmured noncommittal responses.

I steered him back to local matters. We discussed the grand attractions of the Wee Waa district. I told him my mum used to come here as a girl, and if I remembered correctly, used to stay at a station called Native Dog Creek. Oh yes, he knew the place. A slight narrowing of the eyes: might I perhaps have an interest? Before I could think of the right answer, he went on to say that if I did have an interest, he could let me know the name of a good agent in town. The way things were in Wee Waa, he said, confidentially, *everything* was for sale, all the time, whether it had a sign out front or not. So I gave him to believe that, as a matter of fact, a friend had asked me to have a quick look at it on his behalf, since I was passing through. He nodded, smiling. He *knew* it. He'd picked me as Sydney, he said. Satisfied, he gave me directions to the place. And if I wanted to look at any others, I should come back and he could give me some good tips.

The car still wasn't ready – another hour – but the mechanic, a different one today, obligingly said I could take the old Austin over there if I wanted, so long as I paid for the petrol I used.

Ten miles north of town the bitumen road became a well-graded dirt road, then a bumpy, rutted track. I went through two gates and over a couple of grids, reached a final gate with a weathered, once-ornate sign: Native Dog Creek.

There was no one there, hadn't been for a while. The old house was deserted, locked up, a window broken. I strolled over to the shearers quarters, where Max and the hoochie coochie girls had been so famously marooned back in 1952. It was an old stone building divided into a series of little compartments – spidery, dusty, wasp-infested – that obviously hadn't been used for a long time. Except the last one, which had been swept in the last year or so. There was an iron bed frame with no mattress, a blackened kero lamp next to it. Nothing else at all, except in the corner, next to the bed, a dog-eared copy of Meher Baba's *Discourses*.

I went out and sat on a stump, let the wave of defeat wash over me. Sucked in once again by a Max Perkal scam. I'd allowed myself to believe there might be a way out of the Troubles, that he really might have the goods this time. It was pure, vintage Max – the cloak and dagger, the needless complications, the misdirections, the blurry divide between truth and fantasy. Then at the end, the no-show.

But he had been here all right, and maybe he *had* entertained the idea of squaring up with me. If he really had a housebrick of compressed smack – which was feasible – how long would it take before he went back, dug it up, started nibbling at it? At any rate, he was long gone from this place.

I went back to the hardware shop. The owner brightened when he saw me. "See anything you like?" he said. He obviously knew I'd driven out to Native Dog Creek.

"Interesting," I said.

He waited.

"Yes, very interesting," I said, hoping to imply that I was quite near making a positive decision on the real estate front. "Something maybe you can help me with," I said.

He nodded, ready to oblige.

"I was out there at the wreckers yesterday. Saw an old feller there, might've been a foreigner. A rough old cove. Talking to himself."

He nodded again.

"Well, after I left, it occurred to me he resembled the description I'd heard, of a friend of a friend. I wouldn't mind catching up with my friend while I'm in the district, but I lost his address. It occurred to me that old feller might know where my mate is."

The shopkeeper's expectant smile had been replaced by a look of mild confusion.

I pressed on. "The old straggly-haired bloke, would you have any idea who he might be? If he's the person I have in mind, he has a property out here somewhere. And my mate, a bloke named Max, could be helping him out around the place a bit."

Complete confusion now. I'd obviously overplayed my hand. But it didn't make any difference – the guy clearly hadn't a clue what I was talking about. He shook his head slowly and looked a bit embarrassed, wouldn't quite look me in the eye. "It's a disgrace," he said, with surprising anger.

"Huh?"

"The derelicts and drifters. They wash up in Wee Waa, loiter there down at the river, or in the park, even. No better than blackfellas. The fighting and drinking. And the language! You couldn't go for a walk with your wife around town after dark here. Disgraceful."

"So, the bloke I saw at the wreckers, you don't know him?"

He shook his head. "Town's full of them," he said.

The car was sitting exactly where I'd left it the day before, obviously hadn't been looked at. The mechanic was sorry, but what could he do? Tomorrow morning.

Back to the motel, a boring night watching the local TV.

I picked the car up next morning. After I'd paid, as he handed me the keys, the mechanic said quietly, "Copper was in a while ago, looking at your car. Asked whose it was."

I stared at him a couple of seconds, wondering how could that be. I shrugged theatrically. "Bit of a snoop, is he?"

"Just thought I should let you know." He looked away, down the street, then stole a quick, searching glance at me. Wondering who I was to bring the coppers in.

As I drove away, I wondered the same. Not a soul in Sydney knew where I was. If the cop checked the car rego, he'd find the name of the previous owner, since Terry always turned his cars over before the two-week grace period expired. I could rule out the number plate, and the car itself was completely unsuspicious. So it had to be just time-killing nosiness on the cop's part. Still, it worried me.

I headed back south, kept driving until I was well clear of the district. Late morning I pulled into a garage and rang Terry and Anna's place. The phone rang for a long time, then a breathless Anna picked up.

"Oh, Billy. Thank god you rang. There's trouble.'

My heart thumped hard. "What trouble?"

"You better ring Eloise. Something happened with the kids. Everything's all right, no harm done, but she's shaken up."

"What happened?"

"Someone approached them after school. Nothing actually happened, but the kids were frightened. Wait, Bill. There's something else. We got home last night and there was a dead cat—" She paused, and I heard a gasp of breath, "*nailed* to the front door. And your sleepout had been broken into, messed up a bit."

She sobbed a little, then stifled it again. "We're clearing out, Bill, going to stay with Katie at Avalon."

"I'm sorry, Anna. I really am. I'll deal with it."

Eloise was no less upset. It took a few minutes to get the story from her. She'd found an envelope pinned to the front door when she came home the night before. Inside were polaroids of the kids, taken as they were coming out of their schools.

"Did they know anything?" I said.

"James said a man fronted him outside school yesterday, said *you'd* sent him to pick him up. James gave the guy the slip. But he's was freaked, even though now he's pretending he wasn't. Who *was* it?" Her voice was louder and higher now. "Was it that Barry person?"

"Yeah. Eloise, take the kids and go away. Right now. Somewhere safe out of town. Your sister's, maybe. I'll deal with this, and I'll ring you when the coast is clear. Don't tell anyone *anything*, though. *No* one, understand?"

She was quiet for a second or two, then, more calmly, "Yes, I understand." She'd heard this sort of thing before, the upbringing she'd had. The word comes, go to ground, keep your mouth shut, wait a while. Something here needs dealing with. Afterwards, never refer to it again. She understood.

Then she sighed and said, "Something else. A friend of yours rang here, twice."

"Who?"

"From Melbourne. That musician guy, Lobby?"

"Lobby Loyde?"

"Yeah. He wanted to talk to you."

"He leave a number?"

"No. I told him you didn't live here. And that I wasn't your secretary. But I thought I should mention it."

I made a call to a Sydney number, was told to ring back in an hour. Which I did, from a town sixty miles further down the highway. It could be done, I was told, but not till tonight, eight or nine. I said I'd be there.

It was hard to keep my driving careful and steady like before. My foot would get heavier on the pedal, and I'd find myself going way too fast. I'd slow down very deliberately and stay that way for a while before the cycle started over again.

At sunset I crossed the Hawkesbury, then slowly threaded my way around the western outskirts of Sydney, through Parramatta, down to Fairfield. I stopped at a Caltex on Liverpool Road and made another phone call. Got a quick answer this time. Twenty minutes later I pulled up at a workshop on a scrubby track in Georges Hall. The light was on, so I went in.

It was cluttered inside. Two stripped-down motorbikes, parts spread over the floor. A long-haired, bearded man hunched over a bench grinder. He glanced at me and went back to his work. I waited.

After a minute he turned off the grinder, put down the steel gizmo he was holding. "Bill," he said.

"Rat."

He looked at his oily hands, smiled apologetically.

"Best not shake," he said. He picked up a packet of White Ox and started rolling a ciggy.

Ray King was one of those short, talky men who'd normally be nicknamed 'Mouse' or 'Sparrow,' but since his actual Christian name was Ratko – Ratko Kis, in fact, from Yugoslavia, via Villawood Migrant Hostel – he'd become 'Rat.'

He lit the cig. "Greg's coming over. Shouldn't be long." Shooting quick glances at me from behind his greasy fringe. Curious, but unwilling to ask me anything outright.

Presently a car pulled up outside and a thick-necked greaser came in carrying a plastic shopping bag. He said nothing. Rat took the bag from him, peered into it and held it out to me. The greaser retreated to a stool in a corner of the shed.

I looked in the bag. A Colt and a box of bullets.

"It's army, Bill, American. Safe as houses. Very good nick. Plus you got your concealed carry. Fits in your daks. A nice piece."

It was that, if a word like "nice" could be applied at all to such a thing.

"All right." I rolled up the bag, looked at Rat.

He glanced at the greaser then back at me. "Three Cs?"

I handed them to him. A big chunk of my remaining funds.

Rat smiled, and put the money carefully in his pocket. "Not turning to armed rob, are you?" He kept grinning, so he could pass the nosiness off as banter, should I take his prying amiss.

"There's a thought," I said.

"'Cause every other cunt is," he said, and the greaser laughed.

I looked at him, and wondered.

Rat glanced at the greaser, then said to me seriously, quietly. "He's okay. It's all okay. Same as ever."

And I knew it would be.

It was late when I got to the Cross, late enough to find a parking spot close to the Bourbon and Beefsteak. I needed a shave, probably looked like I'd been on the road all day, but the bouncer let me in with scarcely a glance.

An indifferent band was plugging away at 'Midnight Hour.' The place was half-filled with a rowdy mix of Kings Cross lunkheads, spivs, pros. But no Barry.

Out again and up the road to the Texas Tavern, a subtly different version of the same crowd. A cowboy band was playing 'Looking at the World through a Windshield.' Over in the corner, in a group of drunk and unruly standover thugs, Barry Geddins. I turned and went to the bar, ordered a middy, dropped back behind a pillar.

Barry lurched away from the laughing group, his face

suddenly serious. He scanned the room in a nervous, jerky manner. I dipped further behind the pillar. When he turned back to the group, I finished the middy and left.

I scanned the street up and down, but couldn't see his car. I went back to mine, drove up to Macleay Street, parked a little way down from the entrance to the Texas Tavern. And waited.

Forty minutes later, Barry walked out briskly. He turned left, towards the Cross. I let him walk on – there were few enough people about that I could easily keep track of him. When he got near the corner I started the car, cruised slowly up Macleay Street, nearly caught up with him at the fountain, pulled over and let him walk on again.

A little past the bend in the road he suddenly stopped and turned quickly, looking hard in my direction. I pulled over. He stepped into the road, whistled and shot his arm out, and a Red Deluxe Cab pulled up.

It was easy to follow. Left into Bayswater Road, down the hill into New South Head Road, then the back way through Darling Point, down the hill to Double Bay. The cab stopped outside a block of flats in William Street. I pulled up fifty yards behind, took the Colt out of the bag on the floor, put four bullets in it, stuck it in my daks. Concealed carry. I got out of the car, closed the door quietly and stood behind a paperbark tree there in the nature strip, waited while Barry finished paying the driver. As the cab drove away, he walked towards a building further along the street, reaching into his pocket, drawing out keys. Another car door slammed somewhere nearby.

Barry disappeared into the unlit driveway between two blocks of flats without turning around, but when I got there, I could see him dimly in the shadows, standing still. He was facing me. The driveway smelled of jasmine.

I stopped. We were fifteen feet apart. The gun was in my hand. I lifted it. He raised his arms away from his sides, palms up. At least, that's what it looked like.

There was nothing to say. I pulled the trigger. It roared in the confined space, and surprised me the way it leapt in my hand.

There was a sudden movement and Barry wasn't standing there anymore. A dog barked, someone cried out.

I turned and left.

I drove back towards the city, not sure where to go or what to do. I couldn't go back and see what had happened to Barry. I either hit him or I didn't, it was too late now to do anything more. I continued driving along Parramatta Road, then onto the Hume Highway. I kept going for three hours, right out of town and into the Belanglo Forest, then pulled off on a dirt road. I slept in the car, well out of sight, and drove straight through to Melbourne the next day.

It took me three phone calls to get Lobby's address. A large Victorian building in South Yarra.

At six that evening I knocked hard on the door, waited a few seconds then knocked again. A voice inside called out, "Holy *fuck*, what is it?" then the door swung open fast.

Lobby, in jeans and faded black t-shirt. He looked blankly at me a for a second.

"You were trying to contact me?" I said.

"Billy?"

I nodded.

He ran his hand through his short hair, then over his face. "Yeah, okay, all right. Come in."

I stepped into the big front room. Gypsy scarves hanging from the light fittings, old leather couches, a couple of guitar amps, a stuffed owl on a pedestal, full ashtrays, cups and saucers, an Aubrey Beardsley poster on the wall, the smell of cat's piss and patchouli.

"You want a cuppa then?" he said distractedly. Then with more liveliness, "Or a drink?"

"No."

"Are you okay? Sit down. You're making me nervous."

I exhaled slowly. "Sorry, I've had a long drive." I flopped onto the nearest couch. A tabby cat slunk over to check me out.

Lobby sat down opposite, still shooting quick glances at me.

"Yeah, well I rang your ex's, 'cause I thought she could get a message to you." He smiled. "I didn't know you were in Melbourne."

"Well, here I am," I said.

His turn to exhale slowly. "So, Bill . . . Last time we met would've been at the House of Cards, back in, what, 1968, 69?"

"Thereabouts."

"Great days."

"Yep."

A pause. He sighed. "Yeah, well, it's about this Max business."

"What Max business?"

"The book. Him being alive."

"*Is* he?"

"Well, with that book and all. Seems obvious, doesn't it?"

I shrugged.

"And now with you here," he said.

"I was in town anyway."

There was someone moving about in the other room. A woman's voice called out, "Lobby, you in there?"

Lobby shook his head quickly, looking over my shoulder to the kitchen doorway, and the voice said, "Oh."

I turned around. A tall, good-looking woman. Dark hair, bobbed. Angular features. Looking at me nervously. She smiled. "I'm Jan."

"This is Billy," Lobby said, giving my name a particular emphasis.

I said "Hi" and turned back around to catch Lobby signalling something to her. He grinned at me. "Hey, let's go up the pub. For the one."

Five minutes later we were in the back bar of the Station Hotel. Lobby with a scotch and dry, me with a lemon squash. A packet of Marlboros and a lighter on the table in front of him.

"So?" I said.

"Well, yeah. See, I was asked to make contact with you."

I waited. Lobby got a smoke out, held the pack out to me. I shook my head. He lit his smoke, took a deep drag, exhaled slowly.

"By Denise Baillieu-Munden," he said, finally.

"Ah, 'the heiress revolutionary'."

"Yeah, her. She's an old friend."

"And what does she want with me?"

"She wanted to talk to you. Discuss the whole business."

"What whole business?"

He shrugged. "Denise keeps her head down. Has to, since she's still on parole. No interviews or anything like that. She did one thing with the *Women's Weekly* when she first got out, and that nearly got her slotted all over again. So the family keep her wrapped up. But she wants to meet you, and have a talk. She asked me to get in touch with you."

"I'll talk to her. But I have some questions for you first."

A flash of nervousness, quickly concealed. "Yeah? What?"

"About Max. Back then, Max worked with you, right?" I said. "You're obviously the 'Bobby Boyd' in the book."

"Yeah," he grinned and shook his head. "He took some real fucking liberties there. Max came around and asked me for work. He *did* play with us for a while. Not that long. Actually, he was, you know, a bit old for us. Even with the afro. But he played Hammond for a bit. He makes out he was right at the heart of things, but really he was working mostly with trad jazz bands. Wearing a straw boater and a red vest, playing banjo at shopping centres. Did something with an old rock'n'roll band too, stuff like that. But he worked with Gully too. Gully thought he looked a bit of an elder statesman, like Allen Ginsberg when he still had hair. Or Garth Hudson. So he let him hang around. He was in that film clip on *GTK*."

"What about the speed?"

He looked at me, brightening. "You got some?"

"I mean Max. The dealing."

"Oh yeah. He had *plenty*."

"You've read the book?"

"Denise got a copy. I skimmed it."

"There's a character in it, called Vic. A bikey."

"That'd be Vic the Bikey."

"Speed guy?"

He smiled. "Fuck, was he ever? Yeah, he was the speed guy. And Vic is his real name. Vic Messenger. I haven't seen him for yonks, though."

"Any idea where he might be?"

He shook his head. "He comes from Echuca. Maybe someone there knows him."

"And the one they called the Boy Wonder. The chemistry whizz."

"Yeah?"

"What's his name?"

"Mark. He was *well* on the gear last time I saw him. Not speed. The bad stuff. Haven't seen him in, shit, two years at least."

"How about 'the Captain'? Who's he?"

Lobby shook his head. "Never trusted that guy, myself. Edward something. The Maoists always reckoned he was a spy. Then again, they reckon *everyone* is a spy." He smiled. "Maybe they're right."

"Where's he now?"

"Don't know." He shook his head. "Smack. Not good. Don't like smack or smack sellers."

"So," I said, "if Max really is alive, where is he now?"

He made a quick convulsive movement. "That, my friend, is the question on everyone's lips."

I looked at him for a long moment, saying nothing. Then I leaned forward, and spoke quietly. "Listen, I don't know how many people Max stiffed down here, and I don't know how many people might think they're owed something. But they're going to have to stand in line. Because I'm first. Understand that, Lobby? There are people waiting for me to collect, and if I don't do the right thing by them, they'll want to know why. And they'll find out why, and then they'll come looking, for you or anyone who gets in their way. You get that?"

"Oh shit, Bill, you've got this all arse up," he said. "It's not about the—"

"*Here* they are!" said a cheery voice behind me. A woman with very long, very shiny fair hair sat down busily on my right, her hair flopping around. Behind her stood a bloke who was looking at me, not kindly. Then he pulled out a chair and sat down too. The woman put her bag on the floor, took out a packet of cigs, tossed her hair again, smiled at me.

Lobby was obviously relieved. "Allow me. Denise . . . Richard, this is Bill. Bill, Denise, Richard."

"I'd guessed that much," I said.

I took another look at the two of them. Brother and sister. He was for protection. A few years older, a little pudgy, sun-bleached boyish hair. A sportsman going to seed. Her long hair was parted in the middle. She had large, intelligent brown eyes. An even and symmetrical face, slightly wide. A generous mouth, but a hint of petulance. Not exactly the raving blond sexpot Max had described.

She reached forward and put her hand over mine, gave it a squeeze. "It's so *amazing* to finally meet you. After all I've heard. I really do know you. Feels like it anyway. Max spoke about you so, so much."

"Did he tell you how much money he owed me?"

Not fazed. "Yes, he did, actually. It was on his mind. A lot."

"So," I said, "Lobby said you wanted to talk to me. Here I am. Go for it."

She smiled again. "Bob Gould said *you* wanted to talk to *me.*"

"Yeah, I do. What happened on the highway? How come Max is alive? Did he *really* write that book? Where is he now? What's your interest? And where's my money?"

Denise took a long breath, and the brother piped up. "You should understand that anything Denise says here is strictly off the record. And furthermore, matters that may be *sub judice* will not be discussed. Got that?"

I just looked at him.

He went on, "You should also be aware that any plans you may have for the exploitation of certain events in which my sister may have been involved, however innocently, whether for print publication in the form of a novel or nonfiction work authored by you or as told to a third party, or as the subject matter of a motion picture, radio drama, television play, or any other media format, will be energetically contested by us."

I looked at Denise. "Is he for real?"

Her smile was gone. "All right, Richard, that's *enough*." She turned back to me. "That probably sounded more hostile than it was meant to be."

I felt way behind the play. I looked at Lobby. He shrugged. I took a sip of my beer. "What *do* you want then," I said to Denise.

The brother answered. "No, the question here is what do *you* want?"

"What I said. I want to get what he owes me."

Denise said, "And, I imagine, you'd want to get even?"

"I want the money. That's all. But for you two," I pointed to Denise and then Richard, "money is not that big a deal, right? Got that already. What you want is—"

"Story rights," said Denise. "A novel first, then later a film. If we" – a light nod in Richard's direction – "can get the finance." She reached over and touched my hand again. "It's early, and I don't want to get ahead of myself. But I'd like you to be involved." She smiled again.

There was an H. Messenger in the Echuca phone book, the only listing for that surname. I rang the number first thing in the morning – no answer – and again in the afternoon. This time a weary, older-sounding woman picked up. Yes, she was Vic's mother. Helen. No, she didn't know where he was. Who was I? A friend of Vic's friend Max, I told her. Oh yes, the funny one. I didn't press her on what particular sense of the word "funny" she meant. I told her I needed to reach Vic.

"He shaved his head," she said. "Poor boy, he was no oil painting, *with* hair." She laughed. "He chants with that group of head shrinkers."

"Who's that?"

"The Harry Krishnas."

"In Melbourne?"

"Brisbane, last I heard."

"What about Vic's friend, Mark?

A long pause. "Mark?"

"Yes."

Another pause, then, "The young chap who disappeared?"

My turn to pause. "I hadn't heard that," I said.

"Vic told me. Mark was a nice boy, really. I would've jumped him, if I was few years younger."

"I . . . *What*?"

"Never mind."

"I . . . Sorry, where were we?"

"Caught you off guard, did I?"

"A bit. When did Mark . . . disappear?"

"Well," she sighed, "I last saw Victor three months ago. So about six months before that, I suppose."

"Did Vic happen to mention anything about Max? I mean, recent news about him?"

"What did you say your name was?"

"Bill Glasheen."

"Oh."

"Yes?"

"Victor mentioned you."

"Really? Did he leave a message?"

"Wouldn't you like to know? Where are you ringing from?"

"Melbourne."

"Oh." She went silent for a few beats. "How old are you?"

"What's that got to do with it?"

She laughed. "Mystery man, huh? Well, I'm game. If you're up Echuca way, give me a call."

"You've caught me off guard again."

She laughed throatily, said, "Well, see ya sometime, maybe," and hung up.

That evening I told Denise about my conversation with Helen

Messenger.

"Isn't she a *trip?*" she said. "Vic brought her to a couple of Carlton parties. She fitted right in. Toking joints and whatnot. Everyone loved her. Did she have anything for you?"

"Not really. If I asked her anything she'd change the subject, answer in a flirty way."

"She's no fool."

"Guess not. She told me Mark had disappeared. Like he was dead."

"Mark?"

"Vic's mate. The kid who made the speed. 'The Boy Wonder' in the book."

She shook her head. "Never knew him."

"You must've known Vic."

"He was more Max's mate. We never buddied up particularly. But yeah, I knew him, of course."

We were at the Italian Waiters Club. Plates of pasta and mugs of red wine in front of us. It was crowded and noisy. We'd ended up halfway to being pals the previous night, especially once brother Richard had shot through. We'd stayed in the pub for another hour while Denise and Lobby filled me in on the actual events before and during the Moratorium, as well as the aftermath. Their versions of it, anyway.

This is how they'd laid it out to me: Yes, there were armed robs, but they'd been Stan and Jimmy's thing. Max might have been involved in the post office robbery, but with Max, who knew for sure?

Cathy had been more involved, maybe even masterminded the Moratorium rip, the idea of the simultaneous robberies, the explosion. Denise had remained mostly on the fringes. She *had* tried to film the robbery, the way Max wrote it up, more or less. She hadn't held a gun though, she said. And had never wanted any part of the take. She wanted the story, she said.

So Denise had come through the shenanigans – the drugs, the robberies, the Moratorium Day knockover, the escape, the crash, the ensuing police trouble, the international notoriety – more or less clean. As Bob Gould had told me, the family put her in a nice private hospital, got her a top-notch lawyer, plenty of postponements on the court appearances. By then she had a folder full of sympathetic psych assessments.

Despite the way Max had written it up, Denise had only ever dabbled in the hard drugs. It was just a case of artistic literary curiosity gone wrong. She'd gravitated too close to her subject, lost her objectivity, been swayed towards the gang's perverse values. A problem of being too young, too open, too fearless even. But she was not a criminal, not really.

That was the line her lawyers took, and by the time Denise fronted court she looked good, acted remorseful, was committed to performing social good, et cetera et cetera. Even the cops were speaking up for her. The end result was a short stretch, all things considered, and early parole.

She'd come out of it all as something of a celebrity. But after the ill-advised *Women's Weekly* interview she'd prudently kept her head down. Now her parole was over – and she really *had* always wanted to write a book, make films and such. With brother Richard being a lawyer, and there being a bunch of new government grants for filmmakers in the pipeline, this was the moment. Finish the novel, capitalize on the notoriety, get the funding to make a feature film.

"So what do you actually want me for?" I'd asked.

At which she smiled and grasped my hand again, and said, "The inside story. Authentic background. Colour and detail."

"That's bullshit," I said. "You can get that authentic stuff anywhere. Or just make it up."

She'd hummed and hawed a bit before coughing up the truth.

"I need a signed and witnessed release from Max. Even though the book was pulped, the fact it once existed might be seen as evidence of his rights to the story. Of course, I've got just as much right to the story, but if the film did get up, and if any money came out of it, Max could make legal trouble later on. Investors will want that settled before they commit."

"Right," I said. "So you need Max to sign a paper?"

"But I have to find him first," she said. "Just like you do."

We'd split on okay terms, agreeing to talk things through the next day, so here we were at the Waiters Club.

"That character in the book, 'the Captain,' did you know him?" I said.

She shook her head slowly. "He was a mysterious off-stage presence. Stan and Jimmy might've known him. Cathy too. But I never did."

"Any idea of his real name?"

She slumped back in her chair. "I didn't want to know. I got the idea he was . . . I'm not sure what. Untrustworthy? The men liked him well enough, the women less so. Not a brute or anything. Good manners. But creepy."

"Do you buy that stuff about Vietnam and the refined smack?'

"Well, it's true it used to be very scarce. Now it's everywhere."

"But he wasn't known as the Captain in real life, right?" I said.

She looked at me cautiously. "No, he wasn't."

"What did they call him, then?"

She narrowed her eyes. "What do *you* think? You have an idea, obviously."

"I think it's a bloke who used to be known as the Filthy Blighter."

She sat up straight. "Yes! The Blighter. That's him. A chum of yours?"

I shook my head and put my hand up. Don't ask.

"How did you get out of it at the end, Denise?"

"How did I jump ship?"

I nodded.

"We left Melbourne after the rip. Pretty much as it's written in Max's book. Most of them were strung out. Road blocks were going up. It was horrible in every way. Max was off his face, even more than he describes. Mandies, pot, grog. Muttering loony stuff to himself the whole time.

"I knew it was going to end badly. It had to. I figured it still wasn't too late to get out, so I just asked them to let me out. And they did. How Max described *his* bail out? That was me. Stan stopped the car. I got out. Walked a couple of miles to a servo and rang Richard. He came and got me. We went to the police in Melbourne next day, with a lawyer in tow."

"So you didn't see Max bail out?"

She shook her head. "I heard about the accident later that afternoon. It was all over the news. And as far as I knew, Max, Cathy, Jimmy and Stan had all . . . you know, died together. It was only when I read the book, knew it had to be genuine, that I realised Max must have jumped ship too, sometime after I did."

"Which was when? That you read the book, I mean."

"About two months ago. Bob Gould sent it to me. Asked my opinion. How did *you* get it?"

"I found a copy in the glove box of the cab I drive. I started thumbing through it because there was nothing else. Just killing time. That was a week ago."

"Coincidence?"

I shook my head. "Nah. The other bloke who drives that cab is a Portuguese feller with bugger-all English. The cab owner knows nothing about it. I suppose a passenger might've left it on the back seat, but—"

"But it's written for you. It's written *to* you."

"In parts, yeah."

"So someone wanted to make sure you saw it."

"It's possible," I said. "It wasn't you, was it?"

She laughed and shook her head. "No. But I'm glad we've made contact now." She leaned forward and gave my hand another squeeze. "But why leave it in the cab at all?" she continued. "Couldn't they – whoever – have just sent it to you, anonymously?"

"Yeah, well. Not so easy. I keep my address sort of quiet. It *could* just be coincidence, you know. What about the detective in the book, 'Craig'? He still around?"

"Real name Craig Grossman. He's right out of it, I think. Retired from the force."

"Max shot him?"

She shook her head. "That's what he wrote. But from what I heard, it wasn't so clear cut. Somehow he got a bullet in the thigh. Could've been from one of his mob, even. But it messed him up, in more ways than one." She tapped her head three times. "Once the money went up in the inferno, his interest would've pretty much evaporated, I think."

The place was getting loud. and I was starting to feel the rotgut red. I wanted out of there.

"So what next?" she said.

I saw no reason to be cagey. Or maybe it was the red.

"I'm going bush again. Those hints in the book – I'm going to check them out."

"Again?"

"Huh?"

"You said 'again.' You mean, you've already been out there?"

"I had an idea Max might be in the north west of the state – New South Wales, I mean. I went out looking last week. But it was a dud. He'd been there, but was long gone. I reckon he decided the no-dope thing was bullshit, went and dug up his package, and by now he's happily shooting it up somewhere. But if there's any money left, I want it."

"You want company on this trip?"

"You?"

"Yeah, me. I've got a stake in it. I'd be company, too."

"What about your brother?"

She raised her eyebrows and grimaced. "Just you and me."

I said nothing, which she took as a yes.

"Great! But just to be clear," she said, looking me in the eye. "I'm not going to fuck you."

❖ ❖ ❖

Next day I rang Eloise at her sister's in Newcastle. The boy answered, said straight off, "Eloise is out."

"When's she back?"

"She said before dinner."

"Put your aunt on then," I said.

"She's out too."

"No adult there?"

"No. But we have sandwiches. And I made a cup of tea."

I thought, does he know how to make a pot of tea? Figured he obviously did. Wondered if that was precocious. Figured it wasn't.

"Sorry about the scare outside your school the other day," I said.

"Why are *you* sorry? It wasn't you who scared me."

"Don't be a smartarse," I said.

"You're the one who taught me."

"Did I? In that case – well done, lad. I'll ring back later. Tell Eloise you lot need to stay put for a bit longer. Give your sister a hug and a kiss for me."

I rang Katie's place at Avalon. *Moondance* was playing in the background. Katie told me all was good. Terry and Anna and she were having a jolly old time of it. That was good, I said. She told me Terry wanted a word.

He came on, "So how's that thing going?" His voice low, serious.

"The Barry thing?"

"Yeah, that."

"Well I'm . . . out of town."

Silence from Terry. Putting it together, quick smart.

"And Barry is . . . ?"

"I don't know where or what Barry is."

"Meaning?"

I said nothing.

"Oh. I get it. Sort of. You're not sure."

"I'm not sure."

"But you . . . you took action?"

I said nothing.

"Right. You're just not sure of the outcome."

I gave a noncommittal hmm.

"So, what happens next? Katie's a doll, but Jesus, we can't stay here forever."

"Truth, Terry, I don't know. I wish I did."

"Maybe I should ask around a bit? See if he might be hiding anywhere?"

Terry was a Balmain head, and he looked it. But he was a pub pool champ too, carried a nice cue in a nice case, had a good rep. He could mix with pretty much anyone, including the rougher element, plenty of whom had won big by backing the longhair in pub competitions.

"Keep your distance, but yeah, if you can find out anything at all . . . Thing is, Terry, if the bloke *is* around, he could be, you know, hurt."

"Yeah, I get it. I'll find out what I can. I won't *do* anything. Hey, in other news, I spoke with Mullet last night, long distance."

"Yeah?"

"He's been screening *Crystal Dreams*. He says people love it. Even the bikers don't mind it."

"They can love it till the cows come home, but we need to turn a friggin' dollar."

"That's it." Terry said, warming, "Have you seen that film *American Graffiti*?"

"Nah. Nostalgia."

"What? Is it? Yeah, well, Dennis took Mullet to a party, introduced him to the bloke who directed it. How do you like that? They got on beaut, apparently. Mullet reckons this bloke was *very* interested in our thing."

"So we've got the Beach Boys onside—"

"One of them."

"—and now a director. Listen Terry, Mullet being who he is, yeah, I can see him palling up with other lairs and loudmouths. Good for him. But are they going to give us any money?"

"Patience, mate. Let them nibble at the bait a bit. I know, I know – there's nothing solid yet. But it's all heading in the right direction, that's the main thing."

"All right. Whatever you say. Better shoot through. I'll ring you in a few days."

"Hang on, hang on, before you go. That squat in Annandale."

"Yeah?"

"Still a goer?"

"Tell them it's okay. There's a bundle of keys in the kitchen drawer in my flat. There are front door keys to all three places, but they'll probably need to put new locks on the doors. Phil will be on their hammer, but if you reckon they can deal with it . . ."

"They can, trust me."

"All right. Three weatherboard joints, all in a row. 17, 19 and 21 Guilliat Street, down near the canal. There's a Leb family in 15. They keep to themselves, but they seem all right. Keep my name right out of it."

❖ ❖ ❖

Denise and I drove out of Melbourne the next day, along the highway to East Gippsland. We stopped mid-afternoon in Orbost, an inoffensive little town in dairy country. I found a phone booth with a local directory and got the address I wanted.

Denise was looking at me expectantly when I went back to the car.

"I've got to see a man," I said, and waited. "About a dog,"

She stared at me a moment, not pleased.

"This person will be shy. Let's find a motel. You check in. I'll go do this thing."

"It's one of them, right?"

"Huh?"

She grinned tightly, trying to conceal her irritation. "One of the people Max listed in the book?"

I said nothing.

"Yep, I thought so." She rummaged around in her bag, pulled out the book and thumbed through it. "Page, ah, let's see . . . Okay, got it." She looked at me, pleased. "Page 112, for your info." She put on a hardboiled Joe Friday voice. "*Along the way I looked up some folks from the old Sydney days. I saw the Cat, proprietor of a chemist shop, a picture of respectability. The Multi-Grip Kid was running a big garage down south. Molly had a motel. Mr Bones, Brylcreem, Steptoe, the Reverend, the Sexational Gypsy Woman. Yeah, Johnny, you know them, our people – they send their regards. The old crew. They're all out there."* She put the book down. "Would it be one of them?"

"You'll never know, sweetheart," I said.

She smiled, shrugged as though she didn't care that much. I thought to myself, Damn, she's *quick*. I dropped her and our bags at a hotel/motel on the outskirts which advertised "TELEVISION IN ROOMS" and headed back through town. And out the other side, past the showground, to a scrappy industrial area. I passed a wreckers, a timber yard, a kitchen cabinet maker, and a tackle shop, turned into a yard surrounded by a high barbed wire and corrugated iron fence. A small sign on the open gate read M&G TRANSPORT. A couple of two-ton trucks were backed up to a big rusty shed. Half a dozen more wrecks lay around in different stages of pillage. Other wrecked cars, racks of steel bar, iron sheets, and a small mountain of rubbish off to the side.

There was a fibro office next to the main shed, a dark green Ford Fairmont behind it. I parked next to the Ford and got out. A kid in greasy blue overalls was staring at me from across the yard. His stance seemed oddly hostile. I ignored him and went into the office.

A stocky middle-aged man with steel-wool grey hair sat at the desk. Wearing reading glasses tied to a length of string around his neck, a stack of crumpled papers in front of him, cigarette burning in the ashtray. Could have been a lesser comic character in *Sergeant Bilko* or *McHale's Navy*. He looked up at me, said nothing. His expression was neutral, but he held the look.

"Hiya, Multi."

He shook his head slowly, smiling in a sad kind of way.

"They usually call me Ron these days."

I put my hand out to shake. He offered his with a degree of reluctance. "I had a feeling I'd be seeing you sooner or later."

"Really? How come?" I said.

He gave a "fucked if I know" shrug and smiled. "You're looking well," he said.

"You too." He'd put on a few pounds, was wider around the middle, but he was still the tough, muscled bloke he'd been five years before. "How's business?" I said. "Mind if I sit down?"

"Go ahead. Business is all right."

"*Transport . . .*"

"No need to say it like that," he said. "Those are working trucks out there."

"Yeah, no doubt. What do they transport? Never mind. You were expecting me, were you?"

"Yeah. After I saw Max."

"After you saw Max. Right." And waited.

He didn't offer to elaborate.

"When would that've been?" I said.

His phone rang. He picked it up, listened. "Yeah . . . No . . . Fuck that . . . That's right . . . No, no, no . . . Yeah . . . Tell him I said no . . . All right, bye now." He put it down and shook his head.

"The trials of running a small business," I said.

He looked at me. "Max was here, oh, would've been middle of the year before last."

"When everyone thought he'd been killed."

"Yeah. Bit of a surprise. He was playing with a music group up the golf club. Clang-clang yodel-ay-ee-hoo."

"Hillbilly?"

"Is that what you call it?"

"Would it be too much of a stretch," I said, "if I were to ask if you know his current whereabouts?"

"Ask away, but I couldn't tell you."

"So you and he had a talk?"

"Chit chat, nothing much."

"But you must've been surprised to see him alive, after all the newspaper and TV stuff?"

"Maxxy always was full of surprises."

"He wrote a book, did you know that?'

He gave a sort of world-weary chuckle. "I'm not much of a reader."

"In the book he says there was a bloke he knew then, husband of the bandleader, who was a mad rorter. Sheep and cattle duffing, probably stolen farm gear. Had a few trucks."

He was slow to answer. "And because I have a few trucks, what, I'm supposed to be up with that? Or part of it?"

"Jeez. Settle down, Multi. I was just asking."

He sighed deeply, leaned back in his swivel chair.

"Sorry, you're right, Bill. I'm being a fair dinkum touchy cunt, aren't I? Truth is, I didn't want any contact with Max, or any of the old mob. Includes you too, old son. That thing we did back then, it was good, and it got me set up here. Nicely. We got away with it, but I don't want to push my luck. And Vi likes it out here." He gestured out the window. "I said hello to Max, because I couldn't very well not."

He looked me right in the eye. "Of course, I knew he was supposed to be dead. And I'd read there was money unaccounted for from those robs. Which *maybe* burnt up in the crash, but who knows? Anyway, I didn't want to stick my beak in. And I still don't." He let that hang. "Honest, I was fucking well glad when they left."

Through the little office window I saw a shiny Cortina drive in fast, pull up sharply. A portly, redheaded woman got out and stomped into the office. Middle-aged but not in bad nick, a bit like Shelley Winters. Curly hair, cat eye sunglasses.

"Gawd love 'im," she said. "Look what the cat dragged in." She came over and hugged me, smiling.

"Hello Vi," I said.

"*Lovely* to see you, pet," she said, "as always."

She stepped back and the smile went ever so slightly off the boil. "What brings you here?"

"I was on my way to Melbourne. Thought I'd pop in, say hello."

"From Sydney? On the coast road?"

"I thought you might've seen Max."

She *almost* glanced at Multi for a signal as to how much he'd already told me. She stifled the reflex, but not quickly enough.

"*Max?*" As though that was an outlandish idea.

"Come on, Vi. Multi has already said he was here, that you saw him."

The smile gone. "Did Ron tell you we're squareheads now? And we want to keep it that way."

"And the sooner I shoot through the better? Don't worry."

"Darling, you're *always* welcome here. You know that." She opened her handbag and pulled out an Oroton cigarette case and a lighter. She picked a cig out with her long fingernails and lit it. Took a drag, exhaled a cloud of smoke, folded her arms and looked at me. "Yes, we saw Max, the poor love. He's a caution, isn't he? Still alive after all that . . . and not around to cash in on his fame?"

"He'd be facing ten years in Pentridge if he was found. At least. But the fame thing, yeah. Out of character. Any idea where he'd be now?"

She shook her head. "Wouldn't have a clue. Wouldn't *want* to know." She looked at me conspiratorially. "What about you, Bill? Not gunning for our old Maxxy. are you?"

"Nothing like that. It's fallen to me to tidy up his affairs. Some of them, anyway, the bits that concern me. I just thought you two, on the off-chance. But you don't, so . . ."

I looked back at Multi. His face completely bland now. Calm and amiable as could be. Vi smoked her cig, watchful.

"So I better shoot through." I shook hands with Multi, gave Vi a kiss.

Vi smiled. "Is there any particular lady friend these days, Bill?"

"How could there be, when Multi here bagged the best one going?"

She gave a wheezy laugh, then started coughing.

Denise was waiting for me in the ladies' lounge back at the hotel/motel. Late afternoon sun was slanting in. The beer garden outside was half full, but except for us the lounge was deserted. Denise had showered and changed. Denim jacket, floral blouse. Sort of a hippie look, but not in a way that would attract attention. We had drinks in front of us – a gin and tonic for her, a beer for me.

"They definitely know something," I said. "But they played it very cool."

"So who was this? 'The Cat'? 'Mr Bones'? 'Brylcreem'? 'Motel Molly'?"

"It was the one Max called 'the Multi-Grip Kid.' Actually, we called him 'Multi-Grips.' Or just 'Multi'."

"Yes, simple is better," she said, without a smile.

"Multi used to be a Sydney knockabout. Very good with machinery – motors, cars and that. He could open most safes, was handy with electrics too. Could deal with an alarm system. He'd been an engineer at AWA, got done for a fiddle he worked with equipment spares. No charges were brought. He was – is – very careful, very meticulous."

"And his connection with you and Max was what exactly?"

"We were involved in some, ah, things together. One of them turned out pretty well for us. Multi and his missus were able to move away, set themselves up down here."

Denise's eyes were very wide, pupils large, as she vacuumed up the story.

"You memorizing this for your novel or film script or whatever it is? Multi will provide a bit of underworld colour, right?"

It rattled her for a second.

"Sorry. I don't mean to be so snoopy. I *am* fascinated, though. Genuinely. Max talked about this stuff a lot, talked about *you* a lot. The nightclub. I always assumed it was part-fantasy. To hear the truth now . . ." She let it trail off.

"A lot of this is common knowledge in Sydney anyway. But this is off the record, okay?"

"Okay. But tell me – why Multi, why now?"

"Max mentioned him specifically in the book, like he was sort of directing my attention that way."

A near-shriek from across the room. "*Here* he is, bless 'im!"

We turned around to see Vi bearing down on us.

"And look, a darling little sweetheart with him!"

Denise stared, literally open-mouthed, then smiled. Vi sat

herself down and put out a paw to Denise. "I'm Vi."

"Hello Vi, I'm Denise. Love your glasses."

"Aren't they something?" Vi was reaching for her Kools, shaking her head, turning to me. "Billy, dear. You must think we've become utter *brutes* out here in the bush, letting you go without even inviting you for a drink, generally behaving like savages."

"No harm done, Vi."

"Well, we're not having it. There's a good Chinese dinner at the Golf Club. You come along tonight – it'll be our shout. Don't even *think* about saying no, we absolutely insist. Then a big smile for Denise, "You too, petal."

"How did you know where to find me, Vi?" I said.

"Small town. There are only three places you could be staying, and the other two?" She shook her head. "You wouldn't stay there.'

Denise smiled. "Would you like a drink?"

"No thanks, darl. Just popping through." Vi turned to me. "You will come, won't you?"

"Yeah, that'd be great." I smiled as warmly as I could. "But listen, just give me a chance to tub and so on. See you there at, what, seven thirty, eight?"

A look of doubt flashed across her face. But she smiled and said, "Wonderful! Make it eight. The golf course is straight out of town a quarter mile past Ronny's yard, on the right." She picked up her keys and cigs, waved "Byee!" and bustled off.

When she'd cleared right out, I waited a moment longer then said to Denise, "Are we paid up at the desk?"

She looked at me with surprise. "No, of course not."

"Go and pay right now. Tell them we're leaving at six in the morning. But be casual about it: ask if there's somewhere we can get breakfast here that early. Then go pack, quick as you can. I'll put the car round the back so we can load up without being seen."

She looked at me for a second, then took off.

Half an hour later we were out of town, driving east. The sun had gone down, the Princes Highway was quiet. We were driving through tall eucalyptus forest, our headlights picking out the straight trunks either side of the road. Roos and wallabies were grazing on the grass verge, so I was taking it slow.

We'd slipped away without fuss. And without dinner. After a long silence Denise said, "Are you going to let me in on what that was all about?"

"Back there? That was all wrong," I said. "They were hiding plenty."

She looked at me curiously, but said nothing.

"And why would they do that?" I said, more to myself than to her. "Cover up, evade?"

"Maybe out of general suspiciousness. Stan's friends were like that, some of them. Wouldn't tell you the truth if there was a lie to be told, any lie."

"Could be. But we go back, Multi and me. I'm not just some gig. Their guard should've been down, at least a little bit."

Denise said nothing.

"They were rattled enough to forget the social niceties. Didn't offer me a drink. Vi had a think about it after I'd gone, realised it looked bad, tried to mend it."

"Yeah, right," Denise said. "She was trying too hard. I see that."

"If that character in the book, Jacko, if he really does exist, and if he really was involved in bush rorting and whatnot, then Multi would know something about it. But he played dumb. Said he knew nothing about any book. Wasn't even curious. That just doesn't wash. So I conclude he was covering up. Which means he has an interest. He's *in* it."

"Why are we leaving then? Why not stay and find out more?"

"If we hung around it could only be good for them and bad for us. They're not going to give anything away, but they'd be trying to find out what I'm up to. And thinking about it now, that yard of Multi's – there's *nothing* happening there. No legitimate living being made, that's for sure. He's up to something.

He's not even hiding it, not that much."

"Which would mean he's got good connections."

I gave her a quick glance. "That's right. He could be in with the local cops. Or the Melbourne cops. Or both."

We drove in silence for another fifteen minutes. A set of headlights appeared in the rear-view mirror, on high-beam. The car came up fast till it was about a hundred yards behind us, then slowed and dropped back a quarter mile. I was still doing just fifty. Over the next few minutes it dropped further back.

Other cars passed it and passed me, but that one stayed put.

Denise saw me eyeing the rear-view, turned to look, then back to me.

"Yes," I said. "It's something." I glanced at her. "You think I'm paranoid?"

She considered that. "You don't *seem* to be."

Silence. Then, "How could they know which way we went?"

I shook my head slowly. "Don't fall for the Darby and Joan act. Multi and Vi are smart. I told Vi I was on my way to Melbourne. She smelled a rat straight off. There are three ways out of that town. The highway west back to Melbourne, east to New South Wales, or the road north into nowhere. They've made an educated guess we're headed to New South Wales."

Denise glanced behind again. "If we'd stayed, maybe we could have wrongfooted them. By leaving we tipped our hand."

I didn't say anything. She was right. But still I was glad to be out of there.

Denise said gently, "Like a joint?"

"Christ, no."

"Do you mind if I do?"

Half an hour later the other car was still on our hammer. It had dropped further back and most of the time stayed out of sight, just a glow back there somewhere. But on the long straight stretches I could see its headlights, way behind.

We came to a little town called Cann River. A hotel, a few shops. And an intersection. The Princes Highway straight ahead to Eden and the New South Wales south coast. Or left on the Monaro Highway, through the hills to Cooma and the Snowy Mountains. I swung left, passed the pub, went another couple of hundred yards and slowed right down.

When I saw the headlights appear back at the corner I took off, once I was sure he'd seen me. "I hope I didn't overplay that," I said, more to myself than Denise. She didn't answer.

"Can you reach that carry bag at the back?" I said to Denise.

She turned and hauled the bag onto the seat between us.

With my left hand I opened the clasp and felt around. The Colt was at the bottom. I'd meant to throw it off a bridge somewhere. Another elementary mistake. I knew it was still loaded.

I was going fast now, as fast as I could. When a wide gravel track appeared on the right, I hit the brake and swung into it. The car bumped roughly across a cattle grid. The track was straight, through paddocks, with no tree cover, which meant he could see where we'd gone. Which was what I wanted. I drove fast over the rough surface and into the forest at the other side of the paddock.

A hundred yards in I pulled onto a side track, just far enough to be out of sight from the road. And turned off the lights. Thirty seconds later a car sped past. A dark green Mini Cooper S. Fast, and apparently skilfully driven. I waited a few seconds, reversed out and headed back to the main road.

By the time he realised that I'd doubled back and he'd turned around, he wouldn't know whether we'd gone back to Cann River or turned north. That was the plan. But he was quicker than I thought. By the time I was back on the bitumen I could see him coming out of the bush at the far side of the paddock. He would be able to follow us for as long he wanted.

"Can you drive?" I said.

Denise looked at me, scared but alert. She nodded tightly.

I pulled left, stopped, took the Colt out of the bag, got out.

"Drive back to that town and wait for me there. I'll walk in when I'm done."

She looked at me doubtfully, then nodded and slid over to the driver's seat.

I ran back to the cattle grid and ducked behind the thick tufts of grass at the side of the road. When the Mini approached the gate, the driver slowed right down to get the small wheels over the grid. I stood up and took a shot at the radiator grille. Then another at the lights. The third shot hit the front wheel.

By then the driver was out, shielded by the car. The young overalled apprentice from Multi's yard. I turned to head back to town, but then I heard a thump. The guy was at the back of the Mini, taking something out. I ran at him. When I got there he was loading a sawn-off rifle.

I swung the barrel of the Colt and caught him on the cheek. He grunted and dropped the sawn-off. I hit him again, and he stayed down. I kicked him hard in the chest to make sure he was out of action, then took the sawn-off, found the bullets, and used them on the Mini's remaining tyres.

A car was coming up fast on the main road. Denise in the panel van. When she pulled onto the side track, I was still holding the sawn-off. The kid was on the ground behind the Mini. She quickly got out of the car, then froze, horrified at what she thought she was seeing.

I went over to the bloke and crouched down beside him. He was a kid, nineteen or twenty at most. Thin, with lank, longish dark hair. Blood trickling down his too prominent cheekbone. A narrow, nervous mouth. Seeing him close-up confirmed the impression I'd got back at Multi's yard: an angry young country town loser. "You all right?"

"Get fucked," he wheezed.

"Multi told you to follow me, right?"

"Get fucked."

"You should've stayed further back," I said. "I picked you right off."

"Get fucked."

I stood up, smashed the .22 on the roadway. The stock splintered. I did it again and the barrel bent. I went back to the bloke on the ground.

"Are you able to get up, sit in your car?"

He said nothing.

"Come on, I'll help you."

He didn't help, but he didn't resist. I got him into the driver's seat.

"When you get your breath back, you can walk into town that way," I said. "Or sleep in the car till morning. And you might want to do something with that sawn-off. If a cop happens to come along you don't want to have to explain it."

This time he said nothing.

I went to the back of the car and picked through the junk on the back seat. An overnight bag, a change of clothes. I went back to the kid and leaned over him.

"I figure Multi told you to follow me for as long as you could. Ring in with reports every day. Or maybe you were to follow for a day or so then hand over to someone else. That about right?"

"Get fucked."

I took the keys out of the ignition and tossed them into the long grass of the paddock. I went back to the driver and punched him in the face, not as hard as I might have.

"Tomorrow you should have a long hard think about the line of work you're getting mixed up in. Consider something more regular. Multi and Vi are way too ruthless for the likes of you. If you're not as strong as the strongest – and let's face it, who is? – then you need to be smarter to make up the difference. But mate, you're neither strong nor smart. Just the truth."

When I left he was glaring at me silently.

Denise didn't say a word as we drove away.

A change blew in from the Tasman Sea, cold, wet, windy. Denise stayed at the wheel until we reached Eden three hours later, across the border in New South Wales. We stopped at the first motel we came to, rang the night bell and waited shivering until the cranky proprietor came out.

We booked into adjoining rooms. Ten minutes after I turned the light out my door opened and Denise tiptoed quickly across the room, wearing just a T shirt. She slipped between the covers, slid up against me. Her skin was warm and very soft. She snuggled up, and I felt her warm breath on my neck.

"Remember I said I wasn't going to fuck you?" she said.

"Yeah, I remember that."

"Well, I didn't really mean it."

❖ ❖ ❖

Next day we drove north. No one behind us, a smooth, fast ride through the coastal hills of the far south coast, then a left off the highway into the ranges towards the Monaro Plains. The rain had passed, it was sunny and cool. As we drove through the big open hills, talk between us was easy. Denise slid over next to me on the bench seat.

"So, what was the go with this nightclub of yours? And Max's?"

"For your book, is it?" I said.

She smiled. "Yeah. No. Sort of. Not really. More just background. For me."

"It's a sorry yarn, all right. Max called it the Joker in the book," I said. "He said it was up at the Cross, a grand kind of place, right? Like the Whisky Au Go Go or something. You know what it really was? A drab upstairs room in Darlinghurst. We called it the House of Cards. Big joke, eh?"

"It's a good name for a club. What about Alex the Greek? Was he a real person?"

I looked at her. "You didn't know him? All that time he spent in Melbourne?"

"The smack was mainly Cathy and Max's thing. Like I said, I was just a dabbler. On the fringe. I never knew . . . was Alex his real name?"

"Yeah. Greek Alex. He was part of it."

"He still around?"

"Been up the Atherton Tableland for the past two years. Out of the picture."

"But his family?"

"His uncle is a bad man. Joe Dimitrios. If there's any one reason Bob *really* pulped Max's novel, I reckon it's that. Fear of the Greeks."

"So are you in hock to him?"

"Kind of. Indirectly. He's with a bunch of knockabouts in Sydney who call themselves the Combine. The number one man there is Abe Saffron. It was Abe who bankrolled our nightclub. You've heard of him?"

"Who hasn't? So it's organised crime?"

"Not that organised. They each run their own race, but they discuss things together – mostly to make sure they keep out of one another's way. And they have some deals in common. They do square-ups for each other too, when it's convenient. Do the wrong thing by Abe, you might find there's a Greek after you. And vice versa."

"So, you being in debt to one, means you're in debt to all of them?"

"Yeah. The Troubles, I call it."

"How much you owe?"

"Enough. More than I'd earn gross in two, maybe three years. That's including rorts."

At midday we stopped in the town of Nimmitabel. I went to the public phone, rang Avalon. The phone rang out the first time, so I redialled. Terry picked up on the third ring.

"We were out the back. Beautiful day here. How's it going?" he said.

"Nothing new. Anything there?"

"It's strange," he said, his voice dropping low. "That particular bloke you mentioned, well, he's gone *very* quiet. No one knows anything. I mean, there's *nothing*."

"What do you mean, nothing?"

"I mean nothing. He's not injured. Not dead. Not here. Not there. Not anywhere. Just . . . zip. Gone."

"That can't be good," I said.

"Good or not good, Annie and I are going home tomorrow."

"All right. I'll ring in a couple of days."

Denise was in the milk bar across the road, sitting in a booth by the front window. We ordered a plate of sandwiches and a pot of tea. As we waited, Denise was writing furiously in a notebook.

"For the novel?" I said.

She didn't look up. "I'm keeping a journal . . . very important."

She didn't stop scribbling, and I didn't try any further conversational gambits.

We drove through the treeless Monaro high plains for a couple of hours, pulled into Bungendore late afternoon. Some of the bush towns are nightmare zones: random, shitty streets with ugly, rundown buildings. You'd wonder how anyone could even stay there overnight. Then there are others with wide streets and avenues of century-old trees. They have big rambling Victorian pubs with shady verandas, like in a Drysdale painting, where you'd spend an afternoon playing pool and listening to the hill-billy jukebox. Bungendore was one of those.

We pulled up outside a rainbow-painted shopfront at the far end of the main street. It advertised kaftans, Indian cotton shirts, essential oils, Afghan coats, beads, sandals, handicrafts from Asia, books, magazines, Aquarian bits and pieces. Tarot readings and massage – strictly therapeutic – if that's what you wanted.

Inside was a forty-something woman with a wild mane of salt-and-pepper hair, olive skin, high cheekbones, an orange kaftan. Good-looking still. She saw me, blinked, then broke into a big smile. There were hugs and more smiles.

Denise sauntered in behind me. The woman's eyes opened wide. "And this is . . . ?"

I stepped back. "Shirley Hill. Denise Baillieu-Munden."

They embraced. Denise stood back and said, "You're the 'Gypsy Woman,' right?"

Shirl laughed then looked at me. "What does she know, Bill?"

"You'd be surprised," I said.

Eyes narrowing, she turned back to Denise. "And you'd be the 'Heiress Revolutionary'."

Denise bowed, smiling apologetically. "That label wasn't my idea."

"Well, we're honoured to get a visit from the famous," said Shirl.

If Denise was stung, she didn't show it.

"You staying? Come out to my place. Tons of room. I'm about to close up anyway."

We followed Shirl's multi-coloured VW out of town, and a little while later we were drinking red wine and lounging in cane chairs under a huge oak tree out front of an old stone farmhouse. The hillside sloped gently away in front of us, down to a woolshed and a nearly empty dam. A mob of galahs was picking through the grass, the afternoon sun threw long deep shadows. The air was soft and mild. Goat curry was bubbling in a pot in the kitchen, smelling good.

Swirling her wine around the glass, looking at us shrewdly, Shirley said, "I was expecting you."

"Auguries?" I said.

Shirley snorted. "Common sense."

"Anyone else been around?"

"Other than Max, you mean?"

"I was leaving him out for the moment, but yeah, other than Max."

She shook her head. "Should I be concerned?"

"I dunno. Max wrote a book. Never quite saw the light of day, but a few copies circulated. He mentioned you in passing. 'The Sexational Gypsy Woman'."

She laughed. "I haven't used that name for a while. Not since the 1962 Royal Easter Show. But yeah, he told me he was going to write something."

"When did you see him?"

"Over a year ago. He came through Bungendore with some awful show band."

"Hillbillies?"

"They played the bachelors and spinsters ball that year, back

240

there in the community hall."

"You must've been surprised to see him."

"I was. With him being supposedly dead and so on. He'd changed, though. A bit haggard-looking. Have you seen him?"

"I'm looking for him now."

"I don't know where he is."

"How's country life treating you?"

She smiled. "I *love* it here."

"A head shop. In *Bungendore*?" I said. "I wouldn't have picked this place as that great an opportunity."

"You'd be surprised. Mick Jagger stayed here for a while, making that film."

"One day I'll tell you a story about that," I said.

Shirl looked at me. "That's right, there was that business."

Denise looked very interested. I shook my head.

Shirl's face went totally blank. She gestured at the surrounding hills. "It's nice. People do day trips out from Canberra. Stickybeak at the weirdo's shop. Sometimes the cockies' wives sneak in and buy little bits and pieces, then after a while they ask about a tarot reading. I'm way too hairy-arsed for stripping now, of course. Likewise the other."

She turned to Denise. "And what's your interest, deary?"

"I'm writing a book."

Shirl pulled a face, kind of a mock "Wooo, I'm so impressed." What she said was, "*Another* book." Looked at me, then back to Denise, her voice suddenly steely, "Just leave me out of it, sweetheart, All right?"

"But you're such a colourful figure, Shirl," I said.

"I'm the harmless old beatnik lady here, and that'll do me nicely. The locals wouldn't understand the gun-moll/stripper thing so well."

"Any idea where I should go next, Shirl?" I said.

"To find Max?"

She was silent for a bit. Then suddenly very serious.

"Please, no," I said. "I don't want a tarot reading."

She shook her head. "I was thinking more the *I Ching*."

I'd stopped grinning. "Last time you read the tea leaves I ended up in jail."

Shirl made an airy gesture and left the room, returning with her book and coins.

"I'm serious, Shirl. Don't do it," I said.

She looked at me and her smile vanished. Her head tilted, eyes wide, peering into my face.

"Oh god, what's happened?" she said.

Denise looked at me, confused.

"Huh?" I said.

"Oh Bill, something has happened."

I shook my head, put my hand on top of Shirl's. She let go of the coins. "I need to find Max – that's it, Shirl. Anything you know that'll help, please tell me. He specifically mentioned you in this fucking loony book of his. He's playing some typical bloody unnecessarily complicated Max game. And you're in it."

Shirl kept staring at me, reluctant to let me change the subject so easily. The frown stayed. She turned to Denise. "He needs a lot more than he lets on, this one."

Denise nodded seriously, said nothing.

"Ah, just like everyone else, Shirl," I said.

She turned back to me, and after a few seconds she relaxed, took her hand back, lit a cig. "Our Max. Yep. Only one oar in the water, poor old thing. But he really is a bit psychic, you know."

"Psycho, more like,' I said.

"Not all that different." She sighed. "When he was here, I saw him, he saw me, we said hello. We didn't talk that much. He's on the gear, the bad stuff, you know that?"

"I know. What about the mob he was travelling with?"

"The group? They were called something like 'Dorothy McKay and the,' ah – no, maybe Doris something. 'Doris McCloud and her Silver Linings.' That was it. Like I said, they weren't great."

In the distance a brown Holden Kingswood appeared on the dirt road leading into the property and drove carefully along the rough track towards us. It slowly came to a stop at the closed gate down by the dam, a hundred yards from where we sat. Just the driver, no one else in the car that I could see.

We'd stopped talking.

"A mate of yours?" I said to Shirl.

She shook her head, staring at the car. "Sometimes they drive out to look at the hippies."

I stood up and walked down the path towards the gate.

When I was halfway there, the car reversed smartly, did a three-point turn and was gone. I turned and headed back. My panel van was parked next to Shirl's house, plainly visible from the gate.

Back on the verandah, I said to Shirl, "A favour."

"Yes?" Warily.

"Can we do a car swap? Let us take your VW, we'll leave you the panel van. I'll swap it back in a few days."

"All right, but look after my little car, won't you?"

"Yeah. And leave the panel van where it can be seen from the road. A mate of mine named Terry will be down some time to collect it, okay?"

She nodded. "Will you leave in the morning?"

"Tonight."

"But you'll have some curry first."

We left late. Shirl gave Denise a hug, a warm one, then the icy tones again. "I meant what I said, sweetheart. You leave me right out of whatever it is you're writing."

We stayed in a caravan park in Queanbeyan, the next big town along the road. In the morning I bought an old Holden ute from a car yard in the main street. It had a couple of small dings, but only 100,000 miles on the clock, and the dull grey duco was pretty clean. Had a tonneau cover on the back as well, with no rips in it. Just like thousands of cars on the bush roads, could belong to an old cockie, a tradie, or any sort of rural worker. I left Shirl's car parked outside the Coles, and we took off.

Denise had been pretty quiet since Shirl's parting words, but once we got on the road out of Queanbeyan, it was like the hoo-doo wore off, and she loosened up again. After twenty minutes driving she said, "So what do you make of that car last night?"

"Don't know what to make of it," I said.

She looked at me. "You have a theory?"

I had a couple of them, but I shook my head, kept them to myself.

That night, we were at the RSL Club in Goulburn, two hours away, but that was far enough. The dining room was a quarter-full with country town nobodies, half-drunk sales reps, wool classers, a few cockies. But they were cheerful enough, and a rowdy racket was spilling in from the pokies in the next room.

Denise was more conservatively dressed tonight. Green woollen frock, silver and turquoise necklace, hair pinned back. No one looked twice at us. We each had a plate of steak and chips and a drink – gin for her, beer for me – in front of us.

Denise asked me again about the brown Kingswood. It had looked every bit a cop car, and the distant glimpse I got of the driver – red neck, grey suit – supported that. But it could as easily have been a surveyor or a real estate agent. Even the noxious weeds inspector.

"But who in the world could have known we were at Shirl's?" Denise asked. "That's what I can't figure."

She continued, thinking aloud more than anything. "How about this: Your mate Multi is in with the cops. Local. Maybe Melbourne detectives too. Maybe Armed Robbery Squad."

"*Maybe.*"

"Yeah, maybe. But just say. He could've tipped them off, and now they're following you. Us."

I shook my head. "This is out of their league. Too clever by half."

She looked at me with unconcealed doubt now.

"Your real question is, am I being a paranoid ratbag?" I said.

"If you prefer." She smiled nicely. Her face was bright.

"Sometimes I can't tell, to be honest. But I was dead sure I didn't want to stay at Shirl's after seeing that moreton in the Kingswood."

"'Moreton'?"

"Snoop. Tattle-tale. As in 'Moreton Bay fig.' As in 'gig'."

"'Gig'?"

"Equals 'snoop,' 'tattle-tale.' Like I said."

She nodded.

"For the book?" I said.

"Would that be a problem?"

"Remember what Shirl said to you?" I said.

"Yeah?" Slowly.

"I'd sort of assumed that since you'd hung around with Stan and Jimmy, and you'd seen the inside of a jail, you'd understand without having to be told."

Smile gone, suddenly all business, Denise leaned forward. "Keep my mouth shut?"

"Yep."

She leaned back briskly. "Of course. Betray no secrets. But a little mix'n'match. You *have* to do that, otherwise no books would ever get written. Okay, say I leave Multi and Vi right out – probably will, actually. But what if I made up a whole other character who was kind of a combination of Shirl and Vi?"

"Then they'd both have the shits with you."

Denise finished her plate and pushed it to one side. She lit a cigarette, leaned back, elbow propped on her other hand, ciggy near her mouth.

"People are going to have the shits anyway. Actually, the way I'm thinking, my book's going to be more centred on the main character, a young bookish woman who gets way out of her depth with outlaws and drug addicts and stuff. But she's so taken with the romance of it she can't tear herself away."

"Romance?"

"Criminal chic."

"Like that conversation in Max's book, you and him?" I said.

"Oh *please*."

"Made you out to be sort of—"

"Naïve and stupid."

"And *built*."

She laughed. "Yeah, the blond uni girl with the tits. It's been a long time since I was at uni. And as for the Bardot tits . . ."

"He meant it as a compliment. He's a Jayne Mansfield–Marilyn Monroe man from way back."

She laughed again, and stood up.

I reached out and held her hand. "The ones you've got are more than fine."

She did a little mock-shy curtsy.

We paid up, drifted over to the banks of pokies. Denise dropped five bucks in the Aztecs, then won ten, then lost seven, won another ten.

"You're as lit up as that machine," I said.

"This is fun," she said. "Very Sydney."

"We're nowhere near Sydney."

"You know what I mean. *Not* Melbourne."

She stopped playing, turned to face me.

"You ever rort these?"

"Tried a few times. Some hardheads can work the handle on the old one-armed bandit type. You sort of half crank it, jiggle each wheel into place one at a time. But it's harder than fly-casting. I never got the hang of it. Best way is to have someone inside to help you. If a machine goes off more than once an hour they shut it down, get the mechanic in. They've probably got a bloke here full-time."

She shook her head, smiling, said more to herself than to me, "*So* Sydney."

We left after an hour, went back to our room in the Tattersall's Hotel, the third best berth the pub had.

By now there was no sneak-into-bed-after-lights-out stuff. Denise took her clothes off as casually and unselfconsciously as if we'd been together for months. I sat on the bed watching her. She got down to just her panties, turned to face me. Put her arms out and did a quick shimmy. Then turned sideways, legs straight, bum out, bending forward, girlie-mag style.

"Not Marilyn, huh?" She was smiling.

"You're real," I said.

She straightened up, lit a cig, then slumped on the end of the bed, her arm resting on her raised knee. "I did some photo modelling once. The poses they had you make, no woman in the history of the world *ever* stood like that of her own free will."

Breakfast next morning at the Paragon Café. Denise had the denim jacket on, a different blouse underneath. Pale silk, with a twenties man's knitted vest over that. We were sitting in an old walnut-veneered booth. The place was busy.

"So . . ." Denise, elbows on the table, holding a steaming cup of tea in two hands, eyeing me very closely. "Something I wanted to ask you."

"Yeah?"

"So far, you've very conspicuously *not* mentioned a couple of important cast members in this little melodrama of ours." She took a sip of tea, enjoying herself here. "And I'm wondering why."

"About whom might you be wondering the most?" I said.

"For starters, the character Max calls 'Barry.' Who would be in real life rather like—"

"Barry Geddins," I said. "Standover yob. Did you know him?"

Suddenly quite sober, smile gone. "He was there at the double-cross. The shootout in South Melbourne. It happened pretty much the way Max describes it. But, you know, Max didn't quite capture how freaky that guy really is." She actually shuddered.

"And he somehow turned up at the crash scene, according to Max." I said.

She looked at me meaningfully, but I wasn't quite sure what her meaning might be. "What Shirl said about the psycho–psychic connection? That was true of him. He had . . . *powers*."

I didn't say anything.

"Heroin is evil," she said. "I mean, it's *supernaturally* evil and it attracts evil people. He was evil."

She was silent for a moment, then snapped out of it. "But see, this is what gets me. You haven't once asked me if I know where he is now, what he might be up to."

Again, too quick by half.

"I know him," I said. "And I've had dealings with him. Recently."

She tilted her head a fraction, waiting for me to go on. Then she said, "Barry works for the Combine?"

I nodded.

"And . . . ?"

"And nothing. He's Barry Geddins, loony. Current whereabouts unknown."

She waited for a moment then lit a cigarette. "So, where to today, cap'n?"

"First the department store up the road."

We went to the Dimmeys in the main street, then the disposal store opposite, ended up with a small but sturdy tent, a double sleeping bag, a billy and a primus, a Tilley lamp, groundsheets, a tomahawk, a couple of jerry cans, a thermos. Takeaway sandwiches from the Paragon, and we were off.

It was inexpensive stuff I'd bought, but it cut deep into my remaining road money. I did my best not to think about what would happen if I was to run right out.

Driving north from Goulburn, we saw in the distance the ancient jail Stan had busted out of way back when. Neither of us made any comment. At the edge of town I hung a left onto a back road that took us through thirty miles of rolling pasture to Taralga, a sleepy little town with a main street of old stone buildings. Another of the nice ones. You could imagine bushrangers like Ben Hall and Frankie Gardiner, or Captain Thunderbolt, taking the town hostage, gathering the entire population in the pub, standing drinks for all, roasting a side of beef, with a fiddler playing all day and all night.

Or maybe the locals were scared shitless, couldn't wait for the outlaws to be on their way. Maybe the outlaws were more like Barry Geddins.

The road turned to gravel, went uphill for ten miles or so. The temperature dropped. The pastures gave way to scrubby eucalyptus forest, which became more stunted the higher we got.

The sound of the car's motor went from a quiet hum to a solid throb to a near-roar. Whatever bog they'd put in the muffler had fallen out. I'd long since concluded it was much longer in the tooth than the 100,000 on the clock.

But the driving was nice with Denise sitting next to me, her window half-open, hair flying. The countryside was your typical New South Wales Central Highlands – scrappy pastures, falling-down fences, the occasional rundown house with wrecked cars and tractors strewn about, lumpy brooding hills. Mobs of crows and galahs browsing by the roadside. Very little traffic. Denise chatted happily for a while, then we both went quiet, enjoying the movement.

On the other side, a long, steep, scary downhill drive. The Holden handled like a dining table on roller skates. We crossed a river at the bottom. Halfway up a hill, a truck going way too fast nearly took us out. Then at the top, a flat plateau, open pasture again. We stopped at a sunny spot protected by ancient pines, fired up the primus and boiled the billy. Other than the truck, we hadn't seen another vehicle for the past hour.

We sat on a rock, drinking our mugs of tea.

I said to Denise, "How do you rate Max's work?"

She looked at me, unsure.

"His music?"

"I already know about that. He can play anything, so long as it's in the key of C. No, I meant his writing. You being a professional."

"No need to be snarky." She thought a moment. "It's very . . ."

"Sydney?"

"It's very *Max*. It has voice."

"*Voice*?"

"And he does the unreliable narrator thing really quite well."

"He's certainly proved himself unreliable over many years."

"No, it's a formal term. I mean like the bit at the party where he hallucinates the cops hidden in the trees?"

"Did it really happen?"

She shrugged. "Could've."

"What about the you and Cathy lesbian thing?"

"What about it?"

"Bob Gould thought the book needed more of that. But, I mean, was that bit true?"

She actually looked away.

"Aha," I said. "A rare moment of shyness."

She turned. "Yeah? Well what about *your* 'you and Cathy thing'? Cathy being the *other* person you've conspicuously not mentioned."

"There was a thing, but it wasn't much of a thing. And it was long over by the time Max and Cathy did the drug rip. That was Max spicing up the story. You know, the unreliable narrator."

She took that in, looked off into the distance.

"Cathy was Cathy," she said quietly. "She did whatever she wanted, more than anyone I've ever known. She was a force of nature." She turned to me. "She was hard to resist."

"Is your book about you, or her?"

She was silent for a few seconds. "Neither. Both. I don't know yet."

"Because people think that photo of her, robbing the petrol station, and the movie film, they now think that's you, the heiress. They lose the fact that you *took* the pictures."

"Yeah, but there's a simple marketing, public relations advantage right there. The advice we've had is to go with what the public already knows, or thinks it knows, even if that's arse-up."

We drove on. Dirty grey clouds came over, the bush lost colour. We were silent for a long stretch. We dodged Oberon, headed west off the plateau and pulled into a cold and misty Bathurst at four o'clock.

I slowly drove the length of the main street, then back again, until I saw what I was looking for. I parked, turned to Denise, and said, "You better sit this one out."

"I won't say a fucking *thing*," crossing her heart and presumably hoping to die.

I shook my head. "Doesn't matter. This one most likely won't even acknowledge *me*. And if you're there . . ."

"Okay," she said brightly.

I walked back down the street to a shop with "Bathurst Furniture Bazaar" above the awning. Smaller signs read, "Antiques Bought and Sold," "Curios," "Tools," "Colonial Bric a Brac." Over the door another small sign: "Licensed Dealer G. Conroy."

The inside was a long, wide space with a high pressed-metal ceiling. To the left were rows of tightly arranged tables and chairs, old lounge suites, cabinet radios. On the right were lamps, luggage, upholstered chairs, smoker's companions, ugly paintings, frames, mantel radios, fish tanks, golf sticks, dusty fishing rods, tool boxes, a couple of banjo-mandolins and an Italian guitar with three strings.

No one to be seen. I called out hello, but there was no answer.

I waited a few minutes. Nothing. I went to the back of the shop, where there was a desk with piles of papers, an ashtray, tools. I kept going, through a cramped passageway, past a messy kitchen and toilet, out the back door. To my right the building extended back another thirty feet, an old stone warehouse or maybe a former blacksmith's, with a loading dock. It had a heavy double door with a solid padlock on it. An old Morris van was parked in the back driveway.

I went back into the shop, out the front door, and walked slowly down the street, away from where the car was parked. I turned into a side street, circled all the way round to the back lane and into the yard where the Morris was parked, then tip-toed through the back door.

A gnomish, cranky-looking man of indeterminate age, with a scrunched-up face and a shock of brown and grey hair, dressed in dusty trousers and work shirt, was standing in the shop's front doorway, peering suspiciously down the street.

"I'm here, George."

He spun around quickly, waved dismissively and shook his head. "I'm not bloody well talking to you." A touch of cockney in the accent.

I waited by his desk, but he didn't come any closer, instead took himself off into one of the twisting passageways running between rows of battered wardrobes and kitchen cabinets. I could hear him banging around, but couldn't see him.

I sat down and started leafing through the *Daily Telegraph* on the table. Occasional bangs and thumps came from the maze, but no one showed.

"I've got all the time in the world, George," I called out. "So why not come out now. You'll have to sooner or later."

"Piss off," he said.

A shadow in the doorway. Denise was standing at the threshold, hands on her hips, taking in the scene.

She marched in, turned left, disappeared down a passageway, calling out, "George! You get out here. *Right* now."

The banging stopped. Silence.

"You heard me!"

I couldn't see either of them, but I heard firm footsteps, a yowl of pain, and some clumsy shuffling. A few seconds later George emerged out of the gloom, grimacing, Denise behind him. She had him firmly by the ear, which she'd twisted so that he was walking half-crooked.

She pushed him over to the desk, let him go with a shove. "Don't tell me. This *has* to be Steptoe," she said to me.

"The same. Sit down, Georgie," I said.

Which he did, rubbing his ear, looking from me to Denise.

"Well-known receiver of stolen goods and one-time proprietor of 'Georgie's World of Bargains' of Parramatta Road, Camperdown. Go to Georgie, he'll see you right. He'll give you a price for warmish items, no worries. But then he might just let the jacks know. And then go ahead and sell the same goods and split the take with those same jacks. Right, Georgie?"

Now he was sheepish and ingratiating. "I never done that to you, Billy, you know that."

"No bullshit now, Georgie. Max Perkal was here. I want you to tell me when, and why."

"Year before last. Came in, bought a guitar and an amplifier."

"What sort?"

"Eh?"

"What brand?"

He looked off. "The guitar, oh, the Australian one. Maton. I can't remember the amplifier. Australian-made, though."

"A Moody."

"Yeah, that one, that's right."

"And since then?"

Looked at me quickly. "Never seen him since. That's true, Billy. Never seen him."

"Know what he wanted the guitar for?"

"He had a job. Working with that mob."

"What mob?"

"The old sheila with the group. Can't remember the name. They come through here every year or so."

"When was the last time?"

"Couldn't tell you. Not my cup of tea."

"Now Georgie, I want you to think hard before you answer this. You being who you are, and having seen Max, who was widely believed to be dead – that must've struck you as the sort of information that others might be interested in."

He was already shaking his head. "Nuh, I never, Billy, I never. You and Max – I wouldn't do that."

"Didn't mention it to anyone, ever?"

"No one. Never." Georgie's confidence was growing, each time he repeated the denial, slowly convincing himself.

We camped that night by the Turon River, a mile outside the almost-ghost town of Sofala. I'd knocked on the farmer's door and politely asked permission, which was given. Our tent was set up on a grassy rise above a bend in the fast-flowing river, well out of sight of the road.

We'd eaten a Chinese dinner in town and now we had a good fire going and a bottle of Penfolds red, which we were drinking out of tin mugs, half-demolished. There was still a touch of blue light in the sky, but a sharp, crisp chill was rising. We were propped up against logs, facing each other across the fire. Warm in front, freezing at the back.

I topped up Denise's mug. "I got to say, back there, you flushed little Georgie out of his rathole in fine style," I said.

"I heard that pommy accent and I just knew he'd be a fore-lock-tugger of the old school. My father had a good way of dealing with that type."

"The lower orders, you mean."

"It worked, didn't it?"

"But we got nothing from him. Not really."

Denise straightened herself, pulled a sleeping bag over her knees, patted it down around her curves. "So you figure that none of that list in the book is an accident? There's a point to it?"

"Yeah, I know, it sounds thin all right. But it's the way Max does things: never say or do anything directly if you can go round about."

"Unreliable narrator," she said.

"Yeah, that."

We were silent a while. Denise had written in her journal then rolled a slim hash joint, as she did every night. This time I'd taken a couple of puffs. The night was still, and the river seemed loud. But nice.

"Anyway," she said. "This is what I don't get. We outran the posse in Gippsland. But now . . ."

"We're leaving a trail wider than the Hume Highway?"

"Yeah. Dropping in on notorious give-ups like that character back there. Max and everyone else always told me you were Mr *Super* Secretive. Couldn't be contacted. Lived in a secret hideaway."

"When the Troubles started, I kept out of the way best I could. Then it became a habit. I got to like it."

"And now?"

"Sometimes you have to sneak around to get things done. But other times it's better to shake the bejesus out of everything, see what falls out of the tree."

We sat and listened to the river. The sky got dark. There was no moon, but the stars shone as brightly as ever they did.

After a while Denise said, "You know, you could do a book about *your* life."

"I'll leave that caper to Max. He did one years ago, did you know that? Back in 1960, somewhere around then. Called *Confessions of a Downbeat Daddio.*"

She didn't laugh. "I'm serious, Bill. There's one in the pipeline now, in Melbourne. A bloke named Brian. one-time police informer. Not like Georgie, this is the guy who blew the whistle on police pay-offs at the royal commission. He's working with a journo, but it's the crook's point of view."

"'Criminal chic'?"

"Mock away all you like. But you just wait and see what happens."

"You could be right. Like the old stories about bushrangers and the traps. No one *ever* barracked for the traps, right? But what about your film, that really going to happen?"

She nodded vigorously. "Australian film. There's something brewing there, for sure. I've got a bunch of friends, they're all learning filmmaking. At tech, at the new film and TV school."

"Yeah?"

"They're making shorts and documentaries, mostly. But why not feature films?"

"What about surf films?" I said.

Her face went blank. "What about them?"

"Never mind."

"Anyway," she said, "Australian films, Australian settings. With genuine Australian characters."

"That's what you're aiming at?" I said.

"My fucking oath I am," she said. "The book first, then the film."

"Where does the money come from?"

She smiled, very pleased with herself. "That's the trick of it. Getting the money. My brother will help with that side of it."

"The old boys' network."

"Not only. What you do, you tap all these Johnny-come-latelys

– property developers, TV stars, advertising people, sportsmen – who are cashed up but a little bit unsure of themselves still. You give them a chance to buy into something to do with culture. They get to meet actors, go to good parties. Maybe make some money back. At the same time, Richard and a few of his friends are working on the other side of it, talking with people in the government about creating tax concessions for film investors. So it's in the investors' interests too."

"Your brother and his private school pals. At least the Combine lets wogs in."

Denise went quiet again, then got up and walked off into the gloom, unbuttoning her jeans. "I hope there are no snakes out here," she called out as she ducked behind a bush.

"Too cold," I said.

When she came back, she used her boot to roll the largest log back into the centre of the fire, got under the blanket again as it flared up.

"About that old boys thing—"

"Forget it," I said. "Your brother and his mates are probably all good chaps." I'd meant to sound neutral, but it came out sounding even more bitter than what I'd said before.

"They don't *only* look after themselves," Denise shot back.

"No doubt."

"It's true. These friends of mine who have a housing co-op in Collingwood? Richard put them in touch with the Housing Department, even negotiated on their behalf. The department bought the whole street in the end, set up a bunch of public housing co-ops."

"The state government?" I said.

"Hardly," she said, irritated. "No, the federal Labor boys. After all that time in opposition – twenty-something years? – they don't really know anyone in the business and finance world. Richard voted Labor. Lots of his friends did. Now they have the government's ear. You don't see the Labor boys telling them to piss off – they welcome the help."

I said, "Yeah?" trying to keep my voice even.

"Yeah. There are things happening no one has heard about yet. Not just the tax concessions for making films. Education projects in inner Melbourne. Richard is very involved in all that."

I kept my trap shut. After five minutes of uneasy silence Denise said, "Would you go another joint?"

We didn't return to the matter of Richard and string-pulling.

I woke up sometime late in the night. It was cosy in the tent. The river outside, unrelenting. The cold, the stars. I thought about the reason I'd given Denise for why I wasn't covering our tracks any more. What I'd told her was only half the truth. The other half was that having her along made me feel different. Like things could work out. Like she'd bestowed something on me. I thought I should tell her that in the morning.

I didn't get the chance. First thing, Denise announced she was bailing out, heading back to Melbourne. No, it wasn't because I'd sneered at her brother and his clique (though neither of us addressed that directly). What it was, she needed to get back home, back to her writing. Being on the road with me had been fun, but you know . . . And if I happened to get a hot tip on Max's whereabouts, then let her know and she'd be back in a flash. But meanwhile . . .

She had me drive her back to Bathurst, so she could catch the train to Sydney then a plane back to Melbourne. A long goodbye hug at the station and she was off. She left me a stock-cube-sized chunk of hash.

❖ ❖ ❖

I went to the public phone at the station. Terry and Anna were back in Balmain. All was good, no trouble. Still not a peep, not a whisper from or about Barry Geddins. Which was maybe the worst thing I could've heard.

Then I rang Eloise, still at her sister's. She was irritable, distracted.

"Everything okay there?" I said.

"No, it's not. The sprouts just *have* to go to back to school."

"Hang on another day or two, will you? I'm working on it."

"Where are you?"

"The bush."

"*Working* on it?"

"As a matter of fact, yes. I know it's a pain."

"It is. Anyway, Phil's houses."

"Yeah, what?"

"Well, nothing really solid yet. But it's interesting." Her tone changed, suddenly pleased and conspiratorial. "I asked a young friend of mine, in real estate, if he knew anything—"

"Jesus, I said keep it under your hat."

"It is. My friend will keep it quiet."

"Who is he?"

"No one you know." Somehow I guessed that meant a boy-friend. "Anyway, when I mentioned the street – in a roundabout way – I got a strange reaction. He was surprised, because another party had asked him about that street a couple of days before. He's looking into it now. So wait a couple of days, see what he can find."

"All right. I hope he can keep his trap shut."

"Oh, he can."

"Listen, Eloise. I haven't kicked in for a while, I know. I'm a bit short right now—."

Eloise interrupted me with a long, weary sigh. "When you can." No bitterness there.

I rang a number on the Central Coast, was given another number to ring, which I did, and finally got a name and a number back in Sydney. I made that call, wrote down an address in the town of Wellington, New South Wales. Less than a hundred miles from where I was, according to the NRMA map.

Back on the road, the day was cool and clear. A deep blue spring sky. The car drove well enough if you kept it slow, which I did. The muffler was noisy, but no worse than plenty of other cars on the bush roads.

By day's end I was pulling into Wellington. A mid-sized town at the junction of two rivers. Grain silos at the end of the main street, a grand 1930s pub. Not much else. I found the house I was looking for in Falls Road, on the other side of town, the last building before the paddocks.

The house was turn of the century and surprisingly large, red brick with an ornate timber veranda around it, a huge walnut tree on the left, old plum trees on the right, sitting on a few acres of what looked like good riverside dirt.

I parked on the road and walked the thirty yards up the house. The sun had just set, and the trees cast deep dark shadows. The closer I got, the more I could tell how run-down the house was. A wooden sign in the front yard, red lettering on white background, said "Church of the Living Spirit." Underneath in smaller letters, "Rev. Murray Leonard" and a phone number.

I stepped onto the veranda and up to the heavy front door, which had an ornate knocker and a leadlight glass panel. A dim light somewhere deep inside the house. The trees hadn't been pruned in an age, and no sun had shone on the veranda in a long time.

I knocked loud and slow. Heard footsteps approached almost immediately, and the door opened to reveal a tall, thin older guy with straggly grey hair. A long, mournful face, sad eyes. Alistair Sim with hair.

He looked at me a long time, standing there in the gloom.

"Murray, you old cunt, doing all right for yourself?" I said eventually.

He smiled and shook his head slowly. "*Open rebuke is better than secret love. Faithful are the wounds of a friend, but the kisses of an enemy are deceitful.* Proverbs, 27."

"Too true. Listen, Murray, I've been driving all day and I'm going to fair dinkum cark it if I don't get a cup of tea into me soon."

He put his hand out and we shook, then he stood aside and gestured me into the hallway. "Straight ahead into the kitchen."

I walked down the long wide hall. A large room on the left had fifteen or twenty upholstered chairs and couches arranged in a rough circle around a small table set on a Persian rug. A standard lamp with a weak bulb beside it.

I went to the end of the hall and into the large kitchen. A newspaper on the table, turned to the sports results. Next to that a book, closed. The room was comfortable, well equipped. Frilly stuff hanging from the shelves.

"You married that Salvation Army lass, didn't you?"

He shook his head. "She and I parted company years ago. This is Maria's doing. She's Estonian. She's away at the moment."

I sat down at the table, picked up the book. I read the title aloud. "*The Teachings of Silver Birch*. Becoming a tree surgeon, Murray?"

Murray filled an old kettle, put it on the gas.

"Delightful though it is to see old friends – especially you, Bill – I know you're not here to chat about the old days."

"Maybe I need that special comfort which is offered by the Church of the Spirit," I said.

It got no rise from him. He busied himself at the counter. Then said over his shoulder, "You in trouble?"

"I'm looking for Max Perkal."

Murray waited for me to go on. I waited for him.

He bought two mugs over to the table. "Max was cutting quite a trail for a while there, wasn't he? Armed rob . . . and then writing a book."

"How'd you know about that?"

"He told me."

We sat in silence while the kettle boiled. Then Murray stood up, poured the water into the pot, brought it to the table.

"So, looks like a beaut old rort here, Murray."

He looked at me sadly.

"Oh, I'm being suspicious and unkind, right?"

"You know me well enough to think that, I suppose."

I did. Murray, who used to be known as Murray Liddicoat, had at various times been a private inquiry agent, a drunk, a gambler, a street-corner preacher, and one of the most able bloodhounds who ever drew breath, like the one in the book who could shadow a drop of salt water from the Golden Gate to Hong Kong without losing sight of it. He was a crook and a wastrel who took his religion seriously. Bits of it, anyway. Last seen in Sydney doing late-night television advertisements for a furniture warehouse, promising a percentage of the profits would "go to charity." The gig went well until a journo from *This Day Tonight* decided to follow the money.

"You teetotal, still?" I asked.

"Except when I'm not. I try to save the sprees for special occasions."

"Nice house."

"A grateful member of the flock lets us live here rent-free."

"Right."

"She has cancer. She appreciates my ministry . . ."

"Well, that's nice," I said. "Not having cancer, of course."

A long sad sigh from Murray. "I do no harm," he said. Then in a very different voice, not the god-bothering sing-song but a lower, street-corner tone, "But don't think you can meddle with what I've got here."

"I know, Murray, I'm being an arse. You never did the wrong thing by me. Not to pry, but would cancer generally be involved in what happens here?"

"People need help. All sorts of people. All sorts of need. Illness is a big part of it, but I don't offer cures. I'm not a quack."

"Yeah, fair enough. Anyway, as you guessed, I'm looking for Max. I only found out a couple of weeks ago that he's still alive."

"I didn't think it was *that* big a secret," he said.

"I've been keeping my head down, my trap shut."

"*Whoso keepeth his mouth and his tongue keepeth his soul from troubles,*" he said.

"Well, up to a point, yeah, that was my reasoning. But now . . . now it's gone way past that. When did you see Max?"

"He came through town a year and half ago. I let him stay here a couple of nights. Maria didn't take to him. Said there was evil following him."

Murray glanced at the clock on the wall, and didn't try to

hide it.

"Someone coming?" I said.

"A service tonight at seven," he said. "You're welcome to attend, of course, provided you don't misbehave."

"Thanks anyway. Out of interest, how many mugs coming?"

"Twenty brothers and sisters, thereabouts."

"Not to mention the spirits, eh?"

"You'd be surprised who and what turns up." He fixed me with a look, smiling slightly. I couldn't tell whether it was smugness or something way creepier.

"Sorry to say it, Murray, but you were much more fun in the old skid-row days."

"You too," he said, smiling again. "But *whoredom and wine and new wine take away the heart.*"

"Right."

"Hosea, 4:11."

"Good-o. So, any thoughts on how to find Max? How would *you* go about finding Max?"

"If it were here, at one of our services, and someone asked me that, I'd cite Mark, 11:24. *What things soever ye desire, when ye pray, believe that ye receive them, and ye shall have them.*"

"Yeah? And . . . ?"

"And maybe I'd quote James, 1:5 to 6. *If any of you lack wisdom, let him ask of God, that giveth to all men liberally, and upbraideth not; and it shall be given him. But let him ask in faith, nothing wavering. For he that wavereth is like a wave of the sea driven with the wind and tossed.*"

"Meaning?"

"Then I'd say, the Holy Spirit knows the location of every lost thing and every hidden thing. And He can tell you."

"Meaning, cross Murray's palm with spondulicks."

"Meaning, if you have faith. Meaning, if you listen to the quiet voice. Meaning, if you don't fuck about."

I sat back. "You and the riddles, Murray. How 'bout you stick them up your arse."

Murray had preached at the Sydney Domain and outside

262

Town Hall Station, and he wasn't so easily heckled. He dropped his voice and leaned forward. "Max is somewhere. He knows where he is."

I got up, shaking my head..

A knock at the door. A woman's voice calling, "Woohoo? Hello?"

A muffled man's voice, too. And a car door slamming.

I headed down the hallway to the front door. Murray followed me.

A middle-aged woman and a beaten-looking old guy with a plastered-down comb-over stood on the porch. Three more people were walking up the path.

"Ooh, hello," the woman said when she saw me. "Another seeker?" she said to Murray.

"Yes, a seeker, a poor wayfarer, like all of us. Regrettably, Brother William won't be staying."

He opened the screen door, smiling. I stepped out, they stepped in, and so did the next lot.

"Go on through," Murray said to them. "I'll join you shortly." And before they were out of earshot he said to me in a wise and kindly stage whisper, "You have the answer you seek, brother."

"Huh?"

"You need no new information. The Great Spirit is telling you. You need only to listen."

The old couple had stopped. They were loving it.

"With your heart," Murray said.

"Meaning he's already told me? Or he's going to tell me?"

We were on the verandah now. The old couple's car was near the door. A Mercedes, not old.

I was still looking at it when Murray slipped something into my shirt pocket. I glanced down. A folded wad of money.

I looked at Murray.

"*Be not forgetful to entertain strangers,*" he said. "*For thereby some have entertained angels unawares.*" He closed the door on me.

263

I drove till midnight, camped on the dirt half a mile off the main road. Moved on the next morning, through long lonely stretches of flat country. Tall, straggly gums gave way to the lower, wide-spreading river redgums and coolabahs. Then long tracts of cypress, then mulga. Great mobs of cockatoos. Hawks and eagles in the sky. As the day wore on, the fences disappeared and I hit the saltbush country. An occasional emu by the road.

That night I camped by a river, and was woken in the morning by the birds: herons, egrets, swans, ducks, pelicans. Goshawks perched on the tallest dead trees. The land where the crow flies backwards, as they say. The river was thick and muddy, but it had a flow. I heated some baked beans, boiled an egg, then was gone.

I hit a far western town that afternoon, but Molly – "Motel Molly" – had long since abandoned the place. No one knew what had become of her and her teenage son. Or if they knew, they weren't telling the outsider. I drove out of town late afternoon into the desert country. The bitumen gave way to gravel. The car had meaty treads and gripped the loose surface well enough, but it was a slow, bumpy ride.

I camped that night in the saltbush, watched the sun set over the two thousand miles of nothing between me and the Indian Ocean.

I followed the single road north the next day. At lunchtime I filled up at a garage and went to use the public phone out front. It only offered operator-connected calls, which almost certainly meant there'd be at least one silent listener. So I drove on.

Next morning I stopped at the first town I came to. There was a public phone outside the single-person post office, and it was direct dial. I went to the milk bar, bought a sandwich and walked back to the phone booth with a pocketful of change. The day was cool, breezy.

My first call was to Sydney. Eloise and the kids were back home. The daughter came on the phone, told me a knock-knock joke, then the boy. Then Eloise.

"Sounds like everything's okay," I said.

"There's been no trouble," she said.

"Good."

"And I've got a little story for you."

I could hear the triumph in her voice.

"What?"

"Phil's houses. There *is* money involved. Quite a bit. Seems the state government might want those houses. The Department of Main Roads has big plans to build a flyover from the city right through Glebe and Annandale, to join up with Parramatta Road. A freeway right through the guts. The Western Distributor, they're calling it."

"Fuck me! First I've heard of it."

"It's still a secret. The government hasn't made anything public, but the word is out. Among *some* people, anyway. No one knows the exact route yet, because allegedly it still hasn't been decided. Phil and Joe might know something the others don't."

"Gee. Okay. That's good. If you hear any more, let me know."

"How would I do that, dear one? I don't even know where you are?"

"I'll ring in a few days."

"Hang on, something else."

"What?"

"Dad came around."

"Yeah?"

"Joe and Phil are upset, he said."

"Are they indeed?"

"Upset with *you*, that is."

"Yeah."

"At first, it was because you'd just vanished, when you're supposed to be on Phil's payroll."

"That's not exactly true, but go on."

"But then someone else on the payroll has become, ah, *scarce*, as it were. Some friend of theirs." She left a meaningful pause. "And now they're suspicious about what that might mean." She put a certain emphasis on the last bit, showing *she* understood what that meant, and wasn't going to spell it out. Old-time skills.

"Hmm," I said. "You didn't tell Donny about . . . recent events?"

"No." Said very quietly. "Anyway, as far as they're concerned, you've gone AWOL."

"That's not right, but whatever. If they've sent Donny along to you, that means they're putting something on the table."

"Yes. Without all the padding, it came down to: Come home now, all will be forgiven. You'll even get back pay for the missing weeks. Things will be sorted out."

"Otherwise?"

"Donny didn't say."

Next I rang Terry. It was 9 a.m. and although he was up, he was still yawning. I heard him light a cigarette.

"So," I said. "What's the mail?"

"It's fucking weird," he said. "Still no sign of your mate. But the dogs are barking."

"How so?"

"You speak to one source and you'll be told that certain crims decided Barry was just too much trouble and took action. Another will tell you the police did it. He's a rock spider, you know that?"

"I'd heard."

"A third line of thought is that the cops and crims got together and dealt with him."

"So everyone thinks he's gone?"

"Unless you go with yet another theory. That someone *did* have a go at him, it didn't take, and he's licking his wounds, preparing for a comeback."

"That's not what I want to hear," I said. "But it's the only explanation that really makes sense. Okay, what about Guilliat Street?

"Right." The heaviness left his voice. "The women's group moved into the biggest house. The first one. The bloke who lives just around the corner from them is a harbour worker, a good bloke, and he got the Seamen's Union to help out. Brought around some furniture, cots and beds and things. Probably hot, but who cares? The union got them a lawyer too."

"All right, And they'll piss off when I give the word?"

"Well, yeah. I think so."

"You *think* so?"

"The women are onside. It's the others."

"Go on."

"There's a group of musos setting up a studio in one place. And some silkscreen poster collective in the other. They might be harder to shift."

"Jesus. Fuck. That cat's right out of the bag."

"Funny thing, it started a bit of a land rush. Squatters are moving in all over the area. Those old houses in Glebe? Up near the uni? There's half a dozen or more squats there now. Another bunch down near the dog track. People are moving in – heads, students. They put new locks on the doors. Get the electricity and gas connected."

"No wonder Phil and Joe are spewing."

"I thought that's what you wanted."

"It is. I guess. But you've got to keep my name right out of it."

"I have. You're a hero, but an unknown one. All the kudos is coming to me."

"You're welcome to it. Hey, and thanks, Tez. For everything. It's big."

"It's okay. We're partners."

"Tell the squatters to keep a lookout."

"I told them that already. But I'm wondering, what's your grand plan here?"

"Stand by for updates," I said.

My grand plan? Good question.

A road train filled with cattle rumbled down the street. The first vehicle to pass the whole time I'd been there. It rolled right on through without stopping, leaving in its wake a smell of diesel and cow shit, and utter silence.

I walked back to the shop, bought a packet of cigs, got another handful of change and went back to the phone.

I rang a contact in Sydney, got a phone number for one Neville Wran, who had just become leader of the state Labor opposition. And the way things were shaping up, the likely next Premier of New South Wales. It took some blarney from me to get through to him, but I got there eventually. Last time we'd spoken was years ago, when he'd been a young law student and a bookie's penciller on the side. But like any good politician, he remembered exactly who I was and came on the line saying, "Good morning, Bill," with a balanced mix of friendliness and formality. "What can I do for you?"

I told him I'd heard some mail that the state government was planning to bulldoze huge parts of Glebe and Annandale to build a freeway. People whose houses might be in line for demolition were obviously very alarmed about the plans, which they said had been kept under wraps for sinister reasons. They'd heard that the current government, via the Department of Main Roads, was secretly buying up properties, doing deals with developers who'd bought up cheap housing after being tipped off in advance. So I was wondering, I said, what Labor's position on that business might be, should they win the upcoming election.

Wran cleared his throat, like he was talking to the TV news, not just lowly W. Glasheen, before delivering his reply. "Well, Bill, as you know, I come from Balmain myself. And I and the Labor Party would be opposed to any hasty plans for demolition of working-class housing which would destroy the social mix, character and heritage values of old inner Sydney. That's on the record as Labor policy."

I was silent for a moment. I'd obviously gone in the wrong way, and now he was talking on the record, in bullet-proof lingo. "That's very official-sounding, Nev," I said. "Are you blokes going to press ahead or not?"

"Could I ask what your interest in that might be, Bill?"

Did he know I had links to the Combine? "Some people I

268

know have, ah, have an involvement," I said.

Wran laughed. That was all I was going to get.

After I hung up I considered what he'd said. Decoded it *maybe* meant, all things being equal, they'd most likely go anti-freeway. Which also meant they could probably be persuaded to swing pro-freeway too.

I lit a cigarette, tried to follow my thoughts to their logical conclusion. Not so easy. I didn't know how this sort of shit was done. Phil, Joe, even Abe, they pulled strings all the time, bending circumstances to suit their interests, getting the mail from weak politicians and officials. I'd achieved nothing by ringing Neville. Maybe I'd even made things worse.

I rang Denise in Melbourne. She sounded happy that I'd called and asked how it was going, I said okay. I told her about my visit to Murray and described his spook act. She laughed.

"You should see this place I'm at," I said, looking out at the flat, dusty street, the endless nothing beyond that. "It's sure not Melbourne."

After a few minutes of chitchat I said, "So, your brother and the Federal government . . ."

"Oh Billy, let's not start that again," she said wearily. "He's who he is. He's my brother."

"No, no, it's not that. I didn't ring to be a shithead, I promise. This is something else. You told me how he went into bat for your friends in Collingwood. With the housing co-op? I've been wondering how he got the government interested in buying those houses."

Speaking carefully now, she said, "I might've overstated that a bit, trying to put you in your place." She laughed. "That particular deal didn't come off in the end. At least, it hasn't yet."

"Feel free to put me in my place anytime I'm being a dick."

"Hmm. Interesting way of putting it . . ."

"Right. Yeah, that too. But back to Richard. How did he go about it?"

"What do you mean?"

"Did he just ring up the department and say to the public

servant who happened to answer, 'Hey, my name's Richard and I've got a spiffing idea'?"

"Hardly." She laughed. "He dealt directly with the federal minister. Tom Uren. They're friends."

Bingo, I thought. "All right. Great. I need your brother's phone number."

"What the fuck, Billy?"

I was counting out ten-cent coins to make another call when I saw a figure come out of a building down the street – which had been deserted till then – and stare in my direction. It probably meant nothing, but still . . . I wandered back to the ute. The person – a portly middle-aged woman— was still staring at me, and making no attempt to conceal it. I nodded a good morning in her direction and drove away.

After a dusty few hours driving, I pulled into Brewarrina around lunchtime, stopped at the first public phone I saw and rang brother Richard. He was curious. Denise had told him I might be ringing him. It didn't go so well at first, each of us having major reservations about the other. But we got there. He wasn't the talking law book I'd thought he was. At least, not only that. And I guess I wasn't the lowlife chancer he'd first thought. Not only.

Once he warmed up he was quite keen to talk Labor politics. He cared a lot more than I did, but I was more or less able to keep up. He let on that he had certain ambitions himself in the political area, long term. Good for him. So I told him what I knew and what I suspected, and he responded with more than polite interest. He'd have a sniff around, he said. Could I leave it with him for a while, then ring back?

I had some lunch and bought some supplies. No one in Brewarrina took any special notice of me.

At three o'clock I rang Richard back. We were old comrades now, and he didn't try to hide his enthusiasm. Yes, what I'd suspected was in fact the case, and guess what? There's more. So he'd hatched this plan. What did I think? We mapped out the next few moves and arranged to talk again day after tomorrow.

I pitched my tent by the Barwon River, a mile out of town. Spent the next day fishing and reading. Fishing meant setting a handline and leaving the reel jammed in the crook of a tree while I sat back in the shade reading. No fish troubled the bait all day.

There was a group of blackfellas a quarter of a mile further up the river. In the afternoon an old couple wandered up and said hello, asked what I was doing. I said fishing, which gave them a good laugh. They left me two cod they'd caught. I couldn't see how they'd done it, since the only gear they had was a bit of old line wound around a stick with a rusty hook and a few budgie feathers.

I stayed by the river for the two days as arranged, went into Brewarrina at nine o'clock the next morning. I pulled up outside the Café Deluxe, got some change, went to the phone booth at the post office and dialled Richard in Melbourne. He answered after four rings, said he'd spoken to Tom Uren. Uren was interested. On the face of it. Yes, it all fitted with federal Labor policy regarding public housing and inner city conservation. But he couldn't act unilaterally. He'd need to take it up with the state mob. They might have their own ideas. "But that's a good result. So far," said Richard.

"Maybe not," I said. "I might've tipped our hand there, because I spoke to Neville Wran a few days ago." I told Richard exactly how the conversation had gone.

"Hmm," he said. "You should've left that alone. Oh well, it's done now. But from here on, it has to be hands-off. If the politicians get the sense we're pushing them, that the thing isn't under their control or could blow up, or that someone they don't know about might have an interest, anything like that, they'll dump the whole idea."

"I understand. So how long will that take?"

"I don't know. Three, six months. Maybe a year."

"Oh shit, that's way too long. Listen, Richard, how about we try to speed the process up a bit?"

"How?" he asked cagily.

"With some do-it-yourself-type public relations." I told him what I meant.

He wasn't too jazzed by my idea. "That could blow the whole thing."

"If it doesn't happen soon, it's useless to me anyway," I said.

I killed some time having tea and toast at the Café Deluxe, then just after ten went back to the phone booth and called the Third World Bookshop in Sydney. Bob Gould picked up. The combined vice and drug squad raid had gone splendidly, he said. He was sufficiently happy that he gave me the phone number I needed. That got me to the editor of the *Nation Review*. Who heard me out, though he sounded less than impressed. Still, I had a hunch he *was* interested, despite his show of indifference.

At eleven I rang Denise's number in Melbourne. No answer.

Another cup of tea. I watched truckies come and go.

At midday I rang again and she picked up. After we got the mutual hello dear, how're you going, I miss you, wish you were here stuff out of the way, I said, "Hey, I might have a bit of an ace investigative reporter–type magazine story for you. If you want to write it. Or know someone who does."

"Yes?" she said slowly, with doubt in her voice.

"About a women's refuge holding out against secret real estate deals. Speculators. All against a backdrop of freeways destroying old inner city communities. Very Sydney."

"The fuck, Billy?"

"The *Nation Review* is kind of interested, but not quite a hundred percent sold. Not yet."

"The fuck, Billy?" Laughing this time.

I gave her the *Review* editor's number, then Terry and Anna's. "The second number, that's my friends in Balmain. They'll show you the ropes, introduce you to the women's refuge crowd. If you want."

"Well, I suppose it can't hurt to at least ring them." Her words sounded detached, but I could tell she was fired up. "Thanks Billy. Seriously. So what are you going to do now?"

"I've come this far," I said. "I'll see it through."

"Meaning?"

"Meaning I'll track down the last name on Max's list," I said.

"Oh, forget that. It's a wild goose chase. Come to Melbourne and stay with me."

It was tempting.

"And wouldn't that be *names*, plural, to track down?" Denise asked. "The Cat, Brylcreem and Mr Bones. Right? Not to mention the Croaker."

"Brylcreem and Bones are in the UK, shoplifting. The Croaker died of a morphine overdose early this year. I'm down to just one name: the Cat."

"Maybe he's gone too?"

"He was at the races in Sydney two months ago. And if the book is to be believed, the Cat was the last person to have dealings with Max before he blew his mind. He's around somewhere."

"According to Professor Perkal, that would be—" I heard her riffling through the book, "That would be, ah, this: *A rundown tropical town . . . a dump. There was no surf, just shitty farm land round about. No natural features to speak of. There were no hippies, no trendies. Just white trash and blackfellas.* That would include an awful lot of New South Wales, would it not?"

"Most of Queensland, too. Where I am now, I can cut across to the coast, make my way back south, checking out the likely towns on the way."

"On the other hand, if you come to Melbourne, we'll have fun."

"How long is that offer good for?" I said.

"Not forever." A pause. "But for a little while yet."

"Keep a light in the window," I said.

❖ ❖ ❖

I crossed into Queensland and cut east through Roma, then Chinchilla, sleeping by creeks and billabongs. I pushed north east all the way up to Cooktown. It was definitely tropical. Also drab, untrendy, and without surf. So were Port Douglas, Cairns, Gordonvale, Innisfail, Tully, Ingham, and so on. So was most of northern Queensland.

But there was no Cat.

I checked in with Eloise again after a week. As I'd expected, Donny had been around again. He was frantic. I needed to front Joe and Phil, pronto. Or else.

"Or else what?" I said. Eloise said that's what she'd asked him. At which Donny had just shaken his head and said, This is bloody serious now. Abe's involved. Billy needed to sort this out as a matter of extreme urgency, or he, Donny, couldn't be held responsible. "Any message?" said Eloise.

"Not yet, but stand by."

After another week I'd worked my way down to Central Queensland. I became very familiar with the details of chemist shops, and was probably better provisioned with toothpicks, razor blades and underarm deodorant than anyone in the country.

My money was nearly gone. Canvas was showing through on the tyres, and the starter motor was on the way out. I signed on to do a day's work on a tomato farm, trimming the laterals off the bushes. That night I was sunburnt and sore, went into a dead sleep at eight thirty.

Two days later, further south, I took on three days' work chipping weeds in a sugar cane field. The first day was tough, by the third I felt okay. Then I did a whole week in a sugar mill – scored an easy job checking off the loads of cane that arrived hour after hour, day and night, on the puffing billy rail line. That time of year there was work to be had all over coastal Queensland, all of it low-paid.

I'd got my dress code worked out and become pretty much invisible: a bloke in his late thirties, maybe early forties, dressed in clean, faded King Gee work togs, driving an old but looked-after ute. I came and went, neither welcomed nor farewelled. Got nearly every job I asked for, though. I looked the part.

I avoided pubs, killed time off the road in movie theatres and drive-ins. Saw the year's big ones, *Serpico*, *The Sting*. Finally caught

American Graffiti, which had one scene I liked, hot rods in the pre-dawn, their lights on, driving slowly towards the camera with 'Green Onions' playing on the soundtrack. Saw some other films I liked, *The Long Goodbye* and *The Laughing Policeman.* Also a late-night double feature, *Badlands* and *Two-Lane Blacktop.* The latter was about a pair of longhaired street racers and a girl hitchhiker getting around the boondocks in an old Chevy. The longhairs enter into a driving duel with Warren Oates. One of the drifters was played by Dennis Wilson, the Beach Boy. Both films were a bit on the slow side, and the longhair actors were kind of wooden. But they were okay for late-night viewing.

Then it started raining. Monsoonal rain. A thunderstorm would build up all day, drop two or three inches in half an hour, then clear before evening. It was the same every afternoon. I worked a few days at a mill near Bundy, but the rain halted the cane cutting, so I moved on.

When it got too wet to camp out, I spent a few nights in a motel outside Brisbane. Watched late-night television. Saw an old movie I'd liked when it first came out years before, *Thunder Road.* Robert Mitchum driving moonshine out of the mountains in a hotted up car, outrunning the traps, stopping every now and then to drop in on a hillbilly party.

I crossed back into New South Wales, moved down through the Tweed Valley. There were longhaired, down-at-heel hitch-hikers everywhere. I picked up a couple at Murwillumbah. She was pregnant, he was drinking from a beer bottle, at one in the afternoon.

"Your muffler doesn't sound too good," he said.

I shrugged. "Been that way for a while."

"Pull up in the shade, if you like, I'll have a look."

Twenty minutes later, using a few bits of fencing wire and a pair of pliers, he'd managed to jerry-rig the exhaust, reduced the racket by two-thirds. I dropped them at the Burringbar turn-off, slipped them twenty bucks. I drove off with the radio playing for the first time since I'd bought the car.

I called into Byron Bay, even though it had hippies, trendies, diverting natural features *and* a surf break. There were head shops in the main street. Garish murals here and there. I bought a hamburger in the milk bar and kept going. Drove inland, through Lismore, the instant hippieville of Nimbin, month by month filling up with longhairs, dope-smokers, girls with long flowing hair in long flowing skirts, drooby strummers on street corners, their guitars always slightly out of tune. One kid was singing "Helpless, helpless, helpless, helpless." A cocky walking past caught my eye and muttered, "*Hope*less, more like."

The hills were green and lush, with clear streams running down through hidden valleys. I was told you could snap up an abandoned hundred-acre dairy farm with a rambling old timber house on it for a song. The hippies were realising now what Mullet and Katie had wigged years ago: this was prime dope-growing country. Provided you could hack all that hippie cuteness and macrobiotic chow.

I camped on a beach that night, and the next day drove south again. Just out of town I picked up two girls with backpacks, hitching in the rain, looking to get to the turn-off thirty miles down the way. They were friendly enough, but oddly serious too. In their early twenties, army shirts with the sleeves rolled up, dungarees, work boots. Smoking roll-your-owns. One was on the large side, dark haired, with a faint mo, the other slim, also dark. Both had track marks on their arms, I noticed, fairly recent.

We chatted a bit, and after I had apparently passed muster, the bigger girl, Marcie, sitting by the window, asked if I'd like a joint. I said no thanks, but they could go ahead if they wanted. They did. They dropped some pills, too.

We drove in silence for a while, then I asked where they were off to. A place up in the ranges, Margie said, suddenly half out of it. Thirty or forty women lived there, coming and going. No men, except for some children. She looked at me as she said it. They said they bounced back and forth between there and Sydney every few months.

"That'd be a separatist community, then?" I said.

They looked at me, surprised. Denise had hipped me to the term only the month before.

"Some of the women believe that when the San Andreas fault gives way and the west coast of America slips into the sea, it'll make a wave that's gonna sweep across the Pacific and hit Australia."

Yeah right, I thought. From the Northern to the Southern Hemisphere? I glanced quickly at her. She looked very earnest, no smile, so I said, "Really?"

"Yes. It'll be huge, of course. It'll go way inland. That's happened in the past, you know, it's in the archaeological record. And the wave is going to cause . . . well, chaos, obviously. It'll be the end of nearly everything. The patriarchy and capitalism will be finished."

At which the other girl, Jan, burst into stoned laughter.

"What about you?" Marcie said. "Where are you headed?"

I had to think for a second. "Nowhere much. I'm on a working holiday."

In the end I drove them all the way to the commune. Took the turn-off, threaded through the ranges all the way to their place. The rainforest closed in over the road, wild green hills, steep valleys and swollen streams. It looked okay from the driver's seat: by day there'd be birds, at night gliders and all the forest marsupials. But I imagined what it'd be like living rough in there, the damp, the ticks, the leeches, the snakes.

I gave a ride to a couple of teenage blackfellas hitching back down the hill. One had a guitar, no case. He snappily picked out instrumentals, 'Apache,' 'Theme for Young Lovers,' 'The Third Man,' all the way down the mountains, but scarcely said a word. After the kid had finished a version of 'Maria Elena,' his mate laughed and said, "Wesley's a guitar-playing Jesus, eh?" I agreed that he was.

As I was going to sleep that night, I thought about what I'd told the hitchhiker, about being on a working holiday, and the twinge of guilt I'd felt when I said it.

I drove on down to Kempsey, just a day's drive from Sydney. Out of the tropics now. Out of habit I stopped outside the chemist shop in the main street. The Cat was standing behind the counter. Fifty or so, well-fed, with a good head of neatly trimmed ginger hair, looking competent in his starched white coat and horn-rimmed specs, the sort of country town small businessman you wouldn't glance at twice. But if you did look a second time, you'd see he was a little over-groomed, the hair too neatly cut, nails too neatly trimmed. The eyes a little too wary and calculating. Look closely and you'd see the Darlinghurst spiv.

He was a crook from way back. When he'd had his shop at the Cross, the Cat was the person you saw to arrange an abortion, fill a dodgy script, sell you a syringe – even patch up a bullet wound, no questions asked, then slip you some pethidine to help with the pain. He had good relations with the racing fraternity, could get hold of the exotic substances they needed from time to time. The entertainment industry had occasion to call on him too, for instance when visiting celebrities found themselves without certain things they needed. All that had come undone when he was charged with indecent behaviour after putting the acid on an undercover cop in a public toilet in Hyde Park. His friends fixed it the first time. The second time he had to pay big to get out of it. The third time he went bush.

The Cat gave the merest flicker of the eyes when I came in, then extended his hand and said, "William. *So* wonderful to see you." He was smiling, but rattled.

I shook his hand. The shop was empty except for us.

"I was hoping I might run into you," I said.

"How did you know I was here?" he said.

"Plain old dumb luck, I guess."

"Really? Anyway, you want something, no doubt. People always do."

"I'm looking for Max Perkal"

He relaxed a little.

"Seen him recently?"

"I have. Twice, in fact. He came in and bought a glass syringe and black hair dye a couple of years ago. He was working as an entertainer at the time." His voice dropped. "Then I saw him again, about a year and a half ago."

"He'd run out of hair dye?"

He shook his head. "I filled a script for him."

"For?"

"Physeptone. That's methadone to you." His voice dropped further. "And some other things in that line."

"Know where he is now?"

He shook his head slowly.

"Any idea where he was headed?"

A long look, then a quick shake of the head. "He was rather a mess."

I thought it best to not push too hard, so I left. Told the Cat I might pop back later before I moved on. Do, he said.

Passing through Crescent Head that night, I saw a public phone with a queue outside it. I waited my turn for a free call, rang Terry in Sydney.

"Mullet's back home. With bad news, and good news," he said.

"Bad news first, please."

"Dennis Wilson and that *American Graffiti* guy, George? Looks like they're maybe not going to pick up *Crystal Dreams*. They think it's a bit too Aussie, or too strange, or maybe not strange *enough* for Yank audiences," Terry said.

"So it's all down the brasco?"

"The good news is that they're still interested. But they want something else."

"Such as?"

"Another film. Something a bit like *Crystal Dreams*, but with more of a proper story. With surf, dope, cars. And maybe a bit of fantasy, too. Thing is, I've been thinking about it, talking with Mullet. We could reuse some of the footage from *Crystal Dreams* – the big surf stuff, the sunrises over the Pacific Ocean, all that. We'd have to film some other bits to string it all together, though.

Add some motor bikes and car crashes. And more drugs."

"Cars, bikes and dope?"

"Yeah. And Australian settings. Outback, abos, koalas, that sort of thing. With tits."

"Mullet's all right at surfing and smoking joints, and filming other people surfing, but is he any sort of real director?"

"I dunno. Are you?"

Next morning I went back to the Cat's pharmacy.

"You're still here?" he said.

"When Max was in town did he see anyone else?"

"Not to my knowledge. But then, what do we know of others," he said, "and the things they get up to?"

"Food for thought," I said. "You're not in the phone book. The Pharmacy Guild didn't have you on their books."

"My, you've been busy. I suppose I should be flattered you've taken such an interest. No, I'm not in the book. And this place isn't mine, technically. It's a friend's. But now I'm intrigued. Why did you so want to find me?"

"Max wrote a book about his exploits in Melbourne. The book never really got around, but a few copies were circulated. He mentions you."

"By name?" Now he was alarmed.

"Just your nickname. Said you were hiding out in a drab coastal town in the tropics, with no trendies, no surfies."

"I was for a while. But can you see me living for long in a town with no surfie lads?"

"Right."

He got serious. "I got the distinct impression Max had a base of sorts, somewhere inland, and was heading back there after he'd cleaned up. I mean, *well* inland. A one- or two-day drive."

"That includes a lot of country."

"I did ask him where he was going, out of politeness. He said he'd make a suitable announcement when the time came. 'But meanwhile,' he said, 'the superior man must be on guard against what is not yet in sight.'" The Cat was grinning now.

"Always with Max, the riddles!"

"You said it."

"He was quite nuts, you realise. And he looked a fright."

I said toodle-oo but before I got to the door the Cat called out, "You could ask the music boys."

I turned back.

"The music boys," he said again, when I got back to the counter. "Max was in the district for a month or more before he did the detox. He became friends with the music boys. They used to play up at the pub on Saturday afternoons."

"Where are they now?"

"I wouldn't know, but maybe you could track them down. They called themselves the Mugs. With good reason, I understand."

No one I spoke to at the pub seemed to remember them or know them, and I left town. Next day, in a newsagent window in Taree, I saw a crudely done handbill: a dance at the Forster community hall the following night featuring the Muggs.

The Muggs were something different, only not in a good way. Surfie types, but not wholesome. They wore old-fashioned black stovepipes – no flares – and were clean shaven. Their hair was long and lank, and they wore pointy-toe boots, like a band from ten years ago. They played loud and fast, but with no finesse. The drummer was loose, the guitarist was just a bit out of tune and played mostly downstrokes – he couldn't really play lead. Still, there was a good crowd on hand. The singer kept telling them what a bunch of fucking idiots they were, but the more shit he put on them, the more they liked it.

During a break I asked the drummer if he knew Max Perkal, but he was well drunk and just looked at me blankly.

Late that night I called Terry.

"Jeez, where've you been?" he said.

"Around. What's new?"

"Lots. Your friend Denise was here," he said. "She stayed in your room, actually. We took her around to the squats. She met the women. Stayed there all day, went back the next day. I think she spoke to your political mate too."

"Who?"

"Neville Wran. And the story turned out pretty good. Did you see it? In last week's *Review*?"

"Where is Denise now?"

"Back in Melbourne."

"All right, thanks—"

"Wait!" said Terry. "She rang here yesterday, left a message for you. Kind of urgent, she said."

"Tell."

"She said a bloke named Fred has been in Melbourne, asking after you."

"Fred Slaney?"

"I don't know. A fat old bloke, she said. Menacing."

"Yeah, Fred Slaney. A cop. Did Denise see him?" I said

"No. But she heard he'd been to some place in Echuca. Saw someone named Helen."

"Helen Messenger." Bikey Vic's mum.

"Apparently he frightened the daylights out of her."

"What did he want?"

"Don't know."

"When was this?"

"A week ago. Anyway, Denise said to tell you Helen Messenger wants to talk to you. But she'll only talk in person."

Echuca was a long, long way from where I was.

"Terry, you still got that panel van?"

A weary sigh. "Yeah, I have. After sloping all the way down to fucking Bungendore to pick it up, yeah, I thought I'd hang on to it for a while. Why?"

"Sorry pal, but I need it. I can leave you a ute in exchange."

Next morning I managed to round up a copy of the previous week's *Nation Review*. The front page had a picture of a bunch of ragtag hippies in front of the Guilliat Street houses. Raised fists, anarchist flags, banner hanging from the veranda,

"HOUSING FOR PEOPLE! STOP DEVELOPERS!" The main story about real-estate shenanigans in inner Sydney had Denise's by-line. The next page included a picture of Neville Wran frowning, as though he was particularly pissed off about those housing shenanigans. I quickly skimmed the piece: all good.

I filled up, and hit the road. The tyres were totally bald now and I dared not go above thirty-five miles an hour. It took all day and some of the night to reach Sydney.

Late that night I pulled up outside Terry's place in Balmain. I bipped the horn and he came out grinning. He looked at the ute I was giving him. Till that moment I'd regarded it as my steadfast old faithful, but seeing it now through Terry's eyes, coated with four different shades of dirt (from dark red outback dust to light grey tropical mud), the tyres showing more canvas than rubber, the motor idling noisily because once stopped it would need to be push-started, exhaust pipe blowing blue smoke, it didn't look too impressive.

I said, "Can't beat the old FJ you-beaut. They go forever."

Terry looked at me but made no comment.

"I know. It's a shit heap," I said. "Funny, until now I thought it was a pretty good car. Listen Tez, I need a few bucks too."

Terry said, "Ah, it's all right," gave me the keys to the panel van and peeled some twenties off a roll. We shook hands and I was gone. At four in the morning I pulled off the Hume somewhere south of Sydney and slept.

The next day I took it slow, even though the panel van was like a rocket ship after the clapped-out article I'd been driving. I made it as far as Albury easily, slept by the river.

At ten the next morning I was in northern Victoria, knocking on Helen Messenger's door.

She was fifty or so. Blondie-grey haired. You could tell she'd had looks, but she was sad and careworn now, living alone.

"Vic was here," she said, after we'd got the introductions out of the way, "And he wants you to talk to you. Said for me to give you his number in Melbourne."

"What's he want with me?"

"He said your friend Max is still alive. That he wrote a book, even. Vic wants to find him."

"So does everyone."

"I don't," she said. "That bloke was nothing but trouble. I wish Vic would keep clear of him. He's better off with the tambourine-bangers in Sydney than with that shithead."

"I thought you'd taken a shine to our Max," I said.

She shook her head. "That mad old greybeard collywoggle?"

I looked hard at her. "When did you last see Max?"

"Eh?"

"You heard me."

She looked at me for a long moment then said quietly, "About six months ago."

"What did he want?"

"He was trying to get in touch with young Mark."

"Did you tell anyone you'd seen Max? Have you told Vic?"

She shook her head. "Didn't want him to get mixed up in all that again. I still don't."

"Where's Mark now?"

"I let him stay here for a while. He was a nice boy, really. He left with Max."

"Did you tell Vic that?"

She shook her head.

"Where are they now?" I said.

She looked at me and shook her head, her mouth tightly closed. She knew.

"I went looking for him in Wee Waa," I said. "Only found a place that Max had been, but ages ago."

"They're around there somewhere," she said quietly. "On some farm."

"'Plain View'?"

"Eh?"

"The name of the property."

She shrugged.

❖ ❖ ❖

It took me two and a half long days of driving north, back up the guts of New South Wales.

On the third day I pulled into the wreckers at Wee Waa where I'd bought the water pump. The same kid was there behind the counter.

He looked up when I walked in. No recognition.

"I was here a few months ago, bought a water pump."

He said, "Yeah?" apathetically.

"There was some crazy old bloke out the back there, mumbling to himself. Didn't talk English."

He brightened. "Oh yeah. The old bastard."

"You told me then you didn't know him."

"I didn't. But after you asked about him, I sort of remembered him the next time he came in. After that I kept noticing him around the district. Strange, eh?"

"Know where he lives?"

He shook his head. "Last I saw him he was driving an old shitheap out on the Spring Plain Road."

I spent the next day driving around north of town. Drove the length of the Spring Plain Road, then down every track that ran off it. I asked a cocky on a tractor if there was a mad old bloke lived somewhere out this way, he shook his head.

The country was dead flat, with only a few scraggly trees dotted about, but the soil looked brown and rich. There were billabongs and meandering creeks, some muddy bogs here and there. The paddocks were big. Cattle, cotton, sheep, wheat. All high and ripe. Some big harvesters working paddocks, but most of the crops were already done.

I pitched my tent next to a billabong, drove further south the next day. The rich soil gave way to sand, and suddenly I was in a thick forest of cypress pine. The Pilliga. I turned around and headed back into open farm country. I camped by a creek that night, and first thing next morning continued criss-crossing the countryside.

Around nine o'clock I passed an old, half-wrecked, once-fancy gate, big brick pillars either side. Arching above it was an old sign in rusty wrought iron with the name 'Plain View.'

I reversed back and drove slowly down the muddy track, through a stand of coolabahs and past some older trees into a neat parking area. There was a house and some orderly outbuildings, a couple of dusty cars parked in a shed.

A bent, craggy-faced old bloke with stringy grey hair was fiddling with a pump mounted on the back of a old Dodge truck.

The geezer from the wreckers. He scarcely glanced my way as I drove in.

I pulled up, got out of the Holden and walked over to him. He was still stooped over, mumbling to himself. He didn't look at me.

"You look like shit," I said.

He looked up, stared emptily at me for a few seconds and said, "You took your fucking time."

He *nearly* went. His tongue lolled back in his head, his eyes closed. I had his scrawny frame pinned to the dirt beneath me, my thumbs deep into his windpipe. He'd stopped fighting back.

Then I was waking up in the dirt, dizzy and nauseous. Max lay limp on the ground ten feet away, with a young guy and a well-dressed older fellow bending over him. The young guy was trying to pour water into his mouth. Max coughed a couple of times then started to retch.

I propped myself up on one elbow. There was a shovel lying next to me.

"Let the prick die," I said.

I sat up. They ignored me. The back of my head hurt like crazy. I put my hand to it. A wet bump. Blood on my fingers, but not too much.

Max opened his eyes, put his hand to his throat. He mumbled "Jesus fuck" in a raspy voice and started coughing again.

The younger guy turned around to me and said, "Bloody hell. You nearly choked him." He sounded almost hurt.

"It was a spur of the moment thing," I said. "If I'd been thinking straight, I would've just shot him."

The older man stood up, still looking at Max. "He'll be all right," he said, his voice clipped and precise.

He faced me then. Round-faced and tanned. Little black mo, dark hair oiled and brushed back. A little swarthy. Sports shirt and pressed trousers. A neat and no-nonsense sixty-something.

I got to my feet, brushed the dust off me, and faced him.

"You must be the Old Cunt," I said.

He laughed richly and put his hand out to shake. "Charles – Charlie – will do," he said. "Pleasure to meet you, Bill."

We shook.

The younger one stood up. A thin, rangy lad in his twenties. Dusty work clothes. A little weatherbeaten and hunted-looking. Longish fair hair. Not unlike Dennis Wilson.

"And you're the Boy Wonder," I said.

"Mark, actually." We shook.

"You ever do any acting?" I said.

He shrugged, which could've meant, Yeah, a bit. Or, Who cares? Or, I don't understand you. "You sure did a job on the old boy there," he said, nodding in Max's direction.

Max stood up slowly, still rubbing his neck. He looked at the three of us and smiled. "No real harm done, I suppose. Charlie, how about a pot of coffee for us all?"

"No coffee," I said. "No tea and scones. No talk. No nothing. Give me the money and the smack, and then I'm gone."

Max was nodding, too fast, too enthusiastically. "Yes, yes, of course. You've got the shits. I understand, I understand. Jesus, after everything? Yes, yes, only natural. We're going to get the stuff, sure thing, no risk. A hundred percent, *yes*. And the money. Oh boy. So glad you made it. But it *did* take you a fucking long time, you'll have to admit—"

I rushed at him again, but he quickly backed away and the other two stepped in front of me.

Charlie said, "Max. Shut up, will you?" He turned and said to me, "Come inside." And to Max and the kid, "I think we'd best show Bill the money." He waited.

Mark looked at Max and said, "Fair enough." Max nodded. They got in the truck, Mark in the driver's seat, and took off out the front gate.

"Let's get inside," said Charlie. "They'll be an hour at least."

It was closer to two hours before I heard the truck return.

Mark dragged a very full army kitbag into the kitchen, Max trailing behind him. He tipped it up, and a pile of neatly tied bundles of ten- and twenty-dollar notes tumbled onto the lino.

He stood back. Max hovered behind him, looking sheepish and hopeful. I sat and stared at the hill of money. I couldn't begin to guess how much was there. A hundred thousand? More. *Hundreds* of thousands. Enough. I could feel the eyes of the other three on me, waiting.

They would each be claiming a piece. In my head I cut the pile in half. That could be mine. The other half could be split between the three of them. My half would still be a good whack. A get-out-of-trouble whack, with plenty left over.

Maybe they'd argue for an even four-way split. Not so good, but a quarter of the whole would still be a lot. Get me out of trouble, invest a little something, and with luck a year or two of no work.

"More than you let on in the book," I said to Max.

"Jimmy gave me the bulk of the loot to look after. When I split from the others."

I turned back to the mountain of money. Maybe Max and Mark had already taken out a nice sly share anyway.

"Is this it?" I said.

Shocked looks on all their faces.

"Isn't it *enough*?" said Max. "Of course it's *it*. The whole fucking lot."

I looked around at the three of them.

"What about the smack?" I said.

After a bit of back and forth it was decided all four of us would go, in two cars. Max and Charlie in the Dodge, Mark and I following in my panel van. Late morning we drove off the farm, back down the dirt road and onto the potholed bitumen. A mile along we passed a council truck and a pair of linesman boiling a billy. We saw no one else on the road.

Mark didn't seem inclined to start a conversation, just stared ahead, his lank hair hiding half his face, smoking roll-your-owns.

"So it was you who took the manuscript to Gould?" I said, after we'd been driving for ten minutes.

"Yes. That was me."

"Did you also put the book in the cab for me to find?"

"Yeah," he said, glancing at me, smiling slightly. "That girl Steph, Gould's offsider, she pocketed a few copies, slipped some to me."

"That's way more money back there than Max lets on in the book," I said.

"What he told me, when they made the getaway from Melbourne, day after the Moratorium, and Max decided to bail – well, Jimmy had the flash idea of splitting the swag, for safety's sake. The big bit ended up with Max. When they all got killed, everyone figured the robbery money had gone up in smoke at Violet Town."

"Old Max is full of surprises," I said.

"Wait till you see the smack," he said.

"The compressed brick?"

He shook his head, smiled. "The *suitcase*. The suitcase *full* of compressed bricks." He turned to me, grinning. "So Max says."

"Do you know where it is?"

He shook his head. "I've never been there."

We were silent for a few minutes, then I said, "Who's Charlie?"

"He owns the property. What Max had in the book about coming out of his blackout, driving the tractor, not knowing who he was – that's pretty much how it really happened, he says. He took some liberties, obviously."

An hour along the bitumen, we turned onto a dirt track towards a row of hills. The track wound into the rises, through a gate, and another. Then the Dodge pulled over. Max and Charlie got out. We did likewise.

Max got a shovel and a mattock off the back of the truck and smiled, "We'll need these." He turned and marched across the paddock towards a low saddle between two hills, two hundred yards away. The three of us followed through the long grass.

Max, twenty yards ahead of us, got to the ridge first. And came to a halt.

We caught up. The hillside dropped away a little more steeply on the other side, down into a gentle natural depression. A D8 excavator was parked at the bottom. The natural rill draining the two hills had been dug out recently, and the many tons of black dirt piled at the low end to make a dam wall. The new dam was large, but the wall hadn't been levelled off yet. For a hundred yards either side, the entire hillside was torn up by the caterpillar tracks.

Max, walking strangely, headed down the hill. We followed.

There was a large pile of tree stumps, twisted roots, bits of rock and torn-up vegetation to the right. Max walked over, leaned into the muddy mess and pulled out what looked like part of a Samsonite suitcase. He held it up, then dropped it and marched towards the dam wall. Again, we followed. No one said anything.

We walked around the right side of the newly shaped dam edge, onto the unfinished wall. Max looked closely at the dark, moist dirt beneath us. There were little white flecks through it, here and there a fine dusting of white, like icing sugar on a chocolate cake.

Max stood staring at the ground, then bent and picked a bit of torn plastic out of the dirt. Chinese writing on it. He let it drop again. Then he found another bit, five yards the other way. Then he shook his head, turned to the three of us of and said, "Sorry. Fucked that *right* up."

We wandered around aimlessly for a while, each of us probing the dirt, pulling out shreds of plastic. Charlie found the other half of the suitcase. Mark dug up a shred of the plastic groundsheet Max had wrapped the packages in. The white flecks were visible, if you looked hard, over a wide area.

After half an hour Charlie said to no one in particular, "Well, I suppose a cup of tea back at the house is in order." His smile was weak and forced.

We turned and without another word began to trudge back to the cars. And then stopped.

Standing at the top of the rise were four figures, silhouetted against the sky.

We walked slowly up the hill towards them. My gun was in the panel van.

As we got closer, the differences between them became clear. An older bloke, thickset, with a big gut and red face, in a fawn sports shirt, permanent press trousers, white shoes. Fred Slaney. Next to him a younger, wiry-looking, ginger-haired feller in a black t-shirt. Scarred face. Then a thirty-something squarehead, and at the end a pudgy, jaded-looking older guy with long straight grey hair and a droopy moustache, wearing a beaten-up linen suit and a straw hat. He had pale, loose, almost colourless flesh.

They separated out a little as we approached. When the four of us reached the ridge, each of us was more or less face to face with one of the men.

"G'day, Fred," I said to Slaney. To the redhead next to him I said, "Vic, is it?"

He nodded guardedly.

Mark made a sound, like a hound baying at the moon. Vic gave him a look but said nothing. Mark did it again.

I looked closely at the third man, the squarehead. I had no idea who he was. Then I faced the big guy with the mo. Something about the way he was standing, the way the others were standing, indicated he was in charge.

"Blighter," I said. "I had a feeling I'd be seeing you."

"William. My dear, dear, fellow." He shook his head slowly, smiling broadly, as if marvelling at how splendidly everything

291

was turning out. He walked across and tried to give me a bear-hug. I writhed away, hit him in the face with my elbow, saying "Fuck off!" He stepped back again, still smiling, no offence taken.

Then he looked at the ground between us, panned across slowly till he got to Max, then gave him a leisurely once-over, from the feet up.

He came to Max's face. Long strands of grey hair, the haggard features, half-crazed, hollow eyes. "You look like utter shit," he said quietly. Not smiling now.

Max kind of squirmed a little, then grinned apologetically. "Well, it's all gone now," Max said. "That's for fucking sure." He pointed back down the hill behind us. "The worms got it all."

The four of them looked at the earthworks, the new dam, the mud. No one said anything for a long few seconds. Then the squarehead said, "No matter. We'll make do with the money."

"And you would be . . ." I said.

Fred Slaney stepped between us. "Craig Grossman, Bill Glasheen."

"Alias 'Craig the Copper'," I said. "I thought you were out of the running, retired hurt."

"I was," he said. "But I thought about my situation, talked with wiser heads." A slight nod towards Slaney. "Thought about what I'd been through, and what I was owed." He spoke with a strange earnestness.

"I thought you were working for me, Fred," I said to Slaney.

He smiled a little. "I am, Bill, believe me." To the whole group he said, "Let's go back to the farmhouse and get this all shit straightened out. What do you say?"

The four of us stayed where we were. I glanced at Max. I guessed he was thinking about guns. Something in his expression told me he had something in the truck. And he knew *I* knew what was on his mind.

Slaney watched me, watched Max, then said in a slightly overhearty way, "Well, I'm getting out of this sun." He started to walk back down the hill towards where their Falcon was parked behind our vehicles, then stopped and turned around again. "Oh, for Christ's sake, we already found the kitbag of money, if that's what you're worried about."

Max said quietly to Vic, "So you turned dog on us?"

Everyone was dead still. Vic said nothing.

"Jimmy rang you from near Violet Town," Max said. "He told you he'd given the big end of the swag to me for safekeeping. You were the only one who knew it hadn't all gone up in smoke. Apart from me."

Vic looked at the dirt in front of him.

Max nodded. "Yeah, thought so."

Slaney walked back to the group. "You're disappointed," he said. "But all in all it's better this way. Everyone gets a little something. It'll save trouble later on. No point blaming Victor. Come on. Let's get this whack-up done."

He walked off again, and this time the rest of us followed, silently and uneasily, through the dry grass back to the cars.

Mark, walking next to me, muttered, "Eight shares now." I was probably the only one who heard it.

When we reached the cars, Max gave me a quick glance, his hand resting on the truck's door handle. Slaney was ahead of the others, nearly at the Falcon. Glancing back, he too caught my eye. I couldn't quite read his look, but my best guess was, he was signalling he was onside, ready to go with my call, whatever it was. Maybe.

Time to act.

Then the sound of a car motor, and a green Honda Civic came around the bend, weaving along the dirt track towards us. Everyone froze, watching it approach. The car pulled up and Denise got out in her denims and R. M. Williams, smiling.

Mark sighed quietly, "*Nine* shares."

My thought was, "I wonder if she's got a gun."

As if she'd heard me, Denise called out, "I've got a lawyer!" She put up her hands. "Don't shoot!" Still smiling. Then she looked at us one after another. She peered at Max standing uncertainly next to his truck, grey and crazy-looking, then ran over and hugged him, buried her head in his shoulder, crying and laughing. Then she went to Mark, hugged him too, more briefly, but warmly. Then she came to me, said a quiet hello, kissed me. She hooked her finger into one of my belt loops and casually, affectionately, leaned against me. Under her loose shirt, something stuck in her waist. A gun. Concealed carry.

"So what happens now, boys?" she said. Still smiling, but dead serious.

We were back where we'd been a moment before. I could start shooting. I played it out in my head. Slaney and Max would have guns in their hands within seconds. Slaney would be a good shot, but Max would just as likely panic and accidentally shoot one of us. As a marksman I was barely adequate, even on my best days. The Blighter was probably tooled up, carrying. Would Vic go with him or with us? Hard to say. Grossman definitely with the Blighter.

We had the numbers. But the Blighter would shoot anyone here, including Denise, without a second's hesitation. And he was *very* good with guns.

Did he read my thoughts? He was smiling slightly now, waiting.

I shook my head. No blue.

"Yeah, let's get out of here," I said, and got in the car.

❖ ❖ ❖

We drove back to Charlie's place in a slow convoy. Slaney's Falcon in front, then me in the van with Mark, Max and Charlie in the truck, Denise in her Honda at the rear.

We pulled into the yard. The others all left their cars, headed into Charlie's kitchen. I went over to Denise's car as she came to a stop. She got out, and we hugged again. When I was sure no one could hear us, I said quietly, "I saw your story."

"Did you read it?"

"Yeah. It's good," I said. "Wran was okay?"

She smiled. "A bit stand-offish at first. I told him I was a friend of yours. That helped. He said you were a 'truly unique Sydney character'."

"Smartarse."

"He called *you* that too." Denise glanced towards the farmhouse, dropped her voice even further. "Anyway, I carry an important message from brother dear," she said, smiling.

"Go on."

"Top level, super hush-hush. The government boffins are onside. Federal people spoke with the state people. There's a budget allocation being arranged. *Millions.* It's a big thing now. They're looking at buying up most of Glebe. Save the heritage houses from developers and freeways. Preserve the working-class character of the area. That sort of thing. The story in the *Review* tipped the scales."

"Terrific. But I don't give a shit about Glebe. Will they buy that street in Annandale?"

"You just say the word."

We went into the farmhouse kitchen. The Blighter was standing against a wall. Max and Mark hovering. Charlie opening bottles of beer, a kettle on the stove. Sao biscuits on the table.

Slaney sat down first, and with elaborate indifference, took a gun and car keys out of his back pocket and put them on the table. And smiled. He wasn't worried about a thing.

Craig looked at him nervously, then reached in his back pocket, put a small gun on the table. He sat down. Then Max did the same. A .38. By now it was a ritual, and everyone was waiting for the next person. The Blighter shrugged, removed his shabby jacket, put it over the back of a chair. He took a Webley, also a .38, out of his belt and dropped it on the laminex. Then he pulled out a copy of *Lost Highway to Hell* from the inside jacket pocket, put it next to the gun. To Max he said, "I'll get the author's signature on this later, if you don't mind." Max grinned, unsure if he was joking.

My turn. Everyone waiting. I looked at Denise. She lifted the front of her blouse, took the .38 out from right in front of her belly button, and thumped it down. Much laughter. But nervous laughter, no one really knowing what the correct protocols were.

Mark tipped the contents of the kitbag onto the table and proceeded to dole out the fifties, then twenties, tens, fives, twos and ones, until there was a nice, not too small pile in front of each person.

Denise said, "You know, that was always the idea. Cathy's idea, actually. Co-op. Everyone involved gets an equal piece."

When it was done, Max, Mark, Charlie and Denise each disappeared with their portions of swag. Then Vic left with his. The Blighter, Slaney, Grossman and I sat at the table.

I took a sip of tea. "I'd figured it was you tracking me across the countryside," I said to the Blighter. "The follow was too well-handled to be just cops."

He shrugged modestly.

"You were in touch with Multi?"

The Blighter gave a slow nod.

"The brown car at Bungendore? The linesmen out on the road there yesterday? Your men?"

He nodded. "I got some help from local authorities. And from others, of course," He nodded at Slaney.

"You tipped off the Blighter, Fred?"

Slaney put three spoons of sugar in his tea and carefully stirred it. Then he looked at me over his glasses. "This was all heading to a very bad conclusion. So yeah, I took a hand. But no, I didn't tip him off, or anyone else."

"In fact, I sought Fred out," said the Blighter. "But I was already closer than you would have ever guessed. You may or may not remember, I grew up just down the road from here."

"Right, Gunnedah. I'd forgotten."

He nodded. "I would've found this place on my own in another day or two."

"You're still a government man, obviously."

He shrugged, as if saying, well, yes and no. "Not always so clear cut."

We fell silent. I heard Denise's car door slam outside, and a few seconds later she came in, followed by Max and Mark.

The Blighter pushed his copy of *Lost Highway to Hell* to Max. "Author signature?" he said, cheerily.

Max shrugged, picked it up, wrote something, dropped the book back on the table.

The Blighter nodded, tapped the book, then looked at Denise. "I'll take your copy, if I may." Then to me, "Yours too, Bill." Then to Max and Mark. "And any others you lads might have lying around."

Denise said, "You've *got* to be fucking kidding!"

The Blighter smiled serenely and said, "Frightful bore, I know. But this business—", nodding at the book on the table, "has to stop right here."

"Because you have set yourself up with the Greeks, just like it says in the book?" I said. "From here on in, it's number 4 heroin all round."

"Oh Bill, *please*. The moralising! You know full well that this heroin thing is going to happen, whether I'm involved or not."

Max shook his head.

The Blighter smiled indulgently. "No point being sentimental for the old days: that little bit of powder smuggled in with the luggage. A bit of opium here—" holding up his finger and thumb a millimetre apart, "a few buddha sticks there. A cap of coke brought through customs, jammed up some poor wretch's blurter."

"It wasn't just that, it was—" said Denise.

But Blighter ploughed on. "That's gone now."

Slaney shook his head, speaking almost to himself said, "Yep, it's the age of the druggie, all right. And armed robbery. Drugs and armed rob."

The Blighter, picking up the copies of the book, said, "Indeed it is. And if anyone present cares to be involved in future, ah, enterprises, they need only say the word." He looked around the room, smiling. "Money *will* be made."

Denise shaking her head, "You *are* kidding! We could blow the whistle on you. I've a good mind to."

The Blighter said quietly, "Don't do that. It wouldn't go well. Actually, I think I've been more than fair. Extraordinarily forbearing, really. I've forgiven the theft at gunpoint of a very substantial amount of product." He looked at Max. "And I've persuaded certain mutual Mediterranean friends to overlook past transgressions. Provided there's no more nonsense. Nothing that interferes with current plans." He looked at Denise, then back at Max.

Neither of them said anything.

Blighter nodded, then looked around the room. "So?" Smiling placidly.

No takers.

Then Mark, talking to no one in particular said, "This smack epidemic. If it *is* coming, regardless, maybe the sooner it starts, the sooner it finishes," he said.

Thoughtful nods around the table.

After another moment's silence Slaney sighed, and said, "Anyway, be that as it may . . . You, Mister Glasheen, and your friends here, and I – we can now all go about our business. There'll be no trouble, no come-back."

"The Melbourne jacks?" I said.

"They got their piece of the Sunshine Pipefitters job. Provided Craig here is looked after, they'll go quietly."

Grossman took a sip of coffee and said to no one in particular, "You know, my original plan was to make a grab for the lot. Shoot anyone I had to. But Fred talked sense into me."

Fred bowed his head, modestly acknowledging praise.

An hour later I stood beside the Falcon. Slaney sat behind the wheel, waiting for the Blighter and Grossman to join him. Their bags and travel stuff were spread messily over the seats. Empty bottles of Paracodin Linctus on the floor. Elbow on the sill, Slaney said, "Just so you know, the other matter back in Sydney has been . . . concluded."

"Meaning?"

"A certain mutual associate has gone, and he won't be coming back."

"Barry's gone. That all?"

He did a double-take. "Isn't that *enough*?"

"It was all a set-up, though, wasn't it?"

Slaney was shaking his head.

"Like that old story about George Moore," I said. "You know it?"

He waited.

"The jockeys are in the dressing room, just before the race, and George goes around, gives them each a five-quid note. Each man nods. Yep, he understands. But George leaves one feller out, the most junior apprentice. Then during the race, as they come into the straight, the apprentice flies past the whole field. As he shoots past Georgie, he turns around and yells out, 'Ya never gave *me* nothin', did ya, Mr Moore?' and moves into the lead. And George shouts to him, "Good on you, son, you go for it. We've all backed you!"

Slaney laughed but said nothing.

"The Combine wanted Barry out of the picture," I said. "Set it up so that I would take action. *Had* to, no choice. Someone was watching things. Followed me on the night, mopped up afterwards. Maybe it was you."

Slaney not smiling now, dropped his voice even further. "I was there, but maybe I wasn't doing the Combine's bidding. And maybe I wasn't alone."

I waited.

"Maybe some other people were prepared to off Mr Geddins."

"Such as?"

"Such as a certain family of Leb cutthroats from Annandale. Maybe they didn't like Barry paying his particular type of attention to their kiddies. Maybe they saw some difference between you and Geddins, thought by helping you they'd be helping themselves."

"And why were *you* there?"

"Maybe I was looking after you."

He let that hang there for a few seconds, then said, "So what about these houses? Phil and Joe are cranky about what's happening there. The Lebs are digging in. There are lezzos and longhairs from arsehole to breakfast. Now the journos are sniffing about. They think you have something to do with that."

"The freeway flyover thing is dead. There'll be a change of government at the state election soon. And there'll be no sale to the state government in the meantime. Never going to happen."

Slaney was waiting. Blank-faced.

I went on. "But I can put them in touch with a possible buyer."

Slaney grinned. "Who might that be?"

"I'd rather not say for now. But they'll get a fair price, maybe better than the state government would have given them. And they'll be able to sell the places as they are. The purchaser will deal with the squatters."

Slaney smiled.

"But they need to know that I've saved them there," I said. "Phil needs to call it square between us."

Slaney nodded. "Noted," he said.

"Abe and Joe Dimitrios, they need to drop off too. We're all square."

Slaney stared at me, said after a moment, "You still don't get it, do you?"

"How so?"

"They've long since called it square. Their worry is that you might be nursing ambitions of your own."

"I don't follow you."

"Gangster-type ambitions."

I looked at him, waiting.

"Look at it from their point of view. You got rid of Barry, their number one standover man. If you wanted to you could round up a gang of sorts."

"Who would that be?"

"You'd have me. Grossman too, if you want him. Your bikey mates. Your druggie connections. Donny could provide a few more men, if needed. If you were to ask the Blighter, he'd quite possibly sign on with your merry band of outlaws. He's probably got a couple of pirates on his string too."

I said nothing.

"That would be what they call a gang. You'd be what they call a gangster. At the very least, you could join the Combine, as an equal partner."

"I'd sooner neck myself."

"I'm just saying, with your old-world sense of honour and so on, you've probably taken your obligations to the Combine more seriously than you needed to. Strictly speaking."

"Whatever. It's all square between us now. Let them think what they like."

The Blighter and Grossman came out to the car. The Blighter said we should keep in touch, but even if we didn't, fate seemed to have its own ideas about such things, so *au revoir* for now. He got in the car.

Slaney put on a pair of sunglasses, gave me a look and a nod, started the car and they were off.

Denise and I camped out a mile from the farmhouse that night. I built a fire, even though it wasn't cold. We'd cooked chops and potatoes, and were drinking flagon riesling out of mugs. Denise leaned back with a cig in her hand. "So, the Blighter and you," she said. "Is that subject to a Bill Glasheen D-notice?"

"The Filthy Blighter. Real name, Beaufoy Edward Hawley-White. Drunk, scoundrel, double-crossing slime. Killer. Old-time spook. Didn't Cathy ever talk about him?"

"Not exactly. She always hinted something big had happened in Vietnam, but I never knew whether that part of the book was real or fantasy."

"More real than not, I think. I knew him years ago. He was a kind of spy then, but running his own rorts too."

She shook her head. "And now, the smack."

"I've got a feeling he won't be around too long. He's got a habit now, by the look of it, maintaining on cough syrup. How long can he last once the shipments start? But forget him. a question for you. How did you find Plain View? Vic's mum?"

"Yeah. She didn't know much, but it was enough for me to

find the place. When I got there, I saw the Falcon driving out of the farm. I followed. At a safe distance, as per the Billy Glasheen method." She snuggled into my side. "I missed our camping out. I missed you."

"Yeah, likewise. Any progress on the book or film or whatever it is?"

Denise looked into the fire and said, "I've had a rethink about all that. You know what I reckon?" Looking at me. "It's too late. The Moratorium, hippies, Trots, Maoists. Vietnam. 1970. Old hat. These days, each year is so different from the one before. *Three* years ago is like another planet. I may as well be writing old-time beatnik bullshit like Max. Who would care?"

"It's all dead then?"

"Love, smack, the Melbourne underground. There could be something in that. I won't be the one doing it though. But I reckon I could do something with my, whatever it is, reputation."

"How about a science-fiction surfing road movie?" I said. "With kangaroos."

She looked at me, smiling, waiting for a punchline.

"I'm serious. Got your typewriter with you?"

Back at the farm the next day. Vic was still there, trying to get Mark and Max to forgive him for having thrown in his lot with the Melbourne police. Max didn't seem to care too much. Yeah, it could've gone badly, he said, but that move ended up being what resolved everything. Mark said, fuck him. It's a matter of principle. Every time Vic tried to talk to him he barked like a pooch. Around mid-afternoon Vic gave up and walked away, head bent, intending to hitch back to town.

Later on, Denise, Max, Charlie and me were sitting on fold-up chairs in the shade of a big pepper tree, drinking more of Charlie's coffee. Mark was nearby, fiddling with a motorbike.

Max took a sip of coffee, smiled at me. "So, old compadre, how do we stand?"

I looked at him a long time. But I had nothing to say. I just shook my head, too tired to answer.

Max grinned, or tried to. "A bit of a drink in it there for old Bill. Not what we'd hoped for, but still, a tidy sum. Get you out of trouble, at least."

I turned to face him. "Are you kidding? This'll barely cover what I need to sling Eloise and the kids."

Max looked at me with the same plastered-on vacant grin.

"If you wanted to make it right, why didn't you just ring me?" I said. "Or send me a letter? Or send Mark to fetch me?"

No answer.

"We could've had *all* the money and *all* the dope. Instead of no dope and a ninth of the money each."

Max said, "My idea was, we draw everyone out, see which way they were going to jump. Spot all the players, then deal with each one of them. Now we've got our money, there's no one left chasing us. And so, with your help—" he grinned inanely, "I can prepare my return to society."

"You'll have to do some jail," I said. "You incriminated yourself with that stupid fucking book."

"It's called unreliable narrator, pal. A tissue of fabrication and artistic license. Carries no weight in court. Anyway, Slaney's doing a little sniffing around for me, see what charges I would actually face. Could even be none. Meanwhile, *we* keep steadily building the legend."

"Really?"

"I was thinking of a television documentary about me and my life. Max Perkal, father of Australian jazz-rock. Man of many parts. Beat generation legend. Came through the hell of drug addiction wiser and stronger. There are so many angles to this. Get someone like Rolf Harris to narrate it."

"Not him."

"Bill Peach then. A family friend, you know."

I said nothing.

"I could go round to schools, warn kids about the dangers of drugs."

I stood up. "This is a waste of time. I'm shooting through." I looked at Denise. She stood up.

Max, still in his chair, looked quickly at Mark, then at Charlie. "Maybe now is the time?"

Mark shrugged. Charlie nodded.

Max stood up. "Before you go. Better come for a little look-see."

We drove across the property, all of us squashed into Denise's car. Through a gate, past a row of she-oaks, across a cattle grid, into what looked like another property. A large yard. A tractor parked under an open shed. All neat and tidy. Along the path another shed, much bigger and newer.

We got out. Mark pulled out a set of keys, opened the three heavy padlocks, pushed back the big sliding door.

The smell hit me instantly. Max gestured, be my guest, and stood aside. I walked in. A bank of flouros flickered on. In front of us, rows and rows of steel shelving. Packages like mini-wool bales, tightly wrapped in taped-up black plastic, neatly stacked along the entire length.

On the other side, racks with plants hanging upside down.

Mark was looking pleased now. Proud.

He walked over to the curing rack, picked up a branch, brought it over to us. Dense, gluey heads, with no seeds.

"Sensimilla?" I said.

"Certainly is."

"The booklet from the Third World?"

"I've improved on the method in the book. Quite a bit, actually."

"He's a clever lad," said Max. "We get three harvests a year up here. Could get four next time." He waited a few seconds. "And you've got a panel van."

I walked along the row of shelves, patting the packages.

Max called out, "Equal share for you, Bill. Need I say, it'll be big bickies. All we need to do is arrange my rehabilitation."

I walked back. "Forget the documentary. No one gives a shit about the old days. But you can have a part in our movie. A small part."

"Eh?"

"You're the crazy old coot who runs a cantina in the hills, up in the rainforest. Strictly a cameo, though."

A confused slow shake of the head from Max.

"It's the near future. A few years after the big crash, the big earthquake, big meteor strike. Whatever. Everything's been wiped out. Law and order has broken down. Every so often another bit of California drops into the sea, sends these sets of waves two, three, four hundred feet high across the Pacific to Australia. There's a band of outlaw surfers who wait on the high ground for each new apocalypse set to arrive. That might be the name of the film, actually – *Apocalypse Set*." I turned to Denise. "What do you think?"

"The title is still up in the air," she said.

"That's right. Just a thought. Anyway these surfies catch the big ones when they come through. Try to. Most of them die, actually.

"But that's not the main story. There are all these different communities who live on the hilltops, where the super waves don't quite reach. Anarchists, hippies, heads, blackfellas, musicians, fortune-tellers, separatist lesbians, artists' co-ops, angel-headed hipsters. They perform ritual magic. There'll be some lezzo sex there, but tasteful. Then there are these—"

"I know some musicians who'd be perfect!" Max piped in.

"Johnny Mugg and the Muggs?" I said.

Max was nodding, but surprised. "You see, we see the same things. That was part of my re-entry plan – take Johnny and the boys to Sydney, promote them as the next thing. You've seen them, obviously."

"They were shithouse. Anyway, glam rock is the big thing now. This Bowie feller."

"Ah, but that's about to change. It's your basic dialectics, comrade. Thesis, antithesis, synthesis. The thing gives birth to its other. The Muggs only play three chords, yeah, yeah, I know. But they've got spirit, you'll have to admit. And a new look. They'll be fast, angry, and rough as guts. Gonna call it 'Mug Rock.' First there was Rock. Then Glam. Now Mug Rock."

"Whatever. Maybe we can use them. There's also a blackfella kid on the north coast, name of Wes, who plays incredible guitar. Good-looking kid."

Denise said, "Lobby would be right for this, too."

"And how about this," said Max. "One bunch of the good people, the anarchists or whoever, are growing this sensational pot up in the hills. Every so often they have to do a run to take the harvest to the lowlands."

"There are no lowlands," said Mark. "It's all under water."

"Bellevue Hill, Coogee, the Blue Mountains. Doesn't matter," Max went on. "There are a bunch of survivor communities spread around, but they're starved for dope. So there's this brief moment when the waters recede, before the next big inundation. All the roads are dry for, like, three days. And there's this super-driver, he gets around in an incredibly hotted-up EK panel van, who does the dope run, brings the righteous shit to all the villages."

"And it's weird," Mark said, "because there are octopuses and seaweed and shit everywhere. There's *coral* growing in the main street of Bathurst."

"So a cross between *Thunder Road* and *Twenty Thousand Leagues under the Sea*," I said.

"Yeah. Kangaroos and starfish." Max again. "The bad guys are the drug squad and the CIA. They're evil murderous bastards in big grey government Kingswoods. Deep down they wish they could just turn on and be cool, but they're too fucked-up in the head."

"The drug squad are trying to stamp out pot," said Mark, "so they can force everyone onto methadone, which they get from—"

I cut in. "We'd need a bikey gang in there too. The Devil's Turds, something like that. All the different wayfarers and seekers pull into the cantina from time to time, because it's kind of neutral territory. 'Crazy Max' tells stories about the old days, shooting up with Lenny Bruce and so on. He says stuff like 'copasetic' and 'daddio.' Kind of hipster nostalgia. But he's an oracle. Talks in loony but poetic riddles. You can play some low-down piano in the corner. A cross between William Burroughs and Hoagy Carmichael. Crazy Max, the Lost Troubadour."

"Hell's Sphincters," said Mark.

Everyone looked at him.

"The bikey gang," he said. "And the cars, they're all made out of rusty corrugated iron, tractor parts, old farm equipment, stump-jump ploughs, tree trunks, rocks and shit. Like Ned Kelly on acid. But they go like the *fuck*."

Denise spoke up. "Satan's Arseholes. Easier to say. Anyway boys, there's a lot to be sorted out yet, and we don't want to get too far ahead of ourselves. One thing, though, what if the hell-driver was a chick?"

We looked at her, suddenly silent. Then everyone burst out laughing.

Denise went on, "Like Cathy. With a young blackfella side-kick. The guitar kid, maybe. But like I said, we can fix all the details later."

"You're right. Later," I said. "So, the business at hand. This shit here—" I gestured at the dope inventory, "are we equal partners?"

Mark said, "Sounds all right. Max, me, you and Charlie. This is Charlie's land. Charlie has the water rights we need for the irrigation."

Charlie, who'd been silent till now, smiled.

"All right," I said. "We don't have long. A year or two, three at the most, before they legalise cannabis. And I need some right off – what are they, a couple of pounds each?"

"Five pounds," said Mark. "Exactly."

"I'll need three or four bags," I turned to Denise, "to sweeten the Annandale squatters. The musicians, at any rate, probably the activists too." To Mark, Max and Charlie I said, "So that comes off the top, before the split. Agreed?"

Mark nodding, said, "Okay. Four ways after that." He glanced quickly at Denise.

"That's all right," she said. "This is your thing. But I wouldn't mind a wee little something to share with my friends. A package. Or two."

We all nodded.

"But we'll need to come to a clear understanding about the film," she said. "Rights and whatnot. Who's the producer, who's the director. Who gets a writing credit. What each person's investment stake is. All that stuff."

I said. "My friends Mullet and Kate, Terry and Anna – they need to be in on this thing too. If they want to be. Mullet can shoot the film. The others will help sell the dope – the Sydney branch office."

More nods all round.

"So how *do* we fix all that?" Mark said.

Denise smiled. "Like I said, I have a lawyer."

MORE FROM PETER DOYLE

Peter Doyle's crime novels, featuring irresistible antihero Billy Glasheen, brilliantly explore the criminal underworld, political corruption, and the explosion of sex, drugs, and rock'n'roll in postwar Australian life, and have earned him three Ned Kelly Awards.

THE DEVIL'S JUMP

August 1945: the Japanese have surrendered and there's dancing in the streets of Sydney. But Billy Glasheen has little time to celebrate; his black marketeer boss has disappeared, leaving Billy high and dry. Soon he's on the run from the criminals and the cops, not to mention a shady private army. They all think he has the thing they want, and they'll kill to get hold of it. Unfortunately for Billy, he doesn't know what it is . . . but he'd better find it fast.

"Peter Doyle does for Sydney what Carl Hiaasen does for Miami."
—Shane Maloney

GET RICH QUICK

Sydney in the 1950s. Billy Glasheen is trying to make a living, any way he can. Luckily, he's a likeable guy, with a gift for masterminding elaborate scenarios—whether it's a gambling scam, transporting a fortune in stolen jewels, or keeping the wheels greased during the notorious 1957 tour by Little Richard and his rock 'n' roll entourage.

But trouble follows close behind—because Billy's schemes always seem to interfere with the plans of Sydney's big players, an unholy trinity of crooks, bent cops, and politicians on the make. Suddenly he's in the frame for murder, and on the run from the police, who'll happily send him down for it. Billy's no sleuth, but there's nowhere to turn for help. To prove it wasn't him, he'll have to find the real killer.

"An absolute gem . . . a marvellous read and a truly distinctive piece of Australian crime writing."—*Sydney Morning Herald*

"Think of a hopped-up James M. Cain."—*Kirkus Reviews*

ALSO FROM DARK PASSAGE BOOKS

G.S. MANSON – *Coorparoo Blues & The Irish Fandango*

Written in the spare, plain-spoken style of all great pulp fiction, G.S. Manson's series featuring 1940s Brisbane P.I. Jack Munro captures the high stakes and nervous energy of wartime, when everything becomes a matter of life and death.

BRISBANE, 1943. Overnight a provincial Australian city has become the main Allied staging post for the war in the Pacific. The tensions – social, sexual, and racial – created by the arrival of thousands of US troops are stirring up all kinds of mayhem, and Brisbane's once quiet streets are looking pretty mean.

Enter Jack Munro, a World War I veteran and ex-cop with a nose for trouble and a stubborn dedication to exposing the truth, however inconvenient it is for the -powers that be. He's not always a particularly good man, but he's the one you want on your side when things look bad.

When Jack is hired by a knockout blonde to find her no-good missing husband, he turns over a few rocks he's not supposed to. Soon the questions are piling up, and so are the bodies. But Jack forges on through the dockside bars, black-market warehouses, and segregated brothels of his roiling city, uncovering greed and corruption eating away at the foundations of the war effort.

Then Jack is hired to investigate a suspicious suicide, and there's a whole new cast of characters for him to deal with – a father surprisingly unmoved by his son's death, a dodgy priest, crooked cops, Spanish Civil War refugees – and a wall of silence between him and the truth, which has its roots deep in the past. Friends, enemies, the police – they're all warning Jack to back off. But he can't walk away from a case: he has to do the square thing.

"Great historical detail of wartime Australia mixed with the steady pace of sex and violence . . . keeps the pages turning."—*Brisbane Courier-Mail*

"Rough and gritty, but also vital."—*The Age*

ALSO FROM DARK PASSAGE BOOKS

ARTHUR NERSESIAN – *Gladyss of the Hunt*

January 2003. A killer with a macabre and baffling MO is targeting Manhattan call girls. Detective Bernie "Burnout" Farrell leads
the hunt, though he's not doing so great: his best friend on the force
just died, and he's had a nagging cough ever since working overtime
at Ground Zero. He picks rookie Gladyss Chronou as his new partner—she's tall and blonde, like the victims, which makes her perfect
bait for the trap he wants to set. But Gladyss has ideas of her own, believ-
ing insights from her mystical yoga practice can guide her to the murderer.

Steeped in New York's recent history, its relentless gentrification and the
psychic aftermath of 9/11, *Gladyss of the Hunt* fuses gritty realism and
sharp satire. Their search takes the oddball pair from the last of the hot-
sheet dives off Times Square to society parties on Central Park West—
until finally Gladyss faces the killer alone, in a climax as terrifying as it is
unexpected.

"Darkly comic . . . Nersesian's love affair with lower Manhattan
sets these pages afire."—*Entertainment Weekly*

"Nersesian revisits New York in a tale combining grit and
glamour, poignancy and cynical wit."—*Kirkus Reviews*

"Nersesian's unique psychological vision of the city rates with
those of Paul Auster and Madison Smartt Bell."—Blake Nelson

"Nersesian renders Gotham's unique cocktail of wealth, poverty, crime,
glamour, and brutality spectacularly."—*Rain Taxi Review of Books*

ALSO FROM DARK PASSAGE BOOKS

JUNE WRIGHT

"A Queen of Crime in the tradition of Dorothy L Sayers
and Margery Allingham."—*The Age*

June Wright burst onto the scene in 1948 with *Murder in the Telephone Exchange*, the best-selling mystery in her native Australia that year. She published five more top-quality novels over the next two decades, all of which were out of print when she died in 2012. But when *Murder in the Telephone Exchange* was reissued in 2014, Wright was hailed by the *Sydney Morning Herald* as "our very own Agatha Christie," and a new generation of readers worldwide fell in love with her inimitable blend of intrigue, wit, and psychological suspense, not to mention her winning sleuth, Maggie Byrnes.

Dark Passage Books will publish new editions of all seven June Wright novels. The following three are available now.

MURDER IN THE TELEPHONE EXCHANGE

"A classic English-style mystery . . . packed with
detail and menace."—*Kirkus Reviews*

When an unpopular colleague at Melbourne Central is murdered – her head bashed in with a buttinsky, a piece of equipment used to listen in on phone calls – feisty young "hello girl" Maggie Byrnes resolves to turn sleuth. Some of her co-workers are acting strangely, and Maggie is convinced she has a better chance of figuring out the killer's identity than the stodgy police team assigned to the case, who seem to think she herself might have had something to do with it. But then one of her friends is murdered too, and it looks like Maggie is next in line.

Narrated with verve and wit, this is a mystery in the tradition of Dorothy L. Sayers, by turns entertaining and suspenseful, and building to a gripping climax. It also offers an evocative account of Melbourne in the early postwar years, as young women like Maggie flocked to the big city, leaving behind small-town family life for jobs, boarding houses and independence.

(336 pages, with a new introduction by Derham Groves)

ALSO FROM DARK PASSAGE BOOKS

SO BAD A DEATH

> "The irrepressible Maggie is probably the most candid
> woman in contemporary crime."—*The Mail* (Adelaide)

Maggie makes a memorable return to the fray in *So Bad a Death*. She's married now, and living in a quiet Melbourne suburb. Yet violent death dogs her footsteps even in apparently tranquil Middleburn. It's no great surprise when a widely disliked local bigwig (who also happens to be her landlord) is shot dead, but Maggie suspects someone is also targeting the infant who is his heir. Her compulsion to investigate puts everyone she loves in danger.

(288 pages, with a new introduction by Lucy Sussex, plus her fascinating interview with June Wright from 1996)

DUCK SEASON DEATH

> "Some darn good detection, fine character work . . . , [and] a healthy sense
> of humor sprinkled throughout the mayhem."—Pretty Sinister Books

June Wright wrote this lost gem in the mid-1950s, but consigned it to her bottom drawer after her publisher foolishly rejected it. Perhaps it was just a little ahead of its time, because while it delivers a bravura twist on the classic 'country house' murder mystery, it's also a sharp-eyed and sparkling send-up of the genre.

When someone takes advantage of a duck hunt to murder publisher Athol Sefton at a remote hunting inn, it soon turns out that almost everyone, guests and staff alike, had good reason to shoot him. Sefton's nephew Charles believes he can solve the crime by applying the traditional "rules of the game" he's absorbed over years as a reviewer of detective fiction. Much to his annoyance, however, the killer doesn't seem to be playing by those rules, and Charles finds that he is the one under suspicion. *Duck Season Death* is a both a devilishly clever whodunit and a delightful entertainment.

(192 pages, with a new introduction by Derham Groves)

JOHN M. CUELENAERE PUBLIC LIBRARY
33292900092697
The big whatever

DARK PASSAGE BOOKS
CHECKLIST

☐ **PETER DOYLE**: The Devil's Jump $14.95

☐ **PETER DOYLE**: Get Rich Quick $13.95

☐ **PETER DOYLE**: The Big Whatever $14.95

☐ **G.S. MANSON**: Coorparoo Blues & The Irish Fandango . . . $13.95

☐ **ARTHUR NERSESIAN**: Gladyss of the Hunt $14.95

☐ **JUNE WRIGHT**: Murder in the Telephone Exchange $15.95

☐ **JUNE WRIGHT**: So Bad a Death $14.95

☐ **JUNE WRIGHT**: Duck Season Death $12.95

also available as ebooks

darkpassagebooks.com
facebook.com/versechoruspress